LOVE OFFLINE

LOOKING FOR ROMANCE IN REAL LIFE

OLIVIA SPRING

HARTLEY PUBLISHING

Dedicated to my darling PD.

CHAPTER ONE

Normally, I love social media.

The endless fancy food and envy-inducing holiday pics on Insta, the witty conversations on Twitter, the funny memes on Facebook—I adore it.

When I've got important designs to create for clients and deadlines to meet, I can often be found spending many minutes (truth be told, more like hours) scrolling through strangers' feeds rather than *actually* working. After all, who doesn't like staring at photos of cute kittens?

Like I said. Normally, I *love* social media.

Well, I *did* until precisely 9.29 a.m. today.

The day started off like any other Monday morning. Hitting the snooze button a dozen times before finally crawling out of bed. Having a shower whilst wondering why the weekend flashes by in what seems like five minutes, whereas Monday to Friday lasts for half a century. Throwing on whatever looked clean and didn't need ironing, then dragging myself to my local coffee shop to get the caffeine-and-sugar hit I needed to help me feel remotely human, or at least alert enough to start work.

I'd sat at my desk, taken a generous bite of my blueberry muffin, sipped on my steaming latte and switched on my computer. I had considered going through my emails but, in true procrastination style, decided to check Instagram first instead, because of course that was *much* more important than doing actual work.

And there it was.

That photo.

The picture, which had already amassed thirty-six likes.

The image that instantly made my head spin and my stomach sink.

Captioned with just three words that sent my world crashing down.

She said yes!

My ex-boyfriend Eric, who I always believed would be the man I'd spend the rest of my life with, had proposed to Nicole—the woman he'd been cheating with for the last six months of our relationship—and she'd said yes.

Great.

There they were on what looked like some tropical beach, waves crashing against the golden sand, gazing into each other's eyes, lips locked, her left hand strategically placed on his shoulder, showing off the giant rock adorning her ring finger.

Exactly what I *didn't* need to see on a miserable grey March Monday morning in South London.

After staring at my screen for longer than was healthy, I'd tried to do what any smart, sensible, level-headed, pragmatic woman would if she heard the news that her unfaithful ex was marrying the younger model she'd been traded in for. I'd told myself I couldn't care less, that it was his loss, there were plenty more fish in the sea, karma would catch up with them and to just get on with my day.

Did it work?

Of course it bloody didn't.

So instead I'd dragged myself the ten steps from my home study to my bedroom, put on the 'Life Sucks' Spotify playlist, curled up into a ball and sobbed until my mobile rang.

It was Chloe. She'd heard the news from a friend during the school run and was on her way over. *With cake.*

I'd told her I wasn't sure that even a Victoria sponge the size of the Atlantic Ocean could make me feel better, but she'd insisted. And now she had let herself into my flat using the key I'd given her for emergencies. I suspected that she was probably mentally preparing herself for the sight that was about to greet her.

Chloe knew how much I loved Eric and how I'd struggled to get over him, so she'd realise that this wasn't going to be pretty.

'Emily Robinson!' she shouted, bursting through the bedroom door. 'Up you get!'

I slowly peeled my head from the pillow and tried to gauge whether I really had to force myself off the bed and deal with the situation or if I could get away with lying here for the rest of the afternoon and convince Chloe to give me a bucketload of tea and sympathy.

Who am I kidding? This was my no-nonsense best friend. And she did *not* do self-pity. Especially over an unfaithful man.

'Come on, Em. We're not doing this again. Remember?' She picked up my iPad from the bedside table, frowning as she bashed away haphazardly at the screen before eventually managing to pause the playlist. 'No more listening to sad songs. No more tears over Eric. He's not worth it,' she said, edging closer to the bed. 'You can do *much* better than that tallywag.'

I slowly dragged myself upright, scraped my thick, dark curly hair off my face and tucked my knees under my chin.

'I know he's a loser, but seeing that picture, of *him*, with *her*, proposing after knowing her for all of two minutes, when he *knew* I'd wanted to get married for *years* and constantly fobbed me off, it just—it really hurt,' I said, using the sleeve of my grey jumper to wipe the tears streaming down my cheeks.

'I understand that,' said Chloe as she smoothed down the back of her 1950s-style polka dot dress and sat down on the plain magnolia duvet. 'But you really need to move on, Em. It's been seven months. It's time to start a new life. Unfollow the fool like I told you to ages ago and make new friends.'

'I make new friends all the time,' I scoffed. 'I'm up to almost six hundred on Facebook. Admittedly, Insta is lagging behind a little as I'm low on content, but—'

'For crying out loud!' Chloe crossed her arms. 'I don't mean friends on social media. That's nonsense. I'm talking about *proper* friends. You know, people that you speak to face-to-face in a restaurant, rather than clicking the stupid love heart button on a post of some person from Timbuktu that you've never met.'

Trust Chloe not to understand. She's so old-fashioned, she doesn't even own a smartphone. Can you imagine?

'I know you have an aversion to technology and anything online, Chloe, but social media has been my life-line. If you think I'm bad now, I would have been *much* worse without the support of my online community.'

'Your *online community*?' Chloe rolled her eyes. 'Good grief! Sounds like some sort of cult!'

'Laugh all you want, but their likes, comments and uplifting posts have kept me going.'

'*If you say so*,' replied Chloe, reaching in her bag and pulling out two forks, serviettes and a container before taking out a large slice of chocolate cake. The rich scent filled the room. *Mmmm*. It smelt delicious. 'Like I've said before, I really think you should venture out of these four walls and try new things. You work from home all day, and apart from coming round to mine, you never seem to go anywhere. If you had a load of hobbies and were out making new friends in real life, you wouldn't have time to think about what that idiot is doing. You'd be too busy having fun.'

Here we go again. It's the *you need to get out of the flat more* lecture. I love Chloe, I really do, but she just doesn't get it.

My whole social circle revolved around my life with Eric. His friends became my friends, and after the breakup, that disappeared overnight. Now it was almost impossible to find anyone to go out with. On the rare occasions that I *did* get invited out, all the people in the group were coupled up and I was the odd one out. I got treated like either a weirdo or a potential husband thief. That's when I wasn't getting pitied or being shown photos of other random single men they were convinced would be ideal for me, purely because we'd both been 'condemned' to a life of solitude. I shuddered just thinking about it. *No, thanks*. I'd rather sit at home and have conversations online than be subjected to that hell.

'It's not that simple,' I huffed as I reached for my own slab of sponge and took a large bite. I wasn't in the mood to use a fork and serviette like Chloe. 'Everyone I know is married and has kids and doesn't have time to go out.'

'I appreciate what you're saying,' said Chloe, stroking her raven bob, which she'd styled into her signature vintage waves. 'But you are not the only thirty-five-year-old singleton in London. There are *loads* of other people out there just like you, so if your old circle of friends doesn't fit your life anymore, make a new circle. Find new friends. Look.' She stood up. 'I hate to leave you like this, but I've been called into work today, so I've got to run. I'll call you later, but please—don't sit here moping. Go for a walk to clear your head and have a think about what I said. There's a whole world out there. So many exciting things you could be doing with your life, but you need to actually step outside of this flat to discover them. Promise you'll give it some thought?'

I looked up at her, fighting the temptation to roll my eyes after hearing her make the same suggestion for the millionth time.

'Yes, yes,' I said. 'I'll think about it.'

'And you'll stop thinking about Eric too?'

'Yes,' I muttered reluctantly. What was I supposed to say? It wasn't like I *wanted* to think about him. Eric was just always there. Right in the front of my thoughts.

'Excellent!' She smiled. 'You'll feel *so* much better when you do. You don't need his toxic energy around you. Anyway, I'd better go.' She leant forward and hugged me tightly before rushing towards the door. 'Make sure you get stuck into the cake. Love you!'

I stretched over to the container and grabbed another helping of sponge, shamelessly stuffing it into my mouth, then wiped my fingers before wrapping the duvet tightly around me. Getting out of these four walls? Going for a walk? *Not a chance.* That was the last thing I felt like doing. I planned to stay right here in this flat until I ran out of food or was forced to evacuate due to a state of national emergency. Whatever happened first.

CHAPTER TWO

I *thought I could do it, but I can't.*

After spending all day yesterday wallowing and devouring the entire chocolate cake, I was still feeling low. Wondering why Eric had chosen her and not me. That image of his proposal was going round and round in my head. I was desperate for a distraction. I didn't dare go back on social media, but I had to do something to take my mind off things.

I needed to find a way to feel wanted again. Desired. So last night, after dragging myself to the kitchen and pouring myself a large glass of Southern Comfort and lemonade, I'd climbed back into bed, logged onto OKCupid and started messaging Kane.

Clearly I'd got carried away and wasn't thinking straight, as I'd agreed to meet him. *Tonight.*

Bad idea. *Very, very bad.*

Kane and I had been chatting online since the beginning of last week. Even though I wasn't the fastest texter, as I thought about everything carefully before replying, which stunted the flow, I liked our conversations. It had been nice having someone to exchange messages with in the evenings and keep me company. Usually we'd talk about something that had been trending on Twitter, share links to new songs we'd found on Spotify or exchange memes. Our marathon messaging sessions had become the highlight of my day. But then the subject of taking our discussions offline had come up again. And even though I'd agreed to meet him face-to-face and told myself I really *would* this time, now in the cold light of day, I didn't think I could go through with it.

I *should*. I knew that. Not just because it might help me stop thinking about the Eric engagement nightmare, but also because I'd already cancelled on Kane. *Twice.* It would be unforgivable to do it a third time.

I was supposed to meet him last Wednesday, but I'd messaged him the night before to ask if we could reschedule, as I'd come down with a nasty bout of the flu and didn't want to pass on my germs.

Okay, *granted*, I'd only sneezed a couple of times that day and that might have been because I'd stood too close to the flowers on display in the coffee shop. But you know, you can never be too careful about these things. One minute you're sniffling and the next you're laid up in bed with a packet of paracetamol and a box of tissues. It was much better all round that I stayed at home. He said he understood.

Then we were due to meet on Friday, but I'd cancelled again. A client had sent a last-minute brief through at 6 p.m. on Thursday, so I'd told Kane straight away that I wouldn't be able to make it, as I'd have to work late the following evening. I suppose I could have finished it over the weekend as the deadline wasn't until Monday, but sometimes I got a burst of creativity on Friday afternoons, so if that happened, I needed to be at my desk to put it to good use.

In my job as an illustrator, you had to strike whilst the inspiration was hot, as you never knew when it might hit you again. I mainly did illustrations for magazines, adverts, leaflets, that kind of thing. And it wasn't unusual to have to fit in jobs at short notice. I'll admit: I was only drawing an egg timer for a pensions advert in a financial magazine, which required *zero* creativity. Much like a lot of my work these days, and as it turned out, I'd finished it by Friday lunchtime, so I *could* have still made the date. But I'd already messaged him and it would've looked bad if I changed my mind again. I didn't want to mess him around. That's why I always tried to give at least twenty-four hours' notice when cancelling a date to give the guy time to make other plans. Kane was understanding, and we'd agreed to meet this week instead.

So now it was 11 a.m. on Tuesday. Eight hours away from the meeting time of the first real-life date I'd agreed to after breaking up with Eric, and I was freaking out.

Although I didn't want to cancel again, surely it wouldn't be fair to meet Kane when I was in full *upset about my ex* mode?

When I'd messaged him last night in my pyjamas he couldn't see my puffy eyes or the sadness that that was written all over my face every time I thought of that Instagram photo. He couldn't see what a train wreck I was. But if we met in person, he'd take one look at me and run a mile. I just wasn't ready.

And anyway, when I'd glanced out of my bedroom

window earlier, it was really overcast, so it was probably going to rain. It *definitely* seemed like torrential downpours were on the way. Pretty sure I'd read something about floods somewhere in the world when I was scrolling through the news app on my phone this morning too, so it wouldn't be long before they hit England, surely?

Who knows? It might even snow. It has happened in March before. London was renowned for having multiple seasons and freak weather in the same day. It was always better to stay inside when there were adverse conditions. All the meteorological experts said so. Who was I to challenge their wisdom?

And I was certain there was something else I was supposed to be doing at home this evening. Like rearranging the cutlery drawer or...or...I don't know. *Something.* I couldn't remember right now, but it would come to me if I thought long and hard enough...

Okay, okay. Full disclosure. I'd rather be doing *anything* other than leaving my flat and going to meet Kane in Soho for a drink. It wasn't that I didn't like him. I *did.* He seemed nice. Charming. But that was the problem. They always did at first. Until they showed their true colours and lied to you for months. Just like Eric had done. So it would be better if we just didn't meet. Then Kane wouldn't be disappointed when he saw me in real life and I didn't live up to his expectations. And I wouldn't get my heart broken when he inevitably cheated on me.

We should just keep chatting online. It was safer. We'd been getting along just fine. Messaging for hours. *It's been nice. If it ain't broke, don't fix it.*

Yes. It would be less risky if we carried on exactly as we had been. I'd message him now and ask to reschedule.

Although eight hours' notice was more than most people would give, I still felt guilty. I wouldn't blame him if he didn't speak to me again. But like I said, it was for the best.

Me
   Hi, Kane. Really sorry, but I can't make it tonight. I'm not feeling well, so I need to stay in until I get better. I'll message again once I've recovered. Emily x

It wasn't like I wasn't telling the truth. I didn't feel well. *At all.* I felt like my heart had been trampled on by a thousand angry bulls.

I felt hollow. Empty. And also lost. Now that I'd cancelled my date with Kane, I would be the last person he'd want to message tonight, so who was I going to talk to?

Ordinarily I could cheer myself up by watching Insta-gram stories or joining in on a Facebook conversation, but logging on today would just be asking for trouble. Eric's engagement was sure to be all anyone would be talking about. And it wasn't as simple as just unfollowing him. There were a load of other people we both knew who I also liked to follow, so there was always the possibility they could post about it too.

For all I knew, the happy couple could be back in the UK, throwing a big engagement party, and my timeline would be filled with photos and messages congratulating the bride and groom to be. *Ugh.*

No. Looked like tonight it would just be me, myself and I. Home alone.

One day I'd be ready to get myself out there again. Meet new people. Make new friends. Friends of my own. Start dating. Maybe eventually find a new boyfriend. Learn to trust again.

Yes.

One day.

Soon.

I will.

At some point.

In the future.

Just not now.

Just not today.

CHAPTER THREE

'So?' said Chloe, her eyes widening as she stepped through my front door. 'How did it go?'

'How did what go?' I frowned, taking the container of cake she'd placed in my hands and walking into the open-plan kitchen and living room.

'Your date. With that online guy. What was his name again? Kyle? Kit?'

'Kane…' I replied reluctantly.

'That's the one!' she said, slapping her forehead. 'I knew it was a K something or other. So? Must have at least helped take your mind off your flapdoodle of an ex for a couple of hours. It couldn't have come at a better time.'

Oh dear.

I'd completely forgotten that I'd told Chloe about my date with Kane. It was just that when she'd called on Monday night, she seemed really worried and was convinced that I was just moping at home, stalking Eric's Instagram page (which of course was *exactly* what I was doing, but I didn't exactly want to confess to that), so I needed to tell her something to reassure her I was okay. Except now she was excited about me finally moving on and I was going to have to break the news that I'd bailed. *Again.*

'Shall I make us some tea to go with this cake?' I said, hoping to change the subject. *If only...* I switched the kettle on, then placed the container on the plain white kitchen counter. 'Gosh Chloe, you really do spoil me. This looks lovely. What is it? A banana loaf? Lemon cake?' I opened the container and closed my eyes as I inhaled the sweet aroma. 'Mmm...actually, I think I'm smelling coconut? And maybe pineapple?'

'You didn't go, did you?' said Chloe, crossing her arms as she stood at the dining table..

Busted.

There was no point trying to deny it. Chloe had known me for so long she could read me like a book.

'No...I had to cancel. I just didn't feel up to it, and after I messaged, he didn't reply, so he probably wasn't right for me anyway.' I hung my head. 'But,' I added enthusiastically, trying to rescue myself, 'I matched with two new guys this morning! Seventy-four per cent compatibility for one of them and I think eighty-seven per cent for the other, which is a record for me, so it's looking positive!'

'For the love of Pete!' said Chloe, spouting another of her old-fashioned sayings. 'If you tell me one more time that your love life *is looking positive* or that you've got a *good feeling* about another one of these online strangers, I think I'm going to *positively* pour a bucket of ice-cold water over you to help you wake up and face reality!'

'Charming!' I snapped. *Talk about trying to bring a*

girl down. She was supposed to be cheering me up and making me feel better, not worse.

'Although it's nice that you're so optimistic, at some point, Em, you need to realise that this online dating thing is *not* working for you. It's nonsense! For starters, you are not going to find the love of your life by staring at some guy's abs on your phone. That's not how love works.'

Chloe didn't have a clue about modern dating.

'For the millionth time, it's not just based on looks or just cold-swiping right,' I huffed. 'The dating apps I use have a special algorithm, which processes how you respond to questions to generate a score that measures how compatible you are with different guys.'

'Utter flimflam!' She rolled her eyes and sat down. 'Sounds like they've employed you as one of their sales reps! You don't realise it, but you're just on a hamster wheel, going round and round in circles. You match with these guys, you rave about your compatibility, you tell me things are looking *positive* and then nothing happens.'

'Not true!' I protested. 'We talk.'

'You mean, you chat to guys—*online*. Not even on the phone or in person. Via stupid phone messages. Then what?'

'Well—we…' I stuttered.

'Seeing as you're having trouble remembering, let me refresh your memory. These men that you're supposed to be *so* compatible with never amount to anything. The conversation with them either fizzles out, or on the rare occasions you *have* had someone like Kane who actually wants to meet, you end up cancelling. You give up, before you've even tried.'

'I just find the whole *meeting in person* thing hard.' I

winced. I poured hot water into our mugs, grabbed two plates from the cupboard, took the milk out of the fridge, then put everything on the table. 'I get nervous.'

'I understand, but how do you expect things to get any better if you don't face your fears?'

I sat down opposite Chloe. She was right, I knew she was, but I was scared. Worried about meeting a guy and saying the wrong thing. About disappointing them. About getting hurt. About a thousand different things. Maybe it was still too soon.

'I just need more time, that's all,' I said.

'I love you, Em, but how much longer are you going to keep making excuses? You are an intelligent, beautiful woman with a lot to offer any man lucky enough to meet you. But I'm telling you: you're not going to find him on your blinking phone!'

'How do you know?' I scoffed, picturing all the success stories and posts I'd seen on social media. 'Myriam, one of my Facebook friends, got engaged last month to a guy she met on Tinder—it *can* happen. I just need to go at my own pace and maybe persevere a bit more.'

'As I keep saying, what you *need* to do, is ditch the apps and go offline.'

Oh, not this again…

'And as *I* keep telling *you*, that's a crazy idea.'

'It really isn't. I'm telling you. If you want to find a man, look for one in real life,' she replied.

Honestly. I really don't know why Chloe keeps harping on about this *in real life* stuff. Everyone knows that apps are the way to go these days. She really is stuck in the dark ages.

'That might be how you met Brian nearly two decades

ago, but times have moved on since then. This isn't the nineties! People don't chat each other up in the street or in bars anymore. As I've said every time you bring this up, it's all done online now.'

'Poppycock!' She slammed her hand on the table. 'If you want to find a meaningful relationship, the old-fashioned ways are still the best. I guarantee it.'

'*Guarantee?*' I scoffed. 'Now *you're* talking *nonsense.*'

'Okay, Ms Online,' she said, calmly taking a sip of her tea, 'if you're so convinced meeting someone offline *won't* work, why don't you try it and prove me wrong? You've been doing things your way with these dating apps for five months and you've got nowhere. So I say it's time to do something different.' She placed a slice of cake on her plate. *Yes. It definitely was her delicious pineapple and coconut loaf.* My mouth began to water. 'Emily Robinson, I challenge you to look for dates offline for two months and I guarantee it will change your life,' she said, taking a big bite.

'Now I *know* you're nuts!' I said, reaching for my own slice and getting stuck in. 'That will *never* work!'

'What you mean is, you're too afraid to try. Too weak to accept the challenge. The Emily I met at uni had balls. She was fun and ambitious. She pushed herself. But *that* Emily has apparently been replaced by some scared little hermit who sits here moping over some idiot when she could be out there having the time of her life. Well, *you* might be happy to wallow and waste away your years, but I'm not going to watch you do it. So what's it to be?'

'*Seriously?*' I said, wiping the crumbs from the corners

of my mouth. 'Are you blackmailing me? Threatening to withdraw our seventeen-year friendship if I don't agree to your stupid challenge?'

'No. I'm *helping* you,' said Chloe. 'It's called tough love. If I don't push you, you'll just sink further and further until eventually, you can't even get out of bed. Then you'll lose all your clients, you won't be able to pay your bills, the bank will threaten to repossess your flat and then you'll *really* have something to worry about.'

'Jeez. Talk about dramatic! I'm not that bad.'

'Not yet. But that's where you're heading. You're not in a good place. This isn't just about finding a man. It's about finding your sanity. Getting out of this godforsaken flat. Making new friends. Having fun. Starting again. I'm helping you to rescue yourself and get a life. You should be thanking me.'

I paused.

I admit. Things weren't great. And I did often find myself going stir-crazy surrounded by these four walls in my two-bed flat every day.

Working alone from home had always seemed like the dream when I was commuting and slaving away at the design agency uptown. I used to fantasise about being my own boss.

I loved the idea of not having to be in a noisy environment, deal with office politics or make small talk.

I longed for the day that I could simply roll out of bed and walk a few steps to my desk when I wanted, rather than having to wake up at the crack of dawn, get dressed, trek to the station, wait on the crowded platform for three packed tubes to pass and cram myself onto the fourth one, which would be so hot, I'd feel like I was standing in a sauna fully clothed. I'd then find my head shoved into some stranger's sweaty armpit as more commuters piled on at the next stop. By the time I'd arrive at the office, I already felt like I'd done half a day's work.

Travelling in rush hour was exhausting. So whilst I didn't miss the daily commute, I'd started to realise that when you work, sleep and eat within the same surroundings 24/7, you can start to feel a little claustrophobic.

'Even if I *were* to consider this offline thing,' I said, making sure I didn't commit to anything, 'I honestly wouldn't know where to begin.'

'Leave that to me,' said Chloe. 'I'll find the activities for you. All I need is for you to commit to it for two months. What do you reckon?'

Yes, it sounded interesting and *yes*, maybe it would be good for me, but it also sounded scary. Chloe had been suggesting I try getting out and about more since I'd broken up with Eric, but she'd never put a definite time frame to it. All this talk of a *two-month challenge* sounded so formal. So *serious*. It was *way* too much to take in. Committing to even going out once to try and meet new people was a big deal, so I'd hate to think about what she'd try and cram into eight weeks. Just the thought of it made me feel ill.

'Chloe.' I softened my voice. 'I really appreciate your concern and it seems like a good idea, but I'm okay for now. I just…it's just not the right time at the moment. But thank you.'

'The brush-off. *Again*. Well, it's your life. Not that you can call sitting at home day after day, doing nothing except working and staring at your phone, a life. I can't force you, but I can't promise I'll be able to stand back forever and just watch you go downhill either. I'll let this slide for today, but I *will* bring it up again. In fact, very, very soon, so give it some serious thought. *Please?*'

'I'll do my best,' I said half-heartedly.

'Good. Well, I'd better run. Brian's got the day off too and his parents are going to pick up the kids from school, so he's taking me out for lunch and then we might head back home for some uninterrupted adult time.' She winked.

'Well, enjoy!' I said, giving her a hug.

'*You* could be enjoying some afternoon delight with a lovely man too if you accepted my challenge…'

'*Bye, Chloe.*' I rolled my eyes and followed her into the hallway.

After she left, I closed the door, then leant against it.

Afternoon delight?

With another man? I couldn't even imagine it. Which was probably another reason I'd avoided meeting guys from these apps. I always enjoyed sex with Eric, so the thought of sleeping with someone other than him was terrifying. Surely he must feel weird about being with Nicole too? Even though it'd been months since we'd broken up, it was still possible that he might realise that he'd made a terrible mistake and ask to come back.

I know, I know. I shouldn't even entertain the idea after what he'd done. I'd always sworn that I would never forgive a guy that cheated, but now I was in this situation, as much as I hated to admit it, maybe I could *consider* it… I mean, we were together for five years. That was half a decade. Surely that was something worth fighting for? Or trying to, at least?

Don't get me wrong. I wouldn't just roll over. There's no way I'd cave in immediately. He'd have to grovel. Apologise. Repeatedly. *Sincerely.* Swear he'd never do it again. I'd need to know he was really, really sorry. I'd also lay down some ground rules. I wouldn't make it easy for him. No way.

Of course I knew it would be hard to forgive him completely. To get over the betrayal. The pain he'd put me through wouldn't disappear overnight, and we'd probably need to go through counselling, but with time, it must be possible. After all, millions of other couples had survived infidelity, so why couldn't we?

As crazy as it seemed, in some ways, taking him back might even make sense. I mean, I knew Eric inside out and he knew me. *Better the devil you know.* Right? Surely it would be better to try and patch things up with him rather than going out and meeting someone completely new.

Anyway, no point thinking too much about it right now. I'd cross the forgiveness bridge when Eric apologised. Until then, I would just monitor the situation. That was the advantage of still following him on Insta. I could see how well Eric and Nicole were getting on. And once the novelty wore off and he remembered what we'd had, he'd ask if we could try again. Until then, it would be better if I didn't meet anyone else. I'd only end up letting them down when Eric came back, which wouldn't be fair.

No. I know Chloe meant well, but things were fine how they were. The engagement thing was just a little setback. Temporary. Their relationship wouldn't last.

Maybe I could wait.

Not forever. Just a little while longer. Just to see what happened.

It was only a matter of time. I was sure of it.

Soon Eric and I would get back together and my life would fall back into place again. Just how it was before.

CHAPTER FOUR

It was now Friday and I was feeling better. Stronger. Whilst I'd had a quick peek at Twitter and Facebook a few times earlier today, I'd managed to stay off Instagram all afternoon, so this evening I'd poured myself a drink, taken the last slice of Chloe's cake and climbed under the covers ready for a well-deserved social media binge.

These past few months, I'd been a bit of a passive user. I hadn't really been anywhere to take pictures so was mainly looking at other people's content rather than posting myself, which meant I was losing followers.

Eric was a sales manager for an events company and was often invited to cool bars. Well, I thought they were pretentious, but everyone else thought they were cool, so whenever I posted those pics, I got lots of likes. I'd been able to get away with some Throwback Thursday posts using old photos from my nights out with him, but now I'd run out of images. Maybe putting up an inspirational quote or reposting might give my numbers a boost. I wasn't in the mood for doing any of that tonight, though, so I'd just scroll through Insta instead. Hopefully I could think of something interesting to put up tomorrow.

Thankfully, things had calmed down on the whole Eric and Nicole front. There hadn't been many new comments when I'd checked quickly this morning and he hadn't posted anything new, so I was feeling quite calm about logging back on.

As I scrolled down the feed, there was a photo of a mouth-watering dinner posted by Rachel, a girl I used to work with at the agency, a snap of a blogger posing by the pool in a tiny bikini, which showed off her washboard stomach, basking in the glorious sunshine at what looked like the most amazing luxury five-star hotel, and a photo of a reality star I didn't even remember following, that showed off her no make-up selfie taken earlier this morning. *Blimey*. If I posted a pic of what I looked like after I'd just woken up, it would be panda eyes, dribble around my mouth and puffy cheeks. And how could her hair possibly be so smooth after eight hours of tossing and turning in bed? Mine was always like a bird's nest.

As I scrolled past a photo of another celeb promoting a dodgy-sounding slimming powder which she claimed had helped her get back into shape weeks after having her baby, I froze.

It was a post from Eric.

A photo of him kissing Nicole with the sun setting behind them.

My stomach sank.

I knew I should just log off there and then, but I couldn't help myself. I read the caption:

My darling Nicole: I love you so very much. My life began the day I met you. Before I was existing in darkness and then you came along and lit up my life. I finally feel like I'm living. Like I'm truly alive. Life with you is never dull or predictable. Every day with you is exciting. A new adventure. I can't wait to see where this next chapter takes us. Thank you for agreeing to be my wife. I'm looking forward to spending the rest of our lives together. Always. Eric x

#truelove #engaged #marriage #fiancee #bridetobe #couplegoals #happiness

I'd thought my heart was crushed before with the proposal post, but reading this felt even worse. It was like a hundred knives had been plunged into my heart, then twisted around slowly.

How could he? He'd never said anything remotely romantic to me and yet here he was. *Gushing.* Telling the whole world how much he loved her.

Before Nicole he was *living in darkness*?

So he found being with me depressing?

Life with her was *never dull or predictable*?

Surely he knew I still followed him. How could he be so cruel? Humiliate me so publicly?

What a bastard.

I suppose I shouldn't be surprised. 'Don't be such a bore!' was what Eric used to say every time we were out and I asked if we could go home—even when we'd been somewhere for hours. Or he'd say it whenever I felt like a relaxed evening on the sofa and he wanted to go to one of those horrible bars in the West End.

If we ever did something *I* enjoyed for a change, like going to an intimate gig or visiting an art gallery, then I'd have been more enthusiastic. But that never happened. I just didn't see the point of going to his flashy places. The drinks were overpriced and it was always too noisy to have a conversation. It seemed like everyone just went there to pose, be seen and take photos for the 'gram. I suppose that was all those bars were good for, really. For me anyway. I always felt so out of place. The women there were all super groomed and wore slinky dresses. If I tried to squeeze even one of my bum cheeks into that kind of outfit, it would rip instantly. I just wasn't one of those glamour-puss girls. That's probably why he preferred Nicole. Because of her young, firm, model physique and glossy hair.

I read the caption again.

Every day with you is exciting. A new adventure.

I sighed. He was probably right. I'd seen her Instagram page. I thought Eric went to lots of swanky places, but Nicole was always going to different bars, clubs, and parties, either with a massive circle of friends or with Eric.

Every weekend she posted photos of their romantic brunches—normally somewhere with a view of the Thames or the London skyline. How could I compete with that? All I ever had for breakfast was a blueberry muffin and a latte. Hardly Insta-worthy. Apart from hanging out at Chloe's, the only other place I went was to Sainsbury's Local if I'd missed something off my online weekly shopping order and needed it urgently. And let's face it: posting a photo of a can of baked beans or a loaf of bread wasn't going to make Eric see the error of his ways.

I flopped on the bed.

What am I doing with my life?

It had been ages since Eric and I had broken up, and

whilst he'd been busy proposing to Nicole and having an amazing time with her, going out every night, I'd been sitting here like some saddo, stalking his Instagram page and hoping he'd come back to me. Watching everyone else's exciting lives whilst I sat inside. Talking to guys on dating apps, but never meeting them because I was terrified of getting hurt again.

There must be more to life than this.

This couldn't be it for me? Could it? I bloody hoped not.

I needed to do something. Otherwise it would be.

Chloe had always said she'd help me to get back out there again, but I still wasn't sure. That two-month challenge thing sounded scary. And once I started, there would be no going back.

I looked at the post, again. Eighty-six likes and thirty-two comments. *Jeez.* I scrolled through them.

@IamMarissa123UKX Such a beautiful couple! You two are made for each other.

What a two-faced cow. Marissa had always said Eric and I were made for each other.

Look at them all. Fawning over Eric and Nicole like they were the world's hottest celebrity couple. It was like I'd never even existed.

I should have logged off, as every second I spent online made me feel even worse. But before I knew it, I had refreshed my feed again, and just as I did, a new photo popped up.

It was another post from Eric. Sitting in what looked like a fancy train carriage, grinning with Nicole. I read the caption:

Dinner on the Eurostar! Oui! My beautiful fiancée and I are off to Paris for an impromptu adventure. Just because…We just LOVE being spontaneous. We'll be sure to post lots of photos of our exciting trip. Stay tuned!

#Livingourbestlives   #happycouples   #couplegoals #madlyinlove #engaged #newlyengaged #love #adventures #Paris #Romance #Romantic #exciting

Aaargghh!

That's it.

I couldn't keep torturing myself. I couldn't subject myself to more lovey-dovey posts, pictures of them snogging in front of the Eiffel Tower, drinking champagne in bed from each other's glasses and God knows what else.

Sod it.

I clicked the button to unfollow him, then scrolled through my list and unfollowed each and every person I could find who was linked to Eric.

Done.

Eric might be looking forward to his 'new adventures' with Nicole, but that didn't mean I needed to sit here and watch from the front row.

And what was with harping on about how *exciting and spontaneous* their lives were? Talk about sticking the knife in. It wasn't like *I* hadn't ever done things off the cuff before. Maybe not so much these days, but before I met Eric I wasn't dull. Or predictable. And I wasn't boring. *I wasn't!* Okay, I might *seem* that way right now, but I *can* be fun. If I wanted to. And I *do*. I wanted to enjoy my life. I'd wasted enough of it with Eric, and I didn't intend to waste another second.

I swiped up to close Instagram and tabbed to favourites in my phone contacts.

'Evening, Em.'

'Hey, Chloe…you know you said you'd help me get out more? Meet new people? Make new friends? Does the offer still stand?'

'Absolutely!'

'Well, I'd like to do it. I'm petrified. Totally shitting myself, but you're right. It might be good for me. I want to do it. I *need* to do it. To at least try…'

'That's brilliant news! Don't worry. I'll arrange everything. Meet me at your coffee shop tomorrow at noon and I'll talk you through what I have in mind.'

'Okay, cool. Thanks.'

I ended the call and exhaled.

Boring? Dull? Predictable? Not anymore.

I'll show you, Eric.

The exciting, fun-seeking Emily is making a comeback. And you're going to be sorry you ever left her.

CHAPTER FIVE

What an earth was I thinking?
I was on my way to the coffee shop to discuss Chloe's 'two months to transform your life' challenge and I couldn't help but think I'd been a little hasty.

I know I was upset about Eric's proposal and all his gushy posts last night, which made me snap out of my delusional bubble and finally see that it really *was* time to move on. And I know that got me all fired up about getting myself out there and starting to live my life properly. But that flash of optimism had disappeared and now I was filled with doubts. Let's get real: did I *really* think I could go from being a hermit to suddenly turning myself into some sort of social butterfly in two months?

Come on.

I mean, *of course* I'd like to believe that I could become more outgoing. But if it really was that easy to meet new people, change your life and bag a decent boyfriend, then everyone would have an entourage of hundreds of friends and we'd all be loved up.

I know Chloe meant well, but sometimes when you've been in a relationship for a while, it's easy to forget how hard it is being thrust back onto the single front line. Especially when one minute you thought everything in your world was hunky-dory, and the next, you were arriving home early from a meeting and hearing loud noises coming from your bedroom, only to open the door to see some twenty-something's toned bottom bouncing up and down on top of your boyfriend as he fondled her big pert breasts and groaned that she felt "*so good*".

Ugh! Just picturing it made me feel like someone had taken a chainsaw to my heart all over again. If I thought about it now, I'd fall back into a hole of darkness. *No. Can't do that. I've got to get over him. Deep breath.*

Like I was saying, when you're in a relationship, you can forget how hard it was to find that special someone. I certainly did. It took a couple of months of being single again to realise that finding someone that you were attracted to and had a connection with wasn't going to be a walk in the park. Particularly when you were in your mid-thirties and so many of the 'good guys' were already coupled up.

I reckon Chloe was thinking that just because she happened to meet Brian at a party all those years ago and fall madly in love, I could easily find someone in a real-life setting now too. But things were different these days. Times had changed. And anyway, I wasn't like her. I was an introvert.

Ever since we'd met in the canteen at uni when I was in my first year of studying art and design and she was in her final year of her sociology degree, Chloe had always been super confident and bubbly. Put her in a room full of strangers and ten minutes later she'd know everyone's middle name, their date of birth, what brand of soap powder they used and where they bought their underwear. She was just a natural people magnet.

I, on the other hand, was the complete opposite, and my memory was rubbish too, which wasn't ideal for networking. Someone could tell me their name five times and I would still forget it in seconds.

Don't get me wrong. Eventually, if I relaxed a little and found that we had a few things in common, I'd be okay. I could hold a conversation. I didn't mind going out and socialising if it was one-on-one or with a small group of people I knew. If I felt comfortable with them, I could even talk for hours. It was mainly the initial bit that I found tricky. You know, breaking the ice. Having the courage to go up and speak to strangers, then think of an 'opening line' to get their attention and make them think I was interesting. Not to mention the awkwardness of making small talk. It was hard. And don't even get me started on approaching a man in a romantic sense. The thought of attempting to chat up a guy I fancied was enough to make me break out in a cold sweat.

I'd met all my past boyfriends via introductions from friends in a familiar group setting, so it had never been that scary blind date scenario. But with literally everyone I knew now being part of a couple or married, those kind of relationship referrals had become extinct along with the Walkman and Blockbuster video stores.

That was why I preferred to dip in and out of the apps just to chat to my matches. It kept me company during the evenings and was low-risk. If I didn't meet them, I wouldn't be disappointed. And if I stayed single, then I wouldn't have to worry about being cheated on again.

So, yeah. Given the fact that I was shy around strangers, scared of rejection and terrified about getting hurt, agreeing to a challenge which involved meeting new people, trying to make new friends and attempting to find a boyfriend who would probably break my heart again sounded like the worst idea *ever*. Which was another reason why I didn't know why I was now stepping through the doors of Cuppa, the coffee shop at the end of my road, for what Chloe was calling a 'project briefing'. Crazy didn't even begin to cover it…

It was busy in here today. Lots of couples at the tables for two, and a few families. I looked around, trying to spot Chloe. I loved the interior of this place. It fused rustic original wooden flooring and exposed brick walls with modern shiny white tables and chairs. They had lightbulbs hanging from suspended yellow string over the bright yellow counter, quirky artwork on the walls and tall white bookcases filled with a selection of cookery and food-related books available to buy.

There she was. I spotted Chloe in the comfy brown leather sofa in the corner. The sofas were one of my favourite things about Cuppa. There were only two, so you were never guaranteed to get one, but when you were lucky enough, they were so lovely to sit in. Like resting your bottom on a soft fluffy cloud. By far the best seats in the house.

'You're here!' said Chloe excitedly as she stood up to greet me.

Chloe was wearing a plum dress which nipped her in at the waist with a hemline below the knee. I recognised it as one of her favourite finds from the charity shop, which was where she bought most of her clothes.

'Reluctantly,' I said, giving her a warm hug. 'I'd thought about texting to say I'd been struck down by a highly infectious strain of flu and couldn't make it, but then I remembered that you don't look at your mobile regularly like normal people. And you have a key to my flat, so even if you had to wear a mask and protective clothing, you'd still come and drag me outside.'

'Correct!' said Chloe, letting out a wicked laugh. 'Nothing wrong with speaking to people on the landline, and a deal is a deal. You agreed to do this, so there's no going back now.'

'Well, *yes*, I did agree, but I am still an adult with my own mind, so I don't *have* to do it if I don't want to, no matter how much you blackmail me.'

'*True*, but deep down, you know that I'm right and you know this will be good for you. Remember, I get nothing from this—other than seeing your happiness.'

'More like watching me squirm and fall flat on my face,' I said, shuffling up beside her.

'It's possible,' she chuckled. 'But as the saying goes, *no pain, no gain*. I can't force you, Em, but I really think you should give it a go. And I spent all night researching the first activity to add to your itinerary, even sacrificing my 'adult time' with Brian, so it would be good to know I hadn't gone without for nothing.'

'Wow, you gave up sex with your husband? Now I *know* you're guilt tripping me! I don't know whether to apologise or say thank you,' I said, picking up the latte Chloe had ordered for me.

'Show your gratitude by saying you're up for your first activity next Saturday.'

Next week? Gosh. So soon?

'I don't think I want to go through with it anymore.' I winced. 'Especially now you've mentioned the word 'itinerary'. Sounds very formal and full-on. I thought it was supposed to be fun?'

'Don't worry. It *will* be fun, but if you're going to do this, it's got to be done right. That's why you need a proper itinerary. So,' she said, whipping her sturdy polka dot notebook from her bag, 'as I mentioned before, the plan is to get you out of your flat, making new friends, trying new things and finding love. All offline. We'll meet here every Monday morning at nine-thirty for a weekly debrief once I've dropped Archie and Violet off to school.'

'Or we can just meet at my flat?' I suggested.

'No! That's the other thing.' She rested her cup of tea back on the table. 'I will *not* be coming to your place for the next two months.'

What the hell?

'Why?' I protested. 'We always meet at my flat. I like having you round.'

'That's exactly the problem. You're not going to meet anyone if you're stuck inside all the time.'

'And I'm not going to meet anyone walking fifty metres to this coffee shop either,' I huffed.

'You don't know that. Anyway, let me finish explaining the plan first and then we can go through questions after,' she snapped.

'Yes, ma'am!' I joked, mocking a salute.

'As I was saying, we'll meet here every Monday morning for a debrief where I will give you your assignment for the week…' *Assignment? What is this? University?* 'We'll start off with just one or two activities, just to break you in gently, but by month two, I'll expect you to be going out at least three or four times a week.'

'Four times a week!' I shouted. 'I'll never find the time to do that?'

'Utter flapdoodle!' said Chloe. 'If you've got time to waste on Insta-bland and watching video tapes, you have time to go out every other day. Anyway, let me finish!'

No one watches video tapes anymore, Chloe. It's all about Netflix.

'Okay, okay,' I said. 'Do continue.'

'So—as I was saying, for the first month, I will find activities for you to do and brief you on where to go, what time they start and finish, etc., so all you'll need to do is turn up and make friends. Then the following Monday, as it's my day off, we'll meet up, you can tell me how it all went, get your next assignment etc. Easy-peasy.' She smiled, looking pleased with herself.

'Yeah, easy for *you* to say,' I scoffed. 'And anyway, why does it have to be two months? Seems a bit random.'

'Believe me, *nothing* I do is random.' Chloe raised her eyebrows. 'The challenge is two months because studies show that's how long it takes to change a habit or to adopt a new one.'

'I thought it was a month?'

'That's a myth that came from a book in the 1960s based around a twenty-one-day challenge, but that isn't accurate. A more recent study found that it takes an average of sixty-six days—sometimes even longer. But I feel that two months is fair and in this instance should be sufficient to achieve the required result.'

There goes Chloe with her official sociology talk. Myth or not, personally I preferred the twenty-one days theory, but even that seemed like torture.

'So go on, then,' I sighed. 'Put me out of my misery. *If* I do decide to do this—and I do still reserve the right to say no—what would be my first *assignment*?'

'A singles' party. Next Saturday night at the Gherkin. It sounds like it's going to be brilliant. They'll be over two hundred people there, so lots of opportunities to make friends.'

'Wait, what?' I gulped, my stomach suddenly tangling up into a million knots. '*Two hundred people*? At the Gherkin? The massive building in the city?'

'Well, the organisers said two hundred and fifty people are expected, but you know not everyone will turn up, so two hundred is a safe bet. And yes, the Gherkin, the famous building in the financial district. Sadly not at the top with the stunning views of London. It'll be held in a big bar at the base instead, which is called The Sterling and looks really snazzy.'

'Two hundred and *fifty* people? I'm supposed to walk into a venue with *two hundred and fifty* strangers and just 'make friends'? I won't know a single soul and you think it will be easy to just go and *talk* to them?' I felt the blood draining rapidly from my cheeks. In fact, from my whole body. 'Forget it, Chloe. I know I said last night that I'd do this, but I've changed my mind. It's too much.'

'Don't worry! They have friendly hosts who will make introductions. And remember, everyone there is in a similar boat. They're all single in their thirties, forties or fifties, and a lot of people come on their own, so they'll be nervous just like you. They even have a special ladies' table if you feel like having a wingwoman.'

I saw Chloe's mouth moving, but whatever she was saying wasn't registering. I couldn't remember the last time I'd been around *fifty* people, never mind two *hundred* and fifty. Because I worked from home, apart from popping into Cuppa, I could sometimes go *days* without seeing or speaking to anyone, which suited me just fine. I usually just communicated via email or text because I hated talking to clients on the phone (and meeting them face-to-face was even worse), so the idea of having real conversations with what might as well be a stadium full of people made me want to bury myself under my duvet. *Indefinitely.*

'Nope. Sorry. Can't face it. The only way I'll *consider* it is if you come with me.' Chloe shook her head. 'At least for this event? Just to get me started? *Please?*'

'Sorry, love.' She took a sip of her tea. 'Firstly I'm not single, so I wouldn't be allowed, and secondly, you've got to throw yourself in at the deep end. This isn't your first day at school, for Pete's sake. You're a grown woman. You've got this.'

'Technically, yes, but being an adult doesn't necessarily mean I'm comfortable in a room full of thousands of strangers. I understand why you're encouraging me to do this, and I admit, I can see there might be one or two benefits if it works, which is still a big *if. But*, because I'm an introvert and I'm still on the fence about all this, can't I try something a bit more intimate—you know, *smaller*—for my first activity? To help me warm up to the idea? Break me in gently?'

Chloe shook her head again.

'Nope. This is the perfect first activity. And now you're just being dramatic. There won't be *thousands* of people. Just a few hundred strangers. No big deal. You'll be fine. Trust me.'

Trust me. The two words that immediately made me want to do the exact opposite.

Chloe opened her notebook and started pointing at a table she'd drawn with different timings and colours. Must have taken her ages to do that by hand.

Bloody hell. Going to a party with a million strangers? On my own?

'I, I…' I was struggling to take it all in. My throat went dry, my cheeks began to burn and my mind grew fuzzy.

'So that's all settled, then?' said Chloe, clapping her hands together excitedly. 'Glad you're okay with the plan. Any other questions?' I opened my mouth to try and speak, but not a single word came out. 'Great! I'll photocopy this itinerary for Saturday so you have it to hand. And no need to be nervous. I'm sure everyone will be lovely, and even if they ignore you or aren't that friendly, it will be a good experience and will make you stronger. It's going to be wonderful, Em. Just you wait and see!'

Oh. Dear. God.

CHAPTER SIX

"Slight change of plan," Chloe had said when she'd called me on Tuesday night. "I thought about your comments about me throwing you in at the deep end with hundreds of people and felt a bit guilty. So I found an extra smaller event to add to this week's itinerary. To help break you in more gently, just like you asked. It's a relaxed singles' event. Should be a harmless, easy icebreaker. No more than twenty-five people there, which means you'll find it easier to manage. I know research shows that social-ising can wear introverts out, so as it's your first go at this, you don't even have to stay that long. Just an hour. Two, tops. Here's the details…"

So I'd written everything down (because of course, Chloe was far too old-fashioned to just send me a bloody text) and I had been dreading it ever since.

Yes, meeting twenty-five people was less scary than two hundred and fifty, but for me, that was still a big crowd. One or two people would have been much better.

The event started in less than two hours. I should have started getting ready at least thirty minutes ago, but I had to finish some boring bike illustrations for a cycling magazine. Then I was procrastinating, because I had no idea what I was going to wear or what I was going to say when I met these strangers.

The idea of making small talk was terrifying. Truth was, all I wanted to do was dive under my duvet and hide there until tomorrow morning, but I owed it to myself to give it a go. I had to at least try. And Chloe had gone to a lot of trouble to help me, so I couldn't let her down.

I switched off my computer, went into my bedroom and opened my wardrobe. It'd been so long since I'd even had a proper look in here. Usually, I just wore comfy leggings and a long baggy jumper, which was fine for popping out to the coffee shop or the supermarket, but that wasn't going to cut the mustard for tonight.

Maybe it would be easier to think whilst I was doing my hair. I stared at my head of thick curls in the mirror. It would take an eternity to straighten them with my irons. Ugh.

It had been ages since I'd bothered. That was one of the advantages of spending all my time at home. Knowing that nobody would see me meant I could just throw it up in a bun or even do nothing with it at all. It didn't matter how I looked. But now I was going out properly in public and would be meeting new people, I had to try and make it look presentable.

Eric would have a fit if he saw me like this. He didn't like my hair looking what he called *wild* and *crazy*. He preferred it to be straight and glossy. Not long after we'd started going out, he'd asked one of his colleagues how she got her hair *so gorgeous* and then booked me an appointment at her favourite salon to get a keratin blow-dry, which he said would make my hair look 'much nicer'. That's when I started going to the salon every three months to keep it sleek.

Each time my curls were flattened, I felt like all the personality of the hair I'd been born with was being stripped away. But Eric liked it, and it was much easier to manage. Mum had always struggled to style it when I was younger as the texture was different to hers. When I was growing up, I was the only girl in my class who didn't have straight, silky hair, so I'd never felt beautiful. After all, name one Disney princess back then with curls? Rapunzel? Cinderella? Belle? *Exactly*. None of them had to deal with trying to tame their thick, disobedient hair into submission or being called frizz-ball at school. Their glossy locks just flowed effortlessly in the wind.

I was so happy when straightening irons became available and spent most of my twenties frying my hair to death every morning to try and get it poker straight just like the celebs I'd see on TV and in the magazines.

I knew it was bad for me, so I did consider going back to wearing my hair curly, but by then I was dating Eric and he made his views about his preferences very clear, so even though I hated the salon and how snooty the stylist always was towards me, I kept up my appointments. Well, that was until I'd walked in on him and Nicole.

I was due to get it redone that weekend, as I hadn't had the treatment for four months. But I'd cancelled and never rebooked. After that, I was so down in the dumps, the last thing on my mind was how straight my bloody hair was. Dragging myself out of bed every morning was already enough of a struggle. So now about a year had passed since I'd straightened my hair, which hadn't really been an issue, because I didn't have to go anywhere. Until now. *Oh well.* I supposed if I was going to give this challenge a go, I would have to get back into the whole hair smoothing routine again.

I switched on the straighteners, pumped some serum on my palms and rubbed them into my curls. I tied the top of my hair into a bun and then started running the irons through the rest, section by section.

God. I'd forgotten how annoying this is. After about twenty minutes, I'd managed to get the back of my hair smooth. I tied that into a loose ponytail, got to work on the sides, then finally unravelled the bun at the top, ready to complete the task. Definitely would have been much easier if I'd had a keratin blow-dry. Doing this manually was hard work.

Just as I went to tackle the crown area, there was a loud bang and then the power and temperature lights on the irons went out. *What the hell?* I frantically pushed the buttons, trying to switch it on again. Nothing. I unplugged the irons from the mains and into another socket. That didn't work either.

No, no, no, no! This cannot be happening! Please don't break on me now.

I glared at myself in the mirror. My hair was smooth at the sides and the back and like a big bird's nest on the top. I looked like someone in the eighties wearing a crazy mullet. How could I go to the event with this mop?

Oh God.

If I'd started at the front, it wouldn't look so bad. Then I could have pulled the smooth hair over the frizzy bits. But like this, it just looked ridiculous.

Disaster.

I checked my watch. I'd already spent almost an hour doing my hair, and I now had just over sixty minutes to get dressed, try and do my make-up and get into central London. Surely this was a sign. Maybe the universe was telling me not to go.

I plonked myself down on the bed. It would be so easy just to lay here all night and watch Netflix or log on to Instagram. But was that really how I wanted to live my life?

No.

I couldn't let a bad hair day stop me from trying.

I jumped up and went back to the wardrobe. Still had no idea what to wear. Everything looked so dreary and too small. I probably wouldn't fit into any of this stuff now anyway. I was always so conscious of Eric teasing me about the size of my bum that I was constantly dieting. So after months of eating what I wanted and doing very little exercise, I was even curvier than I had been when I was with him.

Sod it. This was driving me insane. I didn't have time for overthinking. If in doubt, wear jeans. At least I knew they'd fit me.

I pulled a dark blue pair off the hanger, grabbed a smartish black jumper and put them on quickly. Next I swiped on some mascara, which was probably well past its use-by date, applied some clear lip balm, threw my nightmare hair up into a bun, stepped into some flat black shoes and then rushed out the door before I had time to change my mind and stay at home.

∼

I found the bar quite quickly. It was in the city, quite close to Liverpool Street station. My heart was beating so fast I thought it was going to fly out of my chest. I really, really didn't want to do this. Every part of me wanted to turn and run for the hills.

I took a deep breath and stared nervously through the glass windows. From what I could see, it looked fancy. Just like the kind of bar that Eric liked to go to. Probably all loud and imposing inside. But this time, I didn't have Eric's confidence and outgoing personality to hide behind. I was here. *Alone.* I had to walk into this scary-looking place all on my own. Without any of Eric's friends to talk to. No familiar faces. Just cold strangers who probably wouldn't be interested in anything I had to say.

I can't.

Just as I turned to walk away, the door opened and two women who were leaving smiled at me as they left.

Come on, Em, said a voice inside of me. *You can do this. Maybe it won't be so bad. Give it a go.*

I took another deep breath and stepped inside.

I could see there were two levels. I looked around for signs to point me in the right direction, but there was nothing. I had no clue where to go.

I spotted a woman in her early thirties who looked relatively friendly and approached her.

'Excuse me, I'm here for the event. Do you know if it's on this floor or down in the basement?'

'It's over there at the back,' she said, pointing to the far end of the room. 'More people should be coming soon.'

'Okay, thanks,' I replied.

I glanced over. To the left were a few tables with people sitting down having one-to-one conversations. In the middle was a makeshift cloakroom with rails of coats and jackets, and to the right were larger clusters of people chatting away.

At least I was in the right place, which was something. And if more people were coming, it was good that I'd turned up before it got too busy and I couldn't hear what anyone was saying. Might not have been such bad timing after all.

I stood in a corner near the bar. I supposed I should take a photo for Insta first. I'd been low on content for ages. People would think it looked good, and it would kill time, as I definitely wasn't ready to try speaking to anyone yet...

I took several snaps of the crowd, then scrolled through them, zooming in to select the one that I thought looked the best. Obviously there was no way I could take a selfie looking like this, and posting a photo of myself was always so nerve-wracking and time-consuming. I'd have to take dozens of photos, with different poses before I found any I remotely liked. Even then, I'd spend ages picking my appearance to pieces before running it through a face-tuning app. If it was a full-body shot, I'd make my bum and waist a bit smaller, my boobs a little bigger, my hair a bit shinier, my teeth whiter... I'd edit the image meticulously, adjusting the brightness and sharpness and using every filter I could to try and look half decent.

It wasn't because I was vain. Far from it. It was just to

feel a bit better about myself. Every time I put my photo through one of the apps, I cringed. I never used to bother with all the retouching. When Eric first got me on to Instagram, I was naïve. I would just post the photos as they were. But then when he and the occasional stranger commented negatively on how I looked, I started to become anxious. Especially as I began to follow more people. Somehow everyone else always seemed prettier, slimmer, more glamorous and happier than me.

No definitely not the night for a selfie…

I selected a filter for the crowd shot and applied some different effects. Now for the caption. Even though I'd been using social media for years, I always found this bit difficult, but unlike in real-life conversations, at least I had time to think about it first and edit what to say as many times as I wanted without putting my foot in it. I needed to make it sound exciting. Maybe: *Out on the town again*. Or what about: *Another night out on the town*? Yeah, that made it sound like I'd been out a lot and wasn't boring. Or I could say: *Another night out on the town with friends* so I didn't sound like a loner. But then they'd expect to see photos of me with them. *No. Keep it simple*. I can just *imply* it with a hashtag instead.

I checked the image and read over the caption again.

Another night out on the town! #havingfun #drinkswithfriends #Londonnights #cocktails.

Massive exaggeration, but as Eric used to say, it was all about putting forward the best version of myself. No one wanted to know I was here alone or that this was the first time I'd been out in months and that rather than having fun, I was actually contemplating going home two minutes after I'd arrived. No. This was the kind of thing people wanted to see.

I looked at it once more before tapping the blue *post* button.

There. Done. Now that I'd killed five minutes, it was time to face my fears and tackle the hard stuff…

I exhaled and started walking towards the back, my heart pounding.

I scanned everyone's faces to try and gauge which of the groups seemed the least scary. The people at the tables are talking one to one, which might be easier, but they didn't look very friendly or happy. They were scowling and frowning a lot, whereas the groups to the right seem more relaxed and upbeat.

As I got closer to the groups, I saw that I was clearly underdressed. The guys were in suits and the women in tailored dresses. And here I was in jeans, flats and a jumper like I was going for a Saturday stroll. *Gosh.* I really needed some new clothes. I was so out of practise with this going out stuff, it wasn't even funny.

Well, I was here now. I had to try.

I was going to do it. I was going to approach one of the standing groups.

I tried to step forward. Then I froze.

I tried again, but then turned back and started walking towards the exit.

Come on. Come on. Come on.

I can do this. I can. I counted down from five, took a deep breath and then went over to join them.

They were mid-conversation, which was to be expected. Even though I had no idea what they were talking about, I started nodding and smiling, hoping to blend in and desperately prayed they'd mention something that I could comment on.

After a minute or two had passed (which felt like it could have been two hours), various people from the group started to notice that I'd joined them and they began to smile awkwardly, as if they were trying to figure out who I was and why I'd gate-crashed their circle. Unlike me, they'd probably arrived at the event when it had started and had time to find out more about each other.

By the time they'd finished talking about whatever subject they were discussing, it felt as if the entire group were now all staring at me. It was like they'd all shone a 'who is this woman?' spotlight directly on my face. *Great. Being the centre of attention. My worst nightmare.* I had no choice. I had to say something. *Anything.* I needed to speak about a topic that would instantly help them to connect with me and accept me into their group. But what?

My heart began beating faster. I couldn't delay it any longer. They were all waiting. Eyes wide, ears open. I opened my mouth, still not sure what to say. *Here goes…*

'Do you…' I blurted out. 'Do you come here often?'

Oh God. *Seriously?* Was that the best I could come up with? No wonder they were all frowning. It sounded like a bloody chat-up line. *Pass me a shovel so I can bury myself. Now.*

No, no. Come on. Don't give up.

'I mean, is it…your first time…at…at one of these events?' I stuttered, desperately trying to rescue myself from my lame opening line.

I was so rubbish at this.

They looked at me like I was a madwoman, running

through the streets naked, swinging my bra and knickers above my head.

Beyond awkward.

'Well…' said a geeky looking guy in his early twenties. 'I came last year, so this is my second time.'

Last year? Chloe hadn't mentioned that it was an annual event.

'Really?' I said, grateful that he'd bothered to respond. 'Well, that's one up on me. I was so nervous about coming. I mean, it can be so daunting, being in a room full of strangers. But I guess it helps that we're all in the same boat. Knowing that everyone here is single is definitely a bonus!' I grinned. *There.* I'd managed to string multiple sentences together and was still alive. Result!

Although, actually…why was everyone now frowning even more than they were before?

A tall, handsome guy clutched his wine glass tighter with his left hand, exposing a very visible wedding ring.

What a dirty dog. Honestly. These guys are so brazen. They rock up to a singles' event even though they've got their wife and probably a house full of kids at home and don't even attempt to hide the fact that they're a cheater. *No shame.*

'So who do you work for?' asked a snooty-looking lady in a tight dress and heels. *Gosh.* That was a bit of a formal question.

'I'm self-employed,' I replied, thinking I didn't feel like going into the ins and outs of my job right now. This was supposed to be a relaxed, fun event.

'Oh?' she snarled. 'I didn't think they allowed contractors to attend the annual conference.'

'Conference?' *What's she on about? What annual conference?*

'Yes.' She rolled her eyes. 'The LBLA: London Banking Leadership Annual Conference.'

Now it was my turn to frown.

'Banking conference?'

'That *is* what I just said,' she replied in a condescending voice. 'Took place today across the road, hence why we're here having drinks, per the annual tradition. Most people have already left. We're the last leaders standing.'

What on earth…?

'You mean you're not here for the Singles' Meet and Mingle event?'

She threw her head back and laughed loudly.

'Good heavens, no!' She laughed again. 'Do we look like we're sad and desperate?'

Bitch.

This was embarrassing. *Absolutely mortifying.* The woman said it was at the back of the bar, which was where I was. How could I have got it wrong? And more importantly, how could I get out of this without looking like an even bigger plonker?

'I see…right.' I glanced down at the floor. 'Clearly I've come to the wrong place. Sorry.' I shuffled off whilst she carried on laughing loudly, rolling her eyes at her colleagues as if to say *how could she be so stupid?*

It reminded me of how Eric used to laugh at me in front of his friends and make me feel like whatever I said wasn't smart or funny enough. That's why I sometimes withdrew and stayed quiet so that I wouldn't say something silly. And now here I was, making a fool of myself again.

I quickly headed towards the door. I *had* to get out of here. I knew tonight would be a disaster and it was.

Just as I was leaving, the lady who'd directed me to the back of the bar was throwing her cigarette away and coming back in.

'So, did any more people show up?' she asked.

'I don't know,' I replied. 'I came to the wrong place. It was for a banking conference, which I'm not a part of.'

'Not for *that* group. I mean for the singles group. Y'know, the meet and mingle? Did anyone else turn up?' she asked. *Now I'm really confused.* 'They said there would be twenty-five people there, but there's only six.'

'Six?' I asked. I had no idea what she was talking about.

'Yeah. Sitting down at the little tables. That's the group. The people that have turned up. All women. It's a joke! Can't believe I paid a tenner and no one's showed up. I'm surprised the others stayed. They're not happy about it either. I'm asking for a refund,' she said, storming off towards the back of the room.

Oh.

So the angry-looking people to the left were part of the singles group and the ones standing on the right were the bankers? How was I supposed to know there were two different functions going on in the same place?

Anyway, didn't make any difference to me now. There was no way I was staying. I'd suffered enough humiliation for one night. I wasn't going to prolong the pain any longer by sitting at a table with a bunch of strangers making small talk.

I'd tried Chloe's challenge and it hadn't worked. I was throwing the towel in. Sitting at home watching Netflix and scrolling through social media might not be the most exciting existence in the world, but I'd take that over being laughed at, humiliated and made to feel like a desperado any day of the week.

Chloe would be disappointed, but I couldn't help that. It was my life, and it was too short to waste it subjecting myself to another one of those horrible singles' events.

Never again.

CHAPTER SEVEN

'I hold my hands up,' said Chloe. 'I should have stuck to my original plan of making the big singles' party your first activity. But I've triple-checked my research and Happy Solos, the organisers for tonight's event, are definitely more established. Their parties always get rave reviews, and despite what you think about preferring smaller groups, I actually think a bigger crowd will be better for you. You'll feel less conspicuous.'

I was in Chloe's bedroom preparing for the Gherkin party. *Yes.* Don't ask me how, but she'd persuaded me to give the challenge another go.

'And I should have helped you prepare more. I forget how hard it must be for introverts like you to walk into a setting with unfamiliar faces and start chatting to them. I'm sorry, Em. This will be a better bunch of people. *I promise.* Hopefully now, after the conversation starters we went through today, you're feeling more relaxed?'

When I'd told Chloe how awful it was, I'd expected her to tell me to woman up and not be such a wuss. But surprisingly, she was really apologetic, saying she should have vetted the organiser more thoroughly, briefed me on the dress code and given me some talking points. I felt bad that *she* felt bad. And as much as I disliked the idea of socialising with strangers, I hated giving up even more. It made me feel weak, and that's not what I wanted. I wanted to become stronger.

'Yeah, I feel better, thanks. It's just a shame that I couldn't get an appointment at the salon to sort my crazy mop out, though. At least it's under control again now.'

After the nightmare I'd had trying to style my hair and find something decent to wear, I'd said I needed to find a new hairdresser and go shopping to help me feel more confident, and Chloe had agreed to come with me. She'd helped me pick out some nice new dresses, and annoyingly, I also had to shell out a hundred pounds on a new pair of straighteners. Still, maybe it was worth the investment, as it only took me forty-five minutes to get it smooth this afternoon, rather than the hour it used to take with the old ones.

'I honestly don't know why you bother straightening your hair. Your curls aren't crazy. They're *gorgeous*. It's just a case of finding a hairdresser who can show you how to take care of them, that's all. One of the mums at Archie's school has hair similar to yours, so I'll see if she has any tips. There!' said Chloe, looking pleased with herself, as she circled around me. 'You look a million dollars! Don't you think?'

'Well,' I said, staring at my reflection in her large antique bedroom mirror. '*Maybe*. How much is that with the exchange rate these days? Seven hundred and fifty thousand pounds?'

'Very funny!' She threw her head back. 'Take the compliment, Robinson. You look great. A *massive* improvement on the Emily I see holed up in her flat all the time. Your lovely figure isn't disguised by those awful baggy jumpers you insist on wearing. The dress accentuates your waist, and now we've banished that monobrow and your brows have been threaded, it really opens up your big brown eyes.'

'I did *not* have a monobrow!' I said, slapping her playfully on the shoulder. I'd never had them threaded before, but Chloe had booked me an appointment at a place all the mums went to and they were pretty good. 'Seriously, though, thanks. I admit, I *do* feel much better. Having my brows done does make a difference, and I like this dress.'

I was wearing a V-neck pink skater dress. Normally I wore much looser clothes, but during our shopping trip, Chloe had encouraged me to experiment with fit-and-flare dresses to show off my curves.

I looked myself up and down in the mirror. I supposed I looked okay. Still wished I had bigger boobs though.

I turned and glanced at my side profile. There was never any question of me asking if 'my bum looked big in this' as the answer would always be a definite *yes*. I had certainly been given a very generous behind. Not as firm as JLo's or Kim Kardashian's, of course, but if I did more squats every day (even doing *one* would be a good start) and hired a personal trainer to help me work out for the next ten years, then maybe a firm, toned derrière would be mine. But until then, somehow I had to learn to accept my wobbly bottom and cellulite.

I should probably take a pic for Insta. It was rare that I got dressed up.

'Could you take a few photos of me, please?' I said, bringing the camera up on my phone. 'You just need to tap here.'

'Of course.' She frowned as she zoomed in and out, trying to work out what to do. 'It will be good to have a record of your first proper activity.'

As I moved in different poses, Chloe snapped away, then handed my phone back. I scrolled through the snaps. God, my arse really did look huge in that one. And bit of a double chin from that angle too. *Oh dear.* Hopefully there'd be a half decent photo in there. Somewhere.

'What about the colour, though, Chloe? You sure it's not too Barbie?'

'No!' she scoffed. 'You *need* colour to make a statement. Remember, in a sea full of three hundred people, you want to be able to stand out, not blend in.'

'Three hundred?' I shouted as I felt my stomach drop. 'You said *two* hundred. Two-fifty tops!'

'Two hundred, three hundred. What's the difference? You'll be fine.'

'Oh, Jesus!' I said, sitting down at the edge of her bed. 'I don't know if I can go through with this, Chloe. And I thought you just said I'd feel less conspicuous in a large crowd. The last thing I want to do is stand out. I'd be fine in the corner, blending in with the background, sat right next to the exit…'

'That's exactly why you *should* go: to push yourself out of your comfort zone. Help you become more comfortable in bigger crowds. Wearing a dress like that will make you feel more confident. And you'll be more likely to attract the attention of a potential suitor. That's what I mean. Anyway, the ticket is paid for, you're on the guest list and the taxi is on its way. Look,' she said, sitting beside me. 'I know you're nervous, but it's going to be great. We've been through possible conversation starters. Just remember you're an interesting, intelligent woman and people *will* want to get to know you. Smile, relax and be yourself.'

'Okay.' I stood up and took a deep breath. 'I'll try.'

'That's the spirit!'

'It'll be hard to dance or even breathe in this dress, though. It's *really* tight around the waist,' I said, bopping my head to the upbeat love song playing from the latest Spotify playlist I'd saved onto my phone.

'You'll manage. Perhaps steer clear of any booty shaking or twerking, though, if Beyoncé comes on!'

'I'll try and restrain myself!' I chuckled. 'I *love* this song!' I said, trying to swing my hips. 'I'm tempted to unzip myself to have a little jig around now in case I can't later.' I listened to the lyrics. *So romantic.* 'Why can't I find a man who will gush about how much he loves me? Then I wouldn't have to go to this stupid party and make small talk with strangers.'

'Well, maybe your dream man is already at the party wondering where you are, which is exactly why you should leave right now!'

'Yeah, yeah, whatever.' I scoffed. 'I suppose Prince Charming has got a white horse waiting outside the venue for us to ride off into the sunset too,' I said sarcastically as I checked my phone. 'Talking of transportation, my Uber has arrived, so looks like it *is* time for me to leave.'

'Great! Well, have one last look around as you make your way out, as this will be the last time you'll set foot inside this house for seven weeks.' She smirked.

'I really don't see why I can't—' I scanned the Victorian-style grand mahogany bed, furniture and dark carpet. *Oh, forget it.* I didn't have the energy to debate Chloe's stupid 'no home visits' restriction. 'Anyway, thanks again for your help. I'll probably be cursing you when I'm there, though, *suffering.* Better run.'

'Good luck, Em!'

'Thanks.' I gave her a quick hug. 'I'll need it!'

As I stepped out of the Uber, the nervous cramps in my stomach went into overdrive. It had been ages since I'd worn heels, so as well as trying to calm myself down, I also had to concentrate on trying to walk confidently without twisting my ankle and falling flat on my face.

Help.

I just want to go home and snuggle up in front of the TV in my PJs.

A steady stream of people were walking around the base of the building. They must be going to the party too. As the financial district of London, this area was always quiet at the weekends, so the only reason for anyone to be here was for a special occasion.

I followed behind from a distance and watched a group of guys head towards the grand glass doorway. I saw the sign for The Sterling. Yep, this was it. I took another deep breath and stepped inside.

'Hi! Welcome!' said the smiley redhead at the entrance with a clipboard. 'I'm Melissa, one of the Happy Solos hosts. Can I take your name, please?'

'Yes,' I said, feigning confidence. 'It's Emily. Emily Robinson.'

'Radison, Raymond, Robinson!' she said, running her finger down through the list, then crossing me off. 'Yes. I have you here. Have you been to a Happy Solos event before?'

'No. No, I haven't,' I said.

'No worries! Well, everyone here is single. Lots of people come on their own like you, so there's no need to worry. We have a ladies table over there, just past the bar, where you can sit and chat to other solo females. And if you're nervous about walking up to a group of people by yourself, just find a Happy Solos host, and we'll introduce you to some lovely members who will take good care of you.'

'Cool. Thank you, Melissa,' I said, relaxing a little. At least I knew I was both in the right place and would be talking to the right people this time. 'Where are the loos, please?'

'Just upstairs and on the left. There's a cloakroom up there too, if you'd like to put your coat away.'

'Okay, thanks.'

'Enjoy!' she said enthusiastically.

As I carefully climbed the flight of what felt like five thousand steps, the enormity of it all started to sink in. I glanced down at the main area beneath me. Even though it was only 6.45 p.m., there were already at least a hundred people scattered around. And I was here. On my own. *Oh God.*

It's okay. That Melissa lady seemed nice, and like she'd said, there was nothing to worry about. We were all in the same boat. We were all single. We were all nervous.

I'd check my make-up and hair in the toilets, put my coat away and then head to the ladies table. Make some friends. It would be *totally* fine.

Yes. The more I tell myself that, the more I'll start believing it.

I hoped so anyway…

After touching up my lipstick and fixing my hair, my dress and literally every part of my face, body and clothing repeatedly to try and kill as much time as possible and avoid returning to the growing crowd, I finally went back downstairs.

Drink. I definitely needed a drink.

I walked through the crowds towards the bar. With two rows of people already in front of me, I could tell it was going to take a while to get served. That wasn't necessarily a bad thing. The more time I spent queuing, the less time I needed to spend networking…

'At this rate, the party will be over by the time we get a drink!' said a petite brunette thirty-something woman beside me.

'I know,' I replied. 'It's *so* busy!'

'I'm Kat,' she smiled.

'Nice to meet you, Kat,' I said, thinking of a way to etch her name into my brain. 'I'm Emily. Is it your first time at one of these events?' I asked, using one of Chloe's recommended conversation starters. Definitely an improvement on my disastrous *do you come here often* line.

'It is, actually. And I'm shitting myself!' she laughed.

'Glad I'm not the only one!'

'I've had to stop myself from leaving at least ten times in the last twenty minutes because I'm so nervous.' She moved into a gap nearer to the bar. 'If I hadn't already paid the babysitter, I'd be on the next bus home!'

Hallelujah! Someone who understands my pain...

'I've been hiding in the loos for the past twenty minutes, so I know how you feel! How many kids do you have, Kat?' I asked, adding her name to the end of my question in the hope that would stop it evaporating from my memory.

'Three. My eldest daughter is eighteen and away at uni, so now I've got just the two at home. A nine-year-old boy and eleven-year-old girl.'

'Oh wow—you don't look old enough to have a daughter who's eighteen.'

'Thanks!' Kat blushed. 'I started young, which is my diplomatic way of saying that I believed the rubbish my first boyfriend fed me about not being able to get pregnant the first time you have sex. Gosh, I was so naïve! I also believed that he loved me, but that's a *whole* different story. Suffice to say, nine months later, just before my twentieth birthday, I gave birth to Becky.'

'I'm sure you wouldn't be without her now,' I said.

'Yeah, she's alright. Most of the time. When she's not asking me to lend her money. I can't believe she's all grown up already. It's gone by *so* quickly. Anyway.' She rolled her eyes. 'What am I doing nattering on about my kids? This is supposed to be my night off. Which, these days, is about as rare as finding a decent man, so I better enjoy it whilst I can.'

'I know what you mean! I've recently come out of a relationship and it's hard to find someone with that spark —you know, that I have a connection with.'

That was true, but if I was honest, I couldn't deny the

fact that maybe if I actually went out on more dates, I'd have a much better chance…

'Tell me about it.' She nodded. 'My friends keep saying not to give up hope, because they insist that there *are* still good men out there. But frankly, I reckon they're already taken.'

'Exactly! My best friend, who is married to one of the good ones, says the same thing and is convinced that I just need to get off the dating apps and put myself out there, so here I am.'

'Oh, don't even go there with the apps.' She rolled her eyes. 'I'm so sick of them. They were driving me mental, so I thought it was time for a different approach. I've never been to one of these singles dos before, but I'm up for trying anything once—well. Maybe not *anything*!' she cackled.

'What can I get you?' asked the barman.

'Finally!' she replied. 'I thought you were going to leave us to die of thirst! Vodka and orange, please. *Actually*, let's liven things up a bit. It's still two for one on cocktails, so I fancy a Sex on the Beach. What do you reckon, Emily? Would you like one?'

'Well,' I said, scanning my memory to think what was in it, 'I've never tried that cocktail, so yeah, why not. Thanks!'

'You've never had Sex on the Beach before? You haven't lived! It's my favourite! And it's much better than the real thing. No sand up your bum, for a start!' she cackled.

I never made it to the ladies' table. After we got our drinks, Kat and I found a corner and spent ages chatting about our experiences of dating—the initial rush of getting a match on the apps, the awkward texting, the challenges of moving from messaging to meeting in real life. Full disclosure: I didn't confess that in fact I was my own worst enemy and it was *me* that avoided meeting. She didn't need to know that just yet…

Whilst I thought it was hard being single, clearly being a single mum was much harder. Especially if, like Kat, you didn't have a big family network around you. Whenever she wanted to go out on a date, she had to rely on finding a good babysitter who wouldn't cost her a fortune, or beg her sister to look after her kids.

And whenever she *did* meet a man she liked and wanted to take things further, everything would have to be planned carefully. When she could meet him depended on overnight childcare, which obviously involved footing an even bigger babysitter bill, going to his place or a hotel (yet more of an expense as she'd insist on going Dutch). Plus, the guy could never just casually pop round to hers on a whim to 'Netflix and chill', as she didn't want to risk introducing him to her kids until she could be certain (well, as much as you can be), that they were a serious, long-term prospect.

It certainly put things into perspective. There was Kat, who *wanted* to go on dates but struggled to due to childcare and finances. And then there was me, who *had* opportunities to go on multiple dates but wasted them because of my shyness and fear of rejection. I seriously needed to work on that. At least being here, which initially I'd found terrifying, was a step in the right direction.

As Kat popped to the ladies', I scanned the room. It was filling up fast. Like Chloe had predicted, there was a real cross section of people. It was roughly an even gender split. Perhaps even sixty per cent men and forty per cent women. The age range spanned from late twenties up to mid-sixties. Most had made an effort to dress up, ladies in heels and dresses and men in trousers and shirts. The majority of people were smiling and chatting either one-on-one or in small groups.

There was a scattering of people standing alone nervously clutching a drink, scanning their shoes or glancing at their phones. If I hadn't bumped into Kat at the bar, that would have probably been me too.

In fact, now would be a good time to post the photo Chloe took of me. I'd edited it in the taxi, so it should be ready to go. It was Eric who'd introduced me to the photo editing apps. I remembered tagging him in a photo of us together and him telling me to delete it and retouch it first before putting it up again. He'd downloaded an app to my phone, then gone through every part of my face and body in the photo, showing me how I could make myself look *better*. Since then, I'd never posted anything without tweaking it in some way first.

As I wrote the caption and my thumb hovered over the post button, my heart started beating faster. I always got anxious before I posted an image of myself, worrying about whether it would get any likes or if I looked terrible. And once it was out in the wild, I'd question whether I should delete the post before anyone saw it. Yeah. I wasn't sure if this photo was good enough. Best to save it to drafts and look over it again later before posting. Just to double-check it was okay…

I put my phone back in my bag and exhaled. Right now, I was feeling alright. Dare I say it, even starting to have a good time? Although I was now by myself in a corner beside the end of the bar, waiting for Kat to return, I no longer wanted to escape and run home. I was going to see this through. I wanted to make the most of it.

I glanced around the room again, remembering Chloe's advice to smile as I did so that I would look 'open' and approachable. Downstairs was now full to the brim. There were easily the two hundred and fifty people she'd said were on the guest list. Maybe even more. Surely out of the, say, one hundred and fifty men that were here, there *must* be *someone* that I'd like? *Surely*.

There *were* a couple of guys that caught my eye. One in particular who was wearing a smart burgundy suit (he clearly also followed Chloe's advice to wear colour to stand out from the crowd). Tall, dark, *very* handsome, and I got the feeling that he knew it too. Every time I looked over, which was probably more often that I should have, he was surrounded by a flock of women. They were obviously more confident than me, as I wouldn't have had the courage to approach him. Certainly not on my first proper solo rodeo. And would I really want to anyway? He had *heartbreaker* written all over him.

Just as Kat returned from the toilet, the Happy Solos hosts brought a few men over to meet us.

There was Ray, a bald accountant I guessed was in his early fifties, Will, who was maybe mid- to late thirties, who had scruffy brown hair and was a PE teacher, and Rob, a forty-something train driver who had a shaved head. No physical attraction, at least not from my side, but now that I had Kat with me, I was feeling a bit more relaxed about chatting to other people and listening to their experiences.

As it turned out, men seemed to face the same dating

challenges. They also had a love/hate relationship with apps and said they too struggled to find someone they clicked with.

'Women have unrealistic expectations,' moaned Will.

'How so?' asked Kat.

'Well,' he huffed, 'they have four kids and more baggage than an airport terminal, and yet want a guy who looks like Brad Pitt and earns at least a hundred grand a year to come and look after them all. And if that's not bad enough, as well as having terrible personalities and the IQ of a peanut, they don't even look like Angelina Jolie or Jennifer Aniston. It's a *joke!*'

Whoa. He certainly wasn't shy about telling us what he thought.

'Oh, come on!' Kat protested. 'That's a massive exaggeration!'

'Yeah, come on, mate,' said Rob. 'We've all had our fair share of dodgy encounters, but not all women are like that.'

'I have three kids and I'm not looking for an oil painting or a millionaire. Just a decent, honest guy to share my life with who will also love and respect me and my children. That's not too much to ask, is it?'

'No, Kat,' said Rob. 'I don't think it is.'

'You *think* I'm exaggerating!' protested Will. 'But I've met some *very* strange women on these apps. Half of them are already married and looking for a bit on the side. They have no morals. And I bet the ones here tonight are exactly the same. Women are a complete and utter nightmare!'

'Now hold on!' Kat scowled. 'You can't go around making sweeping statements like that. I mean, yeah, I might be guilty of saying that guys on these apps are rubbish, or saying bad things from time to time when I'm feeling frustrated. But deep down, I *hope* that's not the case for *every* man. Whereas you've pretty much said that *all* women are categorically money-grabbing, dumb, look like the back end of a bus, or are cheats, which is out of order!'

Well, this is kind of awkward, I said to myself, taking a large gulp of my second cocktail and trying to avoid being drawn into the conversation. It was embarrassing to admit it, but in a way, how Will felt about women was a little bit how I felt about men.

Naturally, I disagreed with the specifics—especially the money-grabbing nonsense, the baggage bits and the outrageous comments about our IQ. *Definitely uncalled for.* But just as Will thought most women were the same, if I was being completely honest, right now, I *did* think that men were more likely to be unfaithful, and I *did* believe that they had unrealistic expectations.

Eric had always wanted me to be slimmer and prettier, have better hair, and be funnier and more outgoing. I'd always felt like I was falling short. And because I couldn't meet his high expectations, he'd cheated on me with a woman who could.

I knew it was completely wrong of me to tar every man with the same brush. It was sexist, and it wasn't something I was proud of. But after such bad experiences, and having my heart ripped apart, it was really, really hard not to...

'I just think,' said Kat, 'that we have to hope any strange men or women we encounter on these apps, or even in real life, are the exception rather than the rule and that the nice, normal people like us are all here tonight.

Otherwise, what was the point of us coming to the party in the first place?'

She had a point. And I wanted to believe her. Truly. But I still wasn't convinced that a decent, faithful man really existed. I supposed, like Kat said, we had to try. Be optimistic. Easier said than done, though.

'I reckon you're right, Kat. You and Emily certainly seem like two lovely ladies.' Rob smiled.

'Thank you.' Kat blushed.

'*Whatever*,' snarled Will. 'I'm off to the bar.'

'See ya!' Kat sneered as he walked away. 'And good riddance. Yes!' she screamed as the DJ switched to a Rihanna classic. Whilst he'd kept the music low for the first couple of hours to give people a chance to talk, now that it was almost 9 p.m., he started to crank up the volume. I tapped my toes in time to the beat. 'Tune! Come on, Emily!' Kat took my hand and pulled me towards the dance floor. 'Time to put on our dancing shoes!'

I couldn't remember the last time I'd shaken a leg in public, or in fact done any form of exercise other than walking to and from Cuppa every morning. Sure, I danced around in the shower or at my desk every day when I was playing my latest playlists, but not proper dancing like this. No one ever danced at the parties Eric used to go to. They just took selfies. Actually, maybe now was the time to take some more snaps for social media. Kat could take one of me holding my cocktail. She was right. Sex on the Beach was divine. Or I could get a pic dancing in the crowd like I was having a good time?

Just as I started reaching in my bag to get my phone, Kat grabbed my hand again and spun me around. Once. Twice. Then a third time.

Oh well. I'd have to take some photos later. Right now, I was dancing and it felt so good. I felt free. *Alive.* I whooped every time a song came on that reminded me of my carefree college days.

I've always loved music, so I used to go out fairly often during my late teens and early twenties. I wasn't fussy about the genre. Pop, soul, rock, dance—as long as it had a good beat or a nice melody, I would listen to it.

It was funny. Even though I was reserved in most social settings, I enjoyed concerts, particularly intimate gigs. And if I was with a small group of people I knew and who liked to dance, I didn't mind going to little clubs either. When I was eighteen and had just passed my driving test, me and a couple of friends would head into town on a Thursday night to a small place that would play decent tunes. I used to just lose myself in the beat. I instantly became more carefree. I was a bit more outgoing in that respect. I smiled as I remembered the fun we'd had. Those were the days…

Bloody hell. *Those were the days*? I sounded like a ninety-year-old. I *definitely* had to get out more.

Before I knew it, it was almost half past eleven.

'Emily,' Kat shouted over the music, 'I'm going to have to love you and leave you.'

'Oh no!' I said.

'I've got a Cinderella curfew as the babysitter is only paid up until midnight.'

'Okay. I might not be that far behind you, actually. I'll probably head home soon too.'

'No!' she shouted again. 'You should stay! Dance the night away. Why go home so soon? You're having fun, aren't you? Enjoy yourself. And...you never know who you might meet!' She winked.

'Oh, I don't know about *that*. I *am* enjoying the music, though, so yeah, you're right. No point rushing back to an empty flat. I'll see how I get on. I have to admit, I've had a great time.'

'Me too!' said Kat, shaking her shoulders. 'Listen, you've got my number. Let's keep in touch. I don't get to go out that often, but you know, maybe we can meet up once a month or something. Go for a drink. Vent about whatever we need to get off our chests and exchange stories about life and *men*.'

'Of course! I'd really love that.'

'Great!' she said, reaching over and giving me a hug.

'Get home safely.' I squeezed her tight. 'And I'll message you tomorrow. Fill you in any gossip that happens after you've left.'

'Brilliant! Right,' she said, glancing down at her phone to check the time. 'There's a bus in four minutes, so I better run. See you soon!'

Awww. Kat seemed lovely. It was definitely worth coming tonight just to meet her. Right at that moment I decided that I was absolutely going to stay and enjoy myself.

After dancing to a few more songs, I headed to the loo. Just as I was leaving the ladies' toilets and went to push the swing door in the corridor forward to go back downstairs, it flung backwards towards me.

'Whoa! Careful!' I said as the door narrowly missed hitting me in the face.

'Oh God, I'm so sorry!' said the perpetrator. As I looked up, I saw Mr Burgundy Suit in front of me. My eyes widened. 'I wasn't expecting the door to be so light. Pushed it a bit too hard and nearly knocked you out. Are you okay?'

My heart jumped. *Play it cool, Em.*

'Um, yes. Fine, thanks.' I tried to compose myself. 'That was close, though.'

'I know, sorry.' He gently took my hand and rested his on top. 'Let me make it up to you. Let me buy you a drink. I'd *love* to have a dance too, if I'm not pushing my luck and you could find it in your heart to forgive me?' He tilted his head and gave me his doe eyes. *What a charmer.*

'Sure, why not,' I said as casually as I could muster whilst doing the running man in my head. I know I said before that he had *heartbreaker* written all over him, but he was the hottest guy at the party. How could I resist?

'Great!' he said, now taking both of my hands in his for a few seconds and then gently releasing them. 'I'll meet you on the dance floor in five!' He glided into the gents.

There you go, Chloe. How was *that* for stepping out of my comfort zone? I decided to put my preconceptions about men to one side. Like Kat had said earlier, not *all* men were bad. Rather than judging him because of my experiences with Eric, I just had to try and keep an open mind. *Believe.*

Maybe Chloe was right. Perhaps it really *was* easier to find a decent guy in real life. After all, tonight hadn't been as scary as I'd imagined, and now a man who I was really attracted to also seemed like he was into me. It was like a meet-cute from a romcom. *Boy bumps into girl outside the ladies', their eyes meet for the first time and he asks her to dance.* Who knows where this could lead? *Exciting!*

As I went back downstairs, Rob and Will spotted me. We started chatting. Well, I spoke to Rob, rather than Will. I was still feeling embarrassed that we both shared negative thoughts about the opposite sex. Anyway, maybe my chance meeting with Mr Burgundy Suit would help to change my mind.

Rob was happy to have secured the number of a 'lovely lady' called Gail, whereas Will was bitching about the music being too loud, there being too many men and people breathing (he didn't really complain about people breathing, but he was so negative, it was the kind of thing that could pop out of his mouth at any moment). *Gosh*. I really needed to avoid ending up as bitter as him.

Whilst I was talking to Rob, I kept an eye on the staircase as I didn't want Mr Burgundy Suit to miss me when he came back down. Shouldn't look too keen, though. Better give it a few minutes before I turned around again…

Ray, who we'd met earlier, was doing some enthusiastic dad-dancing to a 90s track with a very smiley twenty-something who was probably young enough to be his daughter. But no judgement here (well, given that I was dumped for a twenty-six-year-old, that's probably *not* entirely true. I was trying my best, though). Ray and his new friend both looked like they were having fun, and unlike my situation with Eric, they were single, so good luck to them.

Mr Burgundy Suit must have come back down by now, surely.

As Rob and Will headed back to the bar, I subtly scanned the room for the umpteenth time.

Then I clocked him. Mr Burgundy Suit. Under the stairs. Dancing *very* provocatively with a slim blonde. His hands were all over her. *Literally*. Skimming her thighs, stroking her bum and then—*what the hell*?

Within seconds, he went in for the kill, firmly thrusting his tongue down her throat like a hungry lizard chasing its prey.

Wow.

So much for that drink and having that magical first dance.

Looked like I was right all along. Mr Burgundy Suit did indeed have *heartbreaker* written all over him. Just proved what I was thinking earlier: men couldn't be trusted.

Jesus. We'd met less than twenty minutes ago and he'd already decided to trade me in for a better model.

Was a guy ever going to think I was good enough?

CHAPTER EIGHT

'So all in all, not only did you survive your second solo outing, it sounds like you had a great night too,' said Chloe smugly as I finished filling her in about the Happy Solos singles' party.

'Well, kind of,' I admitted reluctantly, bracing myself for a *told you so* speech. 'Let's just say that, overall, it wasn't quite as terrifying as I thought it would be. Then again, maybe it was just a fluke. I got lucky because Kat was so friendly and spoke to me first. Otherwise, who knows? I could have been sat on my own for the rest of the night, just watching Mr Burgundy Suit kissing a string of women on the dance floor.' My stomach sank again as I thought about how easily he'd forgotten about me.

'He sounds like a right little zounderkite,' said Chloe, spouting another one of her old-fashioned sayings. Between being raised by her grandparents and working with the elderly and her fascination with history, she was often prone to using outdated words. I was used to them now. This one I recognised as meaning an idiot. Although I reckoned *total prick* might be a more accurate definition in his case.

'You definitely dodged a bullet with that one!' she added, taking a sip of tea and placing the mug on the table in front of our favourite sofa at Cuppa. 'But there's no way you would've been alone. You said yourself that the hosts introduced you to different people, so it would have been fine. Glad you made some new friends as well. Not too shabby at all. You did a *sterling* job, Ms Robinson,' she cackled.

'Ha ha – *sterling* as in the Sterling Bar. I see what you did there. Don't give up your day job. Cracking jokes isn't your thing.'

'Cheek! Anyway, like I said, you did really well. So with that in mind, I think we can fast-track things a bit.'

'Fast-track?' My eyes widened. 'I'm not sure I like the sound of this. What do you mean exactly?'

'So, rather than briefing you on one activity, I thought I'd run through two instead.'

'*Two?*' I asked, my jaw dropping to the floor.

'Yep. *Two* as in the number that comes after *one*.'

'*Oh joy.*' I rolled my eyes again. 'Spill, please.'

'Okay, so this Saturday, you're going on a walking trip—'

'Walking? Walking where? With who?' I said.

'If you stop interrupting, then I can explain,' Chloe huffed. 'It's a walking group. They explore different parts of London every weekend, so it's a good way to discover new places and meet new people.'

Frankly, it sounded dull. Yes, it was almost April now, the weather was getting warmer, so it would be nice to get out and about, but seriously? A small concert would be more up my street and a lot more entertaining. Just think: I'd get to meet like-minded people, have a sing-along and a dance. Surely that was a better way of finding new friends than trekking around a field with a group of pensioners. I mean, no offence, but I didn't know anyone under seventy who chose to spend their Saturday afternoon walking. Especially not if they were single.

'And young people—I mean, people our age—go walking? *Really?*'

'Yep! I do my research before I suggest these things, you know. That first event was just a blip. When I looked into this one, there was a broad range of age groups, from early twenties upwards. You'd be surprised. I've checked the guest list and some cool-looking people have already signed up. You'll be fine.'

'So you keep saying,' I scoffed.

'And was I right about Saturday or was I right?' said Chloe.

'Enough gloating already!'

I wanted to try and keep an open mind, but a walking group? I supposed it would be more intimate. And maybe now I'd conquered going to a singles' party with hundreds of people, everything else should be easier from here on in. Then again, that all depended on what else Chloe had up her sleeve...

'So what's the second thing?' I winced, dreading what other nightmare activity might fall from her mouth.

'Speed dating,' said Chloe casually.

'Speed dating?' *Sweet Jesus.* Forget what I said about things getting easier. This was much worse than I thought. 'Is this the 1990s? Who goes bloody speed dating these days?'

'*Lots* of single people, and now you'll be joining them too.' She grinned. 'Think of it like a live version of a dating app.'

'What are you doing to me, Chloe?' I felt my face getting hotter. 'You honestly want me to sit in front of a room full of men I probably won't like and chat to them one by one?'

'Yep! At least there's no swiping, waiting for them to reply, sending millions of messages to arrange meeting for a drink, then getting there only to find they don't look like their photo or that there's no connection. With speed dating, you get to cut straight to the chase and meet multiple men under one roof in one evening, which will save you *so* much time and hassle. It's *perfect* for you.'

'Chloe.' I rested my head in my hands. 'You're killing me.'

'I'm *helping* you.'

'No. You're *killing* me. At least with online dating, you get to vet and screen in advance. Pick the guys that you're most interested in, so that when you meet for a date, it's kind of just a chemistry check, because you're already confident that you fancy them and have something in common.'

'Poppycock!' she scoffed. 'Like I said, that's not necessarily the case. What if they don't look like their photo? Eh? What then?'

'Well, yes, that *is* possible, but at least if you date twenty guys you've spoken to online first, you know that you already like something about them. That's why you've agreed to meet in the first place.'

'And how exactly would *you* know when you've never

actually bothered to meet anyone?' Chloe raised her eyebrows.

Touché.

'Okay, okay. Guilty as charged, but *theoretically* speaking. I'm saying that with this speed dating thing, it's a free-for-all. Yeah, you meet twenty guys in one night, which saves time, but what's the point if all twenty of them aren't your type?'

'You're looking at this all wrong, Em. Don't think about what will happen if twenty of them are *not* your type. Think about what will happen if ten of them *are*. In fact, you don't even need ten or five or two to be your type. It only takes *one* magic connection to find love. And isn't it worth investing a few hours of your evening for the chance to find love and happiness that could last a lifetime?' she said, fluttering her eyelashes.

God, she's good. How could I argue when she put it like that?

'Okay, Mrs Cupid,' I conceded. 'Point taken. So when's this punishment happening?'

'Speed dating is all booked for a week on Tuesday. Be there for seven p.m. I'll write down all the details for you.'

'Or you could just email or text me?'

'I'm trying to get you *away* from your computer and mobile devices, not keep you on them.'

Chloe really was born in the wrong era. You wouldn't think she was only a few years older than me. Whilst she had a youthful face, she looked like she'd stepped straight out of the 1950s. Apart from her name—which she hated because she thought it was too modern—everything about her was vintage. She could generally be found wearing retro full skirts and structured blouses, or dresses that were cinched at the waist to accentuate her silhouette. Chloe typically styled her hair in vintage waves or victory rolls and always slept in rollers overnight rather than just using curling tongs or straightening irons in the morning.

Then there was her job. She worked as a project manager at a local charity which provided support to the elderly, so her client base was also vintage. Her car was an old Ford Fiesta, and even the methods of communication she used were from another time. For example, she regularly used a house phone. In fact, she had *three* of them. And whilst the ones in the kitchen and bedroom were marginally up-to-date (by Chloe's standards anyway, which meant they were from the year 2000), the one in the hallway was a bright yellow rotary phone. You actually had to place your finger inside the hole of the number and rotate the dial. *Jesus.*

Outside of working hours, the landline was the best way to reach her. Yes, she had a mobile phone for 'emergencies', but it was one of those bricks from years ago, which only allowed you to make calls and send basic texts. No camera, no internet and forget about apps or social media. Frankly, it would have been better off in a museum than in her handbag (which, of course, was also vintage).

In many ways, it was strange that we'd been best friends for so long when on paper we were so different. She was into classic things and was very analogue, and I was a lover of new things and everything digital. But somehow we just clicked. I loved her. She had a heart of gold. And as frustrating as her old-fashioned ways were, sometimes I liked the fact that she was so unique. It kept things interesting and made me adore her more. I wouldn't tell her that, though, *obviously…*

'One of these days, Chloe, I'm going to get you wearing an Apple watch, ordering your shopping online like the rest of the world, driving an electric car and using a digital calendar. That would mean getting you a phone from this decade first, though…'

'Never going to happen. Nothing wrong with a normal watch, walking to Sainsbury's and writing appointments in a proper diary with a pen.'

'Yes, if you're living in the nineteenth century or are ninety years old.'

'Stop teasing, Robinson, or next week you'll have *three* activities.'

Shoes. Sometimes you can tell a lot from someone's footwear. Glamorous. Professional. Sensible. Right now, mine were saying *novice* amongst a group of seasoned ramblers.

When I read Chloe's instructions to wear *suitable shoes* for this walking group, I thought I'd be okay with my white Converse as they were comfy. But a quick survey of the seventy or so people who were already at the meeting point for this organised walk showed that sturdy hiking boots were in order. Still, at least I was doing slightly better than the woman opposite me, who was in a pair of sparkly thong sandals. It was probably her first time too.

Today's walk was in Sydenham Hill Woods, where we'd explore the ancient forest and some old railway paths, then head to Dulwich Park. Chloe claimed she'd been kind by choosing a walk in South London so I wouldn't have to venture too far out. It *was* handy, as it hadn't taken long to get here from my flat in Kennington. Just a couple tube stops and then a few more on the train from Victoria station. Plus, the start time of 2 p.m. meant I was still able to have a lie-in. Bonus.

When Chloe had first mentioned this activity, I hadn't entirely seen the point of it all. But I'd since done some more research online, and apparently walking groups were all the rage right now. Great for improving fitness (and let's face it, I needed all the help I could on that front), good for getting out into the fresh air (although I'm not sure London air can technically be classified as 'fresh', even if we were visiting a park) and good for meeting people. It was a nice day too. Dry, mild and sunny. Could have been much worse.

I'd promised Chloe I would give it my all, so I made sure I arrived nice and early and tried to bring a positive mental attitude. It's a shame my nerves and shyness decided they wanted to come along too…

It was now approaching 2.09 and there were close to a hundred people. It was like a giant school trip. Looked like Chloe and those websites were right. So much for being an intimate activity. When I'd read about them being popular, I was thinking a crowd of thirty people. Fifty tops. I hadn't realised it would be on this scale.

Doing a quick scan of the group, I could tell that many were regulars. Unlike me, they were wearing appropriate footwear and confidently walked up to other members or groups and struck up a conversation. Then there were the people on their own, shielding themselves by burying their heads in their mobile phones to avoid eye contact.

I stood in the corner of the train station exit, not quite

knowing what to do next. I'd checked social media on the way down here, and the station car park was hardly Instagram-worthy, so creating my own post was out of the question.

The knots in my stomach intensified. There was no friendly Kat to come and rescue me this time. Whilst refreshing my Twitter feed was the most appealing option, if I wanted to meet people, I had to make the effort myself. I would have to bite the bullet. Go and speak to someone. But who?

Let's start by trying someone easy. Break myself in gently. I walked up to the organiser, who was holding a branded 'Discover London' flag. It was his job to be friendly so that we felt comfortable, right? After all, the more relaxed we were, the more likely we'd be to come again and the more money he'd make. Maybe he would introduce me to some people too?

'Hi, I'm Emily,' I said as I handed over the five-pound event fee. 'It's my first time.'

'Welcome, Emily,' he said in his soft Irish accent, scribbling my name on a crumpled sheet of A4 paper. Typing them directly into a spreadsheet on an iPad would have been so much easier. He must share Chloe's technology aversion. 'I'm Kevin. Thanks for joining us.' Just as he was about to ask me something else, he was interrupted by a guy who looked like he was part of his team, as he was also holding a branded flag.

I looked behind me and a queue of people was building. Nope. Kevin wouldn't have time for chit-chat or introductions. He still had a hundred other names to write down and fees to collect. I'd have to find my own people to talk to.

I scanned the group again for someone who looked like they wouldn't blank me if I approached them.

My heart was pounding. *I can* do this. *I survived last Saturday night and I* will *get through this activity too.*

Deep breath.

She looked friendly. *Come on, Em.*

'Hi!' I said as enthusiastically as I could, approaching a smiley lady with striking silver hair. Just because she was older than me didn't mean we wouldn't have things in common. *That's right. Think positively.* 'I'm Emily. Do you mind if I join you? It's my first time here and I'm a bit nervous.'

'Of course, my love,' she said warmly. 'Welcome! I'm Margaret. I've been coming on these walks for about seven years now, so stick with me, kid, and you'll be fine.'

It had been a while since I'd been called a kid, but I suppose I was young enough to be her daughter.

Phew. Someone to talk to. My shoulders loosened and I felt ready to give this walking thing my best shot.

After Kevin had made a note of everyone's names and collected the money, we set off towards the woods. I reached into my rucksack for some snacks.

'So what brings you here, then, Emily?' asked Margaret as we weaved through the trees, trying to avoid the puddles and muddy areas. 'A love of nature? Want to see more of London? Keep fit? Or just looking for a hook-up?' She winked.

I almost choked on my Brazil nuts.

'Sorry, did you just ask if I'd come walking for a *hook-up*?'

'Yes, dear. That's what you youngsters call one-night stands these days, isn't it?' said Margaret matter-of-factly.

'It is, but—'

'It's okay, sweetheart.' She grinned. 'Your secret is safe with me. It's quite common.'

'Really?' My mouth dropped open. 'Not that I'm saying that's what I'm here for. In fact, I'm *definitely* not here for that. I mean, my friend Chloe recommended it. She's the one that suggested this—'

Margaret smirked, clearly amused and taking my stuttering as an admission of guilt.

'We've had lots of couples meet here. They get chatting on the walk, go to the pub, because we *always* finish the walk with a few drinks, then one thing leads to another and off they go into the night. Others start dating and have long-term relationships. It all depends what you're looking for.'

Who knew?

'Oh. That's interesting,' I said, not quite knowing how to respond.

'I'm not immune to it either, darling. I've been known to make a gentleman friend or two on these walks as well. Good for keeping the machine well oiled and all that.' Margaret smirked. 'I *do* of course enjoy discovering new parts of London and getting out of the house. The sex is just a nice bonus.' She winked again.

'Right!' I said, taken aback by her frankness.

'Well, don't waste valuable hunting time talking to me, sweetie. Now I've filled you in, have a good look around at what's on offer and get chatting!'

I was almost tempted to pull at Margaret's face and hair to check it wasn't Chloe underneath in disguise. How else would she know that I was effectively here in a veiled attempt to find love?

As with Chloe, I knew better than to argue, so I took a quick glance in front of and behind me. With this many people, it was hard to see through the crowd. Kevin, the organiser, had said we'd be stopping for a toilet break when we reached Dulwich Park, so it'd be easier to make conversation then.

It was crazy. I'd lived in South London all my life and yet I hadn't even known that Sydenham Hill Woods existed and I'd never been to Dulwich Park. But it was beautiful. Lots of lovely flowers, a boating lake and some cute ducks. I took loads of photos. Pics of nature probably wouldn't be appreciated by the social media followers I had, so I couldn't post them, but I thought these shots were really pretty. They'd look great in a mural painting. Shame I didn't do that anymore.

There were couples lying on the grass enjoying picnics. *Lucky them.* I'd love to spend a lazy afternoon in the sunshine snuggled up on a picnic blanket whilst my gorgeous boyfriend fed me grapes and gazed into my eyes. I'd never done anything like that with Eric.

As Kevin promised, we soon stopped outside the loos. Whilst some of the group queued for the toilets, others went off to get ice cream and the rest hung out on the grass.

I looked around, and it wasn't long before I spotted a potential new 'friend': a cute guy with dark floppy hair. But he was at the opposite end of the group. Wouldn't it be a bit weird to walk all the way over there and just start talking to him randomly?

I didn't know how to do this without looking like an idiot. It just seemed so *desperate* somehow. If I was standing next to someone and just happened to turn my head and start talking to them, that would be more natural, but making a beeline for a guy who was nearly twenty metres away? Hmmm. I wasn't sure…

Suddenly, he started advancing, weaving his way through the group, then stopped just a few feet away from me. My heart started racing. Was this my chance? He didn't seem to be with anyone. He was on his own, just like me.

But maybe he *wanted* to be alone? Some people preferred their own company.

Should I try?

Then again, if he *was* interested in talking, now that he was just a few feet away, surely he would have said hello to me first.

But why should the man have to make the first move? Technically, *I* should have the confidence to go for what I want. I supposed as he was standing so close to me now, it would be less weird to chat to him. I *could* just say hi and ask if it was his first time.

Oh God. But what if he ignored me?

Just as I was contemplating what to do next, another woman swooped in front of me, charged forward and introduced herself to him.

Dammit.

Procrastination and acute overthinking. Two of my weaknesses.

Look! He'd only been speaking to her for all of thirty seconds and he was already smiling and chatting away.

Missed opportunity.

I should have just gone for it. What was the worst that could have happened? Yes, I could think of plenty of embarrassing scenarios, but realistically, he *might* have responded positively. It was always much easier to be wise after the fact, though, wasn't it?

I messed up. I'd probably chastise myself about this for the foreseeable future, but that wasn't going to help me. I had made a commitment to this meeting people thing and I needed to do better. Try harder. Chloe said no pain, no gain, so somehow, no idea how exactly, I had to find a way to up my game and not be so bloody afraid.

Preferably before this daunting speed dating event on Tuesday…

CHAPTER NINE

Why was it that whenever I really needed my eyeliner flick to be straight and even on both eyes, I could never get it right? One side was either too thick, or too flicky, or not flicky enough. *Aaargh!* The fact that I was fretting about speed dating tonight probably wasn't helping to steady my hands.

Speed dating. If someone had told me a few weeks ago that in approximately ninety minutes' time, I would be in a Leon restaurant about to meet twenty different guys in one night rather than ordering their chicken satay hot box, I wouldn't have believed it.

Despite vowing not to be so afraid, I couldn't stop myself from worrying. Sitting across a table from a stranger twenty times was pretty scary. What was I supposed to say? Yes, I know, *hello* and the standard *have you done this before?* would be a good start. But what then? Three minutes or whatever it was could be a long time to fill when you had nothing to talk about. Equally, was it really possible to tell whether you had a connection with someone in the time it took to boil a kettle?

It wasn't just finding the right topics of conversation I was nervous about. It was also the task of coming across as interesting, funny and smart whilst trying to look cool and sexy *and* flirt. All at the same time. *Jeez.* How was I going to pull *that* off? And, oh God—what if I spent the whole evening chatting, then realised afterwards I had something stuck between my teeth? Must remember to floss.

I tied my hair back into a bun. I hadn't had time to straighten it today as I was super busy at work, so I wasn't able to start getting ready as early as I would have liked. In any case, it was raining outside, so if I wore it down and even a few drops of water fell on my curls, they would explode into a ball of frizz almost instantly. *Nope.* Much safer to scrape it all back. I'd even slicked it down with some gel I'd found in the bathroom cupboard, so my hair looked quite tidy for a change, not like the messy bun I wore every day.

Anyway... I needed to pick up the pace. I still hadn't worked out what I was going to wear and was only halfway through putting on my make-up. Not to mention the fact that this wonky eyeliner looked like it had been applied by a two-year-old. Time to wipe it off and start again...

Five minutes until speed dating officially started and I was a bag of nerves. I glanced over at the area at the back of the restaurant that had been sectioned off for the event. I felt my stomach cramping and beads of sweat trickling down my forehead. Gosh, it was hot in here. Or maybe it was just me. I pulled a tissue from my bag and dabbed it over my face.

I'd already been to the toilet and could confirm that there wasn't any spinach stuck between my teeth. I'd also swallowed multiple mints, so my breath was fresh, and thankfully, I'd eventually managed to get my eyeliner relatively even. I had kept my make-up simple—just added some mascara, tinted moisturiser and natural peachy gloss.

Outfit-wise, I'd opted for my new purple skater dress with tights and kitten heels. I looked around at the other women here. A few were wearing low-cut tops, short skirts and skyscraper heels. And as for the make-up, they'd either stopped off at a department store counter to get it done professionally before coming here or had religiously studied contouring and 'perfecting your cat's-eye flick' YouTube videos, as their application was flawless. Maybe I should have experimented with some bright lipstick, like one of the colours Chloe wore.

Then again, if I'd worn red lipstick, I might have ended up looking like a clown, as I'd never found the right shade and if I had attempted that contouring stuff, people would think I'd fallen head first into a giant tub of highlighter. And even with this push-up bra, my modest boobs couldn't compare to the others on display tonight.

I'd now been standing in the corner for almost ten minutes, eyeing up the exit, and that wasn't good. I knew myself. The more I stood here, the more I would start to question my outfit, get nervous or start playing on my phone. I needed to do something. Attempt to be brave and throw myself into this.

I looked around. Now this was my fourth event, my

room-scanning skills were getting a little better. This restaurant was much bigger than the other Leon stores I'd visit whenever I fancied some healthy fast food—hence why they were able to host an event at the back whilst they still kept it open to serve customers at the front. It had the familiar white-tiled walls, wooden flooring and black tables and chairs.

At a guess, I'd say most people here for speed dating were early to mid-thirties—perhaps a few in their twenties. The men ranged from cool bearded hipster types to suited and booted city boys, geeks in T-shirts, and a scattering of *I'm hot and I know it* guys. Probably friends with Mr Burgundy Suit.

Just as I was watching them, they were probably doing the same. It was only natural. I didn't want to seem stand-offish or look like a wallflower. Time to take a deep breath, try to make conversation and loosen myself up a little.

First, maybe I should get a drink. Calm my nerves. I reached into my purse for one of the coupons they'd given us with our name badges when we arrived. A glass of red should do the trick. Then again, the last thing I needed was for someone to bump into me when we were changing tables and end up with a big red wine stain down the front of my dress. Not worth the risk.

'Glass of white, please,' I requested before turning to a lady with long braids standing to the left of the bar.

'Hi,' I said, smiling. 'I'm Emily, how are you?'

'Good, thanks, Emily.' She frowned, then took a sip of her red wine. Obviously less clumsy or paranoid than me. 'I'm Monica. Nice to meet you.' She frowned again, then began wiping the top of her brow aggressively.

Strange.

'Tissue...' she said, her frown deepening even more.

'Oh right, yes,' I said, opening my bag and rummaging around. 'I think I have a spare one... Actually, no. Really sorry. I don't have a fresh one. Maybe you could use a serviette instead?' I said, pointing to the counter.

'Thank you, but no. *I* don't need a tissue... I was trying to say that *you* have some bits of tissue on your forehead.'

Great. That's just peachy, isn't it? Must have happened when I tried to wipe my sweat away. I'd been standing over there for God knows how long with guys staring at me and I had blobs of tissue all over my face.

Nice one, Em. What a way to look sexy.

I reached in my bag for my mirror and quickly picked off the bit sticking to my brow and the other piece hanging just below my hairline. Imagine if she hadn't told me and I'd gone the whole night looking like that? Didn't bear thinking about.

'You're a lifesaver, Monica, thank you!' I said, also feeling grateful for the name badge she was wearing. Made things so much easier.

'No worries!' She smiled. 'Is it your first time?'

'God, is it that obvious?' I stood up straighter in an attempt to appear more confident. Hard to do after having your forehead plastered with Kleenex.

'No, not at all. It's just that I came to the first speed dating event a few weeks ago and don't remember seeing you there, so I just guessed.'

'Oh, I see. What was it like?' I said, relaxing a little. 'I've never done anything like this before to meet guys— I've always relied on the apps.'

'Ah, the joys of online dating!' she joked. 'Personally I prefer events like this. It's a good way to meet a bunch of guys face-to-face without having to swipe first. Yeah, most of them probably won't be for you, but it only takes one, so it's worth a try.'

'That's exactly what my friend said, so I'm hoping she's right,' I replied.

'Hi, everyone!' said Kelly, the hostess, tapping the side of a glass with a knife to get our attention.

'Welcome to our second speed dating event. Nice to see you all. I know you're all eager to get started, so let me just run through how it all works. As you can see, there's lots of you here tonight, so each of you will go on up to twenty-four dates. You'll have four minutes to talk to each other, which should give you plenty of time to introduce yourselves, have a quick chat and decide whether you'd like to see each other again.' She picked up a batch of A4 sheets, along with a box of pens, and started passing them around.

'Thanks,' I said, taking a form and pen, then giving the rest to Monica.

'At the end of the four minutes, if you'd like to see that person again, write their name down on the sheet provided. Gents stay seated and then ladies move along to the next date,' continued Kelly. 'When all the dates are completed, we'll come up to you individually to find out who you like, and if there's a match, we'll pass on your contact details so that you can get in touch with each other. Any questions? No? In that case, let the dating begin!'

Wow—up to twenty-four dates rather than the twenty I'd anticipated? This was going to be even harder than I thought...

I sat down to meet my first date: Ed, an artist from East London. The conversation was okay, but there was no connection. Turns out that four minutes *was* enough to know whether you wanted to see someone again. And I needn't have worried about knowing what to say as they'd put a pile of conversation starters in a little box on the table just in case.

Next was Steven. I'd initially been excited to speak to him as he was certainly ticking my box in the aesthetics department with his smouldering good looks, but sadly zero personality and monosyllabic responses, which was a complete turn-off. No amount of conversation starters could have spiced up our mundane exchange. He wasn't into me, and the feeling was *definitely* mutual.

After a dozen or so more dates, I was getting the hang of things a bit more. No one was really jumping out at me yet, but there was still about half an hour to go. I sat down in front of the next prospect.

'Hello, Emily.' He squinted as he tried to read my name badge. 'I'm Rory, good to meet you.'

Nice and polite. Positive start.

'Good to meet you too,' I replied, relaxing a bit more. Maybe this wasn't so bad after all.

We made some small talk for a couple of minutes about the weather and the fact that we'd both never done speed dating before. He seemed okay. At least he could hold a conversation, which was more than could be said for that Steven guy.

'So, Emily, what do you do?' he asked. 'No, no! Actually, don't tell me. Let me guess!' he said excitedly.

'Okay,' I said, thinking this could be fun. 'Go on, then!'

'Um…' He looked me up and down. I felt a bit exposed but let him continue. 'I've got it! You're an accountant!' he shouted.

'Nope.' I smiled, intrigued by his conclusion. 'Not even close!'

'Oh?' He looked really disappointed.

'You seem surprised, Rory.'

'Yeah, I am. It's just I'm normally good at this.'

'Don't worry about it! I'm an illustrator. Out of interest, what made you think I was an accountant?'

'Um,' he said, looking me up and down again. 'I dunno, I guess maybe it's because of your hair?'

'*My hair?*' I frowned.

'Yeah, it looks kind of, I dunno? Boring? Safe?'

Boring? My mouth fell to the floor.

'I mean, it's fine and all, I suppose. Very neat and tidy. Professional. If you're a designer, I would have thought you'd look cooler. More edgy. Y'know. *Creative.* It's just, take that girl over there,' he said, pointing to a busty brunette who was laughing loudly on the other side of the room. 'Her hair is all flowy and *sexy.* I bet she does something glamorous like, I don't know, modelling underwear or exotic dancing. *Mmm.* You can just tell. Oh and also, you're not wearing any make-up. Well, not enough anyway. You could do with wearing more. And I'd lose those thick tights you're wearing. It's a bit much for this time of year, don't you think? Whereas *that* girl, she's dressed properly,' he said as his eyes scanned upwards from her legs, then fixated firmly on her large breasts. 'She's got on a lovely tight dress and bare legs. She looks exciting. *Adventurous.* Like she takes care of herself. She's *hot.*'

What a creep.

'Are you…?' I gasped. 'Did you really just say…?'

I didn't even know how to respond. I mean, I knew I'd never be described as the life and soul of the party, and I wasn't likely to be invited to model at a Victoria's Secret show anytime this century, but wow.

Yes, I know. We all judge people based on their appearance, myself included. But it was one thing to think it, completely another to say it. Especially in such a rude way. I'd put my hair up for practical reasons and worn the only pair of tights I could find so my legs wouldn't get wet in the rain. Yeah, maybe it wasn't exactly sexy, but he didn't need to insult me. I was offended that he thought I didn't look cool enough to be an illustrator. And was he saying all accountants are boring too?

Men.

Seriously. Eric, that Will guy from the party. Oh, and of course Mr Burgundy Suit. As Chloe would say, what a bunch of zounderkites.

I felt like just getting up and leaving right now. I hadn't even wanted to come to this stupid event, so the last thing I needed was to sit here and get insulted again.

Sod it. I'm going home.

Just as I stood up to go, the bell rang. I didn't even bother to say another word to Rude Rory. *Prick.*

I was fuming. I started walking over towards the organiser's area to get my coat.

'Here's your next date!' said Kelly, resting her hand on my shoulder and pointing towards the empty chair.

'Actually, I was just about to—'

'Hey!' said the guy enthusiastically. I couldn't read his name from this distance. It was written in quite small writing. 'Fancy meeting you here!' he joked in his Cockney accent.

He had dark hair and a thick beard and was wearing a red-and-black lumberjack shirt with the sleeves rolled up, showing lots of large tattoos. Whilst he had the dark features that I liked, he dressed differently to my past boyfriends. Eric had a more simple, classic dress sense. You know, plain white shirt, smart blue jeans and black shoes, that type of thing. This guy was more rugged. He looked like he'd just come from chopping down trees or doing hard manual labour. Kind of sexy, actually. *Gosh.* Did making assumptions about his profession based on his looks put me in the same category as that awful Rory guy? *No.* Like I said, I guess we all did it. The difference was, I would keep my thoughts firmly to myself.

In fact, just to prove that I was *not* judgemental like Rory, I was going to stay. I wasn't going home. I was going to sit and chat with this guy and keep an open mind.

'Yes! Fancy meeting you here…Henry,' I laughed as I leant in to read his badge, then sat down.

'I tell you what, Emily, my mate has a *lot* to answer for setting me up on this thing. I've never even been to a Leon before. He's the one who's into all that healthy food. I'm more of a bacon butty or pub grub kind of guy. And as for this speed dating malarkey, I didn't even know people still did this stuff.'

'Exactly!' I said. 'My friend set me up on this too.'

'Let me guess: she told you to get off the apps and find yourself a bloke before you died alone?' he quipped.

'Well, not *quite* that dramatic,' I said, 'but yes, something along those lines.'

'Well-meaning mates, eh!' he raised his eyebrows.

'So,' he said, smiling warmly, 'how's it going tonight? Any of these blokes tickled your fancy? Apart from meeting me and *of course* realising that I'm your soulmate, you having any joy?' he chuckled.

'Hmmm,' I huffed. 'Let's just say I've met some *interesting* characters.'

'Okay...' he said, understanding my meaning of interesting. 'Enough said.'

'So,' I said, tilting my head to attempt to flirt a little, 'reckon you're my soulmate, then, do you, Henry?'

'I'd like to hope so, but I won't get too big for my boots. I'll let you be the judge of that.' He winked. 'Tell you what, though, that'd definitely make both our match-making mates happy, wouldn't it? And just imagine, when people asked how we met, saying it was in a restaurant would sound *much* better than saying we liked each other's Snapchat-filtered photos on Tinder and decided to swipe right!' He let out a wicked laugh.

'I like your thinking!' I said.

'Glad to hear it. See!' Henry teased. 'I *knew* we were soulmates!'

The four minutes flew by. We didn't even get round to asking all the stock *what do you do for work/where do you live/how long have you been single?* questions. We were too busy giggling about the awkwardness of dating. I liked him. I found him attractive, he was funny and down-to-earth, and it felt like we had a connection. I thought so anyway.

I supposed Chloe was right. If I'd been using a dating app, I might have ruled someone like Henry out just because I'd looked at a few photos and automatically assumed he wasn't my type. Like she'd said, at least with speed dating, I only had to invest a few minutes of my time with each guy rather than spending hours texting, arranging to meet up for a drink, then finding out we didn't click.

The rest of the evening whizzed past. I think I 'dated' about eighteen guys in the end. I didn't feel the same connection as I did with Henry, though. He was definitely going on my shortlist.

At the end of the event I gave Kelly my list of favourites (just Henry, who had left straight away as he had an early start, and another guy called Paul, who to be honest I wasn't sure about but thought I'd hedge my bets). I considered staying but thought I'd better quit whilst I was ahead and make my way home.

I patted myself on the back. I'd survived another solo activity. Yeah, I'd come across a few dodgy guys and had some pretty awkward moments with several others, but Henry had given me a glimmer of hope.

Two and a half weeks in and I'd met a guy that I fancied. Was the feeling mutual, though?

The organisers said they'd email details of matches by noon tomorrow, which meant in approximately fourteen hours, I would find out…

CHAPTER TEN

'So this is *different*. Enjoying breakfast in a coffee shop on a Saturday morning with my bestie. Reminds me of my carefree pre-kids days, which feels like about a century ago,' said Chloe.

'It's different for me too. Not the kids bit, *obviously*. More the fact that I'd normally be chilling in bed, scrolling through Instagram looking at pictures of what *other* people were having for breakfast and debating whether or not to get up before or *after* midday.'

'Lucky cow!' said Chloe. 'Even at six years old, Violet still insists on waking me up at the crack of dawn, including on weekends. I'd *kill* to have a lie-in until noon. If I could, I certainly wouldn't be scrolling through social sodding media, that's for sure. What a waste of valuable life. Speaking of which, how is your digital detox coming along?'

'Well,' I said, taking a bite from my blueberry muffin. 'I'm not going to lie. I'm still using social media—'

'*Oh, Emily!*' tutted Chloe like a disapproving mother.

'It's only been three weeks.' Even though I knew this Saturday technically marked the start of week four, it still hadn't been that long. I didn't know why she was so surprised.

'I reckon you've got that Social Media Anxiety Disorder thing I was reading about. You're one of those people who can't go more than a couple of hours without checking their phones and who lie about how much time they spend online. You're a classic case. If you're spending seven hours a day scrolling, messaging and posting, then you're not going to have enough time to do things in real life.'

'I'm not that bad!' I said. It was true. I *didn't* spend seven hours a day online. According to Screen Time on my iPhone, when I'd checked last week, it was more like *six*. I'd made progress, though. Before, it wasn't unusual for me to check every hour. But now it was around four or five times a day. *Okay*. Maybe more on the evenings that I was at home and perhaps a bit less when I had somewhere to go. I don't remember checking it at all that night I went speed dating.

'Not to mention the damage you're doing to your mental health,' Chloe sighed. 'Feeling depressed because you're comparing yourself to everyone else who has the perfect body, job, husband, home, and children and goes to every fancy place known to man. Oh and then there's the eye strain, neck pains, back problems and putting on weight from just sitting around staring down at your phone all day. Seriously, Em, I don't know why you do it to yourself.'

Talk about Mrs Doom and Gloom. I knew she had a point, though. After posting that photo of me dressed up for the singles' party, I was so anxious. I kept refreshing my feed every thirty seconds, worrying what other people would think. Terrified that I'd either be ignored or criticised. I kept scrutinising how I looked and was so close to deleting the image altogether. And then, when the likes started coming in, I got a rush of excitement. I thought: *Someone likes my photo!*

I was on a high. For a little while anyway. I'd hoped I would have got a few more comments. Maybe I didn't look good that night after all.

Posting photos always felt a bit like weighing myself. If I was happy with the number on the scales, or in this case, the number of likes, my mood went up. But if I wasn't, I felt down. I'd constantly compare the likes I'd received for a new photo to previous posts and check what other people had got for theirs.

Pretty sad really. But even though I knew it was toxic, somehow it was addictive. After using social media for years, it was going to be hard to break the habit, so I'd probably continue to go through the same stressful cycle every time I posted something.

'I hear you, and I'm getting better. Whilst I'm still using social media, I'm not on it as much. Although, does WhatsApp count?'

'Not that I'm an expert of course, but I suppose not, as technically you're having meaningful conversations with people you've actually met in real life.'

'Good, as I've been using that more to keep in touch with Kat and Rob from the singles' party. Rob set up a group chat he's called "The Diamonds," because he said we're two of the loveliest ladies he's met.'

'Ah, sweet!'

'Yeah, it is,' I said. 'He sends us jokes and funny videos to brighten up our day. He also admitted he's using us to help him figure out how women work. Truth is, I'm hoping Rob can give *me* a better understanding of how the male brain works too.'

'Good luck with that! Seriously, though, it's great to hear you've found two new friends. They sound lovely. Okay, so that's social media. What about the dating apps? Have you managed to stay off those?'

'Hmm, if I'm completely honest, I *have* been surfing *occasionally*. But again, not as much. You can't expect me to stop immediately, Chloe—it's a process. I need to wean myself off them slowly.'

On the days that I had activities, I hardly used the apps, but on my days off from Chloe's challenge, I was still at home on my own with nothing to do, and my hands were so used to holding my phone that it was so easy to just log on to see if I'd had any messages—and to, you know, *window shop*. I hadn't actually messaged anyone new since Kane, though, so again, I was making *some* progress.

'Fair enough. Hopefully in the next week or two you'll be so busy with dates that you won't even have time to think about apps.'

'Well. On the subject of dates, looks like I have one tonight—' I said, trying to act coy but doing a happy dance in my head.

'*Tonight?* What? You kept that one quiet! Who with? Where did you meet him? Why didn't you tell me?'

Chloe looked so excited that she could literally burst out of her skin at any second.

'We matched at speed dating on Tuesday, and I didn't mention it because you said we'd catch up on everything today. And secondly, I wanted to wait to see if he'd cancel. We're supposed to be meeting at seven p.m., so there's still approximately eight hours for him to do that, of course,' I said, still embarrassed about bailing on Kane.

'Crumbs! This is exciting, Em! Why did you start off telling me about the walking trip when you had *real* news to share? You've got a date, who you *didn't* meet online. Yes!'

'One latte and a tea?' said the waiter as he put our mugs down on the table.

'Ooh, *hello*! Yes, that's us. Thank you, handsome.' Chloe winked. He blushed and headed back behind the counter.

'You little flirt!' I said. She was right, though. He was cute.

'He's a *dish*!' said Chloe. 'Is he new? Don't remember seeing him before.'

'I haven't seen him before either, so he must be.'

'You should *definitely* get his number.'

'Chloe! I am not asking a waiter at my local coffee shop for his number.'

'Why not? Like I said, he's a real hunk!'

Hunk? Haven't heard that word in donkey's years. *Classic Chloe.*

'I agree, but anyway—how did we even get on to this when I was telling you all about my date?'

'Yes, of course. Sorry! Who is this mystery man? What's his name? Where are you going? And never mind *him* changing his mind. The million-dollar question is are you sure *you* are actually going to turn up for this date?'

'Ha ha, very funny,' I scoffed. 'At the moment, I have every intention of going. I like him.'

'Thank heavens for that. Start from the beginning, then, Em. I need to know *everything*!'

I filled her in on speed dating, including my run-in with Rude Rory, how quickly Henry and I had clicked, the excitement I'd felt when I'd received the email from the organisers the following day to say we'd matched. I didn't match with the other guy, but no big loss.

'So how long was it before he messaged you? Or did you suddenly have a moment of bravery and pluck up the courage to get in touch with him first?'

'If only! Come on. This is me we're talking about. No. I waited, and thankfully he WhatsApped me that evening to say how glad he was that we'd matched. I thought about waiting until the following morning to reply, but I've never been good at that *playing it cool* stuff, so I messaged back more or less straight away.'

'Oh! Fast work, Robinson. Yeah, it's a tricky one. Game-playing can get messy. So what happened next?'

'He messaged back on Thursday evening asking if I wanted to meet for a drink on Saturday night, and if so, when and where was good for me. I said yes and suggested London Bridge, and yesterday lunchtime he confirmed seven p.m. inside the tube station.'

'Excellent! So why are you worried about him cancelling? He sounds keen. He messaged you first and suggested meeting for a drink quite quickly without sending you a billion messages first. What's the problem?'

'That's kind of the thing. He doesn't message that much. With all the other guys I've spoken to, there's more chatting, you know? More contact. Regular back-and-forth. More build-up.'

'Well, I think when it comes to all this messaging stuff,

in some ways, less is more. After all, you're not looking for a pen pal. I think it's *good* that he's not constantly messaging. He's clearly not obsessed with being on his phone 24/7 like you are. He just gets straight to the point. The objective is to meet, so once that's set, what else is there to talk about?'

She had a point.

'Arranging to meet quickly rather than messaging hundreds of times a day for ages is definitely preferable,' Chloe added. 'And think about it—you haven't exactly had a good track record with those text spammers, have you?' She rolled her eyes.

'True. I guess I'm also nervous because I tried looking him up online but couldn't find him on Facebook or Instagram, which is really strange.' Apart from Chloe, I didn't know anyone who wasn't on at least one social platform.

'For Pete's sake! I thought you said you were weaning yourself off that nonsense. Not everyone wants to have an online presence, you know. And anyway, not finding him on there is a *good* thing. Studies show that stalking social networking accounts can lead to increased anxiety when meeting in person. Don't bother trying to find out about him online. I know you only met once for a few minutes, but just let discovering more about him happen naturally. In real life.'

Chloe and her studies. I didn't know how she got the time to read them all in between work and having a husband and kids, plus all the baking she did.

'Well, as he's not online. Looks like I don't have a choice, do I?'

'No, you don't. So come on, then!' Chloe clapped her

hands together like an excited seal. 'What are you wearing?'

'Well, I wore a dress last time, and seeing as we've already met and it's just a drink, I thought I'd keep it casual, so maybe some jeans and a top.'

'Oh, Em!' she said loudly. 'It's *never* just a drink. Save the comfy clothing for when you've moved in together or got married.'

I suppose I couldn't expect Chloe to say anything else. She never slummed it. Take today. She was wearing a red-patterned full skirt and a pristine white top with red lipstick and flats. This was her idea of casual dressing. In all the time I'd known her, I had never once seen her in a tracksuit or jeans like most people wore at weekends.

"If you always try to look your best, it makes you feel good. Stand straighter. Walk taller," Chloe would say. Fair enough, but *seriously*. Who could be bothered to iron big skirts and put on proper make-up every morning? Especially on a Saturday? *Not me.* Converse, jumper and leggings were definitely more my weekend style.

'For a first date, Em, you have to up the outfit ante. You want to get a shag, don't you?'

'Chloe!'

'I'm right, though, aren't I? Unless you've been having some secret liaisons you've haven't told me about, it must be almost eight months since you last had some fun between the sheets.'

'Yes, but—I don't think I can.' I winced. 'It's still so raw.'

'Oh, love,' said Chloe, touching my shoulder. 'What's up? I didn't know you were having trouble down there. What is it? Cystitis? Thrush?'

'No! I don't mean downstairs is raw. I mean *I'm* raw: emotionally. Every time I think about sex, I get those awful flashbacks of walking in on Eric screwing Nicole. I see the look on his face. He was so turned on. He was *really* into it, you know? Having the time of his life. Telling her she felt *so* good. He *never* said that to me. He never had that look with me, so clearly I'm rubbish in bed. That's why he cheated.'

God, I hated dredging up those memories. Even now, it still hurt. Would I ever be able to get over him?

'Eric was a slimeball. He was probably just trotting out some lines from a porno he watched. He always thought he was a stud. *Tallywag*. You know I never liked him. I *tolerated* him for you.'

'I know you did. But you can understand why I'm not in a big rush to jump into bed with another man. I can't bear the thought of being cheated on again.' I felt my stomach knotting up. I'd rather have every hair on my body plucked individually with burning hot tweezers than go through that torture again.

'Hold your horses, Em. One step at a time. I know the Eric breakup was really painful—I watched you go through it. But you can't let one todger's behaviour turn you into a nun or stop you from living your life. Not all men are cheats, and a good bedroom workout would do you the world of good. Trust me.'

'If you say so. It would be just my luck to pick another toe-rag, though. And maybe I do need a workout, but not on the first date. To be honest, like I said, I've been trying not to think about sex and I've kind of got so used to *not* having it. No, I think I need to take things slowly. Ease my way back into this dating thing. I admit. I really enjoyed my conversation with Henry, so I'm willing to at least give this date a go tonight.'

'That's the spirit, Em,' said Chloe. 'Tonight, put on some lacy undies, spritz on your favourite perfume, slip into one of your new dresses and some heels, then go and have some fun!'

CHAPTER ELEVEN

I'd arrived ten minutes early at London Bridge tube station for my date with Henry, and my heart was racing.

It had been ages since I'd done this, and I was *so* nervous. A million questions flooded my brain. Would I fancy him? After all, we'd only met briefly at speed dating and had barely exchanged more than a few words on WhatsApp since then. Would *he* fancy *me*? What would we talk about? Getting here early only gave my nerves extra oxygen, because I had nothing to do but wait...

I think I remembered from the dating 'rules' I'd read donkey's years ago that a woman was supposed to be fashionably late. But apart from the obvious sexism, it didn't sound like a good idea for someone like me. Knowing my luck, if I attempted that, my train would be cancelled, my phone battery would die so I wouldn't be able to text him, then I'd run from the platform, twist my ankle and eventually hobble to the meeting place only to find he'd gone home because he thought I'd stood him up. *Nope. Too risky.*

So, rather than play it cool and follow the rule book (who made this stuff up anyway?), I decided it was better to arrive early. Not least because after spending three hours getting ready (yes, three bloody hours), I'd be thoroughly cheesed off if that preparation was all in vain.

I was still worried about whether he'd actually turn up. Given the fact that I'd cancelled my dates with Kane, there was always a chance that karma would bite in the bum and give me a taste of my own medicine.

By 4 p.m. I'd driven myself crazy, so I bit the bullet and messaged Henry to say I was looking forward to seeing him at 7 p.m. (sounded keen, but I wanted to check I wasn't wasting my time). Thankfully he'd replied to say he was too. *Phew.* That made me feel a little less paranoid. Well, until now of course. With these extra minutes to kill, the possibility of him cancelling had been catapulted straight to the front of my mind again…

Five minutes to go.

My phone pinged. *Oh no…don't tell me…*

Thank God. It was just a message from Chloe wishing me good luck. And checking I hadn't chickened out again. *Cheek.*

I quickly replied. It was rare for her to send text messages, so I supposed I should consider it an honour. Maybe she'd got Archie to type it out. Mind you, her phone was so ancient that he probably wouldn't even know how to use it.

Three minutes to go.

Jeez. This waiting was killing me. Why did every minute feel like six hundred seconds rather than sixty?

I needed a distraction. Phone. Instagram. *No*. I was supposed to be cutting back.

I'd go to one of the shops in the arcade, then come back again. That would kill some time.

Just as I started to walk away, I saw Henry approaching me.

'Hey, you!' He smiled.

'Oh, hi, Henry!'

'Hello, darling,' he said, giving me a kiss on the cheek. 'You look nice.'

'Thanks,' I said, pleased that my three hours of exfoliating, leg, armpit, and bikini line shaving, eyebrow and upper lip tweezing, face-masking, make-up applying, and hair straightening, plus my multiple outfit experimentation, had been appreciated by someone else other than me and my bedroom mirror.

He was wearing a grey-and-blue checked shirt, distressed jeans and big tanned Timberland boots. His beard looked much thicker than I remembered, but he looked good. And I can confirm that I found him attractive. *What a relief.*

'You haven't been waiting long, have you?'

'Just got here,' I lied.

'Good. I thought we could head over to a pub by the river. That cool with you?' he said.

'Sounds great!'

As we walked past Borough Market and towards the river, we chatted about our day. He'd been doing some DIY around his flat, and rather than confess that I'd spent the whole afternoon preparing for the date, I said I'd met up with a friend. Not completely untrue, considering I *had* seen Chloe earlier today.

The pub was split across two floors and was very busy, with a large group of people huddled around the TV screens watching a football match. We headed upstairs, where it was much quieter, ordered our drinks and sat down at a table near the large glass patio doors. I was definitely glad to take the weight off my feet, as my toes were beginning to burn from being squashed into these heels. That said, considering I spent most of my days at home wearing slippers or in Converse when I ventured out to grab coffee, my feet were holding up well. I suspected it would be a *very* different story by the end of the night.

'Ah. I needed that!' said Henry as he took a large gulp of his pint.

'Sounds like a well-deserved drink,' I replied.

'Yep!' he sighed. 'Fixing kitchen cupboards and tiling is thirsty work.'

'Never done it myself,' I said, 'but it doesn't sound like a barrel of laughs.'

'It's not. But the doors were literally hanging by a thread and I'd been putting it off for ages, so it had to be done. Feel better now it's all sorted, though. Anyway, enough about all that. So, talking of fun, what do you do to let your hair down?'

'Hmmm.' I paused, wracking my brain for a suitable answer. Admitting that before I'd agreed to Chloe's challenge, I'd generally spend my free time on Twitter, Instagram, Tinder or Netflix wasn't exactly going to make me sound like the catch of the century, now was it? 'Good question. I've been keeping things a bit low-key on the fun front as I've had lots on at work and I'm also only just starting to come out of my shell again after splitting up with my ex.' That much was true.

'Ouch.' He winced. 'Sounds painful. Say no more.'

'Yep, probably for the best. But to answer your question, when I *do* let my hair down, I like going to galleries, museums and intimate gigs,' I replied, thinking that I hadn't done any of those things in ages. Years, even. Terrible really. 'How about you?'

'Watching the footy, enjoying a few pints with my mates. You know, the usual.'

Sounded similar to Eric, whose primary interests were watching rugby, drinking and of course engaging in extracurricular activities with Nicole behind my back.

God. I've really got to stop thinking about Eric. Henry is not Eric. Not all men are the same. Not all men are the same. Not all men are the same…

'I see. Cool,' I said, focusing again. 'So, how about you? How long have you been single?'

'Erm,' he said, taking another sip of his pint. 'About three or four months. Well, the divorce came through about five months ago, but I've only just started to get back into the dating stuff.'

'Oh, I didn't realise you were married,' I said.

'Yep,' he sighed. 'Seven long years.'

'The famous seven-year itch?' I asked.

'Hmm, something like that.' His voice trailed off. 'How about you, darling?' he asked swiftly. 'Were you married?'

So much for not talking about my ex.

'No, but I—' I paused. *Oh my God.* I couldn't believe I was just about to add that I'd wanted to get married, but Eric didn't, and he'd now chosen to marry Nicole instead. *Seriously.* I needed to get a grip. Chloe was right. A first date was never just a date. I was supposed to be selling myself, not acting like a woman who was still hung up on her ex. Rephrase:

'I was with my ex for five years.'

That's better. Short and sweet. He didn't need to know the ins and outs of my angst and insecurities.

'Any kids?' asked Henry.

Another button unwittingly pressed. I'd always wanted to start a family, but Eric had said we should wait until after we were married, which of course never happened...

'No, you?' I replied swiftly, trying to block out Eric for the umpteenth time.

'Nope. Zero baggage. Just me, myself and I.'

'Right. So, should we get something to eat?' I asked, quickly changing the subject, deciding that I wasn't ready to hear about his past or, more to the point, discuss my own. 'I'm *starving*, and if you've been fixing cupboards all afternoon, you must have worked up an appetite too.'

'Now you're talking!' He rubbed his hands together, then we picked up the menus from the table.

As we tucked into our pie and mash, the conversation flowed freely. We chatted about his job as a carpenter and also a bit about my work. Whilst we seemed to get on and both had awkward dating app experiences to share, I wasn't sure if he was husband material. But I *was* attracted to him. Did he feel the same? No idea.

I mean, he'd said I looked *nice* when we'd met in the station, so that was positive. Then again, unlike enthusiastic adjectives like *amazing* or *fantastic*, *nice* was one of those neutral words people used sometimes to be polite. It was a bit non-committal. Like saying to someone they look *okay*. *Hmmm.*

Henry hadn't given any signs to show that he was

interested romantically. No attempts to touch my hand or suggestive comments. He'd flirted a lot more when we'd met at speed dating.

I wished I knew what he was thinking. They say that women play with their hair or flutter their eyelashes when they're attracted to a guy. I had no idea if I'd been doing either tonight. Maybe subconsciously. But what signals did men give a woman if they liked her?

'Wow,' said Henry, gazing out of the windows, which were facing him. 'The views of London look great. Shall we go on the balcony and take a look?'

'Yeah, why not?' I picked up my jacket and followed him through the patio doors.

We headed over to the edge of the empty balcony. He was right. The views of St. Paul's and Tower Bridge in the distance and the lights from the surrounding buildings glistening on the Thames looked stunning.

'It's pretty,' I said, turning to face him.

'Just like you, darling…' He stepped forward, wrapping his arms around my waist and leaning forward to kiss me.

Oh! I wasn't expecting that.

His kisses started slowly, then became more urgent as he pulled me in closer to him. I could feel his hard-on against my thigh. At least that answered my question about whether or not he found me attractive…

Mmmm. I felt a tingle between my legs. It had been a while since I'd been this close to a man, and after being used to kissing Eric for five years, feeling someone else's lips was kind of—I don't know, weird? Not necessarily in a bad way. Just different.

I could taste the beer on Henry's lips. I still remembered the taste of Eric's breath. He was obsessed with chewing gum, so it was always minty. I liked kissing Eric. I missed him.

'That was nice, babe.' Henry smiled, then it faded a little. 'You okay?'

He'd obviously noticed that I wasn't fully engaged.

I snapped out of my thoughts. I'd told myself earlier that I wouldn't do this. I needed to focus on the present.

'Yeah, I'm fine,' I said, trying to push memories of Eric out of my mind for the hundredth time.

Let him go. Eric isn't here and Henry is. Eric's with someone else now. He's getting married to Nicole.

I had to move on. I *needed* to move on.

I took Henry's head in my hands and started to kiss him. This time I focused on the here and now and the fact that I was with a cool, funny guy who seemed to be into me.

As Henry's hands wandered over my bum, then up to stroke the side of my breasts, I began to let go.

That's better. As I allowed my mind to be free and let my body relax, I started to get more turned on.

Henry pressed himself against me, and as I parted my mouth, he thrust his tongue inside.

'I don't live too far away from here, you know,' said Henry, coming up for air, 'if you want to come back to mine?' My eyes grew wide.

'Sleep with you on the first date?' I said, pulling back gently.

'I'm a proper gent, babe. I wouldn't expect you to do the deed on our first date. That's why I waited until tonight, which technically is our *second* date, to ask you instead,' he winked.

'Funny, Henry,' I said, raising my eyebrows. 'But this *is* our *first* date.'

'Nope,' he said, pecking me firmly on the lips. 'Our first date was at Leon. The fact that you also dated twenty other guys that night doesn't count!' he laughed.

'Cheeky!' I said, kissing him on the lips again.

'Come on…' He started planting kisses on my neck. 'I like you, you like me, we're both adults, so what's the problem?'

'True…' I said, trying and failing to think of a witty response.

'Like I said'—he stroked my chin—'I'm a gentleman, so no pressure, babe. All I'm saying is, neither of us are getting any younger. It's not like we're twenty-one with our whole lives ahead of us. At this age, it's carpe diem and all that. Seize the day, or *night*, I say.'

His hands travelled up my burgundy dress and along my inner thigh.

Mmm…

Gosh. It's been a while. All hope of suppressing sexual thoughts went straight out of the window. Henry had reminded me how much I enjoyed it. How much I'd missed it and how much I wanted it.

Here I was, standing out on a balcony, above a large group of tourists huddled on the pavement below who could glance up at any minute with his hands running all over my body, and yet I didn't care.

What had come over me? Must be lust and extreme horniness rearing its head. *Pardon the pun. Rearing* was definitely the right word to describe the rod resting against my thigh.

Carpe diem was great in theory, but in reality, wasn't it

a bit soon? Maybe I should get to know him a bit more first. That would be the sensible thing to do. After all, I didn't want to get hurt again.

But perhaps if I slept with him *before* I got to know him, if it didn't go anywhere, it might be easier to deal with, as I'd be less attached?

Or maybe, just *maybe*, I shouldn't think so bloody much and should just go with the flow for a change? You know, have *fun*?

Chloe had said a shag would do me a world of good. And now I could feel the hormones racing through my body and my heart pumping, I reckoned she was right.

Oh, what the hell.

'Okay, Henry,' I said quickly before I changed my mind. 'Why not? As it's our *second* date, let's go back to my place. Let's go and seize the night.'

CHAPTER TWELVE

We spilled through the front door, hands all over each other's bodies.

'Which way to the bedroom?' he gasped.

'This way,' I said, walking backwards towards the door, pressing my lips against his.

Dammit. I just remembered, My bedroom was a tip. There were clothes literally *everywhere*. I'd pretty much emptied the entire contents of my wardrobe before I'd annoyingly decided to wear the first outfit I'd tried on. *Typical.*

'One second,' I said, pulling away. 'Wait here—I'll just be a minute.'

I slipped inside, closing the door firmly behind me, opened the wardrobe, gathered up the clothes scattered on the floor and all across my duvet, then bundled them over the top of the rail.

There was a knock at the door.

'Babe?' said Henry.

'Er, just a sec—' Before I got to finish my sentence, the door flew open.

'What you doing?' he said. 'Oh darling, don't bother tidying up for me. I'm not interested in what your room looks like. The only thing I want to see right now is you. *Naked*.'

He strode towards me, planted his lips on mine, then lifted my dress up over my head. Thank goodness I'd taken Chloe's advice to put on some decent underwear.

I sat down at the edge of the bed, my heart racing from the rush of nerves and excitement.

Henry whipped off his shirt, unbuckled his jeans, pulled them, along with his brown boxer shorts, down past his ankles and stood in front of me.

'Suck it, please, babe,' he said, holding himself in his hands.

Wow. Talk about cutting to the chase. I guessed this was what we were here for. After all, he hadn't come back to my place to read me a bedtime story.

I looked down to see his throbbing rod standing to attention and peering out from a very heavy curtain of pubic hair.

He had a lot of hair. A thick, dark covering across not just his torso but all across his shoulders and back too. So different to the wisps of hair on Eric's chest.

Henry placed his hands at the back of my head and gently steered it towards him. I wasn't used to going down on a guy so soon after we'd met, but as tonight was about throwing caution to the wind, I decided to go for it. Might help me feel a bit more relaxed about having sex after-wards. I needed to get more comfortable first, though.

I lay on my stomach across the bed, moved my head

towards him, then opened wide. As I slid him in and out of my mouth, he groaned.

'Oh, darling, you really know how to make me happy. Keep going, babe.'

Seeing that I was turning him on made me feel great. My confidence had taken such a battering after Eric left me. I'd never thought I'd be able to face being with another man again, but here I was, and doing okay it would seem. I couldn't wait for him to go down on me too.

After a few minutes I edged away, gently moving him slowly out of my mouth, turned over, peeled off my knickers and opened my legs, ready for him to reciprocate.

'Kiss me, please,' I said as I opened wider. He climbed on top of me and began kissing my neck.

Not there.

'Um, Henry,' I said, pulling away gently. 'I—I meant I'd like you to *kiss me*,' I said, stroking myself.

He bolted up like a deer who'd just been caught in the headlights.

'What?' He grimaced as if I'd just asked him to suck on a diseased animal's rotting big toe. 'I don't do... I mean, I just...er... *later, babe*,' he said, softening his voice. '*Mmmm*. You're *so* sexy, darling,' he groaned as he started kissing my neck again. 'You almost made me come. You turned me on so much, and now I just want to be inside you.'

Wait.

I tried to process what was going on. Was he going to say that he didn't do that? I was clean. I'd showered before I'd met him. *No.* I must have misheard. I mean, he asked me to give him head literally a millisecond after we'd got into the bedroom, so he must be into oral. Eric certainly was.

Yeah. In these days of equality, it wouldn't be fair for him not to return the favour. Surely that would be considered bad manners? Poor sexual etiquette?

'Oh, babe...' groaned Henry again.

As he started grinding into me, although I was still trying to get my head around what he'd said, I couldn't fight what my body was feeling. As I became more and more turned on, the memories of sex—well, the positive ones anyway—came flooding back.

I loved the feeling of a man on top of me. The anticipation. The longing and the sensation when he first entered you. I felt my body tremble. Henry had got me worked up. I didn't want to stop. Not now. I'd give him the benefit of the doubt and just hope he kept his word to reciprocate later. But first things first. If I was going to sleep with him, there was no way I was doing it without playing it safe.

'Have you got a condom?' I asked.

I'd stopped buying condoms years ago after Eric and I had become serious and I'd gone on the pill. No need for protection, I'd thought. I could trust him. And for years it was fine. Until towards the end of our relationship, when I started noticing an unusual discharge. Nothing had changed in my diet or my routine, but I still thought it was me, so I went to the chemist to get some thrush medication. But that didn't help, and I couldn't understand why. Little did I know at the time it was because he was sleeping with someone else. When I found out, I went straight to the clinic and discovered he'd given me chlamydia. Bastard.

'Yep, course I have, babe,' he said, reaching down to

the floor and taking out his wallet. He ripped open the packet, rolled it on, then thrust himself inside me.

Whoa. Yes. It really *had* been a while. Jesus. Even though he was an average size, it felt like trying to squeeze a thick screw into a pinhole.

We rocked backwards and forwards. He certainly wasn't the silent type. Henry groaned loudly, squeezing his eyes shut as if he was deep in concentration and punctuating each thrust with a grunt that grew louder with every move. *So dramatic.*

He was lost in his own little world.

He pumped in and out. Faster and faster.

His groans grew even louder. 'I'm coming. *I'm coming.* Yes! Yes! *Yes!*' he shouted as if he'd just been awarded gold at the sex Olympics.

He collapsed.

'Wooh-hoo!' he screamed. 'How's *that* for seizing the night, Emily! *Yeah, baby!* That was fucking great!'

He nuzzled his face into my neck and exhaled loudly.

It was okay. Not as long as I would have liked, but it had felt nice, I supposed. But I hadn't come. If he went down on me though, I knew I *definitely* could. Eric could always make me come. Oh, he was *so* good with his tongue…

For God's sake! How many times? Eric is a cheating bastard. You're here. Now. With Henry. Remember? Your date? The guy you've just slept with?

You've put yourself out there after eight months of celibacy and that was your first time back in the game. You can't expect miracles and orgasms to happen overnight. Especially with someone new. You have to be patient.

My inner thoughts were right. I was expecting too

much. Plus, the night was young and Henry said he'd go down on me later, so I could just take another shower and ask him again.

I know they say you shouldn't give to receive, but I'd taken care of him, so I was still hopeful that he would be a man of his word and do the same...

CHAPTER THIRTEEN

'So great to see you!' said Kat, giving me a big hug.

'You too!' I said as we sat down on the sofa at Cuppa. 'I was *really* happy to get your text this morning.'

'Sorry it was last minute, but I was speaking to my sister last night, moaning that I never get to have any time to myself and I think she felt bad so messaged me at the crack of dawn to say she'd have the kids for a few hours this afternoon.'

'Amazing!' I said.

'It really is! She came round and got them at eleven, and I went back to bed for a whole hour and then had a bath. An *actual* bath. I got to pour in some lovely oils and have a nice long soak without Kyle banging on the door to use the toilet or April asking when lunch was going to be ready or if I'd ironed her skirt. It was bliss,' she said, closing her eyes to reminisce.

'I can only imagine,' I said. 'Well, thanks for choosing to spend your precious free time with me. I feel privileged.

I wouldn't have blamed you if you wanted to spend the entire afternoon in bed.'

'That did cross my mind, but I just wanted to get out, you know?'

'Yep, I do. It's funny. Before Chloe set me this going out more challenge thing, I was quite happy to spend all day and night at home. But now, I do get a bit of cabin fever if I haven't been out.'

'Tell me about it! It's nice to be in different surroundings for a change. That's why I was happy to come to your area. I like this café. Very cool,' she said, glancing around the interior.

'I like it too. I've been coming here since it opened a couple of years ago. The coffee's good and the fact that it's literally two seconds from my flat is an added bonus.'

'And I'm sure the delightful views help too.' She smirked, looking over at the hot barista.

'Yes, he is rather easy on the eyes,' I said, admiring his short dark hair, sexy stubble and the white T-shirt which clung to his solid chest and arms. 'He's new.'

'Mmm. Well, this new barista is *very*, *very* fit too.' She winked. 'What's his name?'

'Absolutely no idea.' I shrugged my shoulders.

'You mean you have a gorgeous guy working at your local coffee shop and you haven't even made basic enquiries about his name and how soon he'd like to get married?' She chuckled. 'Shame on you!'

Not Kat too. What was it with my friends?

'Oh my god. You sound just like Chloe.' I rolled my eyes.

'Well, Chloe's right! If I was footloose and fancy-free like you and didn't have to think about whether a man would be happy to have an instant family, I would be *all* over that. Trust me.'

'Nope. Too awkward. Like I said, I enjoy coming here. Imagine if I was forward, started flirting and coming on to him, but he wasn't interested and thought I was some weirdo bunny boiler and rejected me. I'd be embarrassed every time I came here. In fact, what am I saying? If he blanked me, I *wouldn't* be able to come back again. No way.' I shuddered. 'I *need* my daily latte. It's like my morning medication. I can't function without it. It's not worth the risk.'

'Okay, coffee addict! I get it. Still think you should find out the basics though. It's not a crime to ask someone their name,' I rolled my eyes again. 'So anyway, how are things with you?' she asked, taking off her jacket and wisely changing the subject. 'How was your date with lover boy Henry? Did you get lucky?'

'Depends on your definition of *lucky*. If you mean did I get a shag, then yes I did.'

'Amazing! Go, Emily! *And?* How was it?' Kat's eyes widened.

'Good. Well, sort of...' Flashbacks whizzed through my head. 'The sex was, fine, good—*ish*. He wasn't Eric, but obviously *he* had five years to get to know me, my body and what I liked, so it's not fair to compare. It was nice to be back in the saddle, I suppose.'

'I'm sensing a *but*?' said Kat.

'Yeah.' I paused. 'Tell me: if you went down on a guy and he didn't reciprocate, would you think that's acceptable?'

'Definitely not! *Okay, okay*. Let me take a step back

and try to be objective. Did you offer to give him a BJ or did he *ask* you?' asked Kat.

'He asked me,' I replied.

'And did *you* ask *him*?' she said. 'Sometimes as women, we're not vocal enough about what we want in the bedroom, and men aren't always good at guessing.'

'Well, after I'd done him, I lay on my back and sort of asked if he would, *kiss me…*' Admittedly my request had been more subtle than his "suck it" terminology. 'I *think* he understood. He looked horrified and I reckon he was about to say he "didn't do that", but he stopped himself and just said he'd do it *later*. Except *later* never came.'

'Alarm bells!' shouted Kat. 'Sorry, but if his first reaction was that he didn't do *that* after he'd asked you to give him oral, then it sounds like he's one of those selfish sexist pricks who believe it's a woman's duty to do everything to please the man but couldn't give a toss whether the woman is satisfied or not.'

'Yeah, that's what I'm worried about. It was a bit frustrating and kind of humiliating, as I suppose I was so used to Eric doing it willingly, and Henry not wanting to made me feel like there was something wrong with me. Like I wasn't clean. And I was. I *always* make sure. I thought about saying something, but at the same time he'd got me so worked up that I didn't want to risk ruining the mood and not going all the way, so I let it go.'

As I heard myself recounting the story, I cringed. Maybe I should have been clearer about my needs, but it was hard to think of the right way to phrase things when you were caught up in the moment and with someone new.

'So are you going to see him again?' asked Kat.

'Not sure. *Maybe.* When he left, he said we should

meet up in the week, but who knows? Even if I decide that I want to give him another chance, now we've slept together, he might not even message me.'

'Yeah, sadly that is true. When they get the goodies too quickly, there's less of an incentive to stick around.'

'Exactly. That's why initially I wasn't going to sleep with him on our first—or as he called it, our *second* date, but like he said, we're not getting any younger, so we should seize the day.'

'Typical bloke spiel,' Kat scoffed.

'Oh, don't get me wrong. I wouldn't have done it if I hadn't wanted to. That's why I'm kind of pondering the whole going down thing. I gave him a blow job because I don't mind giving them, but if I didn't, I wouldn't want to feel like I *had* to do it. It wouldn't be right for a guy to force me, so is it then wrong for me to expect him to go down on me?'

'I hear you but, it's *how* he reacted. If he'd said it's something intimate that he saves for when things are more serious and he didn't feel ready just yet, then you could say *fair enough*. But if you're saying he was horrified and looked disgusted like you'd just asked him to suck a kangaroo's hairy balls, then that's just rude.'

'That's what I thought.' I took a sip of my latte.

It was rude. Thing was, though, now I'd had a taste of having sex, I kind of wanted more. Like, *now*. Or as soon as possible. And so even though I was disappointed with him not keeping his word, I was feeling like I'd still be willing to give him another go. At least I'd be ready to speak up more second time around.

'So if we do see each other and it happens again and I ask him to go down and he refuses, what do you reckon?

Ask him straight up why he doesn't want to? Say *go down or go home*?'

'I'd *love* to see his face if you phrased it like that!' chuckled Kat. 'It depends. How much do you like Henry?'

'He's okay. We get on and I'm attracted to him. Whether I see him as a long-term thing, hmmm. The jury's out on that one.'

'Okay, I'm hearing fuckbuddy. And how critical is cunnilingus for you? A *nice to have* or a *deal-breaker*.'

'Hmmm. Good question. As bad as it might sound, I'm feeling like it could be a deal-breaker.'

'I get what you're saying.' Kat nodded.

'I've been suppressing all sexual thoughts since Eric, but now I remember I *loved* sex, and sometimes I even preferred oral to penetration. It's tricky because on the one hand, I think it would be a bit harsh to stop seeing someone because they didn't do exactly what I wanted the first time. But then on the other, I think, what's the point of having a friend with benefits if your body isn't actually being given the full benefits package? *God*,' I said, catching myself. 'I can't believe I'm having this conversation in my local coffee shop with someone I just met a few weeks ago.'

'Don't worry!' Kat giggled. 'It would take a *lot* to shock me, my dear. I've had three kids and more disappointing sexual encounters than I care to remember.'

'You'll have to share those stories with me another day,' I laughed.

'*Christ*. I'm not sure I'm quite ready to relive those nightmares again,' said Kat, putting her head in her hands. 'To answer your question about what you should do next time, *if* there's a next time, yes, I agree. Ask him. Find out what his concerns are. In a nice way. If he looks like he's just nervous and needs a helping hand, or should that be *tongue*, then offer to train him. Maybe suggest you do a sixty-nine so you're both giving and receiving at the same time. But if he says *yuck* and it really is a deal-breaker, then consider moving on. Like you said, if you're just in it for the sex and he's not delivering the goods, then you might as well log onto Tinder and find someone who will.'

See? This was why I just stuck to chatting to guys on the apps for so long rather than meeting them. Once you started seeing someone, it just opened up a giant can of drama. First I fretted about whether a guy was going to turn up for a date and, if he did, whether he'd like me. And now, as well as all the angst that came with sleeping with a guy for the first time in ages, I had to deal with what to do if he refused to go downtown.

'This whole men and sex thing is a minefield,' I huffed. 'Makes me wonder if it's even worth all the hassle.'

'Yep. I often wonder the same. But we have to keep on going. Somewhere out there is the man of our dreams. Our true soulmate. The partner we'll spend the rest of our lives with.'

'Do you really believe that?' I asked.

'Truthfully?' said Kat. 'Most days, no. But I try to stay optimistic, because as much as men annoy and frustrate me, I love their company. A man that is kind, caring and talented in the sack can make you feel incredible.'

'Yep. I can't deny it was great to have sex again. Chloe was right. It does relax you. I didn't realise how much I'd missed it until last night.'

'You're lucky. I have no idea when or where my next dick fix is coming from.'

'Dick fix!' I laughed.

'It's no laughing matter, Em.' She folded her arms. 'I'm all out of options.'

'I know what that's like. I'm not exactly swimming in a sea of men either. If I kick this one to the curb, who knows when I'll get it again? That's the only reason I'm thinking of giving Henry another chance. So?' I said, finishing off my latte. 'Nothing came from the singles' party, then?'

'No, not really,' said Kat. 'The best thing to come out of that night was meeting you and Rob. I love our WhatsApp chats.'

'Me too,' I said. 'Rob is a sweetie.'

'Yeah, he is a lovely guy. Happy Solos are having another big party in a couple of weeks, but I'm not sure about going.'

'Oh, really?'

'Yeah,' said Kat. 'I'm just wondering if it's all a bit contrived, you know? *Let's get a load of single people in a room together and they will find love.* I don't think it's that simple.'

'I see what you're saying,' I said. 'On the other hand, it is nice to know that everyone there is in the same boat. The worst thing is to spot a guy you like, only to find out he's married, so it does remove that kind of risk.' *Gosh.* I'd just said something positive about going to a singles' event. *Wonders will never cease.*

'You've got a point. I don't know, though. I'll see. By then I'll probably be climbing the walls and will be so horny I'll grab the first guy who asks for my number.

Better ask my sister now if she can have the kids overnight.'

'A woman on a mission!'

'A woman who knows what she *needs* and isn't afraid to get it. Yep. That's me,' said Kat. 'Guilty as charged.'

'High five to that,' I said as we slapped hands. 'Here's to going after what we want and getting satisfaction both in and outside of the bedroom.'

CHAPTER FOURTEEN

Miracles do happen.
     I was on my way to another Chloe activity and was actually excited. I couldn't wait to get there. Why? Because I was going to an event that I reckoned I'd enjoy: a life drawing class.

I'd always been passionate about art, which is why I was an illustrator. But when I was younger and used to lock myself away for hours on end sketching in my bedroom, dreaming about being a grown up, this wasn't exactly the career I'd hoped for. Don't get me wrong, I've made a good living. It's just that after doing pretty much the same thing for so many years, I was kind of over it. I was bored. I didn't find it challenging. Everyone always assumed my job was super exciting, and it definitely could be. But because I was nervous about pitching for new, more glamorous briefs, I ended up just sticking with the clients I'd worked with for ages or accepting the jobs that no one else wanted.

A recent highlight was doing illustrations for a series

of health leaflets about going to the bathroom. Yep, that's right. How long it should take to do a number two and what the colour, shape, size and consistency of your poo said about your health. When I'd accepted that project, that's when I'd known my career was officially heading down the toilet. Pun totally intended. It paid fairly well, so I shouldn't grumble. It was just that drawing diagrams of body waste and other things I had no interest in all day long wasn't the kind of career I'd had in mind.

I used to dream of creating my own cool designs, bringing exciting ideas to life. Producing huge works of art. Big paintings. Large-scale artwork—much bigger than just an A4 sheet of paper. Doing stuff that was fun. Seeing my creations on people's walls one day. That kind of thing.

I wasn't talking about becoming some mega-popular artist. I had no desire to be famous. For me, it was never about being adored by other artists or having my work displayed in galleries. No, it was more about having the opportunity to truly express myself. To feel passionate and happy about the work I'd produced. And of course for people to pay for my work, as I knew that I needed more than just passion to pay the bills.

I used to paint all the time when I was a kid. It was a ritual. I'd race to finish all my homework so I'd be allowed to spend the rest of the weekend drawing or painting random things. Whatever had inspired me that day or that week. Cartoon characters, animals, landscapes, people. It was the same at college and uni. It became easier then as I was studying it full-time. In the holidays or whenever I had a day off, I even used to help out a couple, Hans and Carrie, who were mural artists, and I learnt a lot from them. I loved doing that. It was a real skill to learn how to be creative on walls and larger surfaces. We used to paint murals in people's homes, hotels, schools, businesses or charities. It was fun to take a boring wall and transform it into something exciting that would entertain people, promote a business or just make people smile.

I painted all through my twenties too. Smaller things, as by then I had to get a steady paying job in London. But when I started going out with Eric, I broke the habit.

Whenever I woke up early to paint, he'd tell me to come back to bed. Or if it was the afternoon, he'd want to go into Central London to have a drink with his friends and insisted I come along. So I didn't get time.

I knew my painting was important to me, so in the early years, I switched up my routine to try and carve out the time. I'd get up when Eric was fast asleep, work late doing day job stuff to give me time to do my own thing the following morning. That tired me out, but I was producing work. What I thought was *good* work. But Eric would laugh at me.

I remember painting a field of tulips on an A1 canvas. There was a green windmill in the background, then rows of red, yellow, pink and orange flowers. It looked beautiful. I'd imagined how amazing it would be to paint it directly onto the wall like I used to do when I worked with Hans and Carrie. Either the bedroom or the living room would be perfect. It looked so cheery. It would instantly liven up the space. Just as I was going to show it to Eric, he'd said, 'What's that? *Way* too many colours! Make sure you don't put that up on any of the walls in here. It'll give me a headache!' In the end I'd given it to my parents.

Eric didn't understand art. I knew that. He liked everything plain. White walls. White sheets. Everything bland.

Zero colour. His prized possession was his Italian cream leather sofa. It was one of the things he took when he left, which gave me an excuse to buy the lovely bright green velvet sofa I have now.

After listening to Eric's comments week in, week out, in the end I'd become more and more demoralised. Somehow it didn't seem to matter that *I* liked my work, or that Chloe and my parents loved my paintings so much that they displayed them proudly in their homes. All I could ever hear whenever I picked up a paintbrush was Eric's voice in my head. 'That's even louder than the last one! I know you're trying, Em, but it's not really good enough to sell. Looks a bit amateur. Best to stick to your basic illustration stuff.' So I did it less and less and then eventually I just stopped.

Every now and again I'd tell myself that I *should* try again and shouldn't listen to him, but by then, I just couldn't find the inspiration. I suppose it was worse because I was working from home and didn't actually go anywhere to get inspired. Eric's social life dominated our weekends. I never really got the chance to go to galleries or do the stuff I wanted.

So little by little, my passion was crushed. Looking back, I knew I shouldn't have put up with it. But I didn't have the confidence to speak up or walk away. I haven't done any painting or drawing outside of work for a couple of years now. That's why tonight was so exciting. I used to do life drawing at college and uni. Hopefully it would all come back to me tonight. I couldn't wait to get stuck back into art again.

The class was taking place in a room at the top of a pub just a few miles from home, so it was pretty convenient. I climbed the stairs and entered the room. About a dozen chairs were arranged in a semicircle around a larger armchair. We all filed in and took a seat. There was a cross section of ages. A couple of guys in their twenties, several who looked forty plus and one other woman who was probably around my age.

I picked up the A3 pad and the charcoal, ready to start. A few minutes later, the model appeared in a black silk dressing gown. She was around five feet four, with short dark hair, bright red lipstick and large gold earrings. She sat on the armchair whilst the tutor briefed us. He explained that we'd start with some quick-fire rounds with the model holding poses for just a few minutes to help us warm up and then she would do longer poses, building up to forty minutes.

Once he'd finished talking, the model got up, dropped her robe then stood proudly, placing her hands behind her head. *Wow*. She oozed confidence. She had small boobs and a big stomach, thighs and bottom, and she was totally owning it. You could tell just by looking at her that she was completely comfortable in her skin and had no problem getting her kit off. I loved that. *Wish I could learn to feel like that about my body.* In some ways, our chests and bums were a similar size. Difference was, I'd never be brave enough to do what she was doing. I'd be too worried about exposing all my lumps and bumps.

I started sketching. It was great to connect with the paper again. I'd become so used to doing everything digitally, drawing with a tablet and pen. This was so much better. I loved the way I could make big bold black lines and gently smudge them with my fingers to create different shades of grey.

The next couple of hours flew by. It was different to the monotonous work I did for clients. I lost myself in a different world. I forgot about everything. I wasn't thinking about Eric, Henry, social media or dating apps. All my thoughts just slipped away and I was totally focused. It was so relaxing. I felt so free.

The more sketches I drew, the more I started to realise how beautiful the model's body was. Every day on social media, on TV, in magazines or on billboards I was flooded with images of one kind of beauty ideal. Perfect skin and hair, not an ounce of excess fat, zero blemishes. I'd been conditioned to believe that anything outside of those criteria was flawed.

But here was this woman. She wasn't a tall, slim supermodel. Her hair hadn't been professionally styled. Her make-up wasn't immaculate. There was no flattering lighting. No filters or airbrushing to fix her 'imperfections'.

She wasn't holding in her belly so that she wouldn't be labelled fat by strangers. She didn't have big boobs or a pert bum. She had scars on her stomach. Cellulite on her thighs. All things we're told make women ugly. Yet she was anything but. She was radiant. Real. Authentic. Naturally beautiful. Everything from her generous curves to her petite breasts made her special. Different. In a good way. And her confidence made her glow. I could learn a lot from her.

'Thank you,' I said, approaching the model as she wrapped the robe around herself. 'I really enjoyed drawing you this evening. Have you been doing this long?' I was surprised at how comfortable I'd felt about coming to speak to her. I'd never done that before after a life drawing class. I wasn't even sure if it was the done thing. Hope she didn't think I was weird.

'You're welcome!' She smiled. 'What's your name?'

'Emily.'

'Nice to meet you! I'm Paige. And, no, I've only been doing this for a couple of months.'

'I'd have said you'd been doing it a lot longer. Can't be easy standing for hours in your birthday suit, yet you're so confident. It's beautiful to see.'

'Thanks!' She smiled. 'I haven't always been this way, though. I used to be so self-conscious. Constantly dieting. Always comparing myself to others. Wondering about why I wasn't thinner or prettier.' I could definitely identify with that. 'But I got tired of hating myself. Sure. I could have got a loan and spent thousands trying to "fix" the bits I didn't like, and I'm not knocking anyone who does, but I knew that wasn't for me. So I made a vow to be proud of the person I was. Start not just accepting my body but loving it.'

'Easier said than done, though, isn't it?'

'Tell me about it! But rather than focusing on the bits I didn't like, every morning, I replaced negative thoughts with positive ones. When I looked in the mirror I started focusing on the parts I liked and told myself I was beautiful instead. It felt weird at first, but as the saying goes, sometimes you need to fake it before you make it! Eventually it became second nature and I started feeling better. Then my friend Bernie, the tutor tonight, needed someone to step in when a model dropped out at the last minute, and I thought it could be a great way to help me keep building my confidence, so I decided to give it a go.'

'Must have been nerve-wracking.'

'Definitely! The first time, I was shitting myself. I started getting self-conscious again. Less so about my weight and my cellulite, which used to always bug me, but weirdly about even more insignificant things like the fact that because of the short notice, I hadn't had time to do my bikini line. *Crazy.* But after the first few poses, I relaxed and I told myself that a full bush was probably more interesting to draw anyway!' She laughed.

'Well, I think you're amazing,' I said.

'Thanks! I'd never been able to do this a year or even six months ago, but now I'm really glad I did. It's good to push yourself out of your comfort zone.'

'Yeah,' I said, thinking about the activities I'd been doing these past few weeks. 'It really is.'

'The thing to remember, Emily, is that no one is perfect and that's okay. Be proud of your body and who you are. Our differences, our so-called "imperfections", are what make us special.'

Paige was an inspiration. Although I'd made some progress with the way I felt about how I looked, I still had some way to go. Like she said, I also needed to find a way to not just accept the things I didn't like but learn to love them.

She was also right about stepping outside of my comfort zone. It *was* a good thing. I was already seeing the benefits of regularly getting out of the house, and meeting the model here tonight had made me more determined to continue this social streak.

Yep. I might not be stripping in front of a room full of strangers any time soon, but right there and then, whatever she had up her sleeve, I promised myself to embrace the next Chloe-Challenge activity with open arms.

CHAPTER FIFTEEN

W eek six of Chloe's challenge, and as much as it pained me to admit it, she was right. I was enjoying myself. I had made new friends, was using dating apps and social media much less, and whilst I hadn't found love, which, let's face it, was to be expected after such a short period of time, I *had* got back in the saddle. My confidence was growing.

During week four I'd chalked up three activities: a night with Henry, coffee with Kat and life drawing. Last week after enjoying it so much, I'd booked myself onto two more classes and also arranged to go on an organised walk around Battersea Park and Kings Road. This week, I was on track to go out multiple times again.

Chloe's activity-choosing game was strong. Even though I was well into the second month and was supposed to be arranging all of the activities myself, she had kindly booked me on to a dining meet-up tonight. I loved food, so that was definitely something I could get behind.

She explained that there was a group of people that met

up at different restaurants in central London once a month to chat over a nice meal. This month it was a Thai eatery near Waterloo.

I'd heard a lot about this restaurant. It had opened a few months ago and was quickly becoming recognised as *the* place to be. I had always wanted to visit but of course hadn't managed to drag myself out of my flat, so now that I had, I was really looking forward to it. I'd get to eat lots of great food, have a night out and hopefully make some more new friends in the process. Win-win.

Speaking of meeting new people, dare I say it, but I was starting to feel more comfortable about walking into a room of strangers. Just to clarify, it wasn't my favourite thing in the world and I still got nervous, but I no longer needed to hide in the corner or disappear to the loos to kill time. Well, not for the whole night, at least, which was how I'd felt a few weeks ago. Progress.

On the whole, I'd discovered that whilst some people weren't very verbose or friendly, the majority were just like me: worried about turning up on their own and having to speak to strangers. Most *wanted* to have a conversation. I found that having a quick scan of the room and heading over to the person who either looked really nervous or very smiley worked well.

Keeping in mind Chloe's advice to wear colour to feel more confident, I slipped on a sea-green fit-and-flare dress, put on some natural make-up and ran my fingers through my curls.

Earlier this afternoon I'd gone to see Rochelle, the hair-dresser one of the mums at school had recommended to Chloe. She was great. Rochelle had a big head full of beautiful curls herself, so I instantly felt at ease. Originally I'd asked her to straighten it, but she asked if I minded if she went ahead and worked with my natural texture instead. I wasn't sure at first, especially because I was going out tonight and never really wore my curls down, but she'd put me at ease. I also thought about what Paige said about learning to love myself and the things that made me unique, so I agreed.

She took me step by step through how to manage my hair myself at home and recommended some products for me to use, which I'd snapped up straight away. My hair had never looked so good when it was curly. *Ever.* Even so, I still kept looking at myself in the mirror, wondering if I'd be okay going out tonight with such big, bold hair. Eric would have hated it. But the more I looked at it, the more I liked it. I felt kind of … I don't know. More myself? Maybe even a little bit sexy? So I decided to go for it and wear it just as it was. I was definitely relieved that I wouldn't have to spend ages dragging the straighteners through it too.

After a final check in the mirror, I made my way to the station. It didn't take long to get there. I jumped off the tube and went up the escalators, and just before I headed out of the exit, I took off my Converse, changed into my heels and strutted outside into the cool air.

I was feeling good. Confident. And hungry. I'd checked out the menu before leaving and it looked amazing. For lunch I had eaten a sandwich and some of Chloe's coffee cake, and I'd been tempted to have another slice before getting ready but decided to save myself for tonight's meal.

Not far to go now. I'd passed the restaurant before, so I

knew exactly where to find it. I spotted the street. I just needed to make a right at the traffic lights.

But then as I turned to walk down the cobbled slip road, I froze.

No.

It couldn't be.

Surely not.

I looked again. Then once more to be sure.

It *was*.

Standing outside the restaurant it was *him*. With *her*.

Eric and Nicole.

His hands and lips were all over her. He was stroking her bum, kissing her neck...

OMG. Now she looks like she's about to put her hand between his legs.

Oh God, oh God, oh God.

I can't let them see me.

Shit.

I ducked behind the parked car in front of me.

My stomach felt more tangled than my headphone wires. I was finally starting to get over him. Trying to move on. Going out. Had hooked up with someone new and now *this*? Of all the restaurants in London, why did they have to choose this one? Why tonight? Why not after I'd left or before I'd arrived? Why was I being punished like this?

I peered around the side of the car to see if they were still there. Maybe they were waiting for a cab and it had whisked them away? No cars had passed in either direction since I'd been cowering behind this BMW, so probably not. Or perhaps they'd walked towards the other end of the road and gone home? No. The most logical way to walk would be from where I came.

They were still there. Now he was gazing into her eyes and stroking her face. I felt like I was going to be sick.

I vomited at the side of the road. *Gross.* This was too much. I couldn't do it. I thought I'd grown stronger, but seeing him had brought all those emotions flooding back again.

I knew I should just say I didn't care if they were at the restaurant or not, strut past them and go and have a good time, but I couldn't face it. Although tonight would have been an ideal time to bump into them as I was looking good, I couldn't be sure that I wouldn't lose the plot and start screaming or crying.

Tears started streaming down my face.

Oh God. Well, if I had any intention of walking past them, that had gone out of the window now. Cheeks covered in mascara tears was *not* the best look for showing your ex what he was missing.

I poked my head around the bumper again. His tongue was now firmly cemented down her throat. *Why* did I look?

I jumped up and hobbled towards the station in my heels. I couldn't have stayed. They didn't look like they were leaving anytime soon, and the way their hands were all over each other, if I'd waited a few seconds longer, I wouldn't be surprised if they started having sex on the pavement. God. He was really into her.

Thank goodness it was only one tube stop back to Kennington. Hopefully I'd be able to hold it together until I got home.

As I came out of the station and headed towards my road, my mind was still racing. To-ing and fro-ing. Wondering if I'd done the right thing by running away. But there was no point denying it. Even if I went inside the restaurant, tried my best to ignore them and pretended to have a good time, all I would have been thinking of would be the happy couple. His hands all over her. Her touching him. The man who used to be mine. Until she'd taken him away from me.

Who was I kidding? As much as I despised Nicole, if Eric had really loved me, he wouldn't have allowed anything to happen. Even if she'd stood in front of him naked and begged him for sex, if he'd loved me, he would have said no. But he didn't. So he was the real villain. *He was* the one who betrayed me.

My eyes were stinging. I just wanted to get home, put on a Sad Songs Spotify playlist and curl up into a ball. Shut the world out around me. I couldn't call Chloe. She'd tell me to *woman up* and forget about him. I didn't want to disturb Kat. She'd be busy with her kids. Henry? No. He didn't seem like the emotions type. Plus I was seeing him tomorrow. Didn't want to appear too keen.

'Emily?'

Oh God. The last thing I needed was to see someone I knew right now when I had snot, tears and mascara running down my face. It was only a few more steps to my front door. Maybe if I walked quickly and ignored them, I'd get away with it.

'Emily?' said the voice again. 'Are you okay?'

I guessed not. I turned around slowly.

Oh bloody hell. Let me rephrase those thoughts: the last person I wanted to see when I had snot, tears and mascara running down my face was the hot guy from the coffee shop. Could this evening become any more mortify-ing? *Jeez.*

Tissue. I needed a tissue. I rummaged around in my bag. Why didn't I carry a clean tissue? Oh, that's right, I did. But I'd used it to wipe my mouth after seeing Eric and her and throwing up.

Realistically, though, there was nothing I could do. This was the disaster that was my face right now. I couldn't try to hide it. Unless I suddenly developed the ability to stop time whilst a glam squad miraculously stepped in and fixed my make-up, not even a truckload of Kleenex could save me.

'Hi,' I replied, bowing my head in an attempt to avoid eye contact. This was awkward. Not only did I look a mess, but I also didn't know his name. In fact, how did he even know mine? 'I—I'm fine.'

'No offence,' he said, locking the coffee shop door whilst facing me, 'but you don't *look* okay. I mean, you look great, but also a bit upset?'

'I'll survive,' I said, trying to wipe as much carnage off my face with the back of my hand as I could.

'Is that a Gloria Gaynor man trouble *I'll survive*?' He pulled down the shutters, then frowned as if he realised he might have overstepped the barista-customer boundaries. 'Sorry, I didn't mean to pry.'

'No, no, it's fine. It is indeed man trouble. How did you guess?'

'Just a hunch.' He reached into his pocket. 'Here,' he said, taking out a handkerchief. A hanky? *Very old-school.*

'Thanks,' I said, trying to clean the rest of my face and wiping off what remained of my foundation in the process.

'But seriously, are you okay? You look like you could

do with a drink and a pair of sympathetic ears. Shall we go to the pub across the road?' he asked. 'Come on. I hate to see you upset. You're normally always smiling. Let me try and cheer you up.'

'Thanks, er…sorry, this is terrible, but I don't know your name.' I winced.

'It's Josh,' he said, seemingly unoffended.

'Josh. Right. Great. Um, I'm not sure, Josh. Right now, I just want to go home and be alone,' I said.

'That's probably the *worst* thing you can do. Well, *that* and playing break-up songs.' *Busted.* How did he know that was what I planned to do? 'Plus it's my first Saturday night off in ages and I'm gasping for a Jack Daniels but don't fancy drinking alone, so you'd be doing me a favour,' he said.

Josh looked at me with his twinkly brown eyes and I wanted to melt. How could I say no to that face?

'Well…' I paused, considering his suggestion. 'If it means I'll be doing you a favour, I suppose I *could* help you out. I like to do my bit for charity when I can,' I said, managing to muster up a smile.

'Wow, a real-life philanthropist!' he said. 'Well, I am very happy that you've chosen me as your charity case of the week. And to demonstrate my gratitude, if you're lucky, I might even throw in a latte on the house the next time you come to Cuppa.'

'Okay. *Sold*,' I replied, the cloud of sadness slowly starting to lift from my shoulders.

Although it was going to take a while to get over the shock of seeing Eric with Nicole again and block out yet another gut-wrenching vision of them all over each other from my memory, Josh was probably right. Being at home alone, where no doubt I'd just curl up in bed sobbing whilst replaying what I'd seen over and over again, wouldn't be good for my sanity. Whereas going for a drink with the hot coffee shop guy who, as well as having good looks, also seemed to be caring and funny seemed like a much more positive option. Far healthier for my soul. Provided I didn't get all nervous and mess things up, of course…

No, no. I would be fine.

Yes. The evening had started off badly. But now as I walked through the doors the bustling pub, I had a feeling that tonight was about to improve significantly.

CHAPTER SIXTEEN

'What would you like?' said Josh as we approached the bar.

'Sex on the Beach, please.'

Josh's eyes popped out of his head.

'Whoa, *steady*. That's a bit forward! We've only just met!'

'The cocktail…' I blushed.

'Don't worry, Emily, I was only joking.' He grinned. 'Just trying to make you laugh.' That was sweet of him. Good that he had a sense of humour. 'Even though I'm not really a cocktail guy, I've heard of that one. Although, I'm not even sure if they do cocktails in this pub, so if they don't, is there anything else you fancy?'

'Um, a Southern Comfort and lemonade please.'

'Single or double?' He turned to face me. 'Actually, forget I asked. You've had a tough night. Double it is.'

'Good call. And at least if you have to carry me home, it's only across the road,' I joked.

'Am I in the company of a lightweight?' asked Josh.

'Yeah, I am a bit, so don't get me drunk, okay? Remember, I know where you work.' I grinned.

'Yes, you do. I better make sure I'm on my best behaviour.' he smiled.

'Not *too* well behaved, I hope.' I winked.

Goodness. What had come over me? Just over an hour ago I had been crying over Eric, feeling like the world had come to an end, and now here I was flirting and laughing with the hot coffee shop guy (now that I knew his name, I really should start using it). Normally I'd be all tongue-tied with a man I'd just met. Especially someone like him. Not sure how I was managing to stay calm, but I hoped I could keep it up.

Whilst Josh queued to order the drinks, I hotfooted it to the toilets to try and clean my face up a bit and wash my mouth out. Although I was feeling a bit better, the idea of having a drink with him was still pretty nerve-wracking, and there was no way I was going to make things harder for myself by sitting in front of him worrying about having vomit breath and mascara streaks running down my cheeks.

I shoved a handful of mints in my mouth and chewed them as quickly as I could. As I came out of the ladies', Josh was just being served. We picked up our drinks, then found a table tucked away in the corner. Lucky that couple were leaving as we came in, as being a Saturday night, understandably it was busy and we wouldn't have had anywhere to sit otherwise.

I liked it here. It was a typical British pub. Dark wooden interior, burgundy walls and patterned carpet. I hadn't been here for ages, but I remembered it being a nice, relaxed place to come for a few drinks.

'Here's to *surviving*,' said Josh, raising his glass to mine. 'Cheers!'

'Cheers,' I reciprocated. 'And thank you.'

'I haven't done anything yet,' said Josh.

'Oh, but you *have*. I was feeling rubbish before, and already I'm feeling so much better.'

'Blimey. You really *are* a lightweight. One sip of Southern Comfort and you're already getting merry!'

'Funny! You'll know when I'm drunk.'

'C'mon, then. What kind of drunk are you? Rowdy? Depressed? Gushy? *Saucy?*' He smirked.

'Hmmm.' I placed my finger on my chin. 'I'd say happy and gushy.'

'Good. Because on what I earn from Cuppa, I won't be able to bail you out if you trash this pub and get arrested.'

'Okay. I'll do my best to behave.'

'You won't be too well behaved, I hope,' he said, repeating what I'd said earlier with a wink. Quick-witted, cheeky, funny and hot. *Hmm*...I was keen to find out more about him.

'So,' I said, 'Cuppa—what led you to work there?'

His smile faded.

'Oh, no, no, no,' he said quickly. 'Tonight isn't about me. It's about you talking, me listening, then sharing my thoughts.'

'Right,' I said, taking the hint that he didn't want to speak about himself.

'So tell me, what happened?' He paused. 'That is, if you want to, of course. No pressure as I know you don't know me from Adam. I mean you know me from Cuppa, but—anyway, joking aside, you seemed really upset and sometimes it helps to talk to someone you don't know. To get a more objective opinion. I've been told I'm a good listener, and I'm also good at keeping secrets, so whatever you say will stay between us.'

He was right. I didn't know him. I'd only learnt his name literally half an hour ago. Yet somehow I felt like I *could* talk to him, that he *would* be a good listener and be discreet.

'Well...' I paused, reflecting again about whether it was a good idea to tell a complete stranger about my love life. After all, when Chloe and Kat had first suggested I speak to him, I'd told them it would be too messy. That things would become awkward. And that was when they'd just suggested I start by finding out his name. How comfortable was I really going to feel ordering a latte from a guy who knew how badly I had been humiliated? Revealing that I was so undesirable my ex had dumped me for another woman was hardly the best way to endear myself to a hot guy.

But, I reasoned, I was getting carried away. Potential awkwardness would only arise if we dated and then broke up. To date, he'd have to like me, and look at him: beautiful glowing skin, dark beard, eyes that you could get lost in for days, hair I'd love to run my fingers through, and from the way his black T-shirt clung to his muscular chest and arms, a body that looked toned to perfection. He could have any woman he wanted, so what made me think he'd choose me?

I know, I know. I'm supposed to believe in myself, be confident, say *he'd* be lucky to have *me*, think about my *inner beauty shining through* and channel all of that *strong woman* stuff, but I didn't feel strong. Not right now, anyway. I *was* getting there. On the way to the restaurant, I was feeling confident. Happy. I was getting my mojo back. But at the moment, it was like I'd been knocked straight back to square one.

And let's get real. Most mornings that I dragged myself to the coffee shop, I was wearing leggings, a baggy jumper and zero make-up. Hardly sexy. Add to that how terrible I must have looked right now and you'd understand why I would not be feeling remotely desirable.

So I came to the conclusion that there was no danger of any post-hook-up or post-dating awkwardness. He was just a kind guy that saw me looking upset, was at a loose end and thought hearing about my problems would be more entertaining than watching TV and that having a drink with me would help pass the time. Nothing more, nothing less.

And with that in mind, I decided to take a chance. To trust him. Tell him what happened. Warts and all.

'Okay,' I said, taking a deep breath for courage. 'So in a nutshell, I was on my way to a restaurant to attend a sort of organised dining group thing my friend had booked for me and just as I was about to go in, I saw my ex all over the woman he cheated on me with, and I got upset. Oh, and as well as cheating with her for the last six months of our relationship, he also recently proposed to the same woman and splashed it across social media, which is how I found out.'

'Shit,' said Josh, putting his head in his hands. 'That sucks. If you don't mind me asking and it's not too painful to talk about, how did you find out he was cheating?'

'I had to go to Manchester to meet a client I've known for years and wasn't due back until late as they'd originally wanted to take me to dinner and I'd planned to get the train back to London afterwards. But then the client had a family emergency, so I came home earlier that evening and walked in to see him and her going at it like rabbits.'

'That is the *worst*.' Josh winced. 'I can't imagine how *awful* that must have been for you.'

'It was,' I said, reliving the pain. 'Even talking about it now is difficult.'

'Sorry,' said Josh. 'I shouldn't have asked.'

'No, no. It has to be done. I have to get it out of my system. If I'm honest, I knew that something wasn't right. You know, when you look back with the benefit of hindsight, you see the signs. The messages saying he had to work late again. Coming home smelling of shower gel, even though he'd supposedly been slaving away at the office for twelve hours. Just little things. But at the time, you dismiss them. And whenever I quizzed him, somehow he'd have an answer for everything and make me sound like a paranoid, jealous idiot.'

'Bastard,' said Josh.

'Yep. And do you know what? Even when he got caught red-handed, I don't remember him even saying he was sorry.'

'You're joking,' said Josh.

'Nope. His exact words were: "Emily! Shit. I thought you weren't back until after eleven."'

'No way.'

'I kid you not. Then he said, "I know this is awkward, but, Em, I think we need to talk." No shit, Sherlock!'

'What? So did you stay and talk?' asked Josh.

'No. I'd seen more than I needed to. I picked up my bag and went straight round to my friend Chloe's house.'

'I don't blame you.'

'He tried calling me, but I didn't answer. I couldn't. I felt like my heart had been ripped out and fed though an industrial-strength shredder. I didn't eat properly for days. If you're looking for a quick way to lose weight, walking in on your boyfriend screwing someone else will definitely do the trick.'

I didn't add the fact that you end up putting it all back on again and then some after comfort eating to get over the breakup.

'Christ,' said Josh.

I took a large gulp of my drink. God. Talking about this was tough. Maybe I should have ordered a triple rather than a double.

'So anyway, after Chloe force-fed me for a week, I finally had the courage to go back home. She'd already gone round there the day before to check that he'd left and cleared out his stuff. She got the locks changed and straightened up the place for me. She even ordered a new mattress, bless her.'

'That's what you call a great friend,' said Josh.

'The best,' I said.

'And so have you spoken to him since?'

'We had to exchange a few texts to sort out home stuff —you know, get his name taken off bills, admin, that kind of thing. But other than that, no. I loved him, I trusted him, and rather than coming to me and telling me that he wasn't happy, he was unfaithful. Not just a drunken one-night stand, which I'm not saying is any better, but a full-blown affair. For something to go on for that length of time, it involves, plotting, planning, prolonged and very conscious deceit.' My blood ran cold as I thought about the betrayal. 'It was just so hurtful. So painful.'

'Infidelity is the worst.' He shuffled in his seat a little. 'My dad had an affair when I was thirteen and left us for the other woman. It almost destroyed my mum. Seeing someone who was always so strong and happy suddenly crumble and hearing her crying herself to sleep every night was heart-breaking. She tried to hold it together for me, but she was a shell of what she was like before. She didn't want to see her friends, and like you said, she stopped eating, she lost weight. The sparkle in her eyes just disappeared overnight. It was awful. And I couldn't do anything to help her.'

'That must have been hard on you too,' I said. It couldn't have been easy for him to relive those memories or to share them with me, someone he barely knew, either.

'It was. At that age, you're also insecure, so you start thinking, was it me? Was it something I did? Maybe if I got better grades at school, they would have been happier. Maybe if I kept my room tidy or didn't answer back when they asked me to do my chores. All sorts of crazy things went through my mind. I just wanted to make everything better for my mum, but I couldn't. I haven't wanted to have anything to do with my dad since. Infidelity ruins lives. To me, it's that bad. I could never stay with a woman who cheated. And I would never cheat on my girlfriend. No way.'

'Forgive me for asking, Josh, and for stereotyping a little—well, in fact, a lot—but are you saying that you've *never* cheated?'

'Never,' said Josh.

Likely story. I found that hard to believe.

'Really?' I questioned.

'Absolutely. Why don't you believe me?' Josh frowned.

'It's just that—' I paused, thinking about how to word things delicately. 'How can I say this? Women cheat, of course they do, but infidelity is more common amongst men, no? And someone like you, I mean, it must be more of a challenge surely?'

'I don't follow.' Josh frowned again. '*Someone like me?*'

'Well…' I sighed, realising there was no way around saying that he was hot. 'A guy like you must get a *lot* of attention, so it must be harder not to stray.'

'I don't think I get any more attention than the next guy,' he said modestly, 'but even if I did, it wouldn't matter. If I've made a commitment to someone I love, then that's it. I don't care if Scarlett Johansson, Rihanna or Salma Hayek knocked on my door, I'm staying faithful to my lady.'

'If that's true,' I said, convinced that it absolutely *wasn't*—I mean, who would turn down Rihanna?—'then that's really lovely.'

'Lesson number one that I'd like you to take home with you tonight, Emily, is that all guys are *not* the same. We're not all cheats and liars. When you've seen first-hand what infidelity can do, you couldn't even consider putting someone you love through that kind of pain.'

'Deep down I want to believe that. But when you've been hurt, it's really hard to. I know Eric is just one man. Not even a man. *A boy*. A total and utter dickhead. And I've definitely realised that he can't have loved me.'

'I'm sorry to have to agree, but that's probably true. In which case, although it may not seem like it now and I'm sure your girlfriends have told you this a million times, you really are better off without him. Of course I don't condone his methods, but ultimately his actions set you free to find someone who *will* love and value you. Hang on in there, Emily.'

'Thanks.' I smiled. 'You were right.'

'About which part?' he said.

'When you said that you're a good listener.'

'Thanks. And that's why they pay me the big bucks!' He chuckled. 'Not at Cuppa, obviously. We've established that. I mean my patients. I did mention that I was charging you for this shrink session, didn't I?'

'No, you didn't, Dr Josh.'

'Oh, my bad. Still, as you're a Cuppa regular, I'll give you my special discount, so that's a snip at just ninety-nine quid for you.'

'Pff,' I scoffed. 'You'd be lucky! I'm not even sure I have ninety-nine pounds in my bank account. How about I buy you another Jack Daniels and Coke instead?'

'Deal.'

As I headed to the bar, I couldn't stop smiling. This guy was different. Special. Somehow I could *feel* it.

I liked Josh. A *lot*. The million-pound question now was whether there was the slightest, teeniest, smallest, remotest chance that he could possibly consider liking me too…

CHAPTER SEVENTEEN

I lay in bed grinning like a Cheshire cat. Last night was *amazing*. Josh was *amazing*.

No, no. We didn't sleep together or anything like that. *A girl can dream*. I just had a lovely night with him.

Awww.

I closed my eyes and started smiling again as I pressed rewind in my brain and started thinking about us sitting in the pub together. He was *such* a cool guy. I'd poured my heart out. Told him about one of the most humiliating and heart-breaking periods of my life, and he didn't judge or make me feel like a loser. He just listened and gave me his words of wisdom.

And man was he wise. Somehow he knew exactly what to say. Josh had such a positive aura about him. He didn't tell you what you wanted to hear just for the sake of it. He was direct, yet still so *glass half-full*. He understood the crappiness of the situation but focused on how to learn from it. How the pain could make me a stronger person. He really made me feel *so* much better.

Normally I was nervous around new guys, but I felt like I'd known Josh for ages. I had never spoken to a man before who'd put me so at ease. Someone who was so good with words. Not BS, charmer-type spiel, but a person who was genuinely an excellent communicator. Maybe he was a therapist after all.

In fact, who was this guy? There was definitely more to him than met the eye. There had to be.

Whilst I'd appreciated him letting me offload about my problems and the sorry state of my love life, I wanted to hear more about *him*. I had a feeling he wasn't working at Cuppa by choice, more as a means to an end. I was curious to know his story.

I had tried on a few occasions to find out how he had come to work there and what his background was, but each time, Josh turned the subject back on to me. I got the feeling he wasn't keen to talk about it, so I didn't pressure him, especially as he'd been so kind.

Towards the end of the night, though, my curiosity levels were sky-high, and given that I'd had several Southern Comforts by then (yes, all doubles) my inhibitions had flown well and truly out the window. So I'd asked him again why he was being mysterious and wasn't talking about himself. He'd shifted in his seat and said that it was because tonight was about me and that next time he'd tell me more about him.

'Next time?' I'd asked, trying to suppress my excitement.

'Yes,' he'd said before his face fell a little. 'Unless of course you'd rather there not be a next time.'

In my mind I was screaming: *Are you joking? Do you know how hard it is to find an intelligent guy who's easy to talk to, funny, a great listener, kind and drop-dead gorgeous? Of course I'd bloody want there to be a next time. Is tomorrow too soon?*

But instead, to avoid sounding too keen, I'd simply said, 'A next time would be great. I've enjoyed myself tonight, thank you.' Delivered like a pro. Impressive. Particularly considering how much I'd had to drink.

We'd stayed until last orders, then he'd helped me to my door. *Helped* is the operative word as I was a little—actually *very*—unsteady on my feet. If I remember correctly, we'd walked at a snail's pace and I'd almost toppled over a few times as I was still in the heels I'd put on to go to the restaurant, which, combined with the alcohol and me being a lightweight, was not ideal for staying upright.

Things were a bit awkward when we got to the front door of my building. It was that point where you've met someone new, you're saying goodbye but you don't know whether to hug them or do that kiss on the cheek thing. Given the choice, I would have gladly bypassed both options and made a beeline for his gorgeous lips. Thank God I was alert enough *not* to do that. It would have been so embarrassing.

Was that a missed opportunity? If he'd blanked me, I could have just blamed it on the alcohol. Actually, no. That would have been a terrible idea. If I was him, I wouldn't have wanted to play tonsil hockey with a girl who'd thrown up a few hours earlier. Anyway, in the end we didn't kiss or hug.

'Thanks again for the favour and keeping me company tonight,' he'd said. 'See you at Cuppa soon?'

'Of course!' I'd said. 'You know I need my caffeine fix. When are you in next?'

'Monday morning,' he'd replied.

'Cool. Well, I'll see you then for my free latte.'

'Sure. A promise is a promise, so your complimentary latte will be there waiting for you along with your blueberry muffin.'

'Gosh, I'm so predictable!' I'd joked.

'No, It's just my job to remember the orders of special customers.'

'*Special*, eh?' I'd said excitedly.

'Er, yeah, you know,' he'd stuttered. '*Regulars*.' He'd blushed. 'Well, I better get going. Thanks again, and see you Monday.'

'Yeah, see you on Monday, Josh, and thank *you* for being such a great listener.'

He'd smiled (oh, and he had a *beautiful* smile—straight teeth and nice full lips) and then headed off.

I hadn't been able to sleep all night. Not just because I had to get up a million times to go to the toilet as I'd been guzzling gallons of water to prevent myself from having a hangover this morning, (which thankfully seemed to have done the trick), but mainly as I kept thinking about his gorgeous face and how he'd cheered me up and made me laugh. He was *so* lovely.

Whilst part of me was really glad to have something to smile about, particularly as it had helped me to block out the whole Eric and Nicole sighting, I was also worried that if I kept obsessing over Josh, when I saw him at Cuppa, I would start behaving strangely, stuttering or playing with my hair.

I really wasn't good at acting cool. If I tried to lean

casually at the end of a bar to look all demure and sexy, I was the kind of woman whose elbow would slip, then I'd fall flat on my face. I just couldn't do it.

Yes. I must act normal. Which meant as much as I liked him, I had to resist the temptation to start dressing up in the morning just to show him that I didn't always look like I'd dragged myself out of bed or had an ugly crying meltdown after bumping into my ex. If I suddenly started wearing make-up and decent clothes, he'd *definitely* know I liked him.

I needed to calm down and block him out of my mind too. Not least because Henry would be coming round in less than two hours. Which actually might not be a bad thing. Maybe some sex would take my mind off both Eric and Josh.

Yes, Henry. I was surprised to receive a message from him on Monday night. Like I'd said to Kat and later to Chloe during our morning debrief that day, as I had slept with him so quickly, I wasn't sure if I would ever hear from him again.

He'd asked me how I was and if I fancied meeting up on Wednesday night. I had my life drawing class, so I'd told him I couldn't. I'd offered Thursday or Friday as an option, but he had plans. Then he'd suggested Saturday night, which was a no-go as I was supposed to be going on the dining meet-up, so that didn't work either (who'd have thought that my diary would be this busy?), but we'd settled on this afternoon instead.

I'd asked where he wanted to go and he'd said it would be nice to just 'chill' at mine, which was clearly man speak for *come to yours and have sex.*

Whilst I admit that I wanted it too, now that I was

making an effort to get out more, I didn't want to fall into the habit of him just coming here all the time, having a shag and then going home. I wanted to get out and *do* things. Go to gigs, art galleries, markets, museums—that kind of thing. Mind you, who was I kidding? Like Henry had said himself, he was into *men's stuff*, so he'd probably rather spend his weekend drinking and watching football, not visiting the Tate. Definitely *not* husband material as I'd established on our last date. I just had to adjust my mindset and say that this *is what it is*. A person to have fun in the bedroom with. Get some satisfaction under the sheets. Nothing more, nothing less.

On the subject of satisfaction, if I was going to get any of that this afternoon, I really had to tackle this *going down* thing. Get to the root of his reservations. If he was reluctant again, I'd follow Kat's advice about asking him what his concerns were and also suggest the sixty-nine.

I looked at my watch again. He was late. We'd said 1 p.m. It was now 1.35 and he hadn't even texted to say he'd been delayed.

See? Because he was coming here, he didn't think he needed to be punctual, which is another reason why I'd prefer to meet outside of my flat. This was only our second date (well, he would say *third*) and already bad habits were forming. *So annoying.* If we were going out somewhere, I bet he wouldn't be late. He'd take our meeting time more seriously.

I plumped up the pillows for what felt like the hundredth time. A month ago I probably would have just gone online until he arrived. But I'd hardly logged onto social media the last week or so. Turning off my notifications and leaving my phone in another room helped, as did finding other things to do with my hands after work, like painting my nails (after making them look pretty, there's no way I wanted to smudge them by scrolling or typing). Plus, I'd been too busy going out or doing extra sketches inspired by my life drawing classes in the evenings. I suppose I could have taken photos on that rooftop when I was with Henry and posted a photo of the London skyline, or taken a snap of our drinks when I was in the pub with Josh, but I hadn't thought about it at the time as I was so engaged in our conversation. *Oh well.*

I straightened the perfume bottles on my dressing table. *Again.* Ten minutes late was acceptable, but forty minutes without so much as a courtesy message? That was plain rude.

Are you on your way? I texted. Just as I clicked send, the buzzer rang.

'Sorry. Got held up,' he said, strolling through the door. 'Mmmm. You look sexy.' he pulled me into him and gave me a sloppy kiss. I turned away. 'Ah, come on, babe. I said I'm sorry. Let me make it up to you—'

He started to kiss my neck. Dammit. I was a sucker for that. As I was horny, I guessed I could forgive his lateness. Just this once…

Before I knew it, we were rolling around on the bed naked, clothes in a heap on the floor.

As I lay on my back, he climbed on top and edged himself up towards my face.

'Suck it, babe,' he said, rubbing himself.

'Let's do it together,' I suggested.

'What?' He frowned.

'Sorry, that came out wrong. Obviously we can't *both*

suck it. I mean, I do you and you do me. You know, sixty-nine,' I said.

'*Ah, babe*,' he said, stroking my breasts and moving even closer to my mouth. 'You go first and then I'll do you later,' he said as his tip touched my chin.

Oh, no, you don't. I felt frustration rising within me.

'*Later* is what you said last time, Henry, and you didn't,' I said, moving my head away slowly. 'So this time *you* can go first and then I can do you *later*.' I pushed him over on to his back and then straddled him, moving myself upwards, just as he'd done to me. It felt good to show some confidence.

'No, *please*!' he said as if I was holding a massive knife and threatening to chop off his manhood. 'Stop!'

'Why?' I frowned. 'What's wrong?'

'I don't do *that*.' He winced, bolting upright.

'Why?' I asked trying to sound sympathetic, but also feeling rejected and self-conscious. 'I'm clean. I literally just had a shower.'

'I'm sure you are. It's just I'm a *man*, babe. A *proper* man. And real men don't do *that*. It's kind of, you know —*gross*!' He grimaced.

'What?' I said, placing my hands on my hips as every ounce of sympathy evaporated. 'You did *not* just say that. Let me get this straight. You're a *real* man, so you won't go down on a woman?'

'That's right,' he said proudly.

'But you have no problem with *me* going down on *you*?' I frowned again, trying and failing to understand what I was hearing.

'Well, no. Of course not. I *love* it. It makes me feel

great! That's what good women do—to please a man,' he said matter-of-factly.

'Unbelievable!' I shouted, my blood now boiling like a kettle. 'What *good* women do? *Jesus*. Here I was thinking that dinosaurs were extinct! And what about a *man* pleasing the *woman*?'

'What about it?' he scoffed. 'I suck your breasts, you suck my dick, what's the problem?'

He cannot be serious.

'You sucking my breasts is *not* the same, Henry! If it is, then how about I suck *your* nipples instead? That's fair enough, isn't it?' I scowled. 'And what if I say it *is* a problem for me and I'd like it if you considered kissing me down there?'

'No way!' He winced, covering his mouth as if the mere thought of it made him want to throw up. 'Sticking my tongue where blood and babies come out? Eurgh! *No, thanks.*'

'You know what, Henry?' I said, jumping off the bed, picking up my dress and dragging it on over my head. 'I think you'd better leave.'

'Ah, come on, babe!' He climbed off the bed and rested his hand on my shoulder. 'Don't be such a drama queen! Is this all because I was a little bit late? I already said I was sorry. Twice!'

'Are you joking?' I brushed his hand from my shoulder. 'It's not about you being late, although that *was* annoying and rude.'

'Oh, I see. Is the time of the month on its way or something? Is it your hormones that are making you all moany? Don't worry, babe. You'll feel better once you've had this inside you.' He smirked, rubbing himself.

'Sod off, Henry!' I shouted, grabbing his clothes and throwing them at him. 'Put your little lump of chauvinist meat away and get the hell out of my flat!'

'Oh, don't be like that, babe. I didn't have you down as one of those mouthy birds who are always making demands. That's why I chose you at speed dating. You seemed sweet and willing to please,' he said, moving forward to touch me again and then wisely deciding against it. 'Okay, okay, I'm going.' he snarled, picking up his clothes. 'Actually, babe, if you don't want to suck or fuck me, can you at least wank me off? *Please?* Look at this,' he said, pointing in between his legs. 'It's kind of evil to send me home with a raging hard-on, don't you think?'

Speechless.

I scowled and folded my arms. No words necessary.

He hurriedly pulled on his boxers and his jeans, grabbed his shirt and left.

Selfish bastard. Goodbye and good riddance. I might have been horny, but I had my dignity. I'd rather be sexually frustrated than sleep with a Neanderthal who had no consideration for women and their needs. Henry could go and crawl back under whatever prehistoric rock he came from.

I bet he didn't even remember my name. He never even used it once. It was always *babe this* and *babe that*. I've always thought that was something men did when they were seeing loads of women and didn't want to get their names mixed up. After tonight, I wouldn't put it past him.

Like Henry had said when we went out on that date— neither of us were getting any younger, which meant I didn't have time to waste on someone like him.

What I *really* needed was a man who respected women. Was sensitive to my needs. A man who would treat me like an equal as I should be. Someone who was smart, funny and intelligent. Someone decent.

Someone like *Josh*.

CHAPTER EIGHTEEN

'He's *totally* into you Em,' gushed Chloe as we sat in our favourite spot at Cuppa.

'Shh! Stop it. Seriously! You promised you'd behave yourself today.'

'I *am*!' she said, placing her hands on her hips. 'If I wasn't, you'd know about it, trust me! Goodbye, Eric, *hello*, delicious Josh. Just saying!'

Classic Chloe. Honestly. She was a law unto herself.

After Henry left yesterday, I was furious and just had to vent, so I gave her a call and spent the best part of half an hour growling down the phone as she cleaned the kitchen, then started washing up the dishes (yes, Chloe's aversion to technology also extends to dishwashers, which meant she did everything by hand).

I would have spent at least two more hours seething about Eric and Nicole had Chloe not threatened to put the phone down after the first few minutes of the story.

She told me that discussing it would just be giving Eric oxygen and that whilst she didn't normally wish ill on human beings, after what he'd done to me, she'd rather see him suffocate, so that conversation was brought to an end almost instantly. But, once I'd mentioned my evening with Josh, she'd promptly downed the dishes and shouted: "For Pete's sake, Emily! We *seriously* need to work on your storytelling skills. Why have we just wasted forty minutes talking about that sexist pig Henry and Eric the giant fopdoodle when we should have been speaking about the dishy coffee shop guy? Crumbs! Where are your priorities?"

She'd then swiftly made herself a cup of tea, cut a large slice of the lemon cake she'd just taken out of the oven, then sat down ready to be 'entertained', as she put it.

I'd filled her in on our evening together, how nice Josh was, how much I liked him, but didn't think he could like me as I looked like a train wreck. But Chloe was convinced otherwise and revelled in spouting her *I told you so* speech.

It was definitely a smart move to speak yesterday on the phone as, knowing Josh would be working at Cuppa today whilst Chloe and I had our weekly catch-up, there was no way we could have openly discussed what happened.

Somehow we'd managed to fill another hour that evening talking about Josh. The last part of the chat mainly consisted of Chloe insisting that I should ask him out.

'Me? Ask Josh out?' I'd protested, almost choking on the glass of vodka, orange and cranberry I'd poured myself in a half-hearted attempt to make a Sex on the Beach despite not having all the ingredients. 'You've *got* to be joking. I don't even know if he likes me, and you're suggesting that I voluntarily put myself up for rejection?'

'Don't be ridiculous!' she'd scoffed. 'He already asked you out when he spoke about *next time*, so all you'd be doing is just confirming dates. Simple.'

'That's your favourite bloody word. Of course it's *simple* when you're not the one having to do it,' I'd said.

Just thinking about it had made me break out into a cold sweat, so after she kept insisting, I told her I didn't want to listen to her bullying anymore and that I'd see her at Cuppa today. And so here we were.

'For the love of God and all that is good and holy,' said Chloe. If she drooled anymore I might need to give her a cloth to mop the table. 'Check out his bottom,' she added as we both watched him reaching for something on the top shelf. He was wearing black jeans and a fitted black T-shirt. 'And those muscular arms…'

'I know,' I said, shamelessly joining her swooning session. 'I may have been tipsy on Saturday night, but believe me, I checked out that behind many, many times when he got up to get the drinks. *Mmmm*…anyway!' I said, catching myself and my behaviour. 'What are we like? We're acting as though we're in one of those Diet Coke Break adverts from the nineties, going all doe-eyed over the sexy window cleaner. Have we not evolved since then? There's more to Josh than just a hot body. We shouldn't be objectifying him like that.'

'Oh, do be quiet and get off your politically correct high horse! You're enjoying the view just as much as I am. We're not harassing him, just showing appreciation in our own private way. Crumbs! He's coming over. Act normal, Em!'

Yes, *act normal*. Cue me playing with my hair, blushing, wriggling around nervously in my seat as he got closer, followed by grinning like a lunatic. Yeah, *smooth,* Emily. Real smooth. Told you I was rubbish at playing it cool.

'Here you go, ladies. Two lattes and two blueberry muffins. Both on the house as promised.'

'Ah you're such a sweetie,' Chloe jumped in before I had a chance to open my mouth. 'I'm Chloe,' she said, reaching out her hand, 'pleasure to meet you.'

'Nice to meet you too, Chloe,' said Josh, shaking her hand formally. 'I've heard a lot about you.'

'All good I hope?' she replied, smiling so much her cheeks looked like they were about to shatter.

'Yes, absolutely!' he said.

'Good! And I've been hearing a *lot* of amazing things about you too, Josh…'

'Is that so?' He smirked as he turned to look at me.

I kicked Chloe under the table.

'Yeah,' I jumped in. 'I was telling her how kind you were, listening to me drone on for hours about my problems.'

'Well, you were doing *me* a favour, remember? Helping me out so I wouldn't have to drink alone.'

'With a body like that, I couldn't imagine *you* ever having to spend a night alone, sweetheart,' said Chloe, fluttering her eyelashes.

'Chloe!' I shouted.

'Oops, sorry!' she said. 'Did I just say that out loud? I thought I was just whispering it in my head.'

Ground, please swallow me up now. Cue awkward silence.

'Anyway,' said Josh, blushing, 'I better get back. Nice

to see you again, Emily. You look lovely today, by the way.'

'Well, I couldn't look any worse than I did on Saturday! Mascara running down my face and—ouch!' I yelped as Chloe kicked me under the table. 'I—er. Thank you,' I said, correcting myself and remembering that rather than reminding him how shit I looked, I should have just graciously accepted the compliment and shut up. I couldn't help it. I was nervous.

He smiled at me again and then headed back behind the counter.

'*See!*' said Chloe. 'How can you *not* see that he likes you? Are you blind?'

'He was just being nice.'

'What's wrong with you? We need to book you an appointment at the optician, as clearly your eyesight has gone down the toilet. And by the way, if someone pays you a compliment—'

'Yes, yes,' I jumped in. 'I realised that I was supposed to be selling myself and not talking him out of it. You didn't have to kick me so hard, though!'

'What, like when *you* kicked *me* under the table?'

'Well, that was well-deserved. You were practically about to tell Josh that I have a giant crush on him. I had to shut you up somehow.'

'Violence doesn't solve anything. Did you not learn that at school?'

'And what was with that *I can't imagine you spending a night alone with a body like that* comment? You're such a bloody perv! And you're married too. Poor Brian.'

'Brian knows he's my one and only. And Josh knows I was jesting. You're the only one he wants.' She winked.

'Oh be quiet! Anyway, like I said, he was just being polite.'

Then again, I thought about it more closely. I wasn't great at picking up on signals, least of all from guys, but he did seem to look at me like he was interested. And he'd said I looked lovely...

Despite insisting I was going to dress and act normal, unsurprisingly, I had found myself waking up forty minutes earlier than usual just to get ready, which was a *big* deal—especially on a Monday morning. I'd showered, tried to find a decent outfit, put on some make-up and did my hair. I hadn't gone too overboard. Just opted for a casual knee-length floral dress and some tinted mois-turiser, mascara and gloss and teased out my curls, (which I was getting much better at managing thanks to the game-changing products Rochelle had recommended). I thought I'd pulled off the *not trying too hard* look, but it had taken me ages. Ironically, it was the kind of effortless look that required *lots* of effort.

I'd been practising the 'I am beautiful' mantra Paige had suggested in the mirror too. As odd as it seemed, maybe it was helping. I felt good. I was looking better too. More confident and together. I was beyond excited to see Josh again, and of course, wanted him to find me attractive too, so him saying he thought I looked lovely was defi-nitely a bonus. Mission accomplished, it would seem. I'd need to find a balance, though, with this *making more of an effort* thing. Couldn't go overboard. It was still impor-tant to be myself, and I wasn't sure I could keep this up every day. I needed my sleep...

'But, seriously,' I said, bringing myself back into the room, 'do you think he does like me?'

'Yes! I wouldn't say it otherwise. I know you think I'm pushy, but I love you, Em, and I wouldn't encourage you to do something that I thought would hurt you. It's obvious he's into you. I don't know how you can't see it. Apart from the fact that he's looked over here a million times for no other reason than to check you out and got all nervous around you is a big clue. Oh, that and also telling you you're "hot", as you would say.' Sounded so weird hearing Chloe use that word. Bit like your granny using slang and saying *wicked* or *bad* to describe something that was good.

'He didn't say *hot*. He just said *lovely*.'

'Same thing! And when you take into account him saying he'd like to meet up again, it's clearly a done deal. Trust me. I was right about my *get you out of the house* challenge, and I'm right about this too. The question is, are you going to wait around hoping for him to make a move or be brave, show him you like him and actually do something about it?'

'But, I—'

'No buts! I'm sorry, but you've got a nice, genuine, kind guy who also happens to be hotter than chilli sauce and is clearly into you and you're just going to let him slip through your fingers? *Look!*' she said, forcing my head around to look at Josh again. 'For Pete's sake, look at him! Imagine having that man's gorgeous lips roaming all over your body! Imagine grabbing onto his firm naked arse!'

First she'd used the word *hot* and now *arse*. *Jeez*. What had got into her?

'Chloe!'

'Come on, Em. I know I've been going on about his body and how dishy he is, but in all seriousness, it's more than that. I can tell. I can just *sense* it. He's the one for you. He seems like a good guy. Close your eyes and imagine having more nights like Saturday with Josh. Spending time with him. Spending your *life* with him. Imagine it. Just for a second. A millisecond, even. And tell me you will be happy to walk out that door without even trying to set up your next date.'

'Saturday wasn't a date.'

'*Poppycock.* Just *ask* him. Ask him for a drink. Just a few words is all it takes to alter your destiny, *forever.*'

'You sound like a horoscope page!'

'I don't give a monkey's what I sound like. I'm right. Guys like Josh don't come along every day, and loads of girls would *kill* to get his attention. Look!' She pointed at the tables directly opposite the counter. 'Do you think those women with their tongues hanging out are here for the coffee? *No!* They're here for *him.* Have you not noticed how much busier this place has become since he started and how there's been a massive increase in the female clientele? No coincidence, Emily. But, hey, it's up to you. If you want to let those other floozies swoop in and take the man that should be with *you*, then be my guest.'

Dammit. She'd touched a nerve. And I bet Chloe knew it too.

After Nicole had set her sights on Eric and taken him away from me (yes, I know he played his part), if Chloe *was* right and Josh *was* interested, I couldn't let another woman grab the opportunity to be with him. I had to go for it.

'Sod it!' I said, slamming my mug down on the table. I got up and walked towards the counter, where Josh was facing away from me as he unpacked milk bottles into the fridge. As I grew closer, something about the back of his head seemed familiar. I remembered I'd thought the same thing on Saturday night, but I still couldn't place it. Very strange.

He turned around. My heart started pounding. Shit.

'Oh, hi! Sorry, Emily, didn't see you there. Are you okay?'

'I'm fine, thanks. So,' I said quickly, worried that I was going to get too nervous to get the words out if I didn't do it straight away, 'I was wondering, about that *next time* you spoke about on Saturday? Shall we do it?' Poor choice of words. *Try again, Emily.* 'I mean, would you like to meet for a drink again sometime? I promise I won't go on about myself or how much I hate my ex like last time. And you won't need to practically carry me home like you did before. I'll be a model drinking buddy!'

Buddy? Why the hell did I use the word *buddy*? Just put myself firmly in the friend zone. I was *so* rubbish at this.

'Great!' Josh grinned. 'Yeah, I'd really like that.'

'Oh, great! Cool!' I said. *Calm down. Don't show too much excitement.* 'So when's good for you?' I said as casually as I could.

'Erm, well, I have a day off tomorrow if you want to meet up then,' he said. 'Unless it's too soon or you already have other plans?'

Other plans? Even if I had a private meeting with the Queen, I would gladly cancel for a date with you. If it is a date, of course...

'No, no! Tomorrow's perfect!' I said.

'Great! Well, should we exchange numbers, then, and we can message to arrange times and where to meet?'

'Sounds good!' I replied. 'Oh! Before I forget, let me

give this back to you.' I reached into my dress pocket and handed Josh his handkerchief. 'All freshly washed and pressed.'

'Oh, thanks! I wasn't expecting you to give it back. You didn't have to. Really kind.' He smiled. I still couldn't believe I'd ironed a hanky as I hate ironing with a passion, but I didn't want to give it to him all crumpled up, and it was the least I could do after he'd been so sweet to me.

'No, thank *you*!' I insisted.

'You're welcome! I'll come over to your table in a sec. Don't want the boss to think I'm taking advantage of my position by picking up customers on the job. I mean, not that I'm picking you up...' He winced, realising how what he'd said could be misinterpreted. 'I mean...I didn't mean...*anyway*. Yeah, I'll come over once I've taken my foot out of my mouth,' he chuckled.

'Cool,' I laughed. Was he nervous? Because of *me*? So cute if he was.

As I strode back to my table, I felt the eyes of the women who had been swooning at Josh all morning burning into me. *Too bad*, I thought. If there was one thing that this challenge had taught me so far, it was that if you wanted something, you had to go for it.

There was no doubt about it. I undeniably, unequivocally wanted Josh. And if he wanted me too, which I was finally starting to believe, then I was going to try and use every ounce of my growing confidence to make something happen.

CHAPTER NINETEEN

Tonight was the night. The night I was going out with Josh. On a date.

Yes.

After exchanging several messages over the past twenty-four hours, I was feeling more confident that this *was* actually a date. I mean, I knew I'd been out of the game for a while, but I was pretty sure guys didn't normally invite girls they considered just friends to Chez Pierre—the place that had been voted 'Most Romantic Restaurant' for three years in a row.

We were due to meet at 7 p.m., so I'd shut down my computer at five to give myself enough time to get ready and into town, then put on the 'Body Confident' playlist I'd created. A bit of Lizzo, Pink, Meghan Trainor and Sasha would help me feel good.

For once, I knew exactly what I was going to wear: a canary-yellow dress with a cute bow on one shoulder. When I'd originally bought it on my shopping trip with Chloe, I'd worried that it made my bum look big, but actually, now I quite liked the way it clung to my curves. It would be perfect for this evening.

I'd already showered and put on my make-up, so all I needed to do was my hair. On my evenings off, rather than just scrolling through social media, I'd been watching YouTube videos with different hair tips, which had been really useful. I'd washed it last night, applied some gel, then used a technique I'd seen of styling it into two plaits, which I'd kept in all day, so my hair would be extra wavy when it was unravelled. It worked a treat.

How was I feeling? Calm, actually. Excited, but surprisingly calm. Normally, I'd be bricking it. Over-whelmed with nerves. Don't get me wrong, I still had butterflies, but I wasn't worried about Josh not turning up or being late. Somehow I felt I could trust him. Like he wouldn't let me down. And strangely enough, I wasn't concerned about what we would talk about either. Rather than fretting, I just couldn't wait to see him.

I approached the restaurant and saw Josh standing outside. My heart began to flutter.

'Wow!' said Josh, his jaw dropping. 'You look incredible!'

He leant forward and gave me a kiss on each cheek. Gosh. He smelt so *good*. All woody and fresh like he'd just stepped out of the shower.

'Thank you,' I said, remembering this time to simply accept the compliment. 'So do you.'

The word *incredible* didn't even begin to describe how he looked. Talk about scrubbing up like a shiny penny. He was wearing a fitted white T-shirt under a black blazer, with smart black jeans and polished black boots. I'd noticed he wore black a lot. It suited him. Mind you, anything he wore probably would. His beard was perfectly shaped and his hair looked freshly trimmed. I wondered if he'd done it especially for tonight.

'Thanks,' he said, eyes still wide. Promising start. 'Shall we go in?'

'Yes, let's,' I replied.

The interior was very dark and rustic, with floor-to-ceiling thick wooden beams and dimmed lighting. It was an intimate space. There couldn't be more than a dozen tables here. They were all covered with bright white table-cloths, with candles and a single red rose in a vase in the centre. *Nice*. Right at the back in the corner there was a pianist, playing a love song that sounded familiar, but I couldn't remember the name of it.

As the waiter showed us to our table, Josh stepped ahead and pulled out the chair for me. What a gent. We both sat down.

'So,' I said. 'This is lovely. Do you come here often?' Oh gosh. I had to mess it up. You'd think I would have learnt from my faux pas at that disastrous first networking event. I must be more nervous than I thought. 'Sorry, that came out wrong. Sounded like I was trying to come on to you.'

'Why, Emily?' teased Josh. '*Are* you?'

'Now that would be telling…' I smiled, deliberately not giving too much away. Phew. I'd managed to rescue myself. Now I just needed to keep it going.

'Hmmm, I see. You're keeping your cards close to your chest. Not that I'm looking at your chest, of course. *Oh God.* Me and my mouth!' he said.

Ha ha. Nice to know I wasn't the only one who put their foot in it.

'Wow! We haven't even had a drink yet and already you're checking out my boobs?' They did look a little perkier in my new bra and this dress. Or maybe it was because I was starting to like them more. I crossed my arms and pretended to look angry. Josh cringed with embarrassment. 'Gotcha!' I laughed. 'Don't worry. I know the saying. I was only teasing!'

'You really did get me there. So cruel! Let's order some drinks quickly so that if I say something stupid again, I can blame it on the alcohol.'

'Good idea. Same goes for me too!'

'Great! What are you drinking?'

As we waited for the main courses to arrive, we talked about our day. Whilst mine was fairly uneventful, just drawing some boring illustrations for a magazine subscription advert, Josh's Tuesday seemed much more interesting.

He said he'd woken up at 6 a.m. to work on something and had locked himself away for twelve hours to focus on it before coming to meet me.

'Let me get this straight: on your day off, you voluntarily woke up at six a.m?'

'Yep,' he said.

'Are you mad?'

'No!' he chuckled.

'Hmm. I'm intrigued. There's not many things that would get me out of bed at six. Never mind on a day of rest. Must have been important,' I said, hoping that he'd reveal more.

'It definitely is,' he said. Nope. Clearly he didn't get the hint. Time to be more direct.

'So, what was it, then? DIY?'

'Nope,' he replied blankly. Still nothing. This was like getting blood from a stone.

'Gardening?' I suggested.

'Nope. Although I should have actually, as my garden is getting a bit overgrown,' he said.

'Okay,' I said, throwing my hands in the air. 'I give in. I've got nothing. What were you working on Josh?'

'Erm,' he said, shifting in his seat. He seemed to do that a lot. In fact, whenever I asked him questions about himself. Was he hiding something? 'Do you mind if I don't say? It's just—it's kind of a private thing. I don't really like talking about it. Not just yet anyway.' His eyes darted downwards.

'Oh, right. I see. Fair enough,' I said, my stomach sinking. I felt a little hurt that I'd poured my heart out on Saturday and revealed lots of personal things about myself to him, but he didn't feel he could trust me enough to do the same.

Whilst I'd try my best to respect his privacy, if he was genuinely interested in me and if whatever this was could have any hope of going further, I had to know more about him. So far, all I knew was that he worked in Cuppa, was thirty-seven years old and was a good listener. That was it. A conversation had to work both ways. As much as I liked Josh, he was going to have to open up and give me *something*.

'So…if you're not able to tell me about the secret project you work on at home, at least tell me a bit more about you. Like your work at Cuppa. You've only been there a few weeks now, so where were you working before? You seem like the kind of guy that was either working somewhere much bigger or has chosen to be there whilst you work on something bigger. You know, like how you hear about actors and actresses waiting tables whilst they go to auditions, as they have dreams of making it big in Hollywood?' I said.

His face turned cold. Was he angry? I wondered if what I'd said had come across badly. What if he'd always been a barista and enjoyed it? I didn't want to insult him by implying there was something wrong with working in a coffee shop. I wasn't like that. I respected anyone who got out there and earned a living, whether it was as a barista, bartender or an actor.

'Sorry,' I added quickly. 'I hope that I didn't offend you. I wasn't saying that it isn't a good job—'

'It's okay. I know what you meant,' he said. 'And, yes, you're right. It *is* something I'm doing whilst I work on something else. And, yes, you could say I was working in a "big" job before I came to Cuppa.'

'Oh, thank God for that! Not thank God you had a big job or—' *Take your foot out your mouth, Emily.* 'I mean, thank God I didn't offend you.'

'Don't worry. You didn't. I guess I'm not so great about talking about myself, but yeah.' He took a deep breath. 'I used to be a lawyer.'

'A lawyer?' That surprised me. It didn't seem very Josh.

'Yep. A fully fledged, suited and booted lawyer.'

'That's interesting. You don't strike me as the corporate type...' My voice trailed off as I thought about the assumptions that guy at speed dating had made about me. At least I wasn't judging Josh negatively purely based on his looks.

'I'm not. I *wasn't*. I went into law after—well, let's just say I went into it because I saw how people can be taken for a ride without the right guidance, so I had all these idealistic visions about helping people. But somewhere down the line, after I qualified and landed a job at a fancy firm in the city, I got caught up in the whole corporate world. Rather than helping people in need, which was always the plan, I got sucked into the trap of climbing the career ladder. Obsessed with rising to the next level. I was representing horrible, greedy people. I didn't realise it at the time, but I sacrificed myself and my integrity just to get the next promotion.'

'Oh,' I said, taking a gulp of my Sex on the Beach. 'That sounds horrible.'

'It was. But when you're on the hamster wheel, you're none the wiser. You bounce from one successful case to another. My bosses loved me because I was committed. If I take something on, I give it my all. I never want to fail. So I'd work until eleven o'clock at night—sometimes even until three in the morning—to make sure I'd done every-thing possible to win a case. They saw that and took advantage. Well, it's my fault. I *let* them. Before I knew it I was on call 24/7. Late nights became weekends. Working seven days a week became the norm rather than the excep-tion. It was my life. As the years passed and my track record grew, they kept dangling the carrot of making partner and I continued working my arse off.'

'So what happened? What led to you making the change and leaving?'

'I suppose as I became more and more exhausted, getting up in the morning got harder. My friends had always said I was working too much and was losing myself. Eventually I started to realise they were right.

Every day I stepped through those doors, I lost a little bit more of my soul. But the real wake-up call came after my grandma.'

'Your grandma?' I frowned. His expression suddenly changed. It was like a wave of sadness washed over him. I wondered if it was a good idea to keep discussing this. Maybe I'd let him carry on, and if it was too much, I was sure he'd let me know.

'I used to always see my grandma on a Sunday evening for dinner,' Josh continued. 'But one Sunday morning, I got a call from the boss. Some potential clients were coming over from New York. If we landed this account, it would "transform the firm," he said. "Get this account and you'll *definitely* make partner," he said. "I just need you to meet with them this afternoon. Shouldn't take long. You'll be done by six. Seven at the latest," he said. I agreed to it, but only on the condition that I'd be done by seven. as I always went to see my grandma. *Always.*'

'So did you leave on time?'

'No.' His voice cracked. 'I was still with them at eight. I told them as politely as I could that I needed to wrap it up, but they said there were a few more things they needed to run through. By the time we finally finished at ten thirty, it was too late to see her. I called to apologise and said I'd come on Wednesday, which was the other day she liked me to visit to have her home-made soup. But she died unexpectedly that Tuesday night and I never got to see her alive again. All because I'd agreed to that stupid meeting. To land a deal. Just to make partner.' His eyes began to water.

'I'm so sorry, Josh.' I desperately wanted to reach out and hold his hand or give him a hug. Anything to try and comfort him.

'Yeah,' he said, trying to compose himself. 'Nothing like the death of one of the people you love most in the world to make you realise what's really important in life. I was on autopilot the next day. Dragged myself into work, walked straight into my boss's office, told him I was leaving and walked out.'

'Bloody hell! What did he say?'

'I didn't wait around to listen. I remember him being shocked, but I couldn't have cared less. I didn't have to do it in person. I could have just not showed up. But grandma always taught me to be respectful, and under the circumstances, telling him face-to-face, even though it was in an abrupt way, was the best I could manage.'

'I'm surprised you could even get out of bed,' I said. God knows how he went to work that day. 'I'd be a wreck if I lost someone so close to me.'

'I was. After I left the office, I stumbled to the park and sat there. For hours. Staring into space. I couldn't get my head around her not being here anymore. And I felt sick that I'd missed the chance to see her because of work. Because of a job I didn't even enjoy. I'd wasted *years* of my life doing something I hated, and I couldn't waste another minute. I needed to follow my dream. And so that's what I'm doing now. *That's* what I'm working on.'

'Wow, Josh,' I said, trying to think of the right words. 'I don't know what to say. I'm so sorry you lost her. I'm sure she would have been proud of you, though.'

'Yeah,' he said, managing a smile. 'She was my biggest supporter. She loved to… she was sad that I'd stopped and used to always encourage me to pursue it again. But there was just no time for it when I was at the firm. It was too full-on. I was exhausted. It stifled my creativity.'

'Creativity?' I asked, pleased that he'd unwittingly given me a clue. 'So it's something creative, then?' He did his chair shifting thing again. 'Sorry. I didn't mean to pry. You said you don't want to talk about it, so I'll respect your decision.'

I really, really wanted to know, but pushing him probably wasn't a good idea. I just had to try my best not to overthink and trust that he'd open up and tell me the full story. Hopefully sooner rather than later.

'Thanks. I appreciate that. It's a *big* deal for me. It's my life. It's what I really want to do, and now I am.'

'Good for you. So did you start working on it straight away?'

'No. After leaving the firm, I took time out. Didn't work for a few months. I was *exhausted*. Working that hard for so many years really messed with my body, my health and my mind. And then add to that the grief. It was a disastrous cocktail. I had some really dark days. There's no way I could have worked. Thankfully, I had savings. That's the by-product of selling your soul. Having money meant I was able to survive for months without working, invest some cash in my future and make things happen. But doing it right, the way I want to, takes both time and money, so I had to get another job. And I didn't want something that would get in the way of what I need to do to get everything fully off the ground.'

'So that's why you work at Cuppa?'

'Yep. I start at seven and I'm usually finished by two, so I have most of the rest of the day to focus on it.'

'And how is *it* going?'

'Actually, it's great. When I'm doing it, I feel like me, you know? Like this is what I was always meant to do. It's my calling. And things are progressing well. I received really good news earlier about an opportunity that could really help things take off.' His face lit up.

'Sounds amazing!'

'It really is! It's a long journey and really hard to achieve success because it's super competitive, but I'm not giving up. I'm really proud of my work and the feedback so far is encouraging. It feels right. Like it's my time now.'

'Well, you sound really passionate about it, so keep going. Whatever it is, I hope it all takes off in a massive way, Josh, I really do. And I admire you for taking that leap and chasing your dream.' I thought about all the people who'd talked about wanting to do this or do that but never made it happen. A bit like me. Yeah, I'd left the agency and gone freelance, but I hadn't followed through with my goal to do work that I enjoyed. I wished I could be as brave as him. 'Can't have been easy walking away from a big, well-paid job, when you were so close to making partner.'

'Money isn't important to me.' He shook his head. 'Obviously I need to live, but all the rest is bullshit. It sounds lame, but it's people and being happy that matter. My boss couldn't understand that. He thought I was nuts. They tried for weeks to convince me to come back. Said I needed to at least work my notice, but I soon pointed out some things that made them see why it would be better to let me leave rather than fight me on it. The irony is that we won the big New York account and they still tried to persuade me to stay. Offered me partner and a shedload of money. I could have named my price. Had whatever salary

I wanted. But my happiness was worth more than they could ever pay me.'

'Sounds like you did the right thing,' I said. 'I'm really happy for you.'

Josh sat there smiling and completely silent. Was something I'd just said funny? I thought I was being quite deep. Oh gosh. Why was he grinning?

'What's up?' I said.

He smiled again and held my gaze.

'Nothing,' he said.

More silence.

Perhaps I should say something to fill it? Normally the conversation just flowed so freely between us.

'Thank you for opening up,' I said. 'For telling me more about you.'

He reached over the table and gently placed his hands on top of mine. As I felt the heat coming from his palms, it was as if I'd been struck by lightning.

My heart started racing.

'No,' he said, holding my gaze. 'Thank *you* for listening and for respecting that I'm not ready to talk about everything just yet. It means a lot.'

'You're welcome,' I said, staring into his eyes. *God, those eyes…*

'I've been waiting for the right moment to say this… it's not easy for me to do, but after the conversation we've just had, now seems like the perfect time to tell you that—'

'Boeuf bourguignon? For you, sir? And coq au vin for you, madame?' said the waiter, resting our mains on the table. Josh quickly lifted his hands away to make room for the plates.

Nooooo!

Why did the waiter have to bring the food right at that second? Josh was about to say something. Something good, I think? He had an extra sparkle in his eyes. Goddammit.

'Salt and pepper?' asked the waiter.

'I'm fine, thanks,' said Josh.

'Any more drinks?'

'We're okay at the moment,' I said, wishing that he'd leave so we could continue our conversation.

'Would you like any more water for the table?' the waiter added.

Mr Waiter, I whispered in my head, *I know you're trying to be helpful, but please, pretty please, can you go now? We were right in the middle of something...*

'We're fine, thank you. Everything is fine. But if we need anything, we'll let you know,' said Josh politely.

'Wonderful. Okay. Great, well, if you're sure there's nothing else, I'll let you enjoy your meal. *Bon appetit!*' he said before darting back towards the kitchen.

'I thought he was never going to leave,' I laughed.

'I know! He certainly was keen. Must be new. Not used to picking up on when two people want to be alone. That won't be good for their Most Romantic Restaurant status!' He chuckled. 'Anyway, this looks amazing. I'm starving! All I've had to eat today was two slices of toast and a muffin.'

'Blueberry, by any chance?'

'Yep,' he replied.

'Such a copycat!'

'Well, you have one every morning, so I wanted to see what all the fuss was about.'

'And?'

'Delicious!' he said. 'I'm hooked. But if I keep eating those, I'll have to step up my gym routine,' he said, patting his toned stomach.

'Looks fine to me,' I said. Josh smiled and held my gaze again. 'So—you were about to say something before?' I asked. He glanced down at his plate.

'Oh, nothing. It was nothing,' he said. 'Come on, let's eat our food before it gets cold.'

It was as if we'd inhaled our main courses and the tarte tatin we'd had for dessert, because before I knew it, we'd left the restaurant and were outside my flat.

'So…here we are again,' said Josh, standing in front of me.

'Yes, indeed. Here we are,' I said. 'And I'm actually able to stand on my own two feet this time. Bonus!'

'Yes, I must say, you handled your drink *much* better tonight.'

'I did, didn't I? Perhaps I've become a middleweight, rather than a lightweight!'

Josh stepped towards me and brushed a stray curl away from my face.

'You're beautiful Emily,' he said. 'So stunning, kind and funny and smart.'

'Tha—'

Before I had a chance to say thanks, Josh had pulled me into him and gently placed his lips on mine.

As we kissed, it was like the whole world was spinning. Round and round. Faster and faster. Like the wheels of a Ferrari speeding around a racetrack.

Wow.

Maybe I'd spoken too soon about being able to stand on my own two feet.

I felt a rush of blood shoot towards my head and as he wrapped his arms around my waist, my whole body tingled.

Wow. Wow. *Wow.*

I parted my lips and his tongue slid effortlessly inside, gently flicking against mine. His breath was so sweet, and as his kisses grew stronger and stronger, I began to feel him against me.

Oh my God.

I couldn't help it. My hands began to wander. Down his firm back (he *definitely* worked out), then across his bum. That beautiful, taught, sculpted bottom I'd admired many times from afar. It was solid like a Roman statue. *So hot.*

'Wow,' he said, easing away for a second. He pushed me against the front door and started kissing me passionately again.

I want this man so badly. And I mean, really badly.

I wanted him upstairs. I wanted him in my bed. I wanted him inside me. But I liked Josh. A *lot.* Somehow I felt that Chloe might be right. Josh could be special. And if he was, I didn't want to rush into things. I couldn't sleep with him on our first date. Or even our second. We had to take our time. I needed to get to know him. *Properly.* I needed to be sure that I could trust him. I couldn't get hurt. I couldn't go through that pain. Not again. It would destroy me.

'Josh,' I said, taking my hands away.

'Mmmm,' he said, pushing his lips against mine again.

'Josh, we should stop…'

'Sorry,' he said, stepping back quickly. 'Sorry, I didn't mean to—I thought you—I thought you liked me. Did I get that wrong?'

'No, no, no! I do! I *really* do—that's the problem.'

'Problem?' He frowned.

'I literally could stand here all night and kiss you. Actually, no. That's not true. I could probably only manage a few more seconds of kissing you before I invited you upstairs to my flat and then…' My mind began to wander and imagine his hands all over my naked body. Jesus. I couldn't believe I was actually asking him to stop when I wanted him so much.

'Oh no. I wasn't expecting—I didn't…I just *had* to kiss you. I've wanted to kiss you for ages. And I just couldn't wait a second longer. But we can take this as slowly as you want. I know you're still healing from your ex, so if you're not ready…'

'No. Seriously, it's fine. I'm ready. Ready to try at least. So, yeah, if we could take things slowly, that would be great.'

'Of course,' he said, leaning forward to give me a short, firm kiss. 'No problem. I better go. Seven o'clock start tomorrow. Thank you for an amazing evening. I hope I'll see you tomorrow? At Cuppa?'

'Absolutely,' I said, wishing that the night didn't have to end. 'Look forward to seeing you tomorrow.'

CHAPTER TWENTY

There was no point in denying it. I was falling for Josh. *Hard.* If I'd had my way, I'd have gone to Cuppa when it opened at 7 a.m. I couldn't sleep. I'd spent the whole night tossing and turning. Imagining him in bed with me, our hands all over each other. How he looked. How he tasted. Breathing in his delicious scent.

I'd woken up earlier than usual and taken a shower. I'd tried to hold out until nine, which was when I would normally go. First I attempted to distract myself with Facebook but got bored after about twenty seconds, so I logged off. After that, I loaded the dishwasher, then mopped the kitchen floor, but by 8.15 I couldn't wait any longer. I *had* to see him. I did my hair, put on a bit of make-up, threw on some jeans and a top, and by 8.30, I was out the door.

His face lit up as soon as I'd walked inside. He finished serving a customer, whispered something to his colleague, stepped out from behind the counter and headed towards the doors, nodding for me to follow.

As I walked outside, he took my hand, pulled me

around the corner of the shop, pushed me up against the wall and began to kiss me.

'Mmmm…good morning,' I said.

'I haven't been able to stop thinking about you since last night,' he said, gasping for breath.

'Me neither,' I replied, unable to hide my feelings.

'Are you busy later?' he said as he took my head in his hands and kissed me again. 'I'd really like to spend time with you.'

'I'd love to,' I said, my heart pounding with excitement.

'I should really be working—you know, on my stuff— but I don't even know if I can concentrate. My mind is just racing.'

'Mine too,' I said, launching forward and thrusting my tongue in his mouth. I couldn't help myself.

'Jesus. What are you doing to me, Emily? I'm going crazy. But in the most amazing way. I need to go back inside, but I should probably wait,' he said, looking between his legs.

'Mmmm,' I said, glaring at his hard-on whilst resisting the urge to touch it. Doing that wasn't going to help either of us. 'Glad you're happy to see me.'

'Oh, I am. *Believe me.* So,' he said, stepping back. 'Later. What's better for you? We could either meet this evening. That way I could spend a few hours at home working beforehand. Or if you're able to take the afternoon off, then we could go into town, maybe check out a museum or something? There's a new exhibition at the V&A I've been wanting to see for a while if you're up for that.'

Wow. He's into art? I'd spoken briefly about my work

as an illustrator, but I'd never really talked about the kind of stuff I used to like doing. Finally a man that shares my love of museums. *Amazing.*

'That sounds perfect! Actually, it might be good for us to go this afternoon.' I was still determined to take things slowly with Josh. But given the way my legs turned to jelly and my libido went into overdrive whenever I saw him, something told me that if we went out this evening and he walked me home, I might not be able to resist this time.

'Great!' he said, pulling me towards him. 'Looking forward to it already.' We started to kiss again.

Oh gosh. He was just too tempting. If we didn't stop now, things could get really out of hand...

'Come on!' I said, tapping his bum. *Any excuse.* 'You'd better go. There's probably a load of tired customers queuing up to get their caffeine fix. I can't let them be deprived because of me. And I wouldn't want you to get fired either. I don't need that kind of karma.' After wanting to see him so badly, I deserved a medal for my self-control.

He took a deep breath and checked himself again.

'Okay, give me a minute and I should be good. Provided, of course, that you don't kiss me, touch me, look at me, or speak to me and you erase the last twelve hours from my memory.'

'Go!' I replied, resisting the urge to do everything he'd just said not to.

'Yes, ma'am! Are you going to come?' he said.

'What?' I smirked, my mind filling itself with naughty thoughts again.

'I mean for your latte and blueberry muffin. Get your mind out of the gutter, young lady!'

'Yes, I'll be there in a sec. And, Josh?' I said cheekily as he turned back.

'Emily?'

'I think I'll definitely be *coming* very soon.' I winked. 'In a *big* way.'

CHAPTER TWENTY-ONE

The next two weeks with Josh were magical. Like a fairy tale.

No. *More* than a fairy tale. I kept having to pinch myself to check that it was real. That this was happening. That Josh and I were really together.

That Wednesday afternoon, we'd wandered around the V&A hand in hand. I had always said I'd like to be with a man who loved art and museums as much as I did, and the universe had clearly listened, as they'd sent Josh to me.

In fact, at times I wondered if he loved art more than I did. Something I never even thought was possible. The fire that I saw in his eyes as he walked up close to each painting and examined it inch by inch was undeniable.

'I *love* the creativity,' he'd gushed. 'You know? Looking at other people's creations and considering how they brought their visions to life. The whole process they went through. The way what started as a seed of an idea blossoms and then becomes a work of art coveted by millions. I find it so just so *inspiring*.'

I did too. When Josh mentioned that, I couldn't help but wish my work could be on display. Not necessarily in a gallery being seen by thousands of people or anything like that. Even if I knew just one person looked at my art every day and it made them happy, it would have been enough for me. I mean, yeah, loads of people saw my illustrations in adverts or leaflets all the time, but it wasn't anything creative or exciting. It wasn't the same.

We'd stayed there for hours and then agreed that as we hadn't even scratched the surface of what the museum had to offer, we'd have to return again in a few weeks for part two. *Part two*. He was thinking ahead. To the future. Our future. *Together*. Yeah, I knew it was only weeks ahead, rather than months or years, but to me that was a sign that he didn't want this to be a quick fling. He was making plans and including me in them.

Ever the gentleman, he'd walked me back to my door and, despite the fact that my street was still busy, he'd given me the most amazing long, passionate kiss as if the rest of the world didn't exist. *Mmm…*

Eventually we'd pulled ourselves apart. Josh had said he'd better go back home and work, and I'd gone upstairs, then collapsed on my bed, groaning at the torture I was voluntarily putting myself through by resisting the tempta- tion of sleeping with him. It was *soooo* hard, but I hoped the wait would be worth it. I wanted to be sure. Get to know him better. I couldn't risk getting hurt again.

We'd seen each other on the Thursday afternoon too. This time he'd packed some snacks into a box with a blanket and we'd had a picnic in the park. Sounds silly, but it was another thing I'd always wanted to do with a guy. I remembered seeing those couples when I'd visited

Dulwich Park on that walking group and wishing it was me. And now here we were. Josh feeding me bite-sized pieces of my favourite blueberry muffin (if I didn't curb my addiction to them soon, I was probably going to end up looking like a giant bloody muffin), sipping from the bottle of Prosecco I'd brought along, all in between shamelessly kissing and cuddling as if no one else was around.

Josh made me feel so at ease that I'd become less afraid about sharing my feelings with him and suggesting places for us to go. So when he'd walked me home, I'd asked him if he wanted to do something on Friday. As soon as he said he couldn't, I regretted it. I was disappointed but took a deep breath and told myself not to worry. We could hang out on Saturday instead. So, I'd suggested we meet up then.

'Can't do Saturday, I'm afraid, Em,' he'd said. *Gutted.*

'Sunday?'

'I'm working at Cuppa on Sunday afternoon...' Maybe sensing my disappointment at rejecting three suggestions, he'd then said, 'I can do Monday, though. Monday afternoon?'

Monday! I'd thought. My stomach dropped. That was a whole four days away. Sure, I'd see him the following day and on the Sunday if I went for coffee, but why couldn't we meet on Saturday if it was his day off?

Then I told myself to be reasonable. We'd spent three afternoons in a row together and he obviously needed his own space. Well, at least I'd hoped it was that and not because he was getting bored of me already.

Thankfully, I hadn't needed to worry. As he'd suggested, we'd met up again on the Monday afternoon and went for a walk along the Thames holding hands, then sat on a bench and just talked for hours. About our parents (well, Josh's mum in his case, as he hadn't spoken to his dad since he'd left them to live with another woman), who had both chosen to move abroad when they'd retired. His mum had gone to Spain three years ago and mine had headed off to New York last summer. I'd visited them at Christmas, and he'd gone to spend the holidays with his mum too.

I'd explained that I texted my parents once a week or whenever I could. I told him I wasn't sure if I'd go back to New York this year, whilst secretly wondering what Josh's plans for Christmas would be and if he'd like to come with me if I did. But then I told myself not to get carried away. After all, Christmas was in seven months' time and anything could happen between now and then.

Josh was an only child like me. That's why he'd grown even closer to his grandma after his mum had left for Spain. He didn't have much family here. A few distant aunts and cousins, but that was it. His best friends, Doug and Phil, were both married and busy with their kids and work, so he didn't get to see much of them, particularly now he was so focused on pursuing his dream.

We'd gone to the cinema on Thursday afternoon, but we'd spent more time kissing than actually watching the film…

He was busy again last Friday and over the weekend, so we didn't see each other again until Monday, when we'd gone for a walk along the Southbank, and then two days later, this afternoon, as it was another sunny day in May, we'd gone back to the park, found a secluded spot and worked off the sandwiches and apple pie he'd brought along by rolling around on the blanket…

It had got very heated. I mean *very*. At one point when he was on top of me, I was actually ready to whip my clothes off there and then and just go for it. Not even the fear of getting arrested for public indecency was enough to stop me. Thankfully (well, then again, when you're sexually frustrated, it's difficult to feel *thankful*), Josh realised we were very close to letting things get out of control, so he'd jumped up, hard-on bulging beneath his jeans, and said we'd better pack up and head home.

Whilst he'd walked over to the tree opposite us to take a phone call (why he couldn't talk in front of me, I didn't know), I'd called Chloe on her house phone. There was no point texting her. Pretty sure she only checked messages once a month, so the old-fashioned approach, as always with her, was best.

'SOS!'

'Hello to you too, Emily.'

'Are you busy? Please can I come round? Like now? Immediately?'

'Dinner's in the oven and I was just going to sit down with a cup of tea, so I do have some time, but you know the rules. No coming to my house until your challenge is over.'

'Oh, come on! How much longer do I have left? Like two days or something? You've seen how much I've been going out. You know I've changed.' I really had. Couldn't remember the last time I'd gone on social media, and let's face it, there were loads of things I could have posted. Dinner at Chez Pierre or maybe one of the many photos I took at the museums Josh and I had visited. But I didn't feel the need to. If I'd spent time trying to filter the photos and thinking of how to write a witty caption, then I would have had less time to spend enjoying those moments with him, doing extra sketches at home or something more productive.

'Actually, you have three days, if we say you started the challenge that Saturday when I briefed you on it in the coffee shop. You may not have long left, but we can't have you relapsing. A deal is a deal. However, Brian has just got home, so I can pop out for an hour before we all sit down to eat. Is Josh working at Cuppa today?'

'No, his shift finished this afternoon, so we're just in the park, but as it's about him, it's probably better we don't go there. I don't want any of his colleagues overhearing anything.'

'Why don't I just come to the park, then? We can walk and talk.'

'Brilliant! Thanks, Chloe. I need your words of wisdom. We're behind the bushes. You know, at the back of the park.'

'*Classy*. Yes, I know the place. Leaving right now.'

'Everything okay?' said Josh as he walked towards me, then wrapped his arms around my waist.

'Yep! You?'

'Y-yeah. All cool. I just had to…yeah, everything's fine. Come here,' he said, kissing me again.

I felt him against me. *Oh God.*

My hands crept beneath his T-shirt, up and across his smooth chest, then down between his thighs.

He grabbed my bum, then started kissing my neck and along my shoulders whilst he ran his hands under my top and started caressing my breasts. I'd forgotten that somehow my bra had magically become unfastened earlier. Thank goodness this part of the park was secluded.

I didn't know how much more I could take before I quite literally *exploded*. My whole body tingled. Literally every inch of me was crying out for him.

'Em…' he gasped. I loved that he'd now started calling me that.

'Josh…'

'We'd better stop. It's been a long time for me. I haven't been with anyone for a while, and if we keep going, I'm not going to be able to control myself.'

'I know. I feel the same.'

'Shall we head back now?' he said.

'Actually, I'm going to stay. Chloe's coming over to the park. We're going for a walk.'

'Oh, okay. I'll go, then, as I've got loads to do tonight, but do you want to meet tomorrow?'

'Sure,' I said, feeling excited to see Josh again, but also wondering how I could without literally jumping him.

'Great,' he said. 'Any ideas of what you might like to do?'

Rip your clothes off and have sex?

Calm yourself, Emily. You definitely can't say that.

'Erm, can I have a think and let you know later?'

'Sure. Okay, I better go, but one last kiss before I do…'

'Mmm, of course,' I said, planting my lips on his, 'but I thought we were supposed to be stopping.'

'I know, but I can't seem to…I mean, this beautiful behind of yours, for a start,' he said, running his hands over my bottom, 'makes it *very* difficult.' It was good to know he appreciated it. Ever since I'd started saying more positive things about my body in the mirror each morning, I'd begun to grow fond of it too. Hearing someone else complimenting my bum for a change was the cherry on top.

'Yours is rather nice too,' I said, my hands also getting carried away.

'Oi! *You two!*' boomed a deep voice behind us. 'This is a public place, stop it!'

Shit.

We both dropped our hands and span around. Maybe I was about to get arrested after all...

Chloe. Bloody Chloe.

'You frightened the life out of me!' I said. Who knew she could make her voice go that deep?

'Good! Get a room!'

Josh and I looked at each other and then burst into laughter.

'That's my cue to leave. Nice to see you, Chloe. Em, let's speak later, yeah?'

'Yeah, speak later.'

'Erm, Josh...?' said Chloe. 'You might want to wrap your jacket—no, actually, that *entire* blanket—around your waist, you know? To cover the inner thigh area. You might take someone's eye out with that!'

'Chloe!'

'Just saying, Em...'

Josh glanced down. 'Noted. Thanks for the heads up...'

'Yes, Josh. The head is *literally* and most definitely *up*,' said Chloe.

Blushing, Josh scooped up the blanket and his black denim jacket, placed them in front of him, smirked, then began walking off.

'Bye, ladies!'

'Oh my God, Chloe!' I said, slapping her playfully on the back, once Josh was out of range. 'You are *terrible*!'

'*Me?* I did the man a favour. You can't walk around a park swinging a weapon around like that. That's what you call armed and dangerous. One look at what he's been blessed with down there and he could cause innocent cyclists to crash, not to mention women— oh, and prob-ably men—to walk into trees. *Goodness gracious me!* That looks like some piece of equipment he's carrying. You lucky, lucky lady! So when's the big day, or should that be *night*?'

'Well, that's why I called you. I've been trying to hold out for as long as I could—you know, to be sure that he's decent and all that—but I don't think I can do it anymore. I'm just not strong enough. I'm *gasping* for him. I'm driving myself mental. I can't stop thinking about him. About sex. I don't know what's come over me. I can't function when I'm at my desk. I went months without even giving it a second thought. In fact, there were times I couldn't even *consider* being with another man. But now, any long object I see, I start imagining as a phallic symbol. I spent far too long eating a banana yesterday. Things are *bad*, Chloe. I think it's actually making me ill.'

'Sounds like you've got that serious condition—what's it called again?'

'Wait, what? There's an *actual* medical condition?'

'Yes. It's called sexual-frustration-crazy-nympho-lady-itis!'

'Chloe!'

She wasn't far wrong, though. I was like a woman possessed.

'It's perfectly natural. Well, maybe not the banana

thing, but clearly you've reached your limit. No point torturing yourself. From the looks of things, he's definitely, ahem, *up for it*!'

'This isn't a joke!'

'Sorry! I couldn't resist! But seriously, though, he is. He's a man, so he probably was ready to do the deed from day one.'

'No, he's not like that. He's never asked or made me feel pressured. It's been a while for him too, so I think he wants to take his time.'

'Pull the other one! Mr Stud Muffin is saying that it's been a while? He must have women throwing themselves at him every second.'

'Josh explained that because he's been focusing all of his energies pursuing his dream and working on his mystery 'project', he hasn't had time for a girlfriend. And he wasn't in the right place emotionally before because his grandma passed away, then before that, he was always working, so—'

'So is he trying to say he's been celibate for years?'

'Well, no. Not *years*. He said he's dated on and off during that time, but not anything serious, and he hasn't slept with anyone at all for months. Not since Christmas, when he went to see his mum in Spain and hooked up with the daughter of one of her friends.'

Chloe rolled her eyes.

'Stop! Like I said, he told me that up until I came along, he deliberately avoided getting involved with anyone as he didn't want to get distracted, and I believe him!'

'Fair enough. Yes, sorry. I really must stop judging him by his looks,' she said, slapping herself on the hand. 'My gut tells me he's a good egg, Em. How many dates have you been on now?'

'Seven. Well, eight if you include that first drink at the pub, but definitely seven proper dates. And it's been two weeks and one day since our date at Chez Pierre.'

'Not that you've been counting, of course…'

'Stop teasing!' I squeezed her arm gently. '*Help!*'

'I'm not the one who can help you, I'm afraid. As you keep reminding me, I'm married, and as beautiful as you are, Em, we're just friends. You're not my type.'

'*Stop!*'

'Sorry. You're just so easy to wind up right now,' she chuckled. 'Okay, serious Chloe is back in the building and she says go for it! If you're ready, and I believe that you are, then call him later, invite him round to yours tomorrow and just do it for Pete's sake! That's got to be better than you two frolicking behind the bushes like teenagers.'

So true. It was terrible. *Shameless*. But so good at the same time…

'I know. We couldn't help ourselves. I just lose all my inhibitions when he touches me.'

'Clearly!' Chloe laughed again. 'Get yourself home, prep your boudoir and your body for action tomorrow and get it over and done with so that you can put yourselves and me out of our misery. And don't forget to call me on Friday morning once he's left to let me know how it went. Most importantly, relax and try not to worry. If that big display in his trousers earlier was anything to go by, I think you're in for the night of your life!'

CHAPTER TWENTY-TWO

T*his was it.* In exactly seventeen minutes, Josh, who was always on time, would be here. In my flat. And perhaps an hour or so later, once we'd had dinner, if the heat between us in the park yesterday was anything to go by, we would have done the deed. Got down to business. And I could not wait.

Don't get me wrong. Of course I was nervous. I wouldn't be me otherwise. Whilst I felt really comfortable around him, it was much easier to be relaxed on a dinner, museum or park date, when I was fully or even partially clothed. Being sprawled out on the bed in my birthday suit, exposing myself and all my wobbly bits to a man who was drop-dead gorgeous was a different story.

There was so much to think about before having sex for the first time with someone new. Would it be any good? Would *I* be any good? Would *he* be any good? Would we have the same connection in the bedroom, or would it be awkward? The list was endless. Particularly because I *really* liked him. Whilst that quick fumble with

Henry was good practise for being naked in front of a man and getting me back in the game again, I hoped it was going to pale in comparison to the experience I would have with Josh.

Because I'd resisted for so long (well, just over two weeks wasn't exactly *long*, especially as I'd gone several months without it, but considering I would have been happy to indulge from day one, it certainly felt that way), the anticipation had built up even more. And because Josh was so hot, somehow that meant that I expected sex with him to be extra mind-blowing. Completely shallow, I know, but I mean, look at him. He must have had women falling at his feet all his life, so surely he'd had more opportunities to hone his skills than most.

And as Chloe couldn't fail to notice, and I felt every time we got close, he did seem to be *very* well endowed. That has always been billed as the holy grail for a guy, right? Supposedly, the bigger the better? Not always the case in my experience. I remember a guy I slept with in college. What was his name again? Jerry, I think? Anyway, he was very, very well hung and sex was very, very uncomfortable. With every thrust I thought he was going to crush my insides. I couldn't wait for it to end. *Oh God*. I really hoped it wouldn't be like that with Josh.

Like Chloe said, I just needed to relax. Josh has had a good feel of my body, albeit under my clothes, and so would already be familiar with my shape. Yes, maybe I could be firmer in many places. Couldn't we all? But he didn't seem to mind my small boobs and big bum, so I should stop fretting. It was going to be fine…

I wondered how he was feeling. Did guys get nervous before they slept with a woman too? Perhaps they suffered from performance anxiety, wondering if they'd be able to get it up and how long it would stay up. Or did they just take it all in their stride? I think Josh knew that I wanted things to happen tonight. I hadn't said it explicitly, but when we'd spoken last night and I'd suggested that he could come round to mine for a 'night in,' I could feel him smiling down the phone. *'A night in, eh?'* he'd said, as if instantly guessing that I was inviting him around to Netflix and chill.

'Yeah,' I'd added quickly, for some reason trying to throw him off the scent. 'I'm not the best cook in the world, but I do make a mean spaghetti bolognese…'

'My favourite!' he'd said. 'So what time do you want me? At your flat? I mean, what time should I come? Round. To your flat? *Oh God!*'

We'd both laughed.

Yeah. I'm pretty sure he knows what's on the cards…

I checked the table. Looking good. Placemats were laid out, I'd lit some candles to set the mood, had opened the red wine and the bolognese was spot on. Thankfully, this dish never failed me. I would cook the spaghetti when he arrived.

My bedroom was ready. Clean sheets, clothes all neatly hung up in the wardrobe. And my body was ready too. Freshly shaved, freshly showered. Smothered in sweet coconut oil. Primed for action. I'd put on my silky peach lingerie, a colourful floral miniskirt I'd bought at the weekend and sheer white vest top. Sexy but casual, I thought.

The doorbell rang. As always, right on time.

'Welcome!' I said as Josh stepped through the door.

'Thank you,' he said, removing his shoes, then kissing

me gently on the lips. 'I feel very privileged to have received the invitation, especially as you've cooked too. I'm looking forward to sampling your cuisine.'

We burst into laughter. *Such dirty minds.*

'Are you referring to my bolognese?' I said, running my fingers suggestively down his chest.

'*Of course.*' He smirked, kissing me again. 'What *else*?'

'That's a shame,' I said.

'Well, I *am* very hungry, so I'll be ready to devour anything you want to offer me.' He winked.

As I imagined the possibilities, my heart started beating faster.

Reluctantly, I snapped out of my thoughts and regained my focus.

'So,' I said, taking his hand and leading him through the flat, 'this is the kitchen slash dining and living room.'

'Open-plan. Cool,' said Josh. 'Good for entertaining.'

'Yeah, that *was* the idea, but I haven't done much of that lately. And then, this is obviously the bathroom,' I said, opening the door. 'That room there is my office, but it's not fit for visitors at the moment, so I'll save the tour of that for another day, and then *this* is the *bedroom,*' I added, my body tingling again as I pictured us on my bed together.

'Mmm, okay,' said Josh. '*Very* nice. Good to know where everything is. Thanks for the tour.'

'No probs! So. First things first. Drink? I've got red wine for dinner, but I also made sure I got a bottle of Jack Daniels just for you.'

'Awww, thanks. A JD and Coke is perfect.'

He walked around the living room, his eyes scanning

the walls and the furniture. He sat on the sofa, then jumped up again as he pulled out a folder that I'd left down the side. Damn. I'd forgotten to put that away.

'What's this?' he said, picking up one of my old paintings that had fallen out and onto the floor.

'Oh, just some…some of my old work.' I squirmed. I didn't really want anyone to see it. Normally I had it locked away in my office, but I'd taken them out earlier to flick through at lunchtime as I was looking to see if I had any old life drawing sketches in there.

'This is *amazing*! Why do you have this stuff hidden away? You should be selling it!' He eagerly thumbed through the folder. 'Could I have one of these, please? I'd pay for it obviously. These would be perfect. I've got a lot of art, because I…but some of my walls are looking a bit bare and boring, which I hate. No offence,' he said, slapping his forehead as he stared at my magnolia living room.

'No, no, you're right. I hate bare walls too. They're only like this as I haven't bothered to change anything since Eric left. *He* chose the décor for this place. If I had my way, they'd be painted bright colours. I'd have put up lots of art and would have painted a mural in here. I drew something years ago with a colourful field of tulips. I'd have loved to have painted that on this wall,' I said, pointing to the bland décor.

'What?' he shouted. 'You can paint murals too? Straight onto the wall?'

'Well, yeah.' I shrugged. 'I used to help out a couple of mural artists when I was at uni. Did it for a couple of years.'

'That's incredible! I know a fair bit about art—well, not, you know…' His voice trailed off. 'Anyway, I know that most people that paint small, from the wrist, can't paint from the shoulder and do large-scale stuff too. The fact that you can do illustrations *and* murals is very rare. That's a real skill, Em. I wish I could do that.'

Josh's knowledge was impressive. Not many people knew the difference between painting from the wrist and the shoulder. My lecturer at uni had said a similar thing about me having a unique skill set and encouraged me to pursue becoming a mural artist, but I couldn't find a steady paying job in London. And then the opportunity to work in illustration had come up and I'd just focused on that instead.

'Thanks, that's nice of you to say.'

'But it's true! So I don't understand. Why don't you paint murals on your walls, then? What's stopping you?'

'Nothing, I suppose.' That wasn't strictly true. It was mainly because I hadn't had the motivation. And I'd stopped believing in myself. In my abilities. I'd thought about it a couple of times since I'd started life drawing but pushed it to the back of my mind again. 'I guess I got so used to doing things Eric's way, and since the breakup, I've just never really been inspired to change anything.'

'Well, I think it would be criminal to have your talent and not put it to good use. I mean, I knew you could draw, obviously, but not like this! It sounds like you've got lots of ideas about what you'd like to do. And those ideas definitely seem to be more *you*. I mean, you've got such a warm, vibrant, exciting and creative personality. When I think of you, I don't think of blank magnolia walls, or plain white duvet covers. I see colour. A rainbow. So many shades. Forget about Eric and how he wanted things. He's gone. This is *your* home now. You should feel free to express yourself and paint it however you want. Show off your personality. Showcase your skills. Your work is *incredible*, Em,' he said, sifting through the paintings again. 'You've got an *amazing* talent. A gift. Your work shouldn't be hidden away. The world should see it. And at the very least I reckon you should be proud to display your skills on your own four walls.'

Wow.

I was kind of speechless. No one had ever spoken about my work like that before. I mean, yeah, my lecturers had said in the past that they thought I had talent, and both Chloe and my parents had some of my old stuff hanging in their houses, but again, they were biased. When I was a child, Mum often pinned my latest creations on the fridge. Then when I was in college and uni, she'd always put something in the hallway or living room. But she was my mother. That was what mums did. And Chloe was my best friend. Of course she'd want to be supportive. But Josh? He already knew I liked him and that sex was on the cards, so there was no reason for him to lie. After years of being ridiculed by Eric, it felt good to finally find a man who believed in me and my art.

And it was also lovely to hear someone call me vibrant and exciting. Definitely better than the 'boring' tag I'd been labelled with so many times.

'Thanks. I might start doing some stuff again. I've really been enjoying my life drawing classes, and our visit to the V&A gave me some inspiration too.'

'I'm really glad to hear that, Em. Honestly, you're so good. I'd love to buy some of your work. In fact, how do you fancy doing a few murals for me? I've got some walls at home which could do with livening up.'

'What?' I frowned. 'If you really want the paintings, you can have them. I wouldn't charge you! They've been gathering dust for ages. It'd be great to know they've gone to a good home.'

'That's kind of you, but I honestly don't mind paying for these or for you to paint the murals.'

'But you haven't seen any of my mural work. I might have some old photos somewhere that I could show you, but—'

'I don't need to see anything. I believe in you. I just *know* you'll do a great job. We can talk about it properly another time if you like, but in the meantime, will you give it some thought?'

I couldn't quite get my head around the fact that he was even considering effectively commissioning me to do some work for him.

'Um, yeah. Sure,' I said, thinking he was just being nice and that it probably wouldn't happen anyway. 'Well, I better get you that drink.'

'Thanks.'

I poured the Jack Daniels into a glass.

'Nice rug,' he said, rubbing his feet over the thick cream faux fur, then sliding down to sit on it. '*Very* soft.'

'Yeah. Even though it's plain, and I've just been rabbiting on about how much I love colour, after my green sofa, it's still one of my favourite things in this room,' I said as I finished pouring the Coke over the ice. 'My parents bought it for me a couple of years ago to match the cream leather sofa that used to be here. I'm always paranoid about spilling red wine on it, though.'

'Bolognese sauce wouldn't look too good on here either, I'd imagine.'

'Nope,' I said, handing him his drink, 'That's why we'll be eating from the table tonight.'

'I'm fine to eat your spag bol from the table if you like,' said Josh, 'but there's something much more appealing that I'd like to sample on this rug before then...'

Josh held my gaze, took my hands, then gently pulled me downwards and laid me across it without saying another word.

He began to kiss me. First slowly but firmly on my lips and all over my neck. He lifted my vest over my head, then his tongue travelled down my chest until he reached my belly button. Next, his head travelled down my body as Josh peeled off my skirt and thong.

'God, you're beautiful,' he said. I couldn't even speak. My heart was beating so fast. I just couldn't wait to see and feel what was going to happen next.

As he moved his lips upwards from my knees, all along my inner thighs, my whole body trembled with anticipation. I wanted him to kiss me. *There*. I wanted him to bury his head between my legs and kiss me. Passionately. Like his life depended on it.

Thankfully the universe was listening because, before I could catch my breath, I felt Josh's mouth on me.

Thank the Lord. He's not afraid to go down. And I didn't even have to ask.

'Spread your legs wide, please, Em,' he said, licking his lips. 'I really want to taste every inch of you.' I wasted no time doing exactly that.

Josh separated my lips, then rotated his tongue slowly, drawing figures of eight over my clit. Every stroke was like a lightning bolt striking my body.

'*Mmm*,' he moaned. 'I've wanted to do this for *so long*.'

Next came the gentle flicks up and down, left to right, each one more powerful than the last. With every touch, my breathing became heavier and I grew wetter. I knew the signs. I was on my way. It was happening much quicker than usual. I was always guaranteed to climax if a guy went down on me, but knowing it was Josh that was between my thighs, the man I felt such a strong connection with, meant I wouldn't be able to hold on for much longer.

I watched his head moving up and down as he began to suck and release. It was like he'd switched on every nerve ending in my body. I could tell he was enjoying it as much as I was. He wasn't just sampling my cuisine like he'd offered to earlier, he was *devouring* it.

I grabbed his head and gently pushed it further and further into me.

'Oh…*I like that*,' I gasped. 'Keep going.'

As he swirled his tongue round and round in circles faster and faster, that was it. I was catapulted past the point of no return. My knees started to tremble, then my body began to shake as the throbbing sensation grew stronger and stronger. I raised my hips off the rug and closer into him.

'I'm coming…I'm…ooooooohhhh! Josh!'

I collapsed back on the rug.

That was *amazing*.

Thank you, universe.

Josh licked his lips, then moved up to rest his head on my chest.

'Did you enjoy?' he said.

'*Very much*,' I said, my breathing still heavy. 'Thank you. That was *wonderful*.'

'Glad to be of service,' he said. 'I enjoyed it too.'

'Did you now? So you're a man who likes to go *down*?'

'*Love it*. On the right woman,' he said.

'Glad to hear it,' I said.

It took several minutes to regain my composure. I was still on such a high, but as much as I wanted to lie here feeling cosy with him, there was no way I was done yet. After dreaming about us being together for so long, I wanted to continue.

I lifted him off my chest, slid downwards, unbuckled his belt then peeled off his jeans and boxer shorts.

Sweet Jesus.

As suspected, he was a *very* big man. But somehow I wasn't as apprehensive as I thought I would be. In fact, I couldn't wait to feel him. To *taste* him.

I held him in my hands and licked him from base to tip. Josh groaned with pleasure.

I took Josh in my mouth. My head moved up and down and my tongue circled him. As I increased the speed of my rotations, I felt his body rise beneath me.

'Fuck…' said Josh. 'That feels…*incredible*… oh…shit…Em?'

'Mmmm?'

'I-I'm in *real* danger of coming, literally any second if you continue…'

'Mmmm…' I repeated, loving the fact that he was getting so turned on.

'And I'm *really* enjoying it, *but* I wondered if you feel

ready now? Because, if you are, I'd really like to be inside you.'

Ready? I'd been ready since the first day we'd kissed. My stomach flipped at the thought that I was seconds away from feeling him. *All of him.*

I slid Josh out slowly, like I was removing a giant lollipop from my mouth.

'I'm *definitely* ready, Josh.'

That was all he needed to hear. Whilst I lay on my back, Josh reached into his jeans, pulled out a condom, rolled it on, then climbed on top.

As he entered me, I groaned.

Whoa.

'Are you okay, Em?'

'Yes, I-I'm fine,' I gasped. I just needed a moment to get over the initial shock of entry. But when I did, it felt great.

More than great. *Phenomenal.*

He lay on top of me, slowly rocking back and forth, and put his hands behind my back as he unfastened my bra, then tossed it on the rug.

Next he took my nipples in his mouth and sucked them slowly. *Oh so slowly.* Everything he did felt so *deep*, so sensual. The connection between us was undeniable. Although it had taken a few seconds to get used to his size, now everything felt so right. It was like our bodies were made for each other. Everything was in tune. Perfectly in sync. The rhythm. The timing. I didn't have to ask him to move this way or that way. Go harder or slower. He just knew exactly what to do and where to touch without me even saying a word.

What I was experiencing wasn't wild, crazy, soulless,

fast screwing. It was long and slow. Intense. He was taking his time. Savouring every second.

This wasn't just sex. *This* was making love.

Josh slid my nipples out of his mouth and sat up, his hips still rotating and gently thrusting, whilst I mirrored his actions underneath him. He'd stop for a microsecond, then start, then stop and start again. It was driving me crazy. *In the greatest way.*

My hands wandered across his silky-smooth chest and then down to his firm butt cheeks. I grabbed hold of them tightly in appreciation.

'Em,' he moaned. 'I might come pretty soon, but I promise to make up for it next time. One sec,' he said, pulling out quickly. 'Bend over, please. There. Over the arm of the sofa. I want to see your amazing bum.'

I leant over the soft velvet fabric, lifting my bottom in the air. Josh entered me from behind and his gentle thrusts suddenly became more urgent, pulling me into him with every stroke.

He plunged deeper and deeper and the rhythm grew faster. He removed his right hand from my waist and started rubbing my clit.

Oh my God.

Shockwaves shot straight through me. As he carried on stroking and thrusting, maintaining the perfect intensity and pace, my brain started swirling. I dug my nails into the sofa beneath me. I felt like an earthquake had erupted through my whole body. I was powerless to stop it.

Then I felt his body tense. Whilst my limbs wanted to flop onto the cushions and enjoy the warm, fuzzy feeling floating through my bloodstream, I used every bit of energy I had left to continue, pushing back onto him as he grinded into me. Josh's breathing quickly became heavier, until he let out a loud groan and finally collapsed on my back.

'Wow…' he panted. 'Wow! That was *incredible*.'

'It certainly was,' I said, trying to catch my breath. That had definitely exceeded my expectations.

'Did you come?' he said as he stroked my hair.

'I did indeed.'

'Then my work is done. Well, until round two anyway…'

'Looking forward to it already, Mr Carter.'

After a few minutes of holding me, Josh pulled out slowly, kissed me on the lips and went to the bathroom.

I peeled myself off the sofa and lay back down on the rug. My favourite soft and fluffy rug. Looking at it had always brought me pleasure, but tonight it had given me pleasure in a whole new way.

When Josh returned, he lay down beside me and wrapped his arms around my waist, I closed my eyes. This was a moment I wanted to savour for as long as possible. I was floating. Floating on my magical rug with this magical man. Soaring high into the clouds. Seeing stars. The brightest, most beautiful stars and knowing that I never, ever wanted to come back down to earth.

CHAPTER TWENTY-THREE

B est. Night. Ever.

Even though I was lying here on Josh's chest with his arms wrapped around me, I still couldn't quite believe it was true.

I closed my eyes again and enjoyed the flashbacks of last night.

After round one, we'd worked up an appetite, so I'd put on the spaghetti whilst Josh followed me around the kitchen kissing my neck and shoulders, nibbling on my ears, then stroking my breasts. It was all very distracting, but very enjoyable.

We'd eaten, enjoyed a few glasses of wine and chatted more about my art and how he was convinced I should consider getting back into it again when he did his silent stare thing, patted his leg and asked me to come and sit on him. Then round two took place on the dining chair and across the table. Once again, Josh didn't disappoint.

I remember us having more wine then, and everything past that point is a bit hazy. Neither of us could have managed another session after the epic length of round two. All that *exercise* combined with the alcohol finished us off.

I reckon I'd slept for a few hours, but now I was feeling a bit more human, my mind was racing, excitedly pressing rewind on my memories. I'd been dying to go to the loo for ages, but I didn't want to move. I wished I could stop time so that I could just lie here in his arms, forever.

The moment I moved, I would be returning to reality. I'd have to start thinking about what would happen next. Worrying if this would be the first and last time we'd sleep together. Whether things would be different between us. Everything can change after sex. I hoped that for us it would change for the better. Bring us closer. It certainly felt like it had last night.

I wouldn't overthink it. Well, I'd make a big effort to *try* not to anyway. I breathed in Josh's scent, and just as I felt myself floating back to sleep, a loud beeping noise boomed around the room.

Josh bolted up.

'Shit! What's the time?' he said, squinting at his watch. 'Shit! I've got to go.'

He jumped off the bed, cancelled the alarm on his phone, raced across the hall to the living room, then returned to the bedroom, pulling his T-shirt over his head and stepping into his jeans.

'Do you really have to go so soon?' I said, sitting upright. 'It's only five o'clock. I thought you didn't start at Cuppa until seven.'

'I don't, but I've got some stuff to do first and I have to get home and shower and then get there by six forty-five.'

'Not even time for another round?'

'I'd love to, but I really can't.'

'Okay, what about later today, then?'

'Sorry, I can't see you at all today.'

'Tomorrow, then?' I suggested.

'Not tomorrow either. Look, I'm really sorry, but I have to go. *Shit, shit shit!* Should've left sooner. Thanks for an amazing evening, though,' he said, leaning forward and quickly kissing me on the head. 'I'll call you.'

And with that, he was gone.

I sat up in the bed trying to process what had just happened. One minute I was dreaming about Josh, the next his alarm had gone off and he couldn't wait to get away from me.

Thanks for an amazing evening?

I'll call you?

Both classic lines used by guys hot-footing it out the door after a drunken one-night stand. And they'd just fallen out of Josh's mouth.

What the hell?

Was I wrong about him being different? And was I right to think that all men wanted was sex and once they'd got it, they immediately lost interest?

But it hadn't seemed that way last night. There was a closeness. A bond that I'd never felt before. I couldn't have imagined it all, surely?

I glanced at my phone. Only 5.09. What could he possibly have to do at five in the morning? I didn't get it. And once again, he couldn't see me at all today or tomorrow. What was it with Fridays and Saturdays?

I was going to drive myself crazy if I lay here and tried to figure it out. Somehow, I was going to have to get some sleep. After taking so many afternoons off to spend with Josh, I had a mountain of work to catch up on today, so I needed a clear head. Fat chance. Unless I could figure out what the hell had happened this morning, something told me I was going to find it very difficult to concentrate.

∾

'So, how was it? Can you walk?' said Chloe. 'No, Woody! Don't touch that!' she shouted.

'Woody? Who's Woody? And what is he touching?' I said.

'Sorry. I completely forgot that I had a day off and said I'd take a bunch of kids to Legoland today, so we're just at the train station and Woody's decided it would be fun to pick some disgusting dirty pink chewing gum off the floor. He's only three, bless him.'

'Shall I just call you later?' I said.

'If I'm not back too late, then definitely, but we're going to Candy's, one of the other mum's, for dinner afterwards. It totally slipped my mind. But just tell me quickly, was it as wonderful as you thought it would be?'

I paused. A few hours ago I was on cloud nine after the best night of my life. But Josh's abrupt departure had kind of tainted the experience. Too long a story to tell Chloe now as she had her hands full. Keep it simple.

'If you're asking about the sex, then yes,' I replied.

'Brilliant! No, no, no. Leave it. Woody! I said *don't touch that*!'

'Look, you'd better go. Maybe we'll catch up later?'

'Yes, thanks, Em, and glad you had a good workout!' she said, ending the call.

I buried my head in my knees. I felt like shit, and I couldn't even rely on caffeine to make me feel better. There was no way I could go to Cuppa this morning after what had happened earlier. That would be *way* too awkward.

Josh had clearly got what he wanted and then couldn't get out the door fast enough. I'd feel too embarrassed seeing him again in front of all those people. What if he had told his colleagues?

See? This was *exactly* what I was trying to avoid when Chloe had first suggested I talked to him. I didn't want to have to feel uncomfortable about getting my breakfast there if things didn't work out. And now look.

Like I'd said to Kat before, when I wasn't dating and was just chatting online, my mind was calmer. But as soon as I started taking things further, it went crazy.

Kat.

Kat!

Pretty sure she'd messaged me last night, but I was otherwise engaged. I launched WhatsApp.

Kat

Is tonight the big night? Let me know how it goes and if you want a catch-up tomorrow? I have childcare all weekend!! Xxx

Yes! Perfect timing.

Me

Sorry, for the late reply. I was with Josh…A catch-up

today would be brilliant. Head's all over the place and I've got severe overthinking-itis.

Seconds after I clicked send, Kat came online.

Kat

Whoop!

Oh dear! Yep, I get struck with overthinking-itis on a daily basis. I can meet around 7 if that's okay? My sister's collecting the kids at 6 and then returning them at 1 on Sunday!

Me

Wow! What you going to do with all that time? Sleep?

Kat

Well…Let's just say I'm planning to be in bed, but hopefully not sleeping!

Me

Whoop! Is this the same secret guy you went to lunch with last week?

Kat

Yep. And three times this week…Lunch dates are the new dinner dates. Easier to fit in during the working day without having to worry about childcare. Will fill you in later.

Me

Can't wait! Shall I come to your area or do you want to come over here?

Kat

Happy to come to yours. Any suggestions?

Me

There's a pub across the street that's nice. You can't miss it.

Kat

Perfect! See you there at 7 p.m.!

~

The day flew by. I knew I'd fallen behind on my work but hadn't realised how much until I started checking through my emails. It was a disaster.

All those times that I'd stopped working at two to meet Josh, the plan was to see him until seven, then come home and work until ten to catch up on everything I'd missed in the afternoon. But of course that hadn't happened.

Usually I'd come home, lie down on the bed and think about Josh. Get up, make dinner and think about Josh again. Tell myself I shouldn't be thinking about Josh, which would make me think about him even more.

The good thing about having so much to catch up on today was that I barely had time to think about what had happened this morning. It was only now that I was heading inside the pub to meet Kat that everything came flooding back again.

'Hey!' said Kat, walking towards the door and throwing her arms around me.

'Hey! And there I was thinking I was early,' I said.

'Well, my sister came at five-thirty, so I thought rather than wait around at home, I'd just come straight here. I knew you had a lot of work to do, so I didn't want to bother you about meeting earlier. I've just been relaxing here with a nice vodka and orange, which went down like a dream!'

'Good for you! Can I get you another?'

'Ooh, I wouldn't say no!' said Kat. 'I've got us a table over there in the corner.'

'Cool. I'll be over in a sec,' I said.

As I placed the drinks on the table, Kat was just finishing a call and grinning like a Cheshire cat.

'I can't wait either. See you tomorrow…No, you hang up. No, you! *No, you!*'

Clearly talking to her lover man. I'd never actually heard anyone do that *no, you hang up* thing in real life. Thought it was just in films. It was cheesy, but kind of cute at the same time.

'So, young lady,' I said when she eventually hung up. 'Tell me about this mystery man. What's his name and where did you meet?' Kat just sat there grinning. 'Well, come on! Spill!'

'It's Rob.'

'Rob?' I frowned. 'Rob who?' Kat grinned some more. 'What Rob, as in our WhatsApp Rob?'

'Yup!'

'You sneaky little pair! Wow! I did *not* see that one coming!' I said. 'Then again…now that I think about it, some of the recent messages I've seen in the group chat between you two have been quite flirtatious. Hmmm. *You sly little thing.* Anyway, I'm so happy for you! Rob's a great guy.'

'Oh, Em, he really is. He's such a gentleman. He treats me like a lady, you know? So respectful, so lovely, so… gosh, sorry. I'm gushing! I can't help it. I feel nineteen again. Minus the baby bump, of course.'

'Well, conception might happen tomorrow by the sounds of things…'

'Stop it!' she said, slapping me playfully. 'I'm not sure

about having any more kids. We'll just have to see how it goes. Early days, so I don't want to get ahead of myself. Well, I'll remind myself of that tomorrow, when hopefully my head has disappeared into the clouds after we've slept together.'

'Oh yes, I know the feeling of getting swept away after sex,' I said.

'Yes, yes!' she screamed. 'So tell me! How was it? What happened last night?'

I filled her in on the amazing time Josh and I had spent together, followed by him rushing off in the morning.

'Hmmm,' said Kat. 'I can understand why you feel upset. You have the perfect night, you wake up and have visions of having round three, followed by breakfast gazing into each other's eyes and whispering sweet nothings across the kitchen table, but instead, he jumps up and says he wishes he'd left sooner! I mean, yeah, he *could* have had stuff to do, like I don't know *what* exactly at that time, but maybe he was genuinely just late to do something?'

'Yeah, maybe,' I said, not entirely convinced.

'The never meeting on Fridays or Saturdays thing is a bit weird, though. Do you know where he lives, Em? Have you ever been to his house?'

'No, I haven't. Not yet. He lives in Vauxhall, though, so not too far away.'

'Hmm. Okay. Kind of reminds me of a guy I was dating years ago who was really cagey and could never meet me at weekends. Turned out he had a secret family in tow. He'd have his kids stay over at weekends and didn't want me to know. Which was strange, as he knew I had children, so I don't know why he lied.'

'What, you're saying you think Josh is hiding a secret family from me? That he has kids?' I said, my brain whirring.

'I've got no idea. I'm just saying what happened to me. He's definitely hiding something, though. I get that he's working on this secret dream thing, but you need to find out more about him and what he's not telling you before you get any deeper.'

'I know. It's driving me crazy! I don't think Josh has a secret family, though. I mean, we spoke about it. He said he didn't really have any close relatives in London.'

'Well, maybe they live *outside* of London and come down to see him at the weekends,' said Kat.

My head was spinning.

'No. It can't be that. Can it?' I said.

'Look, there's no point us sitting here and guessing. Especially as we're both overthinkers. You need to speak to him. Ask him. Outright. But in the meantime, don't over-obsess or think about it. Keep yourself busy. Don't you have any of Chloe's activities coming up?'

'Yeah, kind of. Tomorrow. Nothing in the daytime— I'd hoped to spend that with Josh, but I've got a gig tomorrow night. Which is something I set up myself.'

'Well, that sounds good,' said Kat, taking a sip of her drink. 'It seems like you and Josh have practically been seeing each other every day—well, apart from Fridays and Saturdays, of course. And whilst that's all wonderful, you have to still keep some of your independence. Don't revolve around him or get swept away too much. Still make time to do your own thing.'

That was a good point. I'd missed the last life drawing class because I'd been out with Josh, so I really should stick to those to make sure I was doing something for myself at least once a week.

'You're right. Maybe I'll see if Chloe fancies meeting up tomorrow for brunch and then I'll go home, play some music as I take my time getting ready and then head to the show.'

I was really excited about it. It had been years since I'd been to a gig.

'Good plan! Who are you seeing?' asked Kat.

'Sounds strange, but I'm not sure,' I said.

'You're going to a concert and you don't know who you're seeing?' Kat frowned.

'Yeah, it's this thing called Sofar Sounds. I found out about it through Spotify. You choose the area you want to go to, but the actual location of the gig is a secret and they don't reveal the address until the day before. It's always an intimate venue, so sometimes it's someone's living room, or it could be somewhere cool like a rooftop in the city,' I said, taking a sip of my drink. Actually, that reminded me: I should have checked my personal email for the details. The organisers would have sent them by now. 'Yeah, so once you find out where it is, then you go and watch a surprise line-up of artists. They've had people like James Bay and Bastille playing there in the past, so it's really exciting.'

'Very cool! Chloe's challenge has been life-changing for you, hasn't it?'

'It has, actually,' I replied, thinking about how far I'd come.

'How much longer do you have left?'

'Tomorrow officially marks the end of the challenge. It's gone by so fast. Don't tell her I said this, as her head will explode and she'll start her *I told you so* speech, but it's been totally worth it. I haven't been on social media properly for God knows how long and I haven't even looked at any dating apps.'

'Well, no need for them now that you're seeing Josh…'

'Yep! He's *amazing*,' I said, forgetting what had happened this morning, then quickly remembering again. 'Oh God! Do you really think he's got a secret family?'

'No idea. There's only one way to find out and that's to ask him. But like I said, try not to focus on Josh for now. Text Chloe and set up your lunch tomorrow, then go and enjoy your gig.'

'Will do. I'll have some me time this weekend, and then if I see Josh on Monday, I'll ask him. I need to know what he's hiding. Once and for all.'

T*-shirt and jeans. That'll do. I'd better bring a jumper too just in case.* It had been a while since I'd been to a gig, but I *did* remember that there was no telling how hot or cold it would be inside, so comfortable layers were always best.

Tonight I was going to my first Sofar Sounds event. When I'd checked my emails last night, the organisers had confirmed the secret residential location. I was excited to find out whether it would be in a flat or a house and what the bands would be like. Wherever it was and whoever was playing, I promised myself to forget about my worries for one night and just embrace every moment.

As everyone could bring their own food and drink, I stuffed my mini cans of pre-mixed Southern Comfort and lemonade and some snacks in my bag, along with a cushion to sit on just in case all the seating had gone by the time I arrived. It probably would have now as I should have left fifteen minutes ago, but I'd been on a bit of a go-slow, mulling over Kat's comments from last night and Chloe's thoughts from this afternoon.

On the whole, Chloe agreed with Kat. Whilst nothing was impossible, she wasn't convinced about the secret family thing, even remembering that when we'd first seen Josh, it was a Saturday. But then we reasoned that if they really *did* exist, they might have been on holiday that weekend. In the end she concluded, like Kat, that I just had to ask him.

As much as her gut feeling still said Josh was one of the good guys, she *did* admit that the fact I hadn't heard from him since he'd rushed out of the door on Friday morning wasn't exactly helping his case.

I'd been over and over it in my head a million times. Questioning why he hadn't messaged or called when a quick *hi* only took a second to write and whether I should call him. In the end, I decided to just focus on myself. So after I'd got home from brunch with Chloe, I'd set a lovely bubble bath, lit some candles, put on some music and just relaxed.

Trouble was, I was so relaxed, I fell asleep. And woke up at six forty-five—the time I was supposed to leave to get there for seven-thirty, which the organisers had recommended. I'd got ready and out the door in half an hour, but considering this was going to be a nice chilled night and no dressing up or make-up were really required, technically, I should have been able to do it in half the time. Instead, I wasted it on overthinking.

I got on the tube. 7.20. Shouldn't take more than half an hour to get to Old Street. Then according to Google Maps, it was nine minutes to walk to the mystery house or flat or whatever it was. If it started at eight, which I guessed it did, as they always liked you to get there a bit earlier, then I should still be okay.

Why aren't we moving? We've been sat here for at least five minutes. Come on...

We still haven't moved. I'm going to be so *late.*

'Apologies ladies and gentlemen,' the driver's voice blared through the carriage. 'We're being held at a red signal due to a passenger being taken ill on the train in front. We hope to be moving shortly.'

It was 7.37 and I was barely halfway. I was going to get there and there would be nowhere left to sit. They might even turn me away. *Dammit.*

7.59. I was outside the station. Directions. What was wrong with my phone? Why was there no reception? *Seriously? Not now. Not when I'm late*. And I was *dying* to go to the toilet. Like, I needed to wee *really* badly. It would be just my luck to turn up late *and* wet myself.

Shit.

Okay, okay. It was 8.11 and I was here.

'So sorry I'm late,' I whispered to the organiser as I stumbled through the door. Wow, this place was impressive. A loft apartment, and from what I could see from the limited view of the large room at the end of the hallway, it had stunning views. I started tapping my feet. The music sounded great too.

'No worries. You've missed about ten minutes of the first artist, who's *amazing*, but there's still a couple of songs to go. It's just in the living room, straight ahead at the end of the hall. There's a teeny bit of space at the back, so you should be able to grab a seat there,' she said.

Thank God. That was really kind of her. I know they liked everyone to be on time to avoid disrupting the artist's performance, so I was really grateful that they still let me in and I didn't have to wait until the interval.

'Thanks so much! I will.' I winced, crossing my legs, 'but I *desperately* need to go to the loo first. I'm bursting!'

'It's just before you get to the living room on the right,' she replied.

'Thank you,' I said, speed walking and ordering my bladder to hold on a few seconds longer.

The music boomed through the bathroom. The sound was *incredible*. So sharp, so clear, so raw. I wasn't even in the room yet but could already tell that this was going to be so much better than being stuck in a stadium or massive commercial venue. As I sat down, I found my feet tapping away again.

Actually, I recognised this song from Spotify. Yes! I remember it was on the Discover Weekly playlist they'd sent me and I'd saved it straight away. I pictured the cover image. The black-and-white image of the guy with his back to the camera. I *loved* this song.

Hurry up! Why was it that whenever you were in a rush, your bladder seemed to decide that it wanted to empty literally every drop of water in your body? It was as if I'd drunk a hundred bottles of Evian and now had a never-ending flow. I needed to get out there before the song ended.

Too late. It was finished. Now he was talking. I liked when they did that. When the singer engaged with the audience. I pulled up my knickers and jeans, washed my hands and shut the door gently behind me.

'The next song I'm going to sing was inspired by someone really special to me.'

Awww, sweet, I said to myself. I loved hearing about

what led an artist to write a song and the inspiration behind it.

'In fact, I only wrote and recorded it last week, so you guys are the first to hear it.'

Hold on.

That voice.

I recognised that voice.

It couldn't be?

I walked into the room and nearly fainted.

'It's called "Rainbow".'

Holy shit.

Sat at the head of the room on a stool, dressed in a white T-shirt, black waistcoat and jeans, clutching a guitar in front of several rows of people seated on the wooden flooring was him.

Josh.

What the hell?

I couldn't believe what I was seeing.

Josh was a *musician*? An *artist*? *That* was his secret? His dream? That's what he meant when he was talking about his *creativity*?

I slid down onto the floor in a corner at the back in a trance. I still couldn't take it all in.

The way he'd gushed about the paintings at the museum and been so enthusiastic about my work, I'd thought perhaps he was an artist, as in a painter. Not an actual *singer* artist. I didn't even know he could sing. Never mind play the keyboard that was sitting beside him, and of course the guitar he was strumming. There was a whole side of him that I knew absolutely nothing about.

Why didn't he just tell me?

And he couldn't be a complete beginner either. I'd

played that song I heard him performing whilst I was in the bathroom to death about two months ago and I remembered seeing his Spotify following. Whenever I added someone new to a playlist, I enjoyed checking out their monthly listeners, seeing what they looked like, where they came from, what other songs they'd made, how many streams each song had... I found it fascinating. I couldn't remember exactly, but I was sure for him it was something like half a million? Or maybe even a million?

I also remember being disappointed that his profile image didn't show his face. Just the back of his head and shoulders.

That's it! That's what was familiar when he was facing away from me and putting stuff on the shelves at Cuppa. I *knew* I recognised something about him.

And there was no information about him in the bio either. I can't even think what his name was. What did he call himself? Did he have a stage name? Or was that just for actors?

Before you, life was black and white
Now everything shines so bright...

God, he's good. That *voice!* How could he keep this from me? Why did he want to? He was *so* talented. I would have supported him. Been happy for him. I didn't get it?

Everything is in colour...

He said he wrote and recorded this song last week about someone that was special to him? Last week? How did you even finish a song that quickly? Didn't it need to go through loads of music producer people or studios or something? I knew nothing about how this record stuff worked. I just liked listening and dancing to music. I hadn't given the rest of it much thought before. I'd never had any need to.

Wait, did he just mention *viewing his favourite art and picnicking in the park*? That's what we did. Was this…? Could this song be about me?

Your eyes, your smile,
Your curls, your style…

Shit! I think it is!

I love you and I want you to know
You are, darling, you are my rainbow…

I couldn't move. I couldn't breathe. This was so much to take in. Josh was a singer. Josh was here performing. Josh had written a song about me. *Little old me?* And wait: he loved me? I was his *rainbow*? Could it be true?

I pinched myself to check I wasn't dreaming. Ouch! Squeezed a little too hard there. At least that confirmed that I was definitely awake. This was actually happening.

Bloody hell.

As he finished the final chord, he gazed into the crowd, grinning at the rapturous applause and whooping from the audience. Then it happened.

He saw me.

Our eyes met.

At first he frowned. Then squinted. Next his eyes bulged out of their sockets as he clearly struggled to believe that I was here. That I'd seen him. That his secret was out.

But then his face softened into a smile. He chuckled, shaking his head in a kind of *what are the chances* way and winked. I couldn't be sure, but I sensed warmth. That maybe he was happy I was there?

I felt butterflies dancing in my stomach, which jolted

me out of my trance. I couldn't quite decide how I was feeling. Shocked? *You can say that again.* Hurt? Yes. Angry? A little. He should have told me. Been honest. I'd opened up to him about my life. Why did he feel like he couldn't do the same? Especially if he loved me.

Oh my God. *He loves me!*

Equally, though, I was relieved. If this was his secret, then it wasn't bad at all. He probably didn't have a secret family. I'm guessing he'd just been busy preparing for this gig. And man was he good. Bloody *brilliant*. His voice was so smooth. *Soulful. Rich.* Josh was super talented.

As well as all of the emotions swirling around me, I was also proud. This was *my* guy. And he'd written a song about *me*. Imagine that? I still couldn't get over it. Well, at least I hoped it was about me. Otherwise, he had even more explaining to do…

The room fell silent as the crowd waited to hear what was coming next.

Josh got up from the stool and moved over to sit behind the keyboard.

'This is my last song. It's about another person who was a major part of my life who sadly passed away. It's called "Make You Proud". '

As he started playing, I took a second to look around the room. Until now, I'd been so fixated on Josh. There were at a guess around sixty people here. Some seated on the large squishy grey sofas, others on some dining room chairs, but most were sitting on cushions on the oak flooring. I'd completely forgotten about mine, which was tucked away in my bag. Well, I wasn't exactly expecting to see Josh was one of tonight's performers, was I? I took it out and slid it underneath me.

When I feel that it's all too much
I keep going and tell myself I can't give up
Because I wanna make you proud
If I'm trying to write a song,
Whenever everything feels like it's going wrong
I tell myself I must stay strong
Because I wanna make you proud...

Oh my goodness. His grandma. Josh had written a song about his beloved grandma. As I listened to the lyrics, my heart began to melt.

Apart from the sound of his voice and the chords he was playing on the keyboard, the room was silent. Normally at a gig people are chatting with their friends, taking photos and posting on Insta rather than enjoying the artist and living in the moment. That wasn't the case here. Everyone was giving Josh their full undivided attention. There was no conversation from the crowd. No unnecessary noise. You could literally hear a pin drop.

Josh was sat in front of the large floor-to-ceiling windows, which had a clear view of the London skyline, but it wasn't the buildings the audience were struck by. Everyone was captivated, utterly mesmerised by his voice. Some were gently swaying to the beat. One lady put her arm around her boyfriend and rested her head on his shoulder. His music was touching people. Moving them. Evoking emotions. What a gift he had.

By the time he'd finished singing the last note, tears were streaming down my cheeks. The song was so beautiful. I felt every word. It summed up all the love I'd sensed he had for his grandma when he'd spoken about her that night in the restaurant. And the way he played those keys. *Wow.*

'That's all from me,' Josh said, mopping his forehead with his hanky and standing up to address the crowd. 'Thank you, Sofar, for having me, and thanks so much to each and every one of you for coming out tonight to support me. You've been an *amazing* audience. My name is JC, goodnight.'

The audience applauded and whooped. The clapping and cheering went on for so long that Josh began to blush. He put his hands together several times to give thanks. I had no doubt that the other two performers would be great, but even an established artist would find his performance a tough act to follow.

'Give it up one more time for JC!' said the host enthusiastically and the cheering continued. He patted Josh on the back and explained to the audience that there would now be a ten-minute break before the next act appeared.

Ten minutes wasn't a lot of time, but it was enough for us to at least have a brief conversation. As proud and as bowled over I was with what I'd just witnessed, I still needed answers from Josh. Why had he kept this from me? And what other secrets did he have? I needed an explanation. And I needed it *now*.

CHAPTER TWENTY-FIVE

'Hey, Em,' said Josh as he walked towards me, then took my hands in his.

'You were *amazing*, man! *Amazing*!' said a guy from the audience as he headed to the bathroom.

'Ah, thanks. Thanks so much.' Josh smiled.

'Can we go somewhere to chat, please?' I said quietly. This was so awkward and confusing. On the one hand, I wanted him to take a moment to soak this all up. Take in the praise and admiration from the audience. He'd given an amazing performance and was probably on a high, so I didn't want to rain on his parade. But on the other, my head was spinning, crying out for answers, and I didn't want to wait any longer to get them.

'Sure. I know this is probably a big shock and you've got loads of questions, and of course I'll explain. It's just, I can't right now, though,' he replied softly. 'I need to clear away my stuff to make way for the next artist and watch them perform. It's important for us to support each other.

But I can sit with you. That is if you can bear to be beside me?'

Whilst I was disappointed, I had to admit that made sense. Everyone was here to watch the artists perform. Josh was here pursuing his dream. Trying to make a good impression. Whatever the reason he'd hidden this from me, I didn't want to jeopardise his future. I would just need to be patient. Wait a bit longer. In the grand scheme of things, I supposed another hour wouldn't make a difference. I shrugged my shoulders without saying a word, which Josh took as a green light, because after he'd picked up his keyboard, the stand and his guitar, then taken them into the room opposite the bathroom, he came back and squeezed into the gap next to me.

Josh was so close I could taste his fresh, woody scent. I really wanted to throw my arms around him. To kiss him. It was only yesterday morning that we'd seen each other, but somehow it felt like it had been forever. I'd missed him.

But I couldn't get all sentimental. This wasn't just some little hobby he'd kept to himself. This was *major*. I know he'd said this dream was *his life,* but I didn't realise it was on this scale.

Once the second act performed, there was another interval, but Josh spent most of the time queuing for the toilet and talking to people who were keen to know where he'd be performing next. After the final act had finished, the crowd got up and began chatting amongst themselves.

Finally we'd get to talk.

'So, can we go somewhere? Somewhere private?' I asked as I stood up and pushed my cushion back into my bag.

'JC!' said a pretty twenty-something as she touched his arm. 'Amazing performance! You're going to be *huge*!'

'Thanks!' Josh smiled, then glanced back at me. 'Sorry. Yes. Yes, we should—'

'JC, this is Alice,' said one of the organisers, who had a beautiful raven-haired woman beside her. 'She'd like to interview you for *Sound* magazine.'

'Great!' Josh's eyes bulged excitedly. 'It's really nice to meet you, Alice.' He shook her hand. 'I *love Sound* magazine!'

'There's a room down on the hall on the left. You know, where you stored your stuff? If you guys need to chat, maybe it will be quieter there?' suggested the Sofar lady.

'Brilliant, thank you,' said Josh before glancing at me again. 'Sorry, Em, back in a minute.'

I waited half an hour. Which then became forty minutes. The audience had disappeared and the only people left were the Sofar team. I even offered to help tidy up so that I didn't look like some sad groupie.

I passed the toilet a couple of times, which was opposite the room, just to see if they sounded like they'd be finishing any time soon. And, yeah, I'll admit, also because I was a little paranoid. It was only natural. The magazine woman, Alice, was attractive and she was clearly impressed with Josh. As they'd walked away I heard her gushing about how *phenomenal* his performance was. And she touched his arm too. What was with all these women touching his arms? Those arms were meant for *me*. Just yesterday they were wrapped around *me*. Now it felt like every woman in London seemed to think she had the right to stroke them.

From what I could hear the last time I walked by, they had no intention of wrapping up the interview anytime soon. All I could hear was lots of giggling and laughter.

Sod it.

Like Kat had said, I couldn't revolve around him. I had to have my own life. This Alice woman seemed influential. This interview was important to him, so he wasn't going to want to rush it. And I wouldn't want him to. This could be great for Josh. I wanted him to do well. I really did. He shouldn't have to be apologising or worrying about keeping me waiting. This sounded like the opportunity of a lifetime. It was just, because of what had happened to me before, I couldn't help but feel insecure. The longer he was in there and I was out here, the more paranoid I was going to become. It sounded like they were getting on like a house on fire, so who knew what would happen next? Maybe she'd make a pass at him and he'd just go with the flow because she had promised him a big spread in her fancy magazine and he would feel that he couldn't say no. Surely a kiss or a quickie was a small price to pay to achieve his lifelong dream?

But no. Josh wasn't like that. He had integrity. He was professional and honest. Wasn't he? Then again, he'd kept all this from me, so what else would he be prepared to hide?

Oh God. Oh God. Oh God.

My head was all over the place. I couldn't handle this. I needed to get out of here before I wound myself up so much that I burst into the room and either didn't like what I saw or ended up embarrassing myself.

I had to go home. *Right now.*

~

I heard a buzzing sound. I opened my eyes and saw my phone screen light up as it vibrated on the bedside table.

Josh.

12.37 a.m.? I must have left around eleven. What had he been doing for the past hour and a half?

I don't like this. I don't like that I'm wondering where he's been and what he's been doing. I hate it.

The phone rang out.

Next the doorbell rang.

I rubbed my eyes, then dragged myself out of bed and into the hallway. I clicked on the intercom.

'Hello?'

'It's me. Can I come up, please? *Please*. We need to talk.'

Those words. *We need to talk.* Exactly what Eric had said to me when I'd caught him with Nicole.

My head was spinning. I wanted to hear what Josh had to say, but I was afraid to. What if tonight was just the tip of the iceberg? What if there were more secrets?

I guessed the sooner I found out, the sooner I could try and get over him. I pressed the buzzer and within seconds he was at my front door.

'I'm so sorry about earlier,' he said as he stepped inside. 'The interview went on for ages, but it was a really great opportunity, so I...Em?'

'So you're only sorry that the interview went on for ages. Not about the fact that you're a bloody pop star and didn't even tell me?' I shouted.

Whoa. That came out perhaps a little more aggressively than I'd intended. But I was nervous. Scared—in fact, *terrified*—of getting hurt again, so I supposed I was lashing out with frustration and fear. I needed to calm down. At least give him a chance to explain. Yes. Try and be reasonable. *Try*...

'I'm sorry. I wanted to tell you.' He stepped forward and rested his hands on my shoulders. 'I was *going* to tell you. When we saw each other on Monday. I just didn't want to jinx it, you know? I wanted to get those gigs out the way first, make sure they went well, and then I was going to tell you. Of course I wanted to.'

'But you *didn't*.' I shook his hands from my shoulders. 'You kept it a secret. Men *always* keep secrets. Just like Eric.' The words flew from my mouth before I could stop them.

'*Oh, Emily*...' Josh's face fell. 'You can't compare me to Eric. I wasn't trying to hurt you or do anything bad or wrong. I just needed to be sure it was going to work out this time. My music career, I mean. Last time, everything was so out of control. I just needed to take things slowly. Do things on my own terms.'

'Last time?' I frowned and placed my hands on my hips. 'What do you mean *last time*?'

'This isn't the first time I've done music. The last time, the *first* time, I was eighteen. I was *really* into my music. *Desperate* to make it. I spent all my time locked away in my bedroom writing songs. I'd done it for years. I think it was my kind of escapism. From all the problems at home. Dad leaving us, Mum being depressed. It was my release. I tried everything to break into the industry. It wasn't like today, where you've got Spotify and so many other platforms to showcase your work. Then I saw an ad. Looking for *talented singers*. I went to the audition. They were putting together a *serious soulful band*, the manager said. *Finally*, I thought. *This is it: my big break*. I got in the group. I was over the moon. He gave me a contract to sign. Said we'd be successful, credible artists. And I believed him.'

'What happened?' I asked, sitting down on the wooden hallway floor. Josh joined me.

'In a nutshell, I got well and truly shafted. Because I was so desperate and hungry for success, to get my voice heard, I didn't check the contract. It wasn't a serious soulful group, it was some cheesy pop boyband. And I hadn't been chosen for my singing or musical talent. They wanted me because they thought the female fans would like me. That it would help sell more records. They gave us shitty songs which we had no input in whatsoever and they worked us like dogs. No, worse than that. I went months without a single day off.'

'But what about your parents?' I tucked my knees beneath my chin. 'Or rather your mum?'

'She was still out of it. She wasn't herself. She was still a mess from Dad leaving. She didn't know the first thing about legal stuff or what the hell was going on. She could barely look after herself.'

'So how did you get out of it?'

'I used the little time we did get off to research contracts and clauses to try and break free. Found a really helpful lawyer who had a son my age and wanted to help. It took ages. By the time I finally got released, I'd been in the band for two years. Two years of absolute hell. I didn't do anything for another year after that. I was broken. Broken by the relentless schedules. Broken by the fame. *Everything*.'

'The fame?' I frowned again.

'Yeah, I guess you could say we were well known. We had a few top ten singles in the UK and were really popular in Asia, so there was a lot of travelling.'

'What was the name of the band?'

'LDN Boys.'

I scanned my memory, trying to think of the groups that were popular at that time. I thought I remembered them, actually.

'LDN Boys? That band with that song…what was it called? "Baby Be Mine"? No. "Baby You're"…?'

'"Baby You're the One",' Josh finished.

'No way!' My eyes popped out of my head. 'That was *you*? That group was pretty big!'

'Kind of,' he said modestly.

Yes, I *definitely* remembered them. They were on all the music TV shows back in the day and on the radio. How they all looked was a bit of a blur, but I did recall hearing their songs. *Wow.* I would have thought he'd enjoyed that experience though, surely?

'But isn't that every eighteen-year-old's dream? Being in a band? Having screaming girls throwing themselves at you?'

'To an extent, yes. But if you've always wanted to be a serious artist and are singing bubblegum pop, doing stupid dance routines and working twenty-hour days, seven days a week, month after month with no way out, with everything you do or say being controlled like you're a puppet, then no. It's not a dream. It's a *nightmare*.' Josh grimaced. 'That's the bit they don't show you. Being stuck with three other guys you hate. Watching them spiralling out of control, off their head on drugs when we're supposed to be some squeaky-clean band. You have no idea what goes on behind the scenes. It can be ugly. Believe me.'

Gosh. He was right. I never would have thought that a group like that would be stoned. Their songs were always so sweet and innocent.

'So when you got out you must have been glad, but you said you were broken? Because of the pressure?'

'Yeah, that and the exhaustion. And also the fame thing. It's hard to explain.' He rested his back against the white walls and stretched his legs out in front of him to try and make himself more comfortable. 'When you're that young and everyone's kissing your arse, telling you what you want to hear and how amazing you are, you start to believe it. Everyone wants to be your friend. All the people that didn't give you the time of day at school and college suddenly tell everyone that you're besties. Guys want to hang out with you to get girls, girls want to hang out with you so they can brag that they slept with a guy from a band and then suddenly you leave the group and no one wants to know you. Worse, they *pity* you. You used to be famous, but now you've failed. When you're barely twenty and you don't have the experience or mental capacity to process that, it's tough. My true friends, Doug and Phil, tried to understand, but they were the same age as me. It was hard enough trying to figure out their own lives, never mind attempting to get their heads around what I'd been through. That's when I started seeing more of my grandma. Without her support, I wouldn't have pulled through.'

'*God.*' I raised my eyebrows. 'I didn't realise. I always thought being a pop star was super glamorous. So I don't understand? How did you get into law, and if the music industry is so awful, why do you want to be part of it again?'

'Well, because I got royally screwed over with that contract, it drove me to look into law as a career. To help other people avoid the same fate as me. That was the ideal-istic view I had, but as I explained before, the reality didn't quite pan out that way. And why go into it again? Because music is my passion. It's who I am. It always has been. I tried to suppress it, but it would always come back. I knew I was happiest when I was writing or making music. My grandma used to love listening to me sing. Sometimes she'd literally say I had to sing for my supper! She wouldn't feed me unless I'd sung her a song.' He strained a smile.

'That's really sweet,' I said, my heart thawing.

'Yeah. So she encouraged me to pursue it. To try again. But my brain was fried. When I was at the firm, I couldn't write. Then on the night after her funeral, I woke up in the middle of the night with an idea for a song and wrote the lyrics for "Make You Proud". It was like she was there with me, pushing me to pursue my dream. So I had to do it. I had to go for it.'

'That's amazing. I love that you're brave enough not to give up. What do you think will be different this time around?' I asked, thinking after what happened before that it would have put him off for good. Once bitten, twice shy and all that.

'The difference now is that this time I'm older and wiser. My eyes are wide open. And I'm doing things on my terms. I haven't shown my face on any of my covers, so people can judge me purely on my music. I don't have a record label. I'm doing it all myself. My own way. I don't have to answer to anyone.'

'That's great. And I'm glad you didn't give up, because you're *so good*. What am I saying? You're not just good. You're *great*!' I moved closer to him. The frustration I'd felt earlier began to slip away. Whilst I wasn't happy that he'd kept it a secret from me, I began to understand. After his past experience, he clearly wanted to make things right this time around and take everything at his own pace. I couldn't be angry with him. Just remembering how well he performed made me excited about his future. 'People *loved* you tonight. I didn't even realise it until this evening, but I was already a fan. I've had your songs on my playlists for months.'

'Really?' he said. 'You've listened to my music? You like my songs?'

'I have, and I really do, Josh,' I said, gazing into his eyes.

'Wow!' His face lit up. 'Thanks. That means a lot. And, Em,' he said, taking my hands in his and squeezing them tight, 'I really am sorry I didn't tell you before. It wasn't done for malicious reasons or to be deliberately dishonest. It's just, like I said, I didn't want to jinx it, and these past few weeks have been so intense. Juggling work at Cuppa, writing and recording songs, preparing for these gigs, but wanting to see you at the same time.'

'I wasn't sure you wanted to see me anymore.' I hung my head. 'I thought once you'd slept with me, that was it.'

'*What?*' His brow furrowed. '*Seriously?* You can't have thought that. Not after Thursday night. That was amazing. Wasn't it?'

'Well, I thought it was, but when you woke up, you

couldn't leave fast enough, and then I didn't hear from you. No call, no text. Nothing.'

'Oh shit. I'm so sorry. You know I'm not normally like that. I always call when I say I will. I just had so much to do. And that morning, I didn't mean to rush off. It's just that although I thought that *maybe* you wanted me to stay the night, I wasn't sure, and I told myself that if something *did* happen, I'd reset my alarm for three-thirty to give myself enough time to get back and get everything prepared. But we had such a great time, the last thing I was thinking of was changing my alarm.'

'But what did you need to leave at three-thirty for?'

'To prepare for Paris.'

'Paris?' What the hell was he doing there?

'Yeah. I did a gig there last night. And it was really tight, but when the opportunity came up at the last minute, it was too good to turn down. What I'd planned to do was to come home in the early hours and pack my guitar, laptop and stuff to bring with me, because as soon as I finished my shift at one-thirty, I had to go straight to St Pancras to catch the Eurostar by three. It was already a challenge, and because I was leaving work earlier than usual, I couldn't turn up late for my shift as the boss was already pissed about me taking time off, which made it extra stressful.'

'So when did you get back to London?'

'I stayed over in Paris, but after the show I spent most of the night trying to do more work on a song on my laptop, then got the Eurostar this morning and slept the whole journey. Came back, finished a track, then started rehearsals for tonight. I literally haven't stopped. That's the only reason why I rushed off and haven't called or messaged. Not because I didn't want to be with you. I thought that was clear from the evening we spent together. Did that feel like a one-night stand to you?'

'No, but—'

'Em,' he said, wrapping his arms around my waist. 'Surely you must know what you mean to me. Did you hear that song tonight? "Rainbow"? I wrote that about you, after we got back from our first picnic. I felt so...so incredible. *You* made me feel incredible. The words just flowed onto the page.'

I still couldn't get my head around it. I remembered him mentioning the word *rainbow* when he was at my place and saying how vibrant he thought my personality was, but never would I have thought he'd have written a song about me. Then again, I hadn't even known he was a singer. *Wow.*

'That's...that's so lovely, Josh,' I said as a warm feeling shot through my body. 'Thank you.' I blushed.

'No, thank *you* for inspiring me. Everything I say in that song is true. The fact that I feel so happy, so bright, so alive when I'm with you, and of course the fact that I'm madly in love with you.'

Is this a dream? Some sweet, wonderful fantasy? It must be. This is crazy.

'You *are*?' I know that's what the song said, but afterwards I'd told myself not to jump to conclusions, as I couldn't be sure he hadn't just added those words to make it sound more romantic.

Wow. Wow. Wow. I'd fallen in love with Josh almost instantly, but never in my wildest dreams did I think he'd fallen for me so soon too. The millions of butterflies that had set up home in my stomach since Josh had come on the scene were jumping around like they were doing a Jive in the *Strictly Come Dancing* finals.

'Yes! *Completely and utterly*. I wanted to tell you on Thursday night, but then I thought because we'd had sex, it might seem a bit, y'know? Disingenuous? Like I was just saying it because I was caught up in the moment. I wanted to wait until the right time, which of course is impossible to find. Didn't quite plan for you to hear me first say those words in front of a room full of strangers...' He chuckled. 'But I love that song. I wanted to perform it because it's all about *you*. Your gorgeous smile, the way you crinkle your nose when you taste something you don't like, how naturally beautiful you look in the mornings when you're all fresh-faced and your gorgeous curls just look so sexy, how comfortable I feel when I'm with you, the way you understood when I said I wasn't ready to talk about my project...God, I love you *so* much.'

Josh pulled me into him, and as soon as his lips touched mine, I felt totally overcome. It was like I'd been swept up in a cyclone. A whirlwind of the warmest, fuzziest, happiest emotions. My stomach fluttered, my heart raced, my head spun relentlessly like a spinning top. Everything felt so light. So *euphoric*.

Josh loves me.

The man that I was crazy about, the man *I* loved, was crazy about me too. He accepted me as I am. My curls, my quirks, my habits, my hang-ups, my insecurities, my uniqueness. He saw them and he still loved me. *All* of me.

I'd loved Josh since, well...it sounds insane, but like I said, it was very early on. I'm convinced that I fell for him the night we went to the pub. *Nuts*. Of course I'd tried to suppress those feelings. I mean, come on: I barely knew him, so how could I even contemplate *loving* him? Especially given the bad experiences I'd had with men before. It made no sense. But the more time we spent together, the more obvious it became. When I was with Josh, I couldn't take my eyes off him. He made me feel high. And when I *wasn't* with him, he was all I could think about. Maybe I was still blinded by the newness of love, but there wasn't anything about him that I didn't adore. Sounded soppy, but it was true.

I'd never have been brave enough to admit my feelings, though. Not without first knowing he felt the same way. Even though I was always so comfortable around Josh and he made me feel like my heart would be safe in his hands, part of me was still cautious. *Sensitive.* Bruised by the past. So like Josh, I'd been holding on. Waiting for the right moment to say those words. And that moment had undoubtedly come. The time was right.

'I love you too, Josh,' I said as our lips parted and my mind and body floated back down to earth. 'With all my heart.'

And just like that it all made sense. I understood.

They say everything happens for a reason, and I could see that every single thing I had been through had led to this. All the pain I'd felt after being cheated on, the fear of dating again, hiding away inside my flat and pushing myself to accept Chloe's challenge, had all been worthwhile because it had led me to this moment.

Led me to finding myself again.

Led me to finding Josh.

My true love.

My soulmate.

CHAPTER TWENTY-SIX

'Congrats!' said Chloe as we clinked glasses. 'You did it!'

'Thanks!' I said, taking a sip of Buck's Fizz, wondering if noon was too early to indulge in drinking alcohol on a Monday.

'You are officially the first graduate of the G.O.O.T.H slash G.E.T.H.O.O.T.H challenge.'

I tried to work out what she meant. *Nope.* Far too many letters.

'Gooth? What?' I frowned.

'Yes. Get out of the House, or Get Em the Hell out of the House,' she cackled.

'That's what you called it?'

'No, not really!' said Chloe. 'I just made that up. Although technically you live in a flat and not a house, but it does have a certain ring to it, though, don't you think?' She winked.

'Funny. And also *rude*,' I chuckled.

'It's true, though. After that whole Eric debacle, I was

worried that if I didn't take drastic action, you'd never see daylight again!'

She had a point. I might have still been in bed now feeling sorry for myself. Wasn't it funny how life was? Something bad happens and at the time, you just can't see a way past it.

'I was pretty low, wasn't I?'

'Er, yes! But let's forget about all that. You've moved on from that todger and being permanently attached to your phone screen.'

'Yeah, thank God.' I winced, remembering that morning Chloe had found me sobbing on my bed.

'So tell me: after two months of living in real life and getting out of your four walls, how are you feeling?'

'Bloody *amazing*!' I gushed. 'And I know you're probably going to spend the next couple of hours gloating, bathing in a river of *I told you sos* and swimming in a sea of self-praise, but do you know what? I don't care, because I'm woman enough to admit that you were right.'

'I was *what*?' said Chloe, clutching her ear.

'I said, you were…you heard what I said, Chloe.' I took another swig of my Buck's Fizz. 'I know I said I'd admit it, but let's not milk it!'

'I'm only teasing! Yes, I could sit here feeling smug, but my pleasure right now comes not from knowing that I was right to set you the challenge, which of course I *was*— sorry, couldn't resist *one* self-plug!—*no*, like I said, it doesn't come from that. It comes from seeing you so ridiculously happy. I mean, look at you! If I got a scrubbing brush the size of America, I still wouldn't be able to wipe that enormous smile off your face. You're *glowing*. Everything. Your eyes, your skin…it's like the entire

IKEA lighting department has just been switched on inside your face. It's *ridiculous*! Ridiculously *brilliant*. I love it!'

'I know,' I said, my grin widening. 'I can't help it…'

'Love will do that to you,' said Chloe. 'And the fact that you've now discovered Josh is some hunky musician who's written a truckload of songs about you being the bee's knees has got to help.'

She wasn't wrong. Never in my wildest dreams had I felt like this level of happiness was even possible. I remembered sitting in my bedroom so many times listening to Spotify and thinking how wonderful it would be if someone adored me enough to declare their undying love for me in a song. But that was just fairy-tale stuff. Not something I'd ever really expected to happen in real life. It was nuts.

'Yeah, it is an incredible feeling. I still can't quite get my head round it all. And him singing to me, actually serenading me, is a whole new level of awesomeness. It's like being a queen. He makes me feel like I'm the most special person in the whole world. Not to mention the fact that it's a real turn-on…'

'I bet! Sounds like as well as giving you a tour of his house last night, he also put on quite a performance…'

'He certainly did,' I said, reminiscing about the memorable encounter on his studio chair.

After Josh and I had finished talking and 'making up' at my flat in the early hours of Sunday morning, he'd suggested that I visit his house that afternoon so that he could show me the home studio he had built using the money he'd saved from his job as a lawyer and get more of an insight into what he did when he locked himself away in there. Not that I had anything to compare it to, but it looked very impressive. There were loads of different instruments—his keyboard, multiple guitars, drums, laptops, microphones, headphones and other technical-looking equipment with all kinds of dials and knobs.

Josh had kitted his studio out nicely. In fact, his whole house was lovely. It was a Victorian property with large rooms. All simple in terms of style. Lots of modern art on the walls, but not much furniture. He had a neutral colour scheme and original wooden flooring throughout. He'd said he'd like me to paint a mural in the studio and in the bedroom, so I promised to start thinking of some ideas.

In the bedroom, the flooring had been painted white and there was a silver/grey colour scheme. *Mmm.* Such a gorgeous bedroom too. It had a big, strong king-size iron bed with a thick silver faux fur throw at the bottom. At least that's where it was when we started…I enjoyed my time there. Almost as much as the impromptu experience that happened after Josh serenaded me…

'Thinking about the studio escapade again, are you?' said Chloe.

How does she always see inside my mind? It's so annoying.

'*Maybe…*' I smiled.

'And all the buttons he was pushing?'

'Stop!' I laughed.

'I'm sure that wasn't what you were saying to Josh!' she cackled. 'More like *don't stop*!'

'Why oh why did I tell you about that?' I rolled my eyes.

'Because I'm your best friend!'

'*Me and my mouth.* I must learn not to tell you anything about my bedroom activities in future…'

'But it happened in the studio, so it doesn't count!' said Chloe.

She didn't miss a trick, that one. Always teasing me.

'Anyway'—I rolled my eyes again—'back to talking about my completion of your challenge! So that's it. Two months of activities done and dusted. Here,' I said, reaching into my bag and taking out a shiny new polka dot notepad. 'I'm guessing you used up a lot of pages in the one you have for the challenge, so I thought you might need a new one.'

'Oh, Em! It's beautiful. You didn't have to get me anything.'

'It's nothing. Thank you for forcing—I mean, *encouraging* me to do the challenge.'

'You're welcome. I'm just pleased it worked. That you got off your phone and back out into the real world, trying new things, meeting new people, making new friends, and of course finding love offline. Now I must admit, I wasn't quite expecting you to meet such a gem of a man too. Especially not that quickly. I thought by the end of the challenge, maybe you'd start courting someone, you know, through just doing things that you enjoyed rather than consciously looking for someone. I thought this would just be a way to get you started. Josh was an unexpected cherry on top.'

'*Definitely*. And the funny thing was, I didn't even meet him at any of the activities you organised. He ended up being right here in front of me, working just a stone's throw away from my front door. I found a man who's into art and loves music like me. We have so much in common. It's amazing. What are the chances?'

'Some things are just meant to be!' She grinned. 'You

just have to believe and put yourself into the path of opportunity. In fact, what am I saying, doubting my match-making and predictive love skills?' Chloe folded her arms. 'Now that I think about it, I *did* kind of predict it.'

'Really?' I rested my finger on my chin. 'I don't remember you getting out your crystal ball and saying that you saw a barista or a musician in my future?'

'No, I didn't *explicitly*. But when I said you wouldn't meet anyone if you were stuck inside all the time, you scoffed and said something like "well, I'm not going to meet anyone walking to this coffee shop, am I?" and I said that you didn't know that for sure. Ringing any bells?'

Hmmm. Now that I thought about it, I think I remembered her saying something like that. *Typical.* Why did she always have to be right?

'Okay, Mrs Clairvoyant. Maybe you should buy us both a lottery ticket.'

'If only I could predict the winning numbers. Then we'd be having a champagne brunch at the Ritz rather than drinking cheap Buck's Fizz at the local pub.'

'Well, I thought it would be better to come here than go to Cuppa. For the purposes of conversation at least.'

'Too right! I wouldn't be able to get two words out of you if we'd gone there. You'd be too busy swooning over Josh or disappearing outside to grope each other or some-thing. Surprised he even made it into work this morning.'

Mmm…now there's a thought.

As much as I loved Chloe, the idea of being with Josh right now was certainly appealing. We'd only been apart for a couple of hours and I was already missing him.

'That's Josh. He'd never pull a sickie. He wouldn't want to let them down. Even though he started at eleven today, rather than at the crack of dawn like he normally does, it was still a struggle to prise ourselves apart.'

'Thought as much, hence you pushing our Monday morning catch up to lunchtime. *Go for it, girl.* You deserve this happiness. I know I tease you, but it's all love. I really am chuffed to bits for you, Em.' She reached over to give me a hug.

'Thanks, Chloe,' I said, giving her a big squeeze.

'You're welcome, sweetheart. It wasn't so bad, was it? Living life offline? When Archie heard about the challenge, he said I was evil. That twenty-four-hour access to social media was a basic human right. When I said I'd send him to a summer camp with no internet access for a month, he soon changed his tune…'

'I bet he did!' I laughed. 'Teenagers wouldn't be able to function without Wi-Fi. I admit, it was really hard at first. I'd become so addicted without even realising it. But as time went on, the easier it became. I do still look at social media occasionally, but it's more of an afterthought. Something I do if I have a spare two minutes, whereas before I used to check Instagram, Facebook, Twitter religiously as soon as I woke up in the morning, multiple times throughout the day and always last thing at night. My life revolved around it. I'd get severe FOMO if I hadn't checked my feeds for more than a couple of hours. Not anymore, though.'

'And do you miss it? Have that fear of missing out? Bet you thought I wouldn't know what FOMO meant, eh?' She chuckled.

'Very good. Well done!' I laughed. 'Your kids taught you well! To answer your question, no, I really don't. In fact, hold on,' I said, reaching into my bag for my phone.

'You're not checking social media now, are you?'

'Nope. The opposite. I reckon now is the perfect time to get rid of the dating apps. To prove to myself how far I've come and show how much I believe in Josh and our future together.' I tapped on each app, one by one, and deleted them. With every click I felt lighter. As far as I was concerned, I'd found the one, so the search was over. No more swiping. No more empty messaging. No more drama. *What a relief.*

'Cheers to that!' said Chloe as we clinked glasses again. 'I'm so proud of you. Next stop, eliminating social media?'

'Hmm. I don't know if I'll get rid of social media alto-gether. Everything in moderation and all that. I've unfol-lowed all the people who made me feel bad and now, rather than being obsessed with watching other people doing fun things, I'm out there creating memories of my own. And I don't feel the pressure to post pictures online to make everyone think I'm interesting or exciting anymore. Instead, I'm trying to live more in the moment, and it actually feels really good.'

'That's wonderful! Although I have zero experience of the Instagram and Backchat stuff you do…'

'Erm, *Snapchat*…?'

'You know what I mean…' She rolled her eyes. 'As I was saying, whilst I've never been into that, I know how much you were, so I'm proud of you for weaning yourself off it and for completing the challenge. But remember, even though you've bagged yourself a dishy man, don't let him become your replacement addiction. Before, your world revolved around social media and courting apps, so as much as I want you to be all loved up with Josh, don't give up all of the activities and things you've learnt from this process for him. Keep doing your lessons and whatever else you fancy. The challenge may have ended, but continue developing and growing.'

Absolutely. I was definitely going to carry on with my life drawing classes, and tomorrow I was going to order a load of paint and supplies so I could make a start on some murals at home. Thanks to Josh, finding new hobbies and picking up on old ones, I was feeling inspired. I couldn't wait to start painting my own creations again.

I also planned to go on some more organised walks depending on where they were visiting, and I wanted to look into learning another language too.

'Yeah, don't worry, I will. I know it's important to keep my own interests and not give up my life for a man. In any case, judging by the reaction from the Sofar gig and the calls Josh has been getting since then, I think he's going to become really busy, so I don't think we'll see each other as often as we'd like, which means I'll need to find plenty of other things to fill my time.'

'You're right, Em. I don't know much about music, and sadly I can't predict the lottery numbers, but based on the songs you played me earlier, I've got a feeling your man Josh is going to do very well. In fact, I'd put money on him becoming a *very, very* big star.'

OCTOBER

CHAPTER TWENTY-SEVEN

To say Josh exploded over the next five months would be the understatement of the century.

After the Sofar gig and Alice's interview came out in *Sound* magazine, Josh's phone didn't stop ringing. His Spotify streams jumped into the millions, and he was inundated with requests from managers and even some record labels.

Josh had ruled out signing with a label again after his first experience and initially wasn't keen on having a manager either, because he was adamant that he wanted to be completely independent. But even I could see that it had got to the stage where it would be impossible to manage everything himself.

One of the managers that contacted him was Adrian. He had just branched out on his own after working for a few of the top music management firms in New York and London and was hungry for success. He wanted to launch his agency with a fresh, talented artist, and Josh certainly fitted the bill. Adrian was pretty sure of himself. Said he had major contacts and knew all the movers and shakers in the industry that'd make Josh's music achieve exposure on both sides of the Atlantic and around the world.

During their many meetings, Adrian told Josh they had a lot in common. After being controlled by large organisations earlier in their careers, he said they were now branching out and forging their own paths as independents. If he helped Josh succeed, then Adrian reasoned that his company would also become huge and they could grow together. Win-win, he'd said.

He certainly was a smooth talker. Josh liked what Adrian was saying—*in theory*. But having been burnt in the past, he wasn't leaving anything to chance. Because of all the buzz around him, Josh was in a strong position. If Adrian didn't give him the terms he wanted, he knew that there were other managers lined up, ready to step in. Josh went through every detail and contract with a fine-tooth comb, going backwards and forwards, and renegotiated until he was completely satisfied. He also negotiated an extended probationary period of nine months to ensure that he'd be happy with Adrian's services. Only then had Josh agreed to go ahead.

So far, he was pleased with Adrian. Josh was impressed at how quickly he'd organised a twenty-date tour across the US, which would be starting in a few days. Particularly as a lot of venues got booked up several months or even a year in advance. They weren't big places. No stadiums or arenas. Not yet, anyway. Adrian said it was best to start off small, build a buzz and then grow from there.

A twenty-date tour meant Josh would be away for five weeks. Five long weeks. With all the interviews, shows and time spent in his studio at home recording songs for his forthcoming album, it was already difficult for him to see me more than a couple of times a week, which I was finding hard. We both were.

Josh had suggested I join him in America, but I wasn't sure. On the one hand, I wanted to be with him and give him my support in person. But on the other, I knew he'd be busy, and these days, I wasn't very good at just hanging around. If I had to sit in a hotel doing nothing all day, waiting for him to come back, I'd go crazy.

Perhaps during my hermit, pre-Chloe's challenge days, I would have happily passed the time on social media. But I was a different person now. I liked to be active. And I've always been independent, so although I supported his career, I didn't want to abandon my work to follow him to the States.

Especially now that I was back into my art, in a big way. For the past few months I'd been spending three days a week painting. I'd reduced my illustration work to four days a week so that I could dedicate Fridays, Saturdays and Sundays to my own personal projects.

That included designing the artwork for Josh's forth-coming album. I couldn't believe it when he'd asked me. He'd decided to make 'Rainbow', the song he'd written about me, the title track, and as he still wasn't keen on having his face on the cover, he asked if I could do a simple illustration of a rainbow instead. I jumped at the chance to do something fun for a change. As well as being excited for his album to be released so that the world could hear the amazing tracks he'd created, I admit, I was also looking forward to seeing my artwork on Spotify and on the advertising posters too.

And that wasn't the only cool thing I'd been working on. True to his word, Josh had given me the go-ahead to paint a mural in his house. I was really nervous about doing it at first. After all, it'd had been years since I'd last painted on a large scale. I was bound to be rusty. So I decided to start by doing a couple in my own flat first. I created a large seafront mural in my office, painting beautiful golden sand and gorgeous blue sea on the wall directly opposite my desk. Every time I looked up from my computer, it made me smile. I felt like I was working on the beach.

In the bathroom, I painted a mural that gave the illusion of looking out of a large window with a sea view. I'd added a cute red-and-white sailboat and lovely clear blue sky. It really livened up the room and lifted my mood when I dragged myself into the shower in the mornings.

I needn't have worried about getting back into it. Once I'd planned out the designs, prepped the walls and got started, it all came flooding back to me. It was like it was only yesterday that I was a student helping Hans and Carrie out with their murals. I felt alive again. Motivated. Happy.

With my growing confidence, I told Josh that I was ready, came up with some ideas, and after he gave me the green light, I got started on the first mural on his studio wall.

As Prince was one of his favourite artists, I created a huge monochrome portrait of him from his *Purple Rain* era, playing his guitar. I also added some doves in honour of one of Josh's favourite songs, 'When Doves Cry'.

It had taken weeks to complete, mainly because I had to fit it around my free time and when Josh was out at a gig or not in the studio, which, given how busy he'd become, was a challenge, but I finally finished it a few days ago and he loved it. I was really proud of it too.

Now that I had a few new murals under my belt, I was planning to build myself a little website to showcase my work and start growing my portfolio. Which was another reason I thought it would be best for me to stay. I wanted to make the most of my newfound creativity. It had taken me so many years to get my mojo back, I was worried that if I just swanned off on tour with Josh, I might lose my momentum.

The doorbell rang. It was Josh. My stomach flipped. He'd managed to schedule the evening off to come round for dinner. Yes, *schedule*. That was what it had come to now. Gone were the days of him working in Cuppa, where we'd have our impromptu afternoons in the park. Because he'd become so in demand, everything had to be booked like an appointment at the dentist just so that he could fit it all in. As I was learning, this was all part of the life of having a talented boyfriend who was becoming more and more famous every day.

'Awww, thank you!' I smiled as I took the bouquet of colourful tulips Josh handed to me. He'd often surprise me with a bunch. He knew how much I loved them, and I think it was also his way of encouraging me to paint the tulip field mural I'd wanted to do for so long.

'Beautiful flowers for the beautiful lady. Mmmm, I've missed you soooo much,' said Josh, wrapping his arms around me before giving me a long, slow kiss.

'Me too. I guess we have to get used to this,' I said, pulling a sad face. 'Just think. It's been three days since I've seen you. Soon it's going to be five weeks…'

'I know. It sucks,' he said.

'Well, this is your dream, so it has to be done.'

'Yeah, of course. I didn't mean *touring* sucks. I mean being without you sucks. *Big time.* Are you sure you won't come?' he asked, stroking my cheek. 'I'd really love you to.'

'I would too, but can't,' I said softly. 'I need to work.'

'I understand,' he said, taking my hand and leading me to sit on the sofa.

'Even if I did come, we wouldn't really get to see each other. You'll be busy rehearsing, in the studio, doing the gigs, then hanging out with all your new celebrity friends and going to all these cool places. I won't fit in, and you won't want me getting in your way. You'll need to focus. Not be worrying about me and whether I'm okay.'

'Yeah, it's going to be busy, but I'd still find time for us to be together. You'd be focusing on your illustration stuff and planning your mural work during the day. I'm sure you'd get loads of inspiration over there, and then if you wanted to, you could come to the gigs each night and then we could be together afterwards. I'll also have a few days off at some point too, so we can go exploring in what-ever city we're in. It'll be fun. And you *know* I'm not into that whole celebrity culture thing. I don't fit into that world either. But *we* fit. The two of us. Em and Josh. Josh and Em. *That's* what matters.'

'I don't know,' I said, thinking that it *did* sound like it would be amazing. 'I want to be there for you, but I need to find a way to develop my new career too.'

'I understand. And I wouldn't want you to give that up for me. I'm your biggest supporter, so I wouldn't even suggest it if I thought it would set you back. I want you to succeed. Your mural work is really going to take off. I really believe that. I love you, Em. I don't want to be without you.'

My heart melted. Just like when he'd told me the first time that he loved me. I loved him too. And that's what made me so afraid. I wanted to go with him, but I was terrified of what would happen if I did.

Josh had already taken me to a few of the industry parties he'd been invited to by Adrian to *network*. It had taken me hours to get ready, and even though I went with Josh and not on my own, it was like going to my first Chloe Challenge event, multiplied by ten million. Whilst I wasn't as bad as I was all those months ago, I was still an introvert at heart, and my nervousness was off the scale. I felt like a fish out of water. All that champagne and those ridiculously beautiful and cool people. Most of the male musicians I spotted were with gorgeous supermodels with legs up to their eyeballs, flawless skin and flowing hair. And I challenge even the most confident woman not to feel insecure in a setting like that.

Josh had held on to my hand tightly, as he could probably see pints of blood draining from my face with every wobbly step I took in my heels, but he was there to work. He couldn't stay with me all night. So when Adrian whisked him away to speak to this person and that person, I was left on my own. And somehow the 'is it your first time here?' conversation starters I'd used for the Happy Solos events weren't going to cut it.

And that was just for a few nights over a period of a few months. Imagine doing that constantly for five weeks. It would be torture. Whilst my confidence had grown, I wasn't ready to throw myself in that deep. I couldn't. And

I didn't want my insecurities to affect Josh and his success. He'd know that I was uncomfortable, then he'd worry and wouldn't be concentrating on what he needed to. And that would be wrong. I'd be selfish to put him in that position.

The other thing that terrified me was taking a leap and falling flat on my face, or rather getting my heart completely crushed. What if I threw caution to the wind, told everyone I was jetting off to the States for five weeks with my wonderful boyfriend, and something happened? What if we didn't get on or had a massive argument? Then I'd come back to London with both my career and my love life down the toilet.

I'd love to be all feisty and say I didn't need Josh and if something *did* happen, I would just get over him. But I loved Josh. *So much.* I had never loved anyone in all my life even half as much as I loved him. That would *crush* me. Yes, Chloe and Kat would be there to support me, so perhaps I'd pick myself up eventually (I'm thinking the year 2050 might be realistic), but the pain. Imagine how excruciating it would feel to lose him. I felt sick to my stomach just thinking about it.

No. I can't. It was safer for me to stay in London. Keep things as they are. *Don't rock the boat.*

'Em?' said Josh.

'Hmmm?' I said, snapping out of my thoughts. 'Sorry. I know you'd like me to be there. I love you so, so much too. You know I'm a hundred per cent behind you, but I'll just need to support you from here. We can Facetime every day, and I'm sure five weeks will fly by,' I said, trying to stay positive. I bet it wouldn't, though. It was probably going to feel like five years.

'I hope you're right. Well, if I've only got forty-eight

hours left in London,' he said, kneeling down on the rug in front of me and leaning forwards, 'we'd better make the most of it…'

~

'All set?' I said, trying my best to stay strong.

'Think so…? I've checked my packing list a million times, so hopefully…' We were standing in the hallway at Josh's house with everything all packed ready to go. 'This is it, Em. I'm so bloody nervous. My first solo US tour! Shit.'

'They're going to love you, Josh. You've already got a strong fan base out there. Your shows all sold out so quickly. It's going to be amazing.'

'I hope so. I'd feel so much better if you could come. I know you've got your reasons, but if you change your mind, just say the word. I'll pay for your ticket. Whatever it costs. Remember, I've also got a couple of dates in New York on a Friday and Saturday, so if you're busy with work and need to focus on building your new career, maybe you could just come for a long weekend or something? You could see your parents then too. Promise you'll think about it?'

'I will. I promise,' I said, kissing him firmly on the lips. God, I was going to miss those lips so much.

'Thanks. And you're sure you won't come to the airport to see me off?'

'I really want to, but I've always hated airport good-byes. Even as a little girl. I get too upset. I'm just about holding my emotions together now. If I see you walking away through those doors, I'll end up wailing, and if you

see me ugly crying, you might never come back!'
Although I was trying to keep things light-hearted, I could
already feel myself welling up.

'You could *never* look ugly,' he said as he took me in
his arms and squeezed me tight.

'I love you so much, Josh. I'm going to miss you,' I
said, tearing up. My stomach was in knots. It was like a
magician was inside, twisting balloons into a thousand
different animal shapes.

'I love you too, Em,' he said, his eyes watering.
'Look!' he laughed. 'You've got me bloody crying now!'

'Go!' I sobbed. 'The taxi's outside. I'll lock up everything for you.'

'The taxi can wait. I need an epic kiss with the love of
my life. Come here.'

As our lips locked, the whole room spun around, just
like it had that first time we'd kissed. Back then, I thought
I would never feel anything stronger or more earth-shat-
tering ever again. But my feelings for Josh had only intensified. There was no doubt in my mind that he was the one.
We were made for each other. Our lips and our bodies
went together like the sand and the sea, like strawberries
and cream. He made me feel happy. So alive. But now he
was leaving to pursue his dream. And I had no idea how
my heart would survive five weeks without him.

CHAPTER TWENTY-EIGHT

Over the past two and a half weeks, I'd thrown myself into as many activities as I could. I had done three life drawing classes, been on a walking group, continued the Spanish language lessons I'd started a few months ago, visited a museum and even begun prepping my living room wall so it would be ready to paint the windmill and tulip fields mural I'd dreamt of doing all those years ago. But, despite that, I still felt so empty. It just wasn't the same without Josh here with me.

Things were going brilliantly for him in the States. We'd Facetime every night after the show when he got back to the hotel and he'd tell me how it went. I could see the joy in his eyes and hear the happiness in his voice. He was having the time of his life. He'd sent me some videos that his tour manager, Bruce, had filmed of him on stage. The crowds went wild for him. They knew all the words to his songs—it was crazy. I was so chuffed for Josh. He was doing it. He was living his dream. Making his grandma proud.

I missed him so much. His smile. His laugh. His warmth. *Everything*. Yeah, it was cool that I got to see him during our video calls, but it couldn't compare to having him beside me. I wanted him to hold me in his arms. To rest my head on his chest and hear his heart beating. To breathe in his scent. Being away from him was unbearable. But I still couldn't bring myself to go over there. It would be selfish. I'd mess things up for him. I knew I would. It was better if I stayed away.

Tonight I was going to Chloe's for dinner. I hadn't been there for a while. Just think. Before she'd set the challenge, I used to go a few times a week and would spend the rest of my days at home working or scrolling through social media or swiping on dating apps looking for love. But now, with work, all my new hobbies and seeing Josh, sometimes I only had time to pop round a couple of times a month. And I couldn't even remember the last time I'd logged onto Instagram. Who would have thought that my life would have changed so dramatically? That I'd be busy going out, trying to start a new career, have new friends like Kat and have found the love of my life? *Crazy*.

'Evening, Em.' Chloe opened the door and gave me a big squeeze. 'How are you, love?'

'Great! I'm fine. All good. Really busy,' I said, squeezing her back.

'Hmmm,' she said, looking at me suspiciously. 'Come and sit down, love.' She walked through to the kitchen and pulled out a chair at the table. 'I've made us a nice chicken stew.'

'*Amazing!*' I smiled. Chloe's chicken stew was as tasty as her cakes. 'I need some good comfort food right now.'

'Yes. I'm sure you do. And some comfort too. How are you? *Really?*'

'I'm fine. Honestly.'

Oops. Adding the word *honestly* to a sentence when speaking to Chloe would automatically be taken as a sign that I was anything but...

'You can tell me how busy you've been and how fine you are and put on the nicest dress and the prettiest make-up like you've done this evening, Em, but your eyes are telling me a different story. They've lost their sparkle. You miss Josh. Terribly. I can tell.'

'Well, *of course* I miss Josh! He's my boyfriend. He's been gone for almost three weeks. That's natural. But I'm not sitting around moping like the old Emily would have done. I'm focusing on developing my future. Keeping myself busy. The time is going to fly by. I know it will. I'm *fine*.'

'Remind me why you're torturing yourself like this again?' asked Chloe as she got the plates out of the cupboard.

'I'm not *torturing* myself.'

She put the plates on the table and folded her arms.

'Okay, I might be a little sad. Like I said, I miss him, but it's okay. It's important for me to stay strong. To remember that I'm just sacrificing some of my happiness for his. Giving him the space to pursue his dream. I'm *helping* him. Trying to be selfless.'

Why is she rolling her eyes?

'You might *think* you're helping him and you might *say* you're being self*less*, but really, Em, you're being sel*fish*.'

'What!' I shouted. 'How can you say that? I'm staying

away *for him*. So he can focus. The last thing Josh needs is some clingy woman hanging around when he's trying to make it big in America.'

'Poppycock!' she shouted back. 'Firstly, you're not some *clingy woman*, you're his girlfriend and he loves you. He *wants* you to be there. Secondly, you say that you're doing it for him, to give him space, but really you're staying away for *you*!'

'For *me*?' I protested. 'What, because I'm trying to develop myself and build a new career rather than running after a man?'

'You and I both know that's an excuse. You can still work on your mural venture over there.'

'I miss him like crazy,' I said, ignoring her comment about working remotely. 'I'd love nothing more than to see him.'

'Flimflam!' She crossed her arms and stood in front of me. 'Words, words, empty *words*. If you wanted to see him, if you *really* missed him, you'd take *action*. You'd be there. Beside him. *Supporting* him. Instead you're just being a big selfish scaredy-cat!'

'I'm not!' I said, still trying to convince myself.

'You're *scared*. Just like that scared little mouse that I found curled up on its bed feeling sorry for itself after Eric the todger proposed to that bimbo. You were in your flat wasting away, crying over some useless man, wishing that you could find a man to love you. Someone to adore and respect you, who you could have a deep connection with. Who you could spend the rest of your life with. And then, after you grew some balls and accepted my challenge, you found the man of your dreams along the way. A man that is everything you'd wished for and more. A man that wants you with him as he embarks on the biggest, most daunting, yet exciting challenge in his life, and what do you do? You run away. You run away and hide because you're too scared. *Again*.'

'I'm not hiding!' I repeated, frustrated that she'd got inside my brain again and shone a giant spotlight on my fears. 'I'm doing what you recommended all those months ago. I'm getting out and about. Developing myself. Doing things, new activities, making new friends.'

'Your *body* may be going out, but your soul and your heart are still stuck inside. Inside a safe little bubble. Too afraid to break free and live life. Don't you see? You're stuck in a comfort zone, just like you were before.' She sat down beside me and softened her voice a little. 'Before, you were afraid to go out and meet people. You've conquered that fear. Fine, good, great, *gold star*. And I'm happy that you're making progress with changing your career. But that isn't enough. You also need to follow your heart. Trust. Take the leap. Go and see Josh.'

'But I *can't*. I've got to work,' I said.

'Sod work!' She jumped up again.

'What? I can't just abandon my clients or stop painting again—give up my dreams. Surely you understand that!'

'You're being dramatic,' she huffed. 'No one is asking you to give up on anything! You can work from anywhere. Isn't that one of the perks of working for your-self? Like I've said a billion times, all you need is your computer, your hands, your brain the internet and a phone. That's it. I'm a technophobe and even *I* know that. You're just making excuses! You can go a few days without painting surely and use that time to work on your marketing. Or I'm pretty sure if inspiration strikes, they sell paint and brushes in America. And if your day job clients need you, they can call you or do that FaceTalk thing.'

'Facetime…'

'You know what I mean. But you and I both know it's not your *customers* that need you right now. It's Josh. *He* needs your support. Keep pushing him away like this, and if you don't want to be there for him, they'll be millions of other women who will…'

'Stop!' I banged my hand on the table. 'I hate it when you say things like that! It's cruel. I shouldn't have to follow him everywhere. If he really loves me, he'll be faithful.'

'I say those things to get your attention and make you *think*. This isn't just about other women or not trusting him. It's about being supportive. This is a *big* deal for Josh. If the roles were reversed, wouldn't you want him to be there for you? Look how much he's been supporting your dream. He helped get you out of your artistic rut. Encouraged you to paint again. The strongest couples, the ones that stand the greatest chance of going the distance, support each other. That's what I'm trying to say. I mean, look at you. You're miserable. Whilst he's happy that things are going so well out there, Josh still knows a big part of him is missing. *You.* If you love him like you say you do, put your fears to one side and go and bloody see him. Even if it's just for the weekend. Didn't you say he's playing in New York this Friday?'

'Yes, but—'

'But *nothing*! Archie!' she shouted. 'Downstairs now, please. And bring that flat computer thingy.'

'Yes, Mum,' he groaned from upstairs in his typical

disinterested teenager tone. A couple of minutes later, Archie skulked into the kitchen, clutching an iPad.

'Do your World Wide Web wizardry stuff and book Aunty Emily a ticket to New York, please.'

'What?' I gasped. 'Chloe! *No!* You can't!' What was she playing at?

'Ignore her, Archie,' she shouted. 'Aunty Emily needs to arrive by Friday morning. Lunchtime at the latest. Here,' she said, reaching into her handbag. 'Use my credit card. As you know, normally I'm a cash person, but I keep this for emergencies.'

She cannot be serious. I couldn't just swan off to New York on a whim. Friday was just three days away. It was too short notice. And it'd cost a fortune. I know Josh had said before that he'd pay, but I couldn't let him or Chloe shell out all that money for me.

And when did Chloe get a credit card?

Archie tapped away on the iPad.

'What's your full name, please, Aunty Emily?'

'Emily Louisa Robinson,' snapped Chloe before I had a chance to answer.

He continued typing, then started entering Chloe's card details.

'Done!' he replied. 'You fly out from Heathrow Friday morning and return on Monday night.'

'Monday night?' My eyes widened. 'But—I *can't.* What about w—?'

'*Thank you, Archie*,' Chloe cut me off again. 'I'll get your aunty to write her email address on a bit of paper so you can send her the details later, or you can write them down for her now?'

'Mum. *Seriously!*' Archie scoffed. 'This isn't the

1950s, you know, or whatever century it was when you were young. Aunty, can you just type in your email address here, please, and I'll send it to you now?'

Type in my email address...? Going to New York this Friday? I was still trying to take it all in.

'Watch your mouth, Sonny Jim!' Chloe shouted. 'I wasn't even *born* in the fifties. And I'll have you know I'm *still* young!'

'Whatever, Mum.' He rolled his eyes.

I took the iPad from Archie, jaw still on the floor, typed in my details and handed it back.

'Sent!' he said. 'You went to New York recently, didn't you?'

'Yeah, last year.'

'Cool. So you won't need the Travel Authorisation thingy. Just read through the details in the email about checking in and whatever and you should be sorted. You're *so* lucky, Aunty Emily. Getting to go to New York. I've *always* wanted to go. Wish Mum would buy *me* a ticket just like that,' he huffed.

'Stop sulking, Archie. Like I said, this credit card is for emergencies only, so don't get any ideas about cloning it or storing it or whatever sneaky people do with card things. This is an emergency of *major* proportions. I had to stop your Aunty Emily from throwing away a chance at lifelong happiness. We needed to get her to New York before she ruined the best relationship she's ever going to have. And as you'll learn when you grow up, Archie, you can't put a price on true love.'

'If you say so, Mum.' He rolled his eyes again. 'Well, if you're not booking me a ticket, then I'm going back to my room. Have fun finding your happiness or whatever,

Aunty. And if you go and live out there, please can you and your rich, megastar boyfriend send me a ticket? Seeing as I helped out and everything?'

'Archie!' shouted Chloe as he smirked, then disappeared from the kitchen.

And just like that, I was going to New York.

I was off to the Big Apple. To see Josh. The apple of my eye and the love of my life.

CHAPTER TWENTY-NINE

'You came!' said Josh, picking me up and spinning me around. 'You're *actually* here!'

I threw my arms around him and we kissed for what felt like hours, but seconds at the same time. Long kisses with Josh were never enough.

I couldn't really believe that he was in front of me either. Since the ticket had been booked, I'd hardly slept. I was so excited to see him, I felt like a kid counting down to Christmas Day. Josh had screamed when and I'd told him over Facetime. 'You're really coming? *Seriously*?' He'd grinned. 'Don't joke, Em. *Oh my God!* That is the *best* news I've heard all day. *No*—all week. *All month!*' he'd shouted. Then we'd say 'just two more sleeps' or 'this time tomorrow we'll be together.' And now the moment we'd waited for had arrived. After three weeks apart, we'd finally been reunited. I was so happy I could burst.

'Sorry I couldn't come and get you at the airport.' He squeezed me tighter.

'Don't worry! I knew you'd be busy today. Thank you

for the tulips,' I said, admiring the bouquet that was on the table. 'They're beautiful.'

'You're welcome!'

'So how come you're here at the hotel? I thought you had to be at the studio.'

'Yeah, I do, but I told Bruce that I *needed* to see you.'

'And he didn't mind?'

'Of course he did! But I reminded him I wasn't going to be a machine like I was in the band. I'm a grown man now. I know that I need to work hard and I'm not afraid to do that, but I also need to take time out for important things. For *special people* that make me happy. In the long run, everyone benefits. If I'm happy, I perform better and write better songs. And I'm better when I'm with you.'

'*Oh my God*,' I said, my heart dancing. 'That is the loveliest thing anyone has said to me. *Thank you.* I bloody love you, Josh. Come here and kiss me again.'

'Kiss?' he said, nibbling my neck. 'I want to do more than *kiss*, young lady. It's been an eternity since I've seen you, so our bodies have got a lot of catching up to do.'

'Yes, they have...' I unbuckled his jeans and pulled them down along with his boxers.

Josh scooped me up in his arms and carried me to the edge of the bed. I yanked my tights and thong off as quickly as I could. He pushed my dress up, then entered me.

Oh God.

I wrapped my legs tightly around his waist and watched him sliding in and out.

Jesus. It felt like heaven.

How had I survived this long without him?

With every thrust, I felt like I was going to come. But

I had to hold on. Even the fantasies of him I'd had floating in my mind whilst he was away couldn't begin to compare to how it felt to have him here, right now, inside me.

'Want to go on top?' he said.

'Yes!'

He pulled out, whipped off his jeans from around his ankles, lay on the bed and then I straddled him. Josh gyrated his hips beneath me whilst I moved up and down.

Josh lifted my dress up over my head, then unclipped my bra. 'Gorgeous,' he said, squeezing my nipples. 'I have missed these so much.'

I leant forward and Josh cradled my breasts, ran his tongue around them before taking each one in his mouth and sucking slowly. We grinded into each other, harder and harder.

He slid his hand into his mouth, then rubbed his wet fingers over my clit.

Holy shit.

He always knew exactly where to touch me.

'You still like it there, I see.'

'Yes…' I gasped. 'Don't you dare stop.'

'Yes, ma'am!'

As I moved my hips backwards and forwards, his strokes became firmer.

Game over.

I tried, but there was no way I would be able to hold on now. I was hanging by a thread. I could feel the sensations building. Like a volcano about to erupt.

'Come with me, Josh…' I panted.

As the words fell from my mouth, I felt the blood rush through me. His body tensed beneath, and as he continued stroking me with one hand, he used the other to grip my bottom.

That was it. I let out a long scream. I couldn't help myself.

Jesus Christ.

It was so good to release.

Josh must have felt it too as he also finished loudly. God knows how noisy we'd have been if we'd waited for two months.

I collapsed on his chest.

'Fuck,' Josh gasped. 'I knew I missed you but...*wow*. That was amazing. I'm so glad you came, Em. You have no idea.'

'*Came* as in the incredible orgasm you've just given me or *came* as in flying here to New York?' I teased.

'Both,' he said, stroking my bum. 'And now that you've *come* all this way, to show my gratitude, I need to do something extra to make it worth your while.'

'Mmm...' I said, planting kisses on his soft beard and along his broad shoulders. 'I like the sound of that. What exactly did you have in mind?'

'Well,' he said, stroking in between my legs again, 'by dedicating the next few hours to making you *come* again and again and *again*...'

After we'd spent some time *catching up* in bed, Josh went to the venue for the soundcheck. I'd offered to join him, but he said he wanted me to see the show for the first time tonight to get the full experience.

I texted my parents to let them know I'd landed safely

and we arranged to have brunch tomorrow. I'd considered inviting them to the show but realised they'd end up grilling Josh, which was the last thing he'd need after performing. And now that I was here (and man was I glad to be), I wanted to spend as much as possible of the precious time we'd have together all by ourselves.

I jumped in a cab and glued my face to the window, looking out for famous landmarks like a typical tourist. Even though I'd been here a few times, I was still filled with excitement. Josh said that he'd be taking Sunday off to spend with me, so we'd see all the sights together. When I was here last Christmas, never did I imagine that the next time I'd visit I would be coming to see my boyfriend performing at a sold-out gig. *Crazy.*

As the taxi pulled up at the venue, Josh's tour manager came out to greet me.

'Hey, Emily, how you doing?' said Bruce, shaking my hand. He was a big guy. His round stomach hung over his baggy blue jeans. I guessed he was maybe late forties. Despite being bald on top, he'd scraped the hair he had at the sides and the back into a short ponytail.

'Great, thanks. You?'

'All good, honey,' he said, leading me through the back door. 'Your boy is just finishing up. He'll be here in a sec.'

'Okay, thanks,' I said, sitting down on the small black sofa and taking off my coat.

'Hey!' As Bruce left, Josh came into the room, picked me up and spun me around. I loved it when he did that.

'Hey!'

'You're wearing my favourite jeans!' he said, squeezing my bum. I'd worn a backless silky red vest top (and no bra was required, which I'd discovered was an advantage of learning to love my small boobs) and my fitted black jeans, which clung nicely to my bottom. As well as being comfortable and making me feel sexy, I knew Josh liked them too, which was a bonus. 'I love when you wear them, but I think I like them even more when I get to take them off. Mmm…' he said, glancing at his watch. 'Do we have time?'

'That all depends on *you*…' I said, stroking his chest.

There was a knock at the door.

'Come in,' said Josh, still holding me tightly.

'Sorry to interrupt, but Bruce asked me to let you know that doors open in half an hour and there's already a line forming,' said a guy in his twenties, hovering nervously.

'Okay, thanks for letting me know,' said Josh as the door closed. 'Well, maybe that's telling us to wait. I can be quick, but I don't want to. I want to enjoy you. *Properly.*'

'Mmm, me too,' I said, staring into his eyes. I still couldn't quite believe I was here. With Josh. In *New York.* 'So do you need me to help you with anything? Get you anything? *Do* anything?'

'No, thanks, Em,' he said, releasing me and then sitting down on the sofa. 'Oh actually, now that I remember, there's three packets of M&Ms on the table, so if you wouldn't mind picking out the red and blue ones and putting them onto a crystal dish for me to eat with a silver spoon, that would be great.'

'Fat chance!' I laughed. 'The day you go all diva on me and start requesting silver spoons is the day I stick that silver spoon where the sun doesn't shine!'

'And I thought you loved me.' He chuckled. 'So you wouldn't pick out my favourite M&Ms? I'm so hurt!'

'You'll get over it!' I poked him playfully in his side.

'But tell me, seriously: do celebs *actually* have assistants to do stuff like that?'

'Yes, it's *actually* a thing. I've heard of people requesting a hundred white doves, for their coffee to only be stirred anti-clockwise…all sorts. There was even a rumour that one rock star asked for a bald-headed toothless prostitute. Now *that* was probably made up! Well, I hope so anyway. *Who knows?* As you can see, I've also become *very* high maintenance since you last saw me.'

'So what's on your rider, then, Mr Big Shot?' I asked, scanning the room.

'Two bottles of chilled mineral water.'

'What else?'

'That's it. Can't drink too much or I'll want to go toilet in the middle of the show, but I still need to keep myself hydrated.'

'Do you need to do your sirening voice warm-up thingy?'

'Already done.'

'You're sure I'm not distracting you?' I stroked his cheek.

'Nope. I *love* you being here. The soundcheck went well. I'm ready. Actually, Em, you know what you could do to help relax me?'

'Name it.'

'Just lie here. Rest your head on my chest. These past few weeks when I've been alone at night, that's what I dreamt about. Just hearing your heartbeat and breathing in your scent and that shampoo you use. I should have taken a bottle just to sniff whenever I missed you.'

'*Weirdo!*' I chuckled. 'My wonderful, sweet, lovely hair-sniffing weirdo.' I kissed him gently.

'So can you do that for me? Just for a few minutes?'

'Of course I can, Josh,' I said, resting my head on him. 'I'd love to.'

~

By the time the support act had finished, the venue was packed. A lot of the places I'd seen Josh play at were just all black walls. This one had more character. It looked like a converted warehouse with a glass-panelled ceiling. Like his London gigs, the staging was kept simple. Just a mic stand, his guitar, keyboard and a drum kit. Bruce had said I could watch from the wings at the side of the stage, but I wanted to be in the crowd and feel the reaction from the audience.

The background music faded out and everyone cheered loudly. As Josh teased the first line of 'Make You Proud', they went crazy. They could hear him singing but couldn't see him. Then he calmly strolled on stage and as he sung the second line and the drummer started playing, they completely lost their minds. It was incredible.

Just like in the videos I'd seen of Josh performing in LA, the crowd knew every word to his songs. Imagine that. Imagine that one day you're sitting in your room in London, scribbling down some lyrics, pouring your thoughts out onto the page, and the next you're in another country, performing to people who have connected with your words and love what you've written so much that they've learnt it all off by heart. That must feel phenomenal.

Hearing Josh perform 'Rainbow' certainly felt phenomenal. It never got old. Watching hundreds of strangers sing along to a song that had been written about me was nuts. Still so surreal.

As Josh sang the last line, he looked directly at me and winked. My heart flipped. *Got me every time.*

Before I knew it, the concert was over. It went so fast. I was already excited to come to tomorrow's show. *Thank you, Chloe*, I said in my head. I needed to be here. I couldn't have missed it.

As the security guard let me through backstage, I spotted Josh talking to Bruce whilst wiping his face with a towel and then his hanky.

I'd asked him why he always carried one. Most people just used tissues. Josh explained they were gifts from his grandma and he liked having a handkerchief with him, especially on stage. It was like a good-luck charm. Something that reminded him of her. So lovely.

After watching him perform and get all hot and sweaty, I totally understood why women threw themselves at musicians. I wished we could go in that dressing room and make love right now. But Josh had work to do. This was about him following his dream, and I was going to do everything I could to support him.

I hung back to give him his space and reached for my phone, for the first time all night. There was a message from Chloe. I was literally just thinking about her. And wow. An actual *text*. That must have been *very* difficult for her.

Chloe

So…? How's it going? Glad you went? Was I right?

Me

Amazing! Yes you were. Thanks again for booking the ticket and forcing me to go. Your methods may be unconventional, but your heart is always in a good place. Love you xxx

Me

PS congrats on sending an actual text message! That's what? The second one I've got from you this year? I'm honoured! And don't worry about replying. I know it must have been painful, so don't want to cause you any more discomfort by making you do it again. Will call on Tuesday. xxx

PPS go to bed! It must be what? Four in the morning over there?!!

I loved that woman. She really was the best friend ever. I looked up to see if Josh was still talking. Just as I did, he spotted me.

He excused himself, walked away from Bruce and straight towards me. 'Hey!' He kissed me firmly on the lips. 'So? How was it? What did you think?'

'A-mazing. Oh my God, you were brilliant! I can't even…there's not a word spectacular enough in the dictionary to describe how fantastic you were!'

'Really? You're not just saying that? You can tell me if you didn't like something.'

'*Seriously?*' I said, rolling my eyes. 'Were you not standing on that stage? Did you not *see* the crowd's reaction? Did you not *hear* them singing along to every word?'

'Yeah, it felt good to me—*great*, even—but you just

don't know. I never want to get complacent. I want to keep getting better.'

'Well, good luck! I don't know how you're going to do *that*! Actually,' I said, 'I do have one criticism…'

'Yeah?' His eyes widened. 'Tell me.'

'Too short. Over far too quickly in my opinion.' I folded my arms.

'Phew! I thought you were going to say something much worse.'

'Isn't that bad enough?' I laughed.

'Well, I apologise. I know you do prefer it when it lasts a long time…' He winked, then leant forward to kiss me again.

Wow. I'd just watched a talented, gorgeous singer perform on stage and then got to snog him afterwards. How lucky was I?

'Josh,' said Bruce. 'Ready? We should get going.' Josh's face fell.

'One sec, Em.'

Josh and Bruce walked over to the other side and seemed to be having a heated conversation for a few minutes. As Josh walked off, Bruce shook his head.

'Come on, let's go,' he said, taking my hand.

'So, which events are we going to tonight?' I asked, guessing that there'd be a string of celebrity parties.

'Our own,' he said as we stepped outside.

'Huh?'

'Bruce had some party thing he wanted me to go to so we could do some schmoozing, but I told him I wasn't in the mood. I'd rather just chill with you.'

'Oh, Josh, don't *not* go because of me,' I said, resting my hands on his shoulders. Even though it wasn't something I'd choose to do, I was fully prepared to do my best to enjoy any function we needed to attend, for Josh's sake. 'This is your career. Your *dream*. It's your first time performing in New York on your own. I totally understand that you need to do these parties to move to the next level.'

'Yeah, maybe. Maybe not. But right now, I don't care. Screw the schmoozing. Sod the parties. The only thing I want to do tonight, all night and all morning is to be in bed with you. So as long as you have no objections, that's exactly what I plan to do.'

CHAPTER THIRTY

It was the end of a *magical* weekend in New York.

After the concert, in the taxi back to the hotel, Josh and I couldn't keep our hands off each other.

The fact that he'd chosen me over going to those parties was a massive deal. I'd felt guilty, but he'd insisted that for him, it was a no-brainer, which made me love him more, if that was even possible.

Having called his earlier stage performance *too short*, Josh made sure his performance in the bedroom more than delivered. That saying about absence making the heart grow fonder and the sex wilder was definitely true.

On Saturday morning, Josh had gone to the studio and I'd met my parents for brunch. They looked well and Dad had brought printouts of the articles he'd been reading on Josh. *Actual hard copies.* Chloe would have been proud.

'I listened to a few of your young man's tunes and they do seem to have nice melodies,' he'd said. 'Very pleasing to the ears.'

'You must be careful of those rock stars though,

Emily,' Mum warned. 'There's always lots of alcohol and women around. Especially with these good-looking ones. I remember when I used to go to concerts and see women throwing their underwear on the stage, so I dread to think how much worse it is these days.'

I'd rolled my eyes and told them that Josh wasn't into the whole sex, drugs and rock 'n' roll scene and they'd see that when they got to meet him *next time* we were over. Yes. I'd said *next time* and used the word *we*. I was finally trusting. Thinking ahead. Planning a future with Josh, without fear. That's what this trip had done. It had helped me to become less afraid.

After brunch, I'd chilled in the hotel and chatted to Kat on WhatsApp. She'd messaged to thank me again for the link to an article I'd sent her last month about introducing a new boyfriend to your kids, which she said was helpful. Her relationship with Rob was blossoming. It was sounding really serious. Not only had he met her children a couple of weeks ago, but last night he'd even stayed over. That was a *big* move for Kat, and not a decision she would have taken unless she was confident it was going to last the distance. Rob was a great guy, though. I had a good feeling about him.

Saturday night's gig once again was flawless. Josh was planning on shunning another after-party again, but when Adrian, who'd flown over for a couple of days, came into the dressing room to say that Sasha—yes, *the* zillion-selling, super-successful, superhuman singer Sasha—was going to be there and was interested in discussing featuring Josh on a single she'd be recording in New York in the next few days, there was no way I could let him pass up on an opportunity like that to be with me. No way.

I'd said I would come to the party, but if she *did* turn up, I'd head back to the hotel to allow him to discuss the details. That way he could go through everything freely without worrying about whether I was okay.

Sasha *did* turn up, and I have to admit, I was in absolute awe. She was *stunning*.

You know when you see someone on TV or in magazines and they look incredible, but you console yourself by thinking that it's partly down to great lighting or airbrushing? Well, having seen her up close, that wasn't the case. She was totally, utterly and undeniably beautiful. In fact, even more so in the flesh. Long legs, big boobs, amazing figure, glowing skin and long flowing dark hair. And she seemed nice. Not at all diva-ish. Just warm, friendly and down to earth. She smelt good too. Ridiculously so. Probably a scent from one of her many perfume lines. She breezed into the room like a queen and just had an aura about her that made you lose the ability to string a coherent sentence together. I can't even remember what I said to her. *Hello?* Yeah, I definitely said that. But whatever came out of my mouth after that was probably a load of jumbled stuff about me loving her and her music. *Cringe.* Even Josh was starstruck, and he was normally quite cool around celebrities.

I'd stayed for a few minutes to be polite whilst everyone did the small talk thing and she'd gushed at how she'd been playing 'Make You Proud' on repeat ever since Adrian had sent all of Josh's music to her manager and how she felt his vocals would be perfect for the song she was recording. That I thought was a good time to make my exit, so I'd said goodnight and left them to it.

Talking of pride, I was proud of myself. In fact, *very*

proud. There I was heading back to the hotel alone whilst Josh was at a party with one of the most beautiful and successful women in the world. Of course, I *did* have worrying, jealous thoughts popping into my head. *Come on.* This was me. *But* each time they did, I batted them away, reminding myself that it wasn't like they were there alone. There were dozens of other people at the party. Not to mention Bruce and Adrian. There was no reason to be insecure—well, apart from her being totally amazing. I reasoned that Josh loved me, and like he'd said loads of times, he wasn't into all that celebrity culture. For him, it was all about the music.

I wasn't sure what time he'd got back that night. I'd knocked out as soon as my head had hit the pillow, but when I woke up at 7 a.m., he'd just come out of the shower and so we'd gone out for breakfast, followed by a walk in Central Park. Then he'd got a call from Adrian and started jumping around like an excited puppy. When he hung up, he shouted,

'It's on! I'm recording a song with Sasha tomorrow! Can you believe it? Can you actually believe it?!'

'Oh my God, Josh! That's *major.*'

'It's *beyond* major. I mean, I couldn't say all of this in front of her yesterday as that wouldn't be cool, but she's been like an inspiration for *years*. Her songwriting skills are just *flawless*. Do you know she wrote "Heartbreak" in fifteen minutes? A billion-streaming, multi-award-winning song in *fifteen minutes*. I mean, who else can do that? *Incredible.*'

'It really is, Josh!' I said, hugging him.

'Me!' he said, pulling away to jump for joy again. 'Me. Recording with *Sasha. Sasha!* Shit. Do you know her band, SASS, were just coming on the scene about a year after my old group started? That's how long she's been around. I remember Carl, Mickey and Todd, you know, the other guys in the band, had a massive crush on her. Well, of course, we *all* did, and when we got booked for festivals and stuff, they were always looking out for them on the bill. And here I am nearly two decades later about to perform a song with her. With *Sasha*. Fuck!'

He was like a hyperactive child who'd just binged on a thousand packets of Haribos. I got it. Sasha was one of the biggest female artists of all time. He'd had a crush on her? *That* I hadn't realised. Then again, who didn't? I remember all the guys I knew back then had been obsessed with her too. And probably still were. She hadn't aged a bit. Like I'd said that night, she actually looked *better… Nope*, I'd said to myself. *I will not let fear or jealously rule my thoughts. I trust Josh. There's no need to worry. Sasha may be a mega star, but she's not me* (clearly). *It's* me *that Josh loves*. After I'd repeated that a dozen times in my head, I'd felt a little better. It was a great opportunity and I was genuinely happy for him.

He told me that often with these collaborations, you just recorded your part separately and sent it over, so you didn't even get to meet in person. So to actually be invited into the studio with the artist was a *big* deal. If his popularity had exploded now, when that single came out, he'd be well and truly famous. A household name for sure. Scary, but exciting too.

It was funny as, not long after that, as if the universe was giving us a taste of what was to come, when we'd stopped for a quick kiss, we'd spotted a guy in the distance taking a photo of us.

'Paps,' tutted Josh.

'Wow, really? You must be famous now if you've got them following you!'

'Nah. They probably just think I'm someone else. Thankfully, my life isn't what the magazines would consider exciting enough to be interested in me. I just make music, do gigs, and apart from the occasional party that I'm persuaded to attend, I go straight back to my hotel. Hardly front-page news.'

'Probably a good thing. I'd *hate* to be famous. All that scrutiny and people picking you apart. Imagine not being able to pop outside for a pint of milk or go to your local coffee shop without having to spend hours getting dolled up just in case some stranger takes your picture and posts it online.' I winced.

'Oooh yeah, imagine! That's why I wouldn't dream of stepping out without my lashes and lipstick on,' he joked.

'*Very funny!* You know what I mean!'

'I do,' he said as we linked arms. 'And I totally agree. I'd hate that too.'

We'd ignored the photographer and continued walking through the park. We'd gone to the Empire State building, then taken the ferry over to the Statue of Liberty. I'd seen it all before, but it was different with Josh. Seeing the sights hand in hand, kissing, cuddling and laughing—it was *so* romantic. I'd felt like I was in an American romcom. It really was the perfect day.

And then in the blink of an eye, it was Monday and the fairy-tale weekend was all but over. After we'd woken up early to have breakfast and spent a few amazing hours together, Josh had left to go to the studio to prepare for his big recording session with Sasha. I'd packed my case, jumped in the taxi to catch my afternoon flight and was now on the plane, London bound.

I would sleep well tonight. With all the walking, the farewell sex sessions we'd had last night and this morning and generally a full-on few days, I was shattered. Probably wasn't a bad thing, as I was already missing Josh, so at least if I was sleeping, I wouldn't be thinking about him and feeling sad.

I would text him when I got home to let him know I'd got back safely, have a shower and then go straight to bed. A long, blissful sleep was exactly what I needed to ensure I woke up feeling refreshed, rejuvenated and ready to face the world in the morning.

I smiled to myself. What a *wonderful* weekend I'd had with my *wonderful* boyfriend. I thought back to that singles' party and how I'd believed that all men were dogs. *How embarrassing.* And now look. Since then, Kat had met a decent man and so had I.

At last I was able to think about planning a happy future with someone special. I was a million miles away from the boring existence I had before, where I did nothing but stare at my phone and stay cooped up at home all day. I had new friends, new hobbies and had met the one. My life was finally exciting. Like a beautiful love story, in a sweet romance novel. And I couldn't wait to turn the page to find out what happened next.

CHAPTER THIRTY-ONE

It's too early! I moaned, putting my alarm on snooze for probably the tenth time. 9.30 a.m. meant it was 4.30 a.m. in New York, so technically I should stay in bed for another five hours, right? I just wasn't ready to get up and return to real life yet. Just ten more minutes…

I was about to close my eyes when I heard a noise.

What was that? Sounded like someone was trying to open my front door.

Shit.

Josh! Maybe it was him. He had a key to my flat. No. He'd given it back before he'd left because he didn't want to lose it. Said he'd like to have it again when he returned. *And hello?* He was in America right now.

So if it wasn't Josh, then who the hell…

'Chloe?' I said as she peeped her head round my bedroom door. 'You frightened the life out of me! What are you doing here? Not that I'm not pleased to see you. It's just you haven't been here since…you haven't used your key for what? Nearly seven months? Not since, in

your words, *I was a quivering mouse crying over Eric!*
Well, I'm glad you're here.' I sat upright. 'Actually, it's
quite poignant that you are. Or should that be *ironic*? I
always get those two words mixed up. Anyway, you'd be
so proud of me. I went to New York and had an amazing
time with Josh. I was *fearless*! I didn't overthink—well,
not as much as usual anyway—and I even acted calmly
and left him to hang out with Sasha—yes, *the* Sasha—at
some showbiz party whilst I went back to the hotel. I
mean, talk about *progress*. Especially as she's ridiculously
beautiful and lovely. She seems *so* cool and...'

I paused.

Why wasn't Chloe talking?

Why was she staring at me like that? Perhaps she was
overwhelmed with my rambling?

Still in silence, she reached in her bag and took out a
container filled with cake and placed it on my bedside
table.

Chloe had bought *cake*. And she'd come to my flat
unexpectedly at 9.30—*in the morning*, when she knew I
was positively *not* a morning person at the best of times.
Never mind after an eight-hour flight, when I'd be
suffering from jet lag.

Chloe had come to my flat after staying away for
months. She hadn't rung the doorbell either. She'd let
herself in. Something she'd only ever do in an emergency.
And she hadn't said a word. Not even *hello*.

Something was wrong. Chloe only usually brought me
a lot of cake if it was my birthday, or to cheer me up if
there'd been bad news, and unless I was more jetlagged
than I thought, it was definitely not my birthday.

And she *never* brought a container that big. Or that

much cake. There was enough there for ten people. This was bad.

Very, very, very bad.

'Chloe? What's wrong?' I jumped up out of the bed. 'Why aren't you saying anything? Is there something wrong? Has someone died?'

'I think you'd better sit back down.'

'Why? Did the world come to an end whilst I was asleep and we're the last known survivors?' I chuckled. Her expression turned to stone.

'Sit down, Em, and here, have some cake.' She opened the box. There was chocolate cake *and* carrot cake.

Oh Jesus.

Code red, people. We have a code red.

If a problem was low to medium on the disaster scale, then Chloe would bring a simple Victoria sponge or banana loaf. But *chocolate cake*, with her salted caramel icing? She hadn't even pulled out that showstopper when I'd seen Eric's proposal on social media, and in my eyes that was at the severe end of the shitty scale. This could only mean World War III is about to erupt. *Imminently.*

No. It must be worse than that, because I spotted brownies too. Whatever it was must be so bad, she needed to bring extra backup.

Shit.

'Seriously, Chloe. You're really starting to freak me out. Chocolate cake, brownies *and* carrot cake? What's going on? Please, can you just tell me!'

'Okay, okay, but please sit down,' she said softly. 'You're really going to need to.'

'Fine.' I climbed back onto the bed. 'I'm sitting down.'

'Good. Good. Um…well, I was dropping Archie to school and you know kids, heads always buried in their phones. That's why I don't like technology. Damaging in so many ways. But he was the one that saw it. He showed me briefly, you know, on his phone whilst I'd stopped at the traffic lights, and I couldn't believe my eyes, so I had to pull over. But then I was worried that we'd be late, so…'

She's waffling. Chloe doesn't waffle.

'Chloe! Can you just get to the point, please!' I snapped, terrified about what she was going to say next.

'Okay, okay. Do you have your phone or the iTablet thing in here, or maybe we could go to the computer in your office and we can—'

'I've got my phone, right here.'

'Okay. But before you do a search and look, I just want to say that maybe it's a mistake. This is what I mean about technology. It can be so—'

'Chloe!'

She took a deep breath. 'Okay, type in *Sasha kisses new mystery man…*'

I felt my heart stop.

'What did you say?'

'I think you heard what I said. Would you like me to do it for you?' she said, reaching for my phone.

'No!' I said, snatching it back. 'I'm perfectly capable of typing a few stupid words into Google.'

My hands started shaking as I punched in the letters. *I honestly don't know what Sasha's love life has got to do with me*, I lied to myself as I started to put the pieces of the puzzle together and understand why Chloe had felt the need to race round here.

As I pressed the 'go' button, my stomach churned and my heart began beating faster.

I clicked on a link and there it was.

Oh my God.

That's Sasha.

With Josh.

Kissing.

I dropped the phone on the floor and got to the bathroom just in time before I threw up.

The whole room began to spin. My heart was now beating out of my chest, my stomach was pulsing as another wave of nausea rose through my body.

Then came the tears. Chloe came and sat beside me and stroked my shoulders, then held my hair back as I threw up again.

'Here,' she said, taking a tissue and wiping around my mouth before pulling me into her so I could cry on her shoulder.

'Tell me this isn't happening, Chloe,' I pleaded. 'Not Josh. Please not Josh too! *Please! No!*'

'Don't worry. We'll get you through this.'

'But why *again*? Why does this keep happening to me? What did I do wrong? I thought he loved me. I really thought this was it. That he was the one. And then he cheats on me? I hadn't even been gone five minutes and he does this? *Why?*'

'You'd really have to ask him.'

'And here I was just telling you how brilliant I'd been by trusting him and leaving him alone with her! What a joke. Maybe that's when it all started. After I left the party. Maybe Bruce and Adrian went home and she invited Josh back to her place to *talk* and he was so in awe of the woman he'd had a massive crush on for decades that he jumped at the chance. Oh my God! How could I have been so *stupid*! Maybe when I woke up and he was in the shower he'd only just got home from screwing her. It was about seven a.m. I was so out of it I didn't even realise!'

'I don't know what to say. I was sure Josh was one of the good ones.'

'So was I! What a fool. And can you believe it?' I said, jumping up from the floor and storming back into the bedroom. 'That first night in the pub, he told me he'd never cheated on a woman, never ever in his entire life. Can you believe that? Mr Hotness had always been faithful? Likely story! I knew it sounded farfetched. "I would never cheat on my lady," he said. What a load of utter bollocks! And I fell for it! Hook, line and sinker.'

'You can't blame yourself.'

'Oh, yes, I can! I should have known not to trust him. I can't trust anyone. Not Eric, not him. In fact, Josh is *worse* than Eric. Josh pretended to be nice and that he loved me more than anything in the world. He made me fall so deeply in love with him. He knew what I'd been through with Eric and then he went and did this!'

'Have some cake, it'll make you feel better.'

'The only thing that will make me feel better right now is a heart transplant. This one I've got right now is well and truly crushed. *Dead*.'

'Oh, Em. Don't say that.'

'It's true! Look!' I said, picking up my phone again. 'That's supposed to be *my* boyfriend. So why is her perfect face pressed against his? Let's see what it says shall we?'

'Don't. No good can come from doing that. You're just

torturing yourself…' I started talking over her as I read the article out loud.

Sasha Smooches with New Mystery Man

The world's most successful female artist of all time was spotted getting up close and very personal with her handsome new man at New York's Owl in a Tux bar last night.

Sasha looked smitten as the pair whispered sweet nothings in each other's ears all night before leaving the club together at midnight.

Sources say the mystery man, believed to be British breakthrough artist Josh Carter, have become increasingly close in recent days, since he came to the States to begin his first US solo tour. A friend said: 'They met at a party after one of his sell-out shows and instantly clicked. They couldn't take their eyes off each other and things escalated from there…'

'Oh, I can't read any more of this, Chloe.' I tossed my phone on the duvet. 'It's too much!'

I collapsed on the bed sobbing again. My phone started ringing.

'I think you might want to get this call.' She passed it to me.

'I can't speak to anyone right now!'

'But it's Josh…'

'I *definitely* don't want to speak to that lying, cheating bastard. He can sod right off. Go and live in Hollywood with that bitch.' I sobbed. 'That's what makes it even harder. I thought she was nice. I'm so gullible. At least that Nicole was a bimbo. But this was *Sasha*. Voted the most beautiful woman in the world a zillion times. I don't know if that makes it worse or better that I've been traded in for her. I suppose he's human after all. Why have plain old me when he could have the woman every man fantasises about?'

'Stop that *right now*! Just because she's famous, that does not make her better than you! Being rich and selling lots of records doesn't make her some kind of superior species. She still shits and farts like the rest of us. The only difference is that she wipes her bottom with more expensive toilet paper! Don't you ever put yourself down like that again. *If* Josh *has* done something with her, then just like Eric, you're better off without him. Rather you find out now than waste years of your life like you did with that other tallywag. Come here,' she said, pulling me to rest my head on her shoulder again and stroking my hair.

'Thank you for coming, Chloe. To break the news to me.'

'I wish there wasn't a need for me to do it, Em, but as soon as I saw it I had to come. It was going to hurt however you found out, but I hoped that at least by being here I could help soften the blow a little.'

'I probably wouldn't even have found out for ages. I don't watch TV, I listen to Spotify all day rather than the radio and I hardly use social media anymore.'

'Good. *Definitely* keep it that way. Especially for the next few days. *Definitely* stay off social media. You really don't need to read that vile flimflam.'

I paused.

Was she speaking *generally*, or about something she'd seen or heard *specifically*?

'Chloe? Is there something else you've seen? Something else you're not telling me?'

She bowed her head. Not like her to be lost for words.

'Yes. There is. But like I said, it's best you don't see it. It will only upset you unnecessarily…'

'What? Upset me more than I am already?'

'Yes. Quite possibly.'

I picked up my phone. It had been ages since I'd been on Twitter. Not since last week. Or maybe even the week before? I did a search for Sasha. A flood of tweets came up. I scanned them quickly.

@Sasha's new man is hot…

@Sasha—yes Queen!

Clearly from fans. Then I came across a post from what looked like a tabloid

@Sasha's new man dumps girlfriend to be with her

Then underneath there was a photo. The photo of us in Central Park. *I was in the photo.* The post that included my image was on social media with thousands of likes and hundreds of comments. I clicked to read them.

He definitely upgraded!

No wonder he left her ugly ass. Aint no one who can compare to Sasha! #Queen

Damn! Look at the size of her butt! Maybe if she went on a diet, he wouldn't have left her.

Look at her frizzy hair. Lol!

The insults went on and on. The tears streamed down my face.

When I'd said last night that I wanted a good sleep so that I would be ready to face the world in the morning, this was definitely *not* what I'd had in mind.

I'd thought I'd experienced pain when I'd gone through the break-up with Eric. But that was nothing. That didn't even register on the scale of complete and utter heartbreak I was feeling now. Even if you laid me down on a bed of a million nails, then got a hundred people to jump on me, set me on fire, then left me to burn a slow death, I could never feel as horrendous as I was right now.

Not only had the love of my life cheated on me and ripped out my heart in the process, but an army of evil trolls were picking away at every part of me. Laughing and ridiculing me and how I looked for their own entertainment. And I couldn't do anything to stop it. I couldn't delete the image of me and retouch it before posting again. I couldn't decide to delete the photo altogether. It brought back all of the insecurities I'd worked so hard to fight. I was vulnerable. Powerless. Chloe was right. Social media could be toxic.

Oh my God. My parents! What if they saw this?

And my clients!

Shit.

Josh called again.

I cancelled the call.

He called back.

I pressed cancel.

He called again.

Cancel.

Then he texted.

Josh

Em, answer your phone. Something's happened that I need to explain.

Me

Fuck off, Josh!

Me

I hate you!

. . .

'What are you typing?' asked Chloe.

'Nothing important. I've just told Josh to sod off, that's all.'

'Don't you think you should talk to him?'

'Why? That's the same thing Eric wanted to do after I walked in on him. *Talk?* What the hell was there to talk about when Eric was there naked inside another woman? Same thing with Josh. I've seen the pictures. He told me himself that he thought she was hot. What else is there to say? He idolised her, they kissed and goodness knows what else.'

'I don't know. I still think you should give him five minutes to hear his side of the story. Give him the benefit of the doubt.'

'No!' I snapped.

'Okay, okay. It's still too raw. I understand. But think about it, okay? Look,' she said, putting her arm round my shoulder, 'I'm really, really sorry. Super bad timing, I know, but I have to go to work now. I feel awful leaving you, but I've got a meeting in half an hour. I can try and see if someone else can fill in for me instead. It's just that one of the ladies has flown down from Scotland especially.'

'Oh, sorry, Chloe. No, no, you go. I'll be fine. I mean, I think I'm just going to go to sleep and then hopefully when I wake up this will all just be a bad dream. I can't face anyone right now. I just want to hide away.'

'I understand.'

'Oh God!' I said as the enormity of this dawned on me. 'That photo will be all over the internet, so do you think they'll be interested in me? The paps won't come here, will they? I couldn't bear it.'

Chloe got up off the bed, crept over to the window and gently flicked open the blinds.

'Coast is looking clear for the moment, but it might not stay that way for long. Leave it to me. I'll contact Archie. He's a whiz at this technology stuff. I'm pretty sure he'll have some ideas on how to throw the paps off the scent. Don't worry, Em. We'll figure this out. Just stay inside. Keep a low profile. I'll be round after work. Until then, get some rest.'

'Thank you again,' I said, hugging her tightly. 'I'm going back to bed now.'

'Good idea.'

'Good luck with your meeting, and sorry if I made you late.'

'Don't be silly. You know I'd do anything for you. And don't let that cake go to waste. Get stuck in. So glad I baked those last night now.'

'So am I.'

By the time Chloe left it was after 9 p.m. She'd brought round some chicken soup and sat with me for hours. Despite sleeping for most of the day, I was still feeling out of it. So many emotions swirling around me. It was exhausting.

Josh hadn't called back or replied to my text. Probably feeling guilty. Arsehole.

Chloe said that Archie had got someone from the States to post on social media to say they'd spotted me in New York, having a heated argument with Josh. It must have worked, as everything was normal outside, but for how long?

I couldn't even think about it. I was too exhausted.

I lay back down on the bed. Apart from getting up to go to the toilet, I hadn't moved all day.

Just as I closed my eyes, my buzzer rang.

Oh no. I hoped I hadn't spoken too soon and the paps had realised I was here. Then again, did paps ring doorbells? I had no idea. This life was all new to me and I didn't like it. *At all.*

I wanted to leave it. But at the same time I wanted to know who it was.

I tiptoed over to the window overlooking the front door of the building and couldn't believe my eyes.

What. The. Actual. Hell.

What an earth was *he* doing here?

Was I asleep?

Was this a nightmare?

I'd thought the day couldn't get any worse, but it just had.

Why?

Because standing at my front door was him.

The world's biggest dickhead. Well, after Josh's shenanigans, I should now call him the world's *second-*biggest dickhead.

Eric—yes, Eric, my lying, cheating ex—was ringing my doorbell.

Shit.

CHAPTER THIRTY-TWO

I sat on the hallway floor, staring at the intercom.

Eric.

What the hell did he want? We'd broken up over a year ago, so why was he here, and why now?

There was *no way* I was letting him in.

If he was thinking that I'd even *consider* speaking to him after what he did, then he was *seriously* deluded.

Not going to happen. Especially not today.

He stopped ringing my buzzer.

Thank God.

Good riddance.

Just as I got up to go back to bed, there was a knock at the door. My flat door.

Please don't tell me that was him. How did he get into the building? I bet it was bloody Keith from the ground floor. They were always friendly. He thought Eric was some kind of god. No doubt Eric had buzzed his flat after I'd refused to answer, and he was only too happy to help.

I'd have to have a word with him. I was sure there was a rule about letting in unauthorised guests.

The door knocked again.

'Hi, Em, it's me. Eric. Please, can you let me in?'

You *must* be joking.

'Em, I know you're in there. Please, can you open the door? I just want to talk.'

'Sod off, Eric,' I muttered under my breath.

'Em, please! It's really important. It will literally take five minutes.'

Life's already too short, arsehole, for me to waste five of my precious minutes on you.

Silence.

I think he's gone. Hallelujah.

Just as I thought the coast was clear, my mobile began ringing. Shit. I'd taken it off silent because Chloe had said she'd ring later to check up on me and I didn't want to miss her call.

'I can hear your phone ringing. I know you're there. You wouldn't go anywhere without your mobile. Open up!' He banged on the door again. 'Look.' He softened his voice. 'I know I hurt you and you probably don't want to speak to me, but I'm *really* sorry. I *really* need to talk to you and I'd prefer to do it inside, but if you'd rather I stand outside this door and say what I need to, then I will. I just didn't think you'd be keen on the neighbours or anyone else lurking around hearing all about our personal lives.'

Well, of course I don't, Eric. But I'm still not letting you in.

I wished he'd just leave me alone. This was harassment.

'Come on, Em. I just want to talk. There's something I need to tell you. It's important. What are you so afraid of?'

I wasn't afraid of Eric. I knew he wouldn't hurt me. Emotionally, yes, as I'd discovered, but not physically. I thought about calling the police. They'd probably think I was wasting their time, though.

'Emily!' he shouted, banging on the door even harder. 'Are you not at least a little bit curious about what I want to tell you? Surely it's better to just let me come in for five minutes and hear me out. I think you'll regret at least not listening to what I have to say.'

'Sod off! I've got no interest in what you have to say!' I shouted. I know I shouldn't have engaged, but he was driving me crazy. I just wanted him to go away. My head was pounding.

'Oh, so you *are* there. I *knew* it! Just let me in, please!' *Let him stop. Please.*

'For fuck's sake. Just let me in!' he snapped. 'I'll stay here all night if I have to. All *week*. I'll keep banging on your door until you let me in.'

Oh God. Eric was as stubborn as a mule. He probably *would* stay here all night.

This was all too much. I felt like there was an army of sumo wrestlers and kickboxers fighting inside my head. A human being can only take so much in one day. *Jesus.* First the photos of Josh with Sasha, then the horrible comments on social media, the fear of paps camping outside and now to top it all off, my cheating ex was banging down my door, threatening to stay there for weeks unless I let him in. It was overwhelming. I just wanted it to stop. I *needed* it to stop.

Even though I really, really knew I shouldn't and I really, really didn't want to, the quickest way to solve this was to just let him in.

Oh gosh. I couldn't believe I was going to do this.

'Em, *please*! Just five minutes is all I need.'

I took a deep breath.

'Just five minutes?'

'Yes! Yes!' he replied excitedly. 'Just five minutes!'

'And then you'll leave me alone and never contact me again?'

'Well, I hope that once you hear what I have to say, you won't want that to be the case, but yes.'

I walked towards the door and unlocked it cautiously.

'Five minutes,' I said, setting the stopwatch on my phone, 'and not a second more.'

'Hi, Em!' said Eric as he stepped into the hallway. 'So good to see you!' He leant forward to kiss me.

'Don't,' I snapped, recoiling sharply and holding up my hands.

'Shall we go in the lounge to sit down and make ourselves more comfortable?' he said.

'No need. Here is just fine, Eric. Now you've only got four minutes and thirty-one seconds, so I suggest you start talking.'

'Okay. So...well, I've been doing a lot of thinking and I realised how much I must have hurt you, and I—I wanted to tell you that I'm sorry. I'm so truly sorry for the way things ended.'

'Right...?' I said, wondering what he expected me to say. Did he want a medal? A thank-you? It had taken him this long to realise that sleeping with another woman when you were already in a relationship was a bad thing to do?

Seriously? There was *so* much I wanted to say to him right now and none of it was pleasant. 'What's this really about? Is this because you're getting married soon and you want to stand in front of the congregation with a clear conscience?'

'No, no. It's nothing like that. Nicole and I are over. Done. Finished.'

Is that so? There was a time I would have loved to have heard those words, but now I couldn't care less.

'And?' I folded my arms.

'And I've been doing a lot of soul searching. I didn't see it before, but I see it so clearly now, Em. It's *you*. It's always been you. You're the one.'

He cannot be serious.

'So let me get this straight,' I said, placing my hands on my hips. 'Because you've broken up with Nicole, who I'm guessing probably got bored and dumped you, you think that you can now come crawling back to me?'

'Come on, Em.' He stepped towards me. 'It's not like that at all. We were so good together. There's no way we could have stayed together for that long if we weren't. Admit it. You *must* have thought about it. About us? Being together again? We had a connection…'

He knelt down in front of me. In what felt like a microsecond, his hands and head darted underneath my nightdress and he'd leant forward to place his mouth between my thighs.

Don't even think about it.

Without even realising, my knee rocketed into the air, straight into his jaw.

'Ouch!' shouted Eric.

'What the hell are you doing?' I said, jumping back.

'That hurt! Why did you kick me? You used to *love* me going down on you. Remember how I always used to make you come?'

The nerve of this guy. Talk about delusional. From the look on his pathetic face right now, he somehow believed I was so desperate that I would want to have his dirty, cheating, lying tongue on me. Just thinking about it made my skin crawl.

'Get out!' I shouted.

'Come on, Em,' he said. 'What's the problem? I'm single, you're single. Why can't we just enjoy the moment?'

'The moment? *What moment?* At the *moment*, I just want you to get out! And you're *so* arrogant. What makes you think I'm single? Do you think I've just been sitting around waiting for you?'

'*Oh, come on.*' He rolled his eyes. 'I do follow the news, you know. I've seen it all over the internet that the pop star guy dumped you because he went and fucked that hot Sasha megastar. Whilst I can understand the appeal—I mean, she *is* incredibly sexy—it still really upset me to see the whole world saying all those cruel things about you, and that's one of the reasons that I wanted to come over. To protect you. Look after you. Oh, and also I wanted to let you know, the whole marriage thing you were always going on about—well, I'm ready. Let's do it, Em. Let's get married. I haven't cancelled the church or the hall that I booked for the reception yet, so we could just do it next month if you like?'

Lost. For. Words.

Stunned.

Furious.

Absolutely fucking furious!

I felt my heart pumping. My blood was boiling. My hands were shaking. The audacity to think that he could just walk in here, say sorry a few times and I'd forget about all the pain he caused me, then take him back. Did he truly believe I would just marry him? Did he *honestly* think I would say yes, just like that? And to add insult to injury, he expected me to be okay doing it in the church he'd arranged to get hitched to Nicole? Same wedding arrangements, just a different bride?

This man was stirring up a dangerous cocktail of angry and potentially violent emotions, and if he didn't leave immediately, I was going to do something that I'd regret.

Stay calm.

Stay calm.

Stay calm.

'Eric,' I said, breathing in deeply. 'If you do not leave this flat in the next thirty seconds, I'm going to do something very, very bad. I've had a shitty day, and seeing you has made it even shittier. To avoid any confusion, let me clarify a few things: I no longer love you. I don't even *like* you. And I *certainly* do *not* want to marry you. Not now, not *ever*. In fact, I can't think of anything worse. Please, can you now get the hell out of my flat and crawl under whatever rock giant cockroaches like you go to? And make sure that it's at least a million miles away from me.' My stopwatch beeped. 'Time's up, Eric. You've had your five minutes, now fuck off and don't come back.'

He left the flat with his mouth on the floor looking wounded. Whatever hurt he was feeling right now was nothing compared to what he'd put me through. I slammed the door shut and slid down on to the floor.

I couldn't believe all the words that had come out of my mouth. Not just the expletives—the change in my feelings towards him. A year ago—in fact, less than that—I would've jumped at the chance to have him back. I used to dream about a reconciliation. He'd leave Nicole and come begging for forgiveness, and I'd make him stew a little but then give in. *Pff.* Perhaps that was why he thought he'd try it. Because he was thinking I was still doormat Em who would've done anything for him. That was then. Those were the days when my world used to revolve around Eric. But since then I'd seen the light. I'd grown. Developed myself. I was a different person now. Stronger.

That was also before Josh. I used to think that I loved Eric until I'd met Josh. Then I'd realised *that* was love. Real, true, *deep* love. Well, it was from my side anyway.

My phone chimed. It was a text. I didn't recognise the number. I clicked on the message.

Unknown

You made a big mistake kicking me out. He'll never take you back. Not now. Not after what just happened! Karma's a bitch…Have a nice life. Alone.

Clearly from Eric. Must be his new number. *So immature.* And what did he mean that he'll never take me back? Josh? *He* was the one that had done something wrong. Eric was an idiot and I'd much rather be alone than with an unfaithful man I couldn't trust. *Eric can go to hell. They both can.*

God. If this was only the first twenty-four hours of this nightmare, I hated to think what it was going to be like in the next few days and weeks.

There was no doubt about it: this was going to be beyond difficult. But I couldn't let these men bring me down anymore. I'd survived being single after a terrible breakup before, and somehow, I was determined that I would find a way to do it again.

CHAPTER THIRTY-THREE

The next few weeks were challenging. It wasn't just the normal emotional trauma that comes with a breakup. Along with the tears and the not wanting to get out of bed and feeling rubbish, I also had to deal with all the other stuff that came with breaking up with someone in the spotlight. You know the usual (*not*): paps, trolls, and seeing your ex's face plastered *everywhere*.

I couldn't escape him. For the first few days, I was literally a prisoner inside my own flat, as once the paps figured out that I *wasn't* in New York, they'd started hanging outside my building.

Obviously going online in any form was a definite no-no. That wasn't hard in terms of social media as I'd deleted all the apps from my phone. Even though I knew it wasn't healthy, in the days after the story broke, I found myself checking every few minutes to see what other horrible comments people had posted about me. It became a toxic addiction. I'd worked really hard to learn to start appreciating my body and I could feel that confidence evaporating with every vicious post and tweet. I didn't want to go back to how I was before. So eventually I realised that the only way to stop getting upset was to remove social media altogether.

At first I was just going to get rid of Twitter. But then I decided to delete Instagram too. Then Facebook. Then Snapchat. They were all gone. No more social media for me. I was over it. *Done.* I instantly felt better.

Reading the news on normal websites wasn't even safe, and I knew I couldn't watch TV just in case Josh or Sasha popped up on screen. I thought I'd be okay with Spotify as long as I avoided my 'Josh' playlist. But he was all over the home page and his songs were included on my New Music Friday, Release Radar and Discover Weekly playlists. There was no escape.

When the paps eventually left, probably to pursue another innocent victim, I decided to venture out. But just as I'd reached the communal hallway, annoying, tactless Keith thought it would be a *wonderful* idea to come out of his flat and tell me 'how well' my ex was doing. He couldn't just leave it at that. *Oh no.* He had to continue, emphasising the fact that Josh was 'everywhere.' No, sorry —I think his exact words were: 'That Josh of yours— sorry, your ex—has been on every TV show known to man: *Graham Norton, James Corden, Good Morning Britain.* He's huge! You must be gutted, Emily.' As much as I wanted to tell him to sod off, I think somehow I managed some self-control, just said 'good for him,' and walked out.

And escaping Josh in the outside world was even harder. At the supermarket, his face was splashed across the front pages of zillions of magazines, and then there were posters on the tube platforms advertising his forth-coming album.

That was definitely a bittersweet moment. After illustrating the cover, I should have been happy to see my work in so many places. Feel proud. But every time I saw it, I felt sick. It just reminded me of him and how much he'd hurt me.

Adrian was certainly earning his keep. Josh must be doing so well that he'd hired a PR too. It was as if he'd taken over the world.

Mum also said the story was big in New York. I was mortified that they had to suffer the embarrassment of their daughter being slagged off in the tabloids. Thank goodness they weren't on social media. Mum and Dad called every day to check up on me and I heard the worry in their voices. Although Mum reminded me that she'd warned me about these 'rock stars' who 'could never be trusted to keep it in their pants', she was really sympathetic. Even offered to pay for a ticket for me to come over and stay with them for a while until it all blew over.

Whilst the paps had gone, there was still the gossiping and pointing from strangers. I'd hear them whispering. 'Isn't she the woman that hot new singer dumped to go out with Sasha?' they'd say as I walked down the street. It was awful.

Oh the irony. Little did I know, when I'd had that conversation with Josh in Central Park about how horrible it would be not to be able to leave the house because of paparazzi or people watching you, that just a few days later, I'd be in that exact situation.

In the end I decided that I couldn't keep hiding away. I

just had to try and ignore everything the best I could and try and get on with my life.

I threw myself into my art, starting with finally painting the field of tulips mural I'd wanted to have on my living room wall all those years ago. I took some time off work and just focused on it completely, making sure every flower, every blade of grass every windmill panel was exactly how I wanted it. It was hard work, but I loved every second. It solidified my decision. This was definitely the career path I *had* to follow. Doing the illustration artwork for Josh's album was fun, and I would have liked to have done more of that type of thing too, but I'd redis- covered my true passion. Mural art was my calling. And this time, I was determined to follow through on my dream and really make things happen.

I also used my time to change up some things around the flat. I took all the plain magnolia bedsheets, cushions and crockery to the charity shop, ready to replace them with something more colourful. Normally I would've sat in bed and ordered everything online. But I decided to venture up into town to see what was in the department stores and in different markets. It was fun. Yeah, online shopping was convenient, but it was also easy to forget the simple pleasures of feeling the different fabrics and textures there and then before buying them.

I came home with bags full of bright red bedsheets, orange cushions, green-and-blue plates and glasses. *Much more me*.

I'd also kept myself busy by continuing my life drawing and going on organised walks. And I'd increased my Spanish lessons from once to twice a week. It was challenging, but I was enjoying it. So much so that I had signed up to go on the two-week language holiday to Fuerteventura in the Canary Islands tomorrow.

Sounded sudden, but after what I had been through, it was exactly what I needed. Some time away from all this craziness. Time to reflect and also plan the next stage of my life.

Two positive things came from visiting New York. Number one: like Chloe had said, I *could* work from anywhere in the world. All I needed was a laptop, a phone and my creativity. I didn't have to be rooted to my desk. Of course, I had always known this but had let fear get in my way. Not anymore. I would go on this holiday, take the lessons in the morning and then work on my mural designs business plan and client work in the afternoons or evenings. Thankfully my clients weren't bothered about the whole scandal. None of them even mentioned it. As long as I produced the work on time, they couldn't care less about my personal life, which was a relief.

Secondly, the trip reminded me that I loved to travel and discover new things. I hadn't done it in ages. I'd been too busy cooped up inside the flat working and crying over Eric. Not anymore. I couldn't let that happen again with Josh. Now that my travel bug had been reignited, I wanted to see more of the world. It would have been nicer to do that exploring with someone special, as that's what made the time in New York so enjoyable. But as that wasn't meant to be, I'd just have to do it on my own. Going away tomorrow would be a good start. The first of many trips abroad. I couldn't wait to escape and try to put this whole nightmare behind me.

I missed Josh. Of course I did. Whilst I *did* want to confront him face-to-face, I decided it was better to leave it. Nothing he could say would change what he'd done, so what was the point? Clearly the connection between him and Sasha was too strong and he couldn't help himself. Sometimes it was just as simple as that.

I mean, let's be honest. We all have crushes. We've all had celebrities, actors or musicians that we've fancied at one point or another. Had their posters splashed across our teenage bedroom walls. Dreamt about them. Fantasised about what it would be like to be with them. Even as adults. So imagine if one of them rocked up at your front door one night, or in this case you met at a party. And *then* imagine you discovered that celebrity liked you too— wouldn't you be tempted?

So even though what Josh had done to me was horrendous, he'd only done what most people would have done in that situation. That's why I've told myself that I would just have to accept that he was weak and move on with my life. Personally, I'd like to believe I was the exception. Even if Chris Hemsworth or Michael B. Jordan rang my doorbell, I loved Josh so much that I would say 'Thanks, but no thanks, I've already got a man' without hesitation. But that was just me.

No.

I couldn't face going to see Josh. I couldn't bear standing in front of him and hearing lies coming out of his mouth. To have to listen to excuses like 'It just happened' or 'I was drunk'. Worse still if he gushed about how he 'hadn't meant to fall for her, but sometimes these things are just meant to be'. Ugh. It would *destroy* me. More than it had already. It was too risky. Much safer to accept that it was over and just try and move on.

It was going to be tough and extremely painful. But I

figured that if I was going to be sad and miss him, I'd rather do it with the sand beneath my feet and the sun shining on my skin. Even at this time of year, it should still be warm, and a nice dose of Vitamin D was sure to do me some good.

The doorbell rang. It was Chloe, who'd come round for dinner and to help me pack.

'Hello, love,' she said as I opened the door.

'Hi,' I replied as I went back into the bedroom.

'How are you? *Crikey, Em*!' she said as she saw the clothes piled high on my bed. 'Are you sure you're going for two weeks and not two *years*?'

'I know it looks like a lot, but I'm not taking all this stuff. I just thought it makes sense to put everything all out on the bed first, then pick what I need from the pile,' I added, trying to convince myself.

'If you say so…'

'Oh!' I said, disappearing into the kitchen, then returning to the bedroom. 'I almost forgot. I picked up a little something for you at one of the markets uptown.'

'Crumbs! It's beautiful!' She held up the antique cake stand. It had a gold trim and delicate flowers. 'You're such a sweetheart, thank you. But what's the occasion?'

'No occasion. I don't need a reason to treat my friend! I saw it and thought you might like it.'

'Well, that's so thoughtful of you, Em. I love it!' She gave me a big hug. 'I'm baking for a gathering this week at work, so this will be perfect. If you weren't jetting off, I would have saved you some cake. Speaking of your travels, are you sure it's a good idea to run away like this? Don't you think you should contact Josh? He's back in

London now. Brian said he's been all over the TV—*Good Morning Britain, Graham Norton...*'

'Yes, yes, I know.' I rolled my eyes. 'Bloody Keith downstairs decided that it would be helpful to tell me all about it.'

'So now that he's back, don't you think you should get an explanation? Find out what happened? Even if you listen to him for five minutes and then tell him to sod off?'

'I gave Eric five minutes of my life and look where that got me.' I shuddered as I recalled that cringey encounter. 'Anyway, to answer your questions, *no*, I'm not running away. I'm taking time out and going to develop myself. Learn new skills. And *double no*, I am *not* going to see Josh. What is there for him to explain? They kissed. Well, they probably did a lot more than that. I saw the photos. The whole world has. It may have been a nightmare for me, but Josh has done really well out of it. He's probably on top of the world right now. Why would he want to spend his precious time explaining himself to me? He's mega famous. He's going out with Sasha, he's the envy of every guy in the universe *and* he's enjoying his dream career. What a great result. Congratulations, Josh!' I said, clapping my hands as if he was in the room. 'You've made it!'

'Look, I understand.' She cleared a space on the bed and sat down. 'Eric really did a number on you. He hurt you. He messed you up for months. But then you got stronger, started going out more and then met Josh and fell in love. You thought you could trust him, that he was the love of your life, but then you saw pictures of him kissing another woman and you feel totally devastated. It feels like your world has come to an end. On the face of it, it looks like history repeating itself. First Eric cheats on you and then Josh does. But to me, something doesn't feel right about this whole Sasha story.'

'Go on...' I stopped folding a T-shirt and plonked myself down on a pile of dresses.

'For starters, I saw the way Josh looked at you—like there was no one else in the room. Like his favourite dish had just been brought to him on a diamond-encrusted platter. He was *besotted*. Even when he was with all those snooty VIP and industry people, he was never afraid to show you affection. He never hid you away. If you look back and think about this situation carefully, *objectively*, you'll see why I'm questioning this whole thing and why I think you should speak to him. Josh loves you, Emily. *Adores* you. So do you honestly think that he would throw all that away, give up everything he has with you, just for an expensive piece of skirt?'

'She's not just an expensive piece of skirt, Chloe!' I huffed. 'She's *Sasha*. Global superstar. I appreciate you saying how much you think Josh loves me, and I believe he *did*, but music is Josh's number one passion. Like he told me, it's his *life*. So when you take that into account and then consider the fact that after years of having a crush on Sasha, suddenly he gets the chance to sing with her. Make music with her. The thing he's most passionate about. Can you imagine the sparks flying, the chemistry and the connection in the studio when they sang together? How can I compete with that?'

'You don't need to compete. Josh loves *you*.'

'Look, I know you're trying to help and you want me to have a nice happy ever after, but Josh and I are over and I'm not going to humiliate myself by contacting him. I mean, can you believe that he hasn't even called or messaged me *once* since this happened? He phoned a few times when you were there—you know, when the story broke—but that's it. Nothing since then. Not a peep. So he can't love me that much if he calls a couple of times and then gives up. He just wasn't into me as much as I thought.' I bowed my head. Just thinking about it made my heart ache.

'Yeah, that does sound bad, but also a bit out of character? In fact, this whole thing seems odd. I mean, let's take all this publicity for starters. I thought Josh *hated* the spotlight. Isn't that why he never put his face on record covers?'

'Maybe Sasha persuaded him about the benefits that mass exposure could bring and he changed his mind.'

'You *do* realise you're talking nonsense, don't you?' She crossed her arms. 'From what I've seen of him and what you've told me, Josh doesn't seem like the kind of guy who wants or enjoys masses of exposure. It's not like he's some attention-seeking reality TV star. Brian said Josh didn't look happy in those interviews. Looked like he hated it. So unless Josh had a complete personality transplant in between seeing you that Monday lunchtime and the early hours of Tuesday morning when this whole Sasha stuff hit the fan or he's the world's best actor, it doesn't ring true. I mean, would Josh really want to be famous for being Sasha's love interest if music and songwriting are his passion? Don't you think he'd hate to be splashed across the World Wide Web and magazine covers for some sordid love triangle and that he'd want to drag you into all of this? Honestly?'

I'd already gone over all those points in my head a

million times.

'I hear what you're saying, and yes, it did seem strange to me and that's what made it all the more hurtful. Because he knows I hate attention and scrutiny. But I've thought about it a lot and sometimes things can't be explained. We're always trying to make sense of things in the world, but we have to face the fact that there's not always a logical explanation. Things just happen. He's human. He's a *man*. Sometimes men just react. Cheat. Lie,' I said, sad that my negative perceptions were right all along. 'And despite having a good track record for knowing the right thing to do and being a good judge of character, you've got to remember, Chloe, that you're human like the rest of us. You don't get it right all the time.'

'Say what you like, Em, but my Spidey senses are usually accurate. I'm telling you, something doesn't add up. I smell a rat, and if you're not going to take action or investigate to get to the bottom of this, then I definitely will.'

Another call from Chloe.

I knew why she was ringing: to suggest I contact Josh. She'd gone on and on about it all night whilst I was packing, and even though she knew I was on my way to the airport, she *still* kept calling me.

That was her again. I wasn't going to answer. I knew her heart was in the right place and that she was trying to help me, which I was grateful for, but I couldn't handle another lecture about going to see him. I just wanted to get out of London, enjoy this holiday and try and move on with my life.

Now she'd sent me a text.

And another!

Wow. She must *really* want me to speak to Josh. Two texts from Chloe was the equivalent of her bringing an entire cake factory to my flat to cheer me up after a world-wide disaster. I suppose I should at least look at them:

Chloe

I've just spoken to Josh and he's told me the whole story.

Chloe

Josh is innocent, Emily! Really!

Don't get on the plane. Come back and go and see Josh. RIGHT NOW! You'll regret it otherwise. TRUST ME!!

No.

I will *not* change my plans and go chasing after Josh.

He might have pulled the wool over Chloe's eyes, but I was stronger now, and I wouldn't be tricked again. Anyway, how did she know? When she said she'd *spoken* to him, did she mean over the phone? She didn't have his number. Maybe she went to go and see him, as she'd dropped me off at his house before. She probably just saw his bum, went all doe-eyed and didn't even listen to what he was saying.

Yes. I *did* miss him and I *did* still love him. I probably always would, but I couldn't put myself through any more pain.

I trusted Chloe and I wanted to believe her. I really did. But what if I got excited that she thought he was innocent, rushed over there only to look Josh in the eyes and realise everything he told her was all a lie? Chloe didn't know him like I did. She wouldn't be able to separate the fact from fiction. But *I* would be able to tell.

Nope.

I was sticking with my plans. I was going away. *End of.*

I put my phone on silent and tossed it back in my bag.

Even though I felt my phone vibrating throughout the journey I ignored it. I was going away on a lovely trip to Fuerteventura. To learn new things and make new friends. Put the past behind me.

We're here. Glad the taxi driver got me to the airport on time. I hated having to rush.

As I approached the check-in desk to queue up, as much as I tried to forget about them, Chloe's texts were still going round and round in my mind.

Josh is innocent. He told me the whole story. Come back.

I was torn. Every fibre in my body wanted to believe her, but I didn't want to keep getting hurt. And anyway, I was here now. At the airport. Standing in the queue. About to check in my suitcase. Even if I wanted to, it was too late.

There were at least fifty people in front of me. Looked like I wasn't the only one keen to get a bit of winter sunshine. The queue was moving at a snail's pace. I wondered if anyone else here was jumping on a plane, hoping that being in a different country would help heal their broken heart. Or was it just me?

Even though I was sad (to put it mildly), at the same time, I had to give myself a pat on the back. I'd come a long way since Chloe had found me in a heap on my bed crying over Eric. Even before his engagement, after we'd broken up, my self-esteem had been minus zero, as had my social life. But this time around, despite my heart feeling like it had gone twelve rounds with Mike Tyson, I could see that I was a much stronger person. I'd grown. I had more confidence, more friends, more self-awareness, self-acceptance and self-worth.

I could have quite easily shagged Eric that night and let him go down on me. Got some pleasure for myself, then asked him to leave to give him a small taste of his own medicine. That could also have been a way to get back at Josh for cheating on me. But instead, I hadn't thought twice about chucking Eric out when he'd come crawling back as I knew I was better than that. That I deserved better than him. And rather than just wasting more of my life wallowing over Josh, I was being proactive. I'd booked myself onto this trip, which I was sure would be amazing. I'd meet new people, get inspiration for my new career direction, see another part of the world and heal my soul. I'd never have been brave enough to do that before.

That was the thing. As well as realising I didn't have to settle for arseholes, I'd also seen that I didn't have to settle for a dull existence. I could be the driver of my destiny. I could do things to make *myself* happier. When I'd finally taken a moment to look up from my phone screen and stopped focusing on the filtered representations of people's lives on social media, I'd discovered there was a whole exciting world out there, filled with good people like Kat and experiences that I enjoyed and that would help me to grow. And it all started offline: outside of my comfort zone. By *feeling the fear and doing it anyway*. All those words that had felt like empty clichés before finally had meaning.

Another cliché that was true was that *I would survive*. It would be hard, yes, but I could do it. Whether I'd be able to trust another man again would be hard to say. Right now it was too soon to even contemplate. I'd never loved anyone like I'd loved Josh, so I didn't know if I could ever get over him, but I was determined to try. And despite how it had ended, all the tears I'd cried and how much he'd hurt me, I couldn't bring myself to regret it. Apart from the last few weeks, my relationship with Josh had given me some of the most magical, happiest times in my life. I would treasure them forever. Until the day I died. I just wished I could have had more of them. That we could have stayed together much longer.

I shuffled forward in the queue. Probably halfway to reaching the desk now. I thought again about Chloe's text.

Josh is innocent. He told me the whole story. Come back.

What if Chloe was right? What if those happy times didn't have to end? My heart wanted to drag me back to the taxi, go straight to his house and fall into his arms. But my head was screaming, *How could you? That would be weak.* I didn't want to be weak.

Anyway, I'd paid for my flight. An extra attendant had just joined the desk, so now the queue was moving faster. In a couple of minutes, my suitcase would be checked in, and I would be going through security and boarding a plane. Then in just a few hours I'd be relaxing on a beach, miles away from all my problems. Hundreds of miles away from Josh.

But that's the thing. Deep down—in fact, not even deep down, right at the surface—I knew in my heart I didn't *want* to be miles away from Josh. I wanted to be right beside him. I wanted to be relaxing on a beach with *him.* Just the two of us. Em and Josh. Josh and Em. *Together.*

Hold on.

It just dawned on me.

I'd been looking at this all wrong.

Yes. I was stronger. That part was true. But, whilst it

was good that I was picking myself up and taking myself away to learn new skills, that was not the only way to be strong. *Being strong* was also about being brave. Having the courage to face up to difficult things, like going to see Josh and listening to his side of the story. Even if what I heard wasn't what I wanted it to be.

I see it now.

Being strong was about taking a chance. Stepping outside of my comfort zone. Again. Trusting. Tuning into my gut. Just like I'd thought and Chloe had also suggested, something was off. The Josh I knew would absolutely *hate* doing any publicity. He would *hate* doing TV shows and being splashed across magazines. He would *hate* people knowing him for just being Sasha's boy toy. He'd *despise* it. In fact, the words *hate* and *despise* weren't strong enough to express how much he would *loathe* it. Josh would want to be recognised for his songwriting skills and his incredible voice, not for his face or who he was snogging.

And he *loved* me. He did. I *knew* it. Even if Sasha did a naked lap dance for him, he would turn her down. But he'd do it in the nicest possible way. Because that was just him. Josh didn't have an evil bone in his body, and even though he was a human being and wasn't perfect, I believed he wouldn't hurt me. I just *felt* it.

I didn't know what the explanation was for those photos, but I was leaving right now. Going back to see him. Because I *loved* him. And I was going to listen because I was strong enough and brave enough to do that, and because I knew that if I *didn't* go, if I didn't find out the truth, not only would I not be able to relax on this trip, I would also regret it for the rest of my life.

I picked up my suitcase, ducked under the barriers and ran from the check-in queue to the exit to hail a cab.

Just as I was about to climb inside the taxi, I heard a voice from behind me.

'Em! Emily! Wait!'

I turned around.

It was him.

It was Josh.

He was here. At the airport.

Looked like I'd be getting that explanation much sooner than I thought.

CHAPTER THIRTY-FIVE

J osh slammed Chloe's car door and started running
towards me.
'Em!' he said as he picked me up and spun me
around. 'I thought I'd lost you!'

As he put me back on the ground and squeezed me
tight. I could hear his heart beating fast. I breathed him in.
God, I missed smelling his scent. It felt so good to be
wrapped in his arms again.

'Hi!' he said, moving his head back to look at me.

'Hey,' I replied. Josh looked tired. Still gorgeous to me,
but tired. His eyes were bloodshot with dark circles
beneath them and he felt slimmer. He was wearing his
signature black jeans and T-shirt, but they seemed looser.
Like he'd lost weight. Josh loved his food and always kept
himself healthy, so it was strange to see him like this.
Maybe with all that that publicity and touring he wasn't
getting time to eat.

'God, I'm so happy to see you, Em. We thought we'd
miss you! Chloe was nervous about driving on the motor-

way, but thankfully she got us here in one piece. I offered to drive instead, but as I hadn't slept, she said it wasn't safe. After she explained everything about Eric and I'd explained everything about the whole Sasha bull, I just *had* to come after you. But we didn't want to wait for a taxi, so we just jumped straight in her car and came here.'

'Eric?' I frowned. 'What's Eric got to do with all this?'

Why on earth was he mentioning my ex?

'We have a *lot* to catch up on. Shall we go somewhere we can talk and then I can fill you in?'

'Okay...' I said as he picked up my suitcase and we headed over to Chloe's red Ford Fiesta.

I was so confused. I couldn't deny that I was happy to see Josh again, but my head was also all over the place trying to make sense of everything.

After being caught kissing another woman, putting me through hell, then not contacting me for weeks, Josh was all jovial and acting like none of it had ever happened and talking about Eric? *Of all people.* And Chloe said there was a logical explanation for all this? Right now it felt like we were existing in parallel universes.

'I thought you'd run off to Fuertev-wherever!' said Chloe as I came over to hug her. 'I tried to get here as quickly as I could, but I don't like driving on the motorway. I only ever use the car to get to and from work, go shopping or for dropping and picking up the kids from school. And I can't believe that you ignored my calls and my texts! You know how much I *hate* sending those things, so you should have realised that it must have been something urgent for me to send two.'

'Yeah, I thought it might be,' I said as I sat in the backseat whilst Josh put my case in the boot. 'But I just needed to get away and clear my head.'

'Well, if you think your head was spinning before, Em, it's going to explode into a million pieces when you hear the whole story.'

Josh got in and sat beside me.

'Come on, you two,' she said, starting her engine. 'Let's get out of here before I get a parking ticket.'

I couldn't wait any longer to hear what had been going on, so Chloe drove into the short-stay car park and pulled into a space at the back. She then climbed onto the front passenger seat and turned around to face us both.

'Right. So you remember I told you last night that if you didn't get to the bottom of this whole Josh and Sasha thing, I would?'

'Yes. I do remember you mentioning it several hundred times, Chloe.' I rolled my eyes.

'Well'—she crossed her arms—'because I knew that you weren't going to do anything about it, when you went to check on dinner, I got Josh's number from your phone and wrote it in my notebook.'

'You what?'

'You heard me. Anyway, so when I got home, I texted him—yes, *texted* him. I tell you what. I've sent more texts since this whole Sasha debacle happened than I think I've sent in my lifetime. Anyway. Josh didn't get my text until five a.m.'

'Because I was in the studio,' he added.

'Yes, that's right, and he responded straight away. None of that texting-back-and-forth nonsense. Josh actually *called* me. At five o'clock in the morning, mind you, so you can imagine Brian's absolute delight when he got woken up by my mobile ringing loudly at that ungodly hour.'

'Yeah, sorry about that again, Chloe. I was just so excited to hear from you as I thought it meant that there might still be a chance with Em and that maybe the whole thing with Eric wasn't how it seemed. Just like the Sasha rubbish wasn't how it seemed either.'

'I still don't get it. What the hell has Eric got to do with anything?'

'Hold your horses.' Chloe raised her hand. 'We'll get to that bit in a minute. Let us continue.'

'Okay, okay. Sorry.' I readjusted myself in the seat. 'I'm listening. Carry on.'

'So I thought as I'm up, I might as well go over to Josh's now to get to the bottom of things,' said Chloe, pulling a bottle of water from her handbag and taking a sip. 'Brian said given all the gossip and controversy, he didn't think it was a good idea for me to be seen going to Josh's house at five a.m., but I said *sod the paps*. They wouldn't dare try and come after me, and anyway, with these rollers in my hair, they're more likely to think I'm his aunt than his hook-up girl. So I went there and Josh explained it all.'

'I did. So now it's time for me to explain it to you too.' He took a deep breath and stared me straight in the eyes. 'In a nutshell, none of it's true. Sasha and I didn't kiss. Well, we *did*, but not like that. It isn't how it seems.'

'Oh, that's what *all* the cheats say,' I scoffed, reverting back to my old thoughts about men.

No, no. Mustn't do that. My gut says to trust him. There's a perfectly logical explanation.

God, I really hope there is…

'Please, Em. Just *listen*, and then you'll understand. Let me start from the beginning. So after I left you at the hotel that Monday. I went to the studio to prepare. That was around one p.m. right?'

'Yeah, I think so.'

'So I went to the studio, and Sasha was supposed to come at four, but she didn't arrive until seven. *Fair enough*, I thought. Well, actually, I thought it was pretty rude, but you hear about big stars being hours late, and it was a great opportunity, so I just put the time to good use. But when Sasha eventually arrived, she was *off*. She wasn't the bubbly person we met at that party. I sang my parts and that was all fine. I was nervous, of course, but I was happy with how it sounded. But when it came to Sasha doing her bit, it just wasn't right. That wasn't the voice that I'd admired for so many years. She just seemed down. *Distracted*. It happens to me sometimes. I might be trying to sing or write something and I *know* I can do it as I've done it so many times before, but it's just not coming. So even though I don't really know her, I can see she's upset, right, and I want to help. Part of me thought she was going to say she didn't need advice from someone like me. I mean, she's got so much experience. Way more than me. But anyway, I thought it was worth a try. So I cleared the room.'

That was bold, I thought to myself.

'I asked if the entourage and all her *people* could leave us alone for a few minutes and I asked Sasha if everything was alright. I told her that when I'm in the studio and things aren't flowing, I normally call you or go and see you and I instantly feel better, but that before that, before I met you, I'd go for a drink, not necessarily alcoholic as that can mess with your voice, but just get out of the studio or go for a walk to clear my head.'

'I couldn't imagine Sasha going for a walk,' I added. 'She'd be mobbed.'

'Exactly,' said Josh. 'So I suggested going for a drink instead. Sasha said we could head back to her hotel, not for any funny business, but just because it would be more private there—no fans or cameras. Even though I knew it would be totally innocent, ironically, I thought that by *not* going to her hotel, I would avoid any scandal or anyone thinking there was something going on. I pictured the headline in my mind: *Sasha Seen Going into Hotel With Mystery Man. Mystery Man Leaves Sasha's Hotel at Midnight.* I wanted to prevent that, so naïve little me thought it would be better to go somewhere public, some-where out in the open, where it would be clear that it was innocent because we were in plain sight. Big mistake.'

'So what happened next?'

'So I asked her, "Are there any bars that you go to, where you feel comfortable? Where you won't get hassled?" So she called her manager and he arranged for us to go to this new bar as he said it would be nice and private. No paps. No cameras. No fans. The place was practically empty. We had a booth in the corner. So we had a drink. We talked. I could tell there was something on her mind. I was guessing it was man trouble. You get to know the signs.'

'Like how you knew when I was upset, when we bumped into each other that night we ended up going to the pub?' I said.

'Yeah, exactly. So I took a big risk. And I asked her. I realised that I was treading on shaky ground. I was a stranger asking Sasha about her personal life. But I just sensed that she needed someone to talk to.'

'And what did she say?' I asked.

'She said, "If I was having man trouble, I think that would keep everyone happy."'

'What?' I frowned. That didn't make sense.

'*Exactly*. At first I didn't understand. And then I did. When a pretty waitress came over, I saw it. And it made sense.'

'What did?'

'The way she looked at her. The way Sasha looked at the waitress.'

'I don't get it.' My face creased with confusion.

'*Wake up, Em*!' said Chloe. 'Sasha prefers the company of *women*.'

'Sasha's a lesbian?'

'Yes,' said Josh.

Poppycock! As Chloe would say.

'No! She's dated *loads* of guys. I've seen it in the magazines. *Come on*.' I rolled my eyes like they were on a spin cycle. 'This is a bit of an elaborate story, isn't it? Is that really the best you could come up with?'

I started to question my decision to believe him again. Maybe my gut was off.

'What do you mean?' said Josh. 'It's true!'

'So, Sasha does what? Smiles at a pretty waitress and that automatically means she's a lesbian? Because lesbians must automatically fancy every woman that crosses their paths? Ridiculous! You two know better than that, surely. And if she's a lesbian, then why were you kissing? This is sounding far-fetched to me.'

'That's because you're not letting him finish!' shouted Chloe.

'Okay, okay. *Do go on, Josh.* Next you'll be telling me that the waitress fell over and it sent Sasha's face flying into your lips!' I scoffed. Chloe raised her eyebrows. 'Okay. Sorry. I'll shut up and listen.'

'Thank you!' Josh huffed. 'As I was saying, I saw it. Just a hint of *something*. It was very, very subtle. It wasn't sleazy or something that would have led to anything, for reasons that I'll explain, it was just—I don't know, call it intuition. It may surprise you, but I'm good at picking up on these things. Anyway, I wanted to be sure. I didn't want to jump to conclusions. So I asked her. I said, "Do you mean that your management would prefer it if you were having *man trouble* as opposed to *women trouble*?"'

'And what did she say?'

'She said, "Yes, Josh. That's *exactly* what I'm saying." And then she opened up to me. I was surprised, but she did.'

'I'm not,' I said as I tried to take it all in. 'You've just got that knack, Josh. Of making people feel comfortable.'

I remembered that night in the pub, I had been *adamant* that I wasn't going to tell Josh anything about Eric, as it was so embarrassing. And the next thing I knew, I'd told him *everything*. He probably could have asked me for my bank account details and security code and I would have told him. Quite scary, actually.

'You're very easy to talk to,' I added.

'Thanks.' He blushed. 'Sasha said the same thing. So anyway, she told me that she's been having to hide her sexuality throughout her whole career and she was tired of living a lie. She's got a girlfriend who wants to settle down with her and doesn't want to be hidden away like a dirty secret. They've been dating for years and her girlfriend told her that morning she'd had enough and wanted to break up. So Sasha had a meeting with her manager, which is why she was so late, about going public and he said it would ruin her image. She'd ruin her career. So understandably she was upset and the *last* thing she wanted to do was go in the studio and sing. All she was thinking about is that the woman she loves was leaving her and she couldn't be who she wants to be.'

That was really sad. Times had changed, though, surely.

'But would it really even matter in this day and age?'

'It shouldn't, but it *does*. Very few big artists ever come out. And because Sasha's image is all about being sexy and she has such a strong male fan base, the manager and industry people didn't want to take that chance. At the end of the day, all they care about is making money. And Sasha is worth a *lot* to them.'

'I think she should forget about all that and do what makes her happy. Life's too short.'

'Which is what I told her. But remember, in this business, it's not that simple. There's the whole contract thing. I mean, look at the trouble I had all those years ago getting out of *my* contract. Someone like Sasha will have one that's iron-clad. She's far too valuable. But equally, she has the money and contacts to try and find a way out of it.'

'Okay, so I get it. You're trying to tell me that Sasha couldn't be interested in you because she likes women. But that still doesn't explain the kiss thing.'

'Right, okay, so the *kiss*. Like I said, it wasn't how it seemed. We talked for hours, and afterwards she said I was such a great listener and how she felt a million times better. So she leant forward to kiss me: *on the cheek*. But you know that awkward thing where your head goes one way and the other person goes the other and then you clash? That's all it was. *Honestly*. If you study the picture carefully, if you zoom in, you can clearly see that. Our lips didn't even touch. But the angle and the point at which the photo was taken makes it look bad.'

'Really?' I glared straight into his eyes as if I'd suddenly been given X-ray lie-detector vision.

'Yes, *really*. Get your phone out and bring up the photo if you don't believe me,' said Josh. 'Zoom in and look for yourself.'

I believed him. I don't know how, but I could just sense that he was telling the truth.

Shit.

What a relief! My shoulders suddenly felt like a ten-tonne weight had been lifted from them. Josh was innocent. He *hadn't* cheated on me. This was *amazing* news. Did this mean we still had a chance?

'I looked, Em, and he's right,' added Chloe. 'That's what I was trying to say from the beginning. These people can do all sorts of trickery with photos. Even Archie told me that. You can't always believe what you see.'

Whilst ordinarily I knew that was true, I was so blinded by my past experiences and scared of getting hurt again that I'd let it cloud my judgment.

'Sasha is a *big* deal around the world,' said Josh. 'Photos of her can earn a lot of money. Neither of us could believe it when we saw it. It was ridiculous. And all that suggestive rubbish about us leaving together at midnight. After our talk, she said she was ready to lay down the track. She asked if we could go to the studio straight away. So that's where we went. And she nailed it. She left and went to her hotel alone and I went back to mine *alone*, then I woke up to that shitstorm. And that's when I called you. I didn't even call Sasha first to tell her. I called you because I knew how upset you'd be. We'd just spoken about paps in Central Park the day before and we'd both agreed how awful it would be to have to go through all of that. So why would I do anything to cause that kind of drama?'

'I just assumed it was because you liked her. You said yourself that you'd always had a crush on her.'

'That was when I was a teenager! I *admire* her, yes. And she's a beautiful woman, yes. But Sasha's not the woman for me. Not because of her sexuality. I wasn't interested in her in that way even *before* I knew that. It was purely professional. I admire her as an *artist*. She's an *incredible* songwriter. That's inspiring. But I was with you. I was madly in love with *you*. Not her.'

'So if you loved me so much, how come you only called a few times and then just left me to suffer and go through that nightmare, the media shitstorm that I did nothing to cause, with all those trolls saying horrible things about me online, without even bothering to see if I was okay?'

There was no way Josh could deny that was a valid question. Just because nothing had happened between them, I couldn't let him off the hook without a proper explanation for why he hadn't tried harder to contact me.

'But he *didn't* just leave you to suffer, Em. Josh came to see you,' said Chloe.

'You didn't!' I glared at him. 'You just stayed in America. You didn't even make an effort to check how I was.'

'Oh, but I *did*! As soon as I got your text message saying you hated me, I dropped everything. *Everything*. I was devastated. Told Bruce and Adrian to cancel the studio time, the interviews booked for that day. I just grabbed my passport and my wallet and I got the first available flight to London. And then I arrived at your flat that evening and saw Eric.'

'*Eric?*' I said, baffled. '*Oh…*'

'He spotted me straight away. "You alright, mate?" he said, zipping up his flies. "If you've come for Em, you're too late. After your shenanigans with Sasha, she was quite upset, so I came over to cheer her up, if you know what I mean. Think she's exhausted now. Things got pretty heated, so I don't think she'll be needing you tonight."'

'He *what*?' I jumped up in anger, hitting my head on the car roof. 'But nothing happened, Josh! He came round and I kicked him out. Bastard!'

So *that's* what Eric had meant when he'd sent me that text saying that after what had just happened, Josh would never take me back. What an arsehole.

'So anyway, Em, you know my views on cheating. I told you when we were at the pub that first night. It's the one thing I can't forgive. When I saw him pulling up his flies and basically telling me that he'd just slept with you, I felt like a bomb had just exploded inside me. It floored me. I'd flown all the way back to London to see you, to explain, and rather than trusting me, you'd just taken some tabloid photos as gospel and jumped back into bed with your ex. So I left. I went home and booked the first flight back to New York for the following morning.'

'*Oh, Josh!* I didn't know.' My heart sank. 'I didn't know that you'd come to see me! How could you think that I would go back to Eric? You should *know* me.'

'And you should know *me*, Em. You should have known that I would never have done anything with Sasha or any other woman. I *told* you. I don't cheat. I also told you that I *love* you. *A million times.* We had an amazing weekend together. So how could you think that I would just say goodbye to you and then go with another woman two minutes later? That's not me. And remember, I listened to you that night in the pub. I could see how much you loved Eric. He really got under your skin. Seemed to have quite a hold over you. So I just thought maybe it was a moment of weakness—he came round and you couldn't resist.'

'No!' I pleaded, desperate for him to believe me. 'No way! He came round banging on the door for ages and he said if I gave him five minutes he'd leave me alone forever, and with everything that had happened that day, I just needed the noise to stop. I needed him to go away. So I let him in. And he *did* try to kiss me and try to get me back, but I told him point blank that I wasn't interested. I hurt his ego, and I think that's why when he saw you, he knew that if he implied we did something, it would be the perfect way to get back at me. To punish me for turning him down.'

'Goodness me!' said Chloe. 'What are you two like? Both jumping to conclusions without actually having a conversation and talking things through. That's what all this technology does to your brains. All this texting. Makes people forget the most effective communication tool of all. *Talking.* Face-to-face.'

'Well, I did *try*. But Madam Emily decided not to answer my calls!' Josh scoffed.

'I'm sorry. But I was upset. Can you blame me?'

'No, I get it. I do. I guess it's easier for me as I understand this industry. I know how it works. So much bullshit. All I want to do is make music. Not get involved with all the other stuff that comes with it.'

'Yeah…what's with having your face everywhere and all the TV shows?'

'I hate it.' He shook his head. 'It's not me. When I got back to New York, I was devastated. I told you the pain that cheating can cause. I'd lost the love of my life to that dickhead and was thousands of miles away from my friends. I felt like I had no one. So I threw myself into work. Both Bruce and Adrian kept going on and on about doing this show and that show and I didn't have the energy to argue, so I just went along with it. Thought it would be a distraction from thinking about you. But I hated every second.'

'And there's more,' said Chloe, raising an eyebrow.

'*More?*' I asked.

Jesus. My head was spinning. If they sprung anything else on me, it was going to fall off my body. I was sure of it.

'Yeah. More to the Sasha story. So when I eventually did get to speak to Sasha, we were trying to work out how that picture was taken. Who had taken it and why. At first we'd just thought it was someone trying to make money selling the photo to the tabloids. But then we realised it ran far deeper. That we needed to look much closer to home.'

'What do you mean?' I asked.

'Our managers.'

'Your managers?'

'Yep. We thought about it. Adrian wanted me to blow up worldwide, right? What better way to get everyone to know about me than by having it look like I'm dating the biggest female star in the universe?'

'And what better way for her managers to cover up her sexuality than pairing her up with the sexy, good-looking British singer?' I added.

Bloody hell.

This was like a devious film plot. *Gosh.* I knew Adrian was ambitious and eager to make his mark in the industry, but resorting to this? Stooping *that* low? *Seriously?* Some people have no morals and will stop at nothing for success.

And as for Sasha's manager going to such lengths to ensure her sexuality didn't come out, that was just disgraceful. Maybe I was being idealistic, but why shouldn't she be free to be who she wanted to be and love who she wanted to? If I was Sasha, I'd tell them to sod off and go and marry my girlfriend. I'm sure her fans would stick by her. Maybe they'd love her even more for taking a stand and following her heart.

'*Exactly.* It's so fucked up.' Josh shook his head again, then perked up as he realised what I'd said at the end of my sentence. 'Thanks for the compliments, by the way. So does that still mean you think I'm sexy, then?' he replied cheekily.

'Maybe…' I tried not to smile, but could already feel my heart melting.

'Told you it would make your head explode!' said Chloe.

'It definitely has. So if you know your managers set you up, what are you going to do about it?'

'Well, in my case, it's already done,' said Josh. 'I've fired Adrian. I said from the beginning that I didn't want to be a puppet. That I wanted to do this on my terms. My way. And he didn't do that. He broke our agreement. That's a clear case of breach of trust. I didn't spend years suffering in that hellhole of a law firm to not make sure that my contract didn't allow me to exit if I needed to. I wasn't going to get stung twice.'

'*Wow*. I can't believe it. But what does it mean for your music? I mean, will it suffer? Can you still have the career you want?'

'Yes. I can. If I *want* to. But,' he said, taking my hands in his, 'I decided today—a few hours ago, in fact, when matchmaker Chloe came knocking at my door and explained the story—that as much as I love music, there's something, *someone*, that I love much more…'

'I think this is the part where I go for a walk,' said Chloe, grinning as she opened the car door, got out, then closed it gently.

'Oh, Josh. I love you too.' I edged closer to him. 'I've been *miserable* without you.'

'It's been awful, hasn't it? The pain was *unbearable*. I wanted to hold you so badly. I even found myself in a supermarket at two a.m. sniffing all of the bottles of shampoo just to find the one that smelt like you.'

'*Weirdo*! My lovely hair-sniffing weirdo.' I squeezed his hands. 'Did you find it?'

'No! I nearly got kicked out by the security guard. He threatened to call the police. Then he recognised my face from all the magazines and said he'd let me off if I signed a copy for his daughter.'

'I suppose being famous does have its perks, then,' I laughed.

'Would've been much easier if you just told me what brand it was.'

'*Aha.* Top secret! That shampoo's made especially for me.'

'Really?'

'Of course not, Josh! I've got loads of it at home. I'll give you a bottle.'

'I'd rather you just give yourself to me, so I can smell you and your hair whenever I like,' he said, twisting my curls gently around his fingers.

'Mmm, I like the sound of that...'

We both leant forward and our lips met for the sweetest kiss. My head and body felt fuzzy. Light-headed in the most amazing way. I was home. I was back with my Josh.

At that moment, a whirlwind of thoughts and feelings also flooded my mind. Desire, naturally. That was a given. I wanted to be with Josh, completely and utterly. But it wasn't just the physical I was thinking about. I was also feeling so grateful. Glad that I'd taken a chance to leave the airport, go after him and listen to his side of the story. Thank God Chloe had been so persistent. If only we'd spoken sooner, we could have saved so much time and heartache. But that was the past. I didn't know what would happen next, but the main thing was, we'd been reunited. We were together again. Which was where I truly believed we were supposed to be.

'God, I've missed kissing you,' said Josh as he brushed a stray curl from my face.

'Me too.' I stroked his cheek. 'Don't ever put me through anything like that.'

'Don't *you* ever put *me* through anything like that again.' He smirked.

'You started it with your celebrity Sasha schmoozing! So what's happening with her? And were you even allowed to tell me all about her private life? Didn't you have to sign some sort of confidentiality agreement?'

'No. I asked her if I could tell you and she said *absolutely*. She understands what it's like to risk losing the love of your life and she felt so bad about the whole thing. She said to do whatever I needed to fix it—even if it meant that you wanted to call and speak to her to check everything. There's even video footage of when we were in the bar. That's the crazy thing. If people checked their sources, they'd see that there was no story. It was all lies. But no one cares about that. They just see a photo and that's it you're guilty. No one verifies these things. People aren't interested in the truth. The fantasy and the scandal are much more exciting and newsworthy in their eyes.'

'*Bloody hell.* So underhand. Chloe always said that a lot of people posted loads of lies online, and whilst obviously I knew it could happen, I didn't realise people would stoop that low. Talking of Chloe, you know she was so desperate to prove your innocence that she even sent multiple texts? I'm surprised she was able to drive here afterwards!'

'Chloe isn't as big of a technophobe as you think, you know.' Josh raised his eyebrow.

'You don't know her like I do. She hates that stuff, and as for anything more advanced, forget it. Chloe would rather donate a kidney than go *surfing* on the World Wide Web,' I giggled.

'That's just what she wants you to believe. How do

you think she booked all those activities for you when you were doing that get out of the house challenge?'

'Well...I don't know...' I scratched my head. 'Maybe she found them in the newspaper or perhaps got Archie to look it up—you know, like she got him to book the ticket to New York...' Chloe had always been resourceful and good at finding and researching things and I'd been so nervous about doing the activities that I hadn't given it much thought, but it was a good question.

'She found all the activities online! On the *Meetup* app. She got Archie to teach her how to use it. For you.'

What a sneaky but amazing friend! Chloe had gone to all that effort for me. Not just with setting the challenge and booking all the activities to stop me wallowing over Eric, and the flight tickets, but also getting to the bottom of the whole Josh and Sasha debacle and then driving him up here to make sure I didn't lose the love of my life. I really didn't know how I could ever repay her.

'God, I'm so lucky to have such an incredible friend.'

'You are indeed.'

'And a rather lovely boyfriend too...well, when he's not dragging me into global tabloid scandals, of course,' I chuckled. 'I can laugh about it now. *Just*. But to be honest, all that celebrity and fame stuff blows my mind. I'm used to leading a simple life.'

'And that's what *I* want too, Em. To live a simple, calm life, with *you*. You're the most important thing to me. *You* are all that matters.'

'But you can't give up your music! You're *way* too talented.'

'Thanks.' He blushed. 'I don't *need* to give up my music, but like I've said from the beginning, I'll do it on my terms. On a smaller scale. Money isn't important to me. As long as I can write songs, make music and have enough to live a decent life with you, that's more than enough. That's what will make me happy. My grandma always said it's about knowing your level. What you want to achieve in life. Some people want global superstardom, but that's never been my goal. I want to be on the level where I put my music out, people buy it or stream it and I maybe tour once or twice a year. Or whatever. Maybe I won't. It all depends on if my lady wants to come with me...'

'Hmm. I think I can be persuaded. Since New York, I feel like I've caught the travel bug. Oh shit!' I said. 'What's the time? I'm supposed to be getting on a plane!'

I rummaged in my bag for my phone. I looked at the clock. I could still make it. *Maybe*. But I didn't want to. I was happy right here.

'Yes, you are.'

'Well, I *was*. That was before some lunatic came chasing after me at the airport.' I smirked.

'Yeah. *Crazy me*. Where were you going, anyway? When I called your name, you were about to get into a taxi.'

'Leaving the airport to go and chase after you, of course.'

'Really?'

'Yes, *really*. I realised that I was going to Fuerteventura to try and get as far away from you as I could, when all I really wanted to do was be right beside you.'

'Oh, Em. I love you so much.'

'I love you too,' I said, placing my lips on him. As my tongue gently flicked against his, the butterflies returned and began dancing around my stomach and my heart raced. I wished that we could stay here kissing. *Forever*.

'So how about it, then?' he said as we came up for air. 'How about we go somewhere right now, just the two of us? *Together*.'

'Where?' I rested my head on his shoulder as he stroked my hair.

'Wherever you want.'

'Wherever I want?' I glanced up at him.

'Yep. Maybe we could go somewhere hot and relax with one of your cocktails by the pool.'

'Oooh, maybe we can *really* have sex on the beach.' I smirked. 'And this time I'm *not* talking about the cocktail…'

'Mmm, I like the sound of that. Honestly, Em, I don't care where I go, as long as it's with you.'

'Awww.' I lifted my head up and kissed him. 'I feel the same. But wait…you don't have your passport. Or any clothes.'

'Oh, yes, I do! Well, I don't have any clothes, but I *do* have my passport. They have clothes shops in other countries, you know.' he chuckled. 'I can pick up something wherever we go.'

'How come you have your passport?'

'Well, I figured that if we didn't get to the airport in time, then I'd just have to jump on a plane and follow you. I've been getting very good at getting on planes at the last minute to come and see you, you know.'

'*Wow*.' I smiled. 'You're amazing, Josh. Do you know that?'

'Thanks. So are you. What do you reckon, then, Em? Fancy going on a nice long holiday with me? We can throw caution to the wind. Just rock up to the desk, pick a flight and jump on a plane to anywhere in the world and plan the rest of our lives together. How about it?'

'My darling Josh,' I said, taking him in my arms. 'I can't think of anything else I'd love to do more.'

EPILOGUE

I put down my paintbrush, took a step back and admired my work: a colourful world map I'd just finished painting in a school classroom. Another mural completed and another satisfied customer.

Since I set up Em's Mural Designs ten months ago, I'd done lots of cool jobs: one of a coffee machine at Cuppa, a summer garden mural at a retirement home and painting cartoon characters inspired by *The Lion King* in a nursery for a new family. So many great projects. I'd even been commissioned to do a mural of the London skyline for the reception area of a cool fashion brand in Soho after pitching for the business myself. I know, right! Little old me actually sold myself not just on email, but also on the phone and in a face-to-face meeting. I'd certainly come a long way.

As well as my mural designs, I'd been doing all the illustrations for Josh's EP and single covers and I loved it. Definitely beat drawing different shapes of poo any day.

Speaking of Josh, everything was going great. After

returning from that impromptu two-week holiday in the Maldives a year ago, I decided to sell my flat and move in with him. It made sense. He had a lot more room there and I could use the large room at the back of his house as my studio. Plus, I was able to put the money I'd made from the sale in the bank, which gave me the financial freedom to set up my business without worrying where my next payslip was coming from.

Josh and I shared the mortgage, which was now in both of our names, and it had become our home. Our base. For now anyway. We'd spoken about maybe living abroad. It was definitely possible. We just had to decide where we'd like to settle. In the meantime, we planned to have lots of fun travelling whilst we did our 'market research'.

Oh, and did I mention that Josh and I were engaged? He proposed unexpectedly during a trip to Spain. His proposal was amazing. So thoughtful and romantic. I couldn't believe it when he dropped down on one knee. Naturally I said yes. We hadn't set a date yet as I've had so much going on with my work and Josh has been preparing for his tour, but we'd start planning soon.

It was crazy to think that if I'd believed that silly tabloid story last year and let myself be ruled by my insecurities and preconceptions, all of this might never have happened. When I looked back on that whole Sasha misunderstanding, I cringed. I should have known from the start that I could have faith in Josh. I suppose back then, I hadn't grown as much as I'd thought. I still believed that all men would cheat and lie. Not anymore, though. I trusted Josh one hundred per cent.

Was it weird seeing thousands of women around the world declaring their undying love for him on a daily basis, trying to hug him after a show or sliding into his DMs with messages telling him exactly what they'd love to do with him (often with explicit photos)? *A little*. But would I be worried if another tabloid rumour linked him to another woman again? *Not anymore*. Because I knew I couldn't believe everything I saw on the internet. It came with the territory, and it was *me* that Josh loved. Me that he came home to. Me who he made love to and whose arms he fell asleep in every night. And for me that was enough. I felt totally secure and calm. Which was a really good feeling.

As well as feeling more secure about my relationship, I was more confident too. I worked out at the gym these days, but for fitness rather than because I was trying to live up to some sort of ideal standard of beauty. After reading all those negative comments on social media last year, I could have easily slipped back into hating my body, but I decided to appreciate the way I was made instead. So what if my bottom was big? Some people would pay good money to get a bum this size. I was proud of my figure, and so I was all for wearing clothes that accentuated rather than hid it.

My confidence also helped me to heal my relationship with social media. I was back on it again, but this time, rather than just looking at what other people were having for breakfast (which I still enjoyed seeing occasionally, by the way), my life no longer revolved around it. I was using it for good. It wasn't about the number of followers or likes. It was more a way to express myself and get inspiration. Instagram allowed me to post photos of my work and follow other artists to stimulate my creativity and people who made me feel empowered. Rather than making me feel anxious, these days it was a source of positivity.

If I felt like it, sometimes I even posted photos of myself. But these days, I didn't spend time agonising over them. I'd wasted so many years worrying about how I looked, getting the right angle, altering my photos and doing anything to make them look 'perfect'. Like Paige, the life model, had said, perfection didn't exist. Having lumps, bumps and cellulite was normal. We're not made of stone. We all came in different shapes and sizes and I shouldn't have to edit my appearance to please others.

Before Chloe had set that challenge, I'd become so used to seeing airbrushed images that I'd thought they were normal. But really it was fake. A lot of what people posted online wasn't a true reflection of reality. Each photo and caption was often carefully planned and edited, so I was comparing myself to things that weren't even real. Trying to be someone I wasn't. Doing things I didn't want to just to impress people I didn't even know. It was silly of me to measure my worth in double taps and to crave validation from strangers. Just because someone else might not think I was beautiful, it didn't mean it was true. That was their opinion. It wasn't a fact.

I didn't need to fit in or pretend to be a fun person to make real friends or find a boyfriend. I just needed to be me. To love myself. And a real man, a man who truly loved me, wouldn't expect me to change my appearance. He'd accept me exactly how I was. Just like Josh did. He loved my bum, my hair, my personality. All of me.

It was funny. Even though we'd stayed together for far too long, I didn't regret my toxic relationship with Eric. It made me value what I had with Josh much more and also showed me the importance of not relying on anyone too much for my social circle. So even though things were brilliant with Josh, I still had my own interests and friends, which actually made our relationship stronger.

I'd kept up my life drawing and Spanish lessons. I met up once a month with Kat, who was still head over heels with Rob. Her kids loved him too and they'd now moved in together and were living as one big happy family.

And of course, I saw my amazing bestie Chloe as often as I could.

I used my first few mural pay cheques and some money from the sale of my flat to book Chloe and her family on an all-expenses-paid trip to New York as a thank-you. Without her and her challenge, not only would I have rotted away alone in my flat, I might never have met Kat or Josh. And after that whole Sasha mix-up, if Chloe hadn't intervened, I might never have discovered the truth.

I also encouraged Chloe to enter a national baking competition. She resisted at first, saying she was happy just making cakes for friends and family. But remembering how persistent she was with convincing me to get out more, I suggested that maybe it was time for *her* to step out of her comfort zone and try something new. In the end she agreed. And she won! Since then, she's had lots of orders from swanky London cafés and even around the UK. It was so exciting. Who knew where it could lead?

I also bought Chloe a smartphone. Last time I checked it was still in the box, though. Baby steps...

Overall, since the offline challenge, I'd never felt happier both with my work and my love life. I still used my phone. There was no way I wanted to give it up. It allowed me to do so many amazing things. Without it I wouldn't be able to use Google Maps when I got lost on my way to see new clients, listen to music on Spotify whilst I was painting, keep in touch with Kat on Whats-App, or Facetime my parents (which I did a lot more now, rather than wasting time typing out essay-length texts).

Plus when Josh started his first solo world tour next month (booked with the help of his much more trustworthy management team) and I was right there beside him, my phone would allow me to check emails, take bookings and do lots of things remotely. I even had some international mural commissions lined up in New York and Barcelona, which funnily enough had come via my Instagram page, so I'd focus on those during the day and I'd be there at each gig every night. It had worked out perfectly. Sasha might even come along to one of the US concerts with her wife. Yep. As well as becoming a good friend of ours (still weird being pals with a megastar), she was now out, proud, married and still massively successful.

So having a phone or using apps wasn't all bad. The difference was that now, I'd learnt to use them in moderation, alongside doing things in the real world. I actually enjoyed visiting a shop to buy things rather than always shopping online and having conversations with people face-to-face (my opening lines had improved a bit these days too). If I was out at an event or one of Josh's gigs, I tried my best to say hello to people who looked like they were lonely or nervous, as I remembered how that felt. Accepting Chloe's challenge and learning to live more of my life offline was definitely one of the best things I'd done.

Yes. Life was good. And even though it had already

changed so much, I still felt like it was only just beginning. I was loving my new career, my new hobbies, my friends and of course spending time with my amazing fiancé. And I couldn't wait to see what the future held for us.

We were looking forward to enjoying lots of new and exciting adventures. Em and Josh. Josh and Em.

Together.

Forever.

Fancy finding out how Josh proposed to Emily?
Join my VIP Club via the exclusive link below and **receive two FREE bonus chapters** with all the details on their romantic engagement!
https://bookhip.com/ZPGMTV

As well as receiving the bonus chapters, I'll also send you the following at a later date, for **FREE**:
1) Yellow Book Of Love: a handy little guide, which features essential dating and relationship tips from multiple experts.
2) A list of *Alex's Top 25 Romcoms*: a definitive guide highlighting 25 top romcoms that are loved by Alex, the protagonist in my novel *Only When It's Love.*
As a VIP club member, you will receive my fun newsletters once or twice a month with details of new releases, special offers and other interesting news.

You can **get the two romantic bonus chapters for FREE right now, by signing up at:** https://bookhip.com/ZPGMTV

ENJOYED THIS BOOK? YOU CAN MAKE A BIG DIFFERENCE.

If you've enjoyed *Love Offline*, I'd be so very grateful if you could spare two minutes to leave a review (it can be as short or as long as you like) on the book's Amazon and Goodreads pages or anywhere that readers visit.

By leaving an honest review of my books, you'll be helping to bring them to the attention of other readers and hearing your thoughts will make them more likely to give my novel a try. As a result, it will help me to build my career, which means I'll get to write more books!

Thank you so much. As well as making a huge difference, you've also just made my day!

Olivia x

ALSO BY OLIVIA SPRING

The Middle-Aged Virgin

Have you read my debut novel ***The Middle-Aged Virgin?*** Here's what it's about:

Newly Single And Seeking Spine-Tingles...

Sophia seems to have it all: a high-flying job running London's coolest beauty PR agency, a long-term boyfriend and a dressing room filled with designer shoes. But money can't buy everything...

When tragedy strikes, Sophia realises she's actually an unhappy workaholic in a relationship that's about as exciting as a bikini wax. And as for her sex life, it's been so long since Sophia's had any action, her bestie has started calling her a *Middle-Aged Virgin.*

Determined to get a life and *get lucky*, Sophia hatches a plan to work less and live more. She ends her relationship and jets off on a cooking holiday in Tuscany, where she meets mysterious chef Lorenzo. Tall, dark and very handsome, this Italian stallion might be just what Sophia needs to spice things up in the bedroom...

But the dating scene has changed since Sophia was last single, and although she'd score an A+ for her career, when it comes to men, she's completely out of her comfort zone. How will Sophia, a self-confessed control freak, handle the unpredictable world of dating? And how much will she sacrifice for love?

Join Sophia today on her laugh-out-loud adventures as she searches for happiness, enjoys passion between the sheets and experiences OMG moments along the way!

Here's what readers are saying about it:

"I couldn't put the book down. It's **one of the best romantic comedies I've read**." Amazon reader

"Life-affirming and empowering." Chicklit Club

"Perfect holiday read." Saira Khan, TV presenter & newspaper columnist

"Olivia has an innate knack for the sex scenes, which are very hot. **This book was steamy**, but with such a huge element of humour in it that when you read it **you will certainly giggle throughout at the escapades**." Book Mad Jo

"Absolutely hilarious! A diverse, wise and poignant novel." The Writing Garnet

Buy *The Middle-Aged Virgin* on Amazon today!

AN EXTRACT FROM THE MIDDLE-AGED VIRGIN

Prologue

'It's over.'

I did it.

I said it.

Fuck.

I'd rehearsed those two words approximately ten million times in my head—whilst I was in the shower, in front of the mirror, on my way to and from work…probably even in my sleep. But saying them out loud was far more difficult than I'd imagined.

'What the fuck, Sophia?' snapped Rich, nostrils flaring. 'What do you mean, it's over?'

As I stared into his hazel eyes, I started to ask myself the same question.

How could I be ending the fifteen-year relationship with the guy I'd always considered to be the one?

I felt the beads of sweat forming on my powdered forehead and warm, salty tears trickling down my rouged cheeks, which now felt like they were on fire. This was serious. This was actually happening.

Shit. I said I'd be strong.

'Earth to Sophia!' screamed Rich, stomping his feet.

I snapped out of my thoughts. Now would probably be a good time to start explaining myself. Not least because the veins currently throbbing on Rich's forehead appeared to indicate that he was on the verge of spontaneous combustion. Easier said than done, though, as with every second that passed, I realised the enormity of what I was doing.

The man standing in front of me wasn't just a guy that came in pretty packaging. Rich was kind, intelligent, successful, financially secure, and faithful. He was a great listener and had been there for me through thick and thin. Qualities that, after numerous failed Tinder dates, my single friends had repeatedly vented, appeared to be rare in men these days.

Most women would have given their right and probably their left arm too for a man like him. So why the hell was I suddenly about to throw it all away?

Want to find out what happens next? Buy *The Middle-Aged Virgin* by Olivia Spring on Amazon.

ALSO BY OLIVIA SPRING

Only When It's Love: Holding Out For Mr Right

Have you read my second novel ***Only When It's Love?*** Here's what it's about:

Alex's love life is a disaster. Will accepting a crazy seven-step dating challenge lead to more heartbreak or help her find Mr Right?

Alex is tired of being single. After years of disastrous hook-ups and relationships that lead to the bedroom but nowhere else, Alex is convinced she'll never find her Mr Right. Then her newly married friend Stacey recommends what worked for her: a self-help book that guarantees Alex will find true love in just seven steps. Sounds simple, right?

Except Alex soon discovers that each step is more difficult than the last, and one of the rules involves dating, but not sleeping with a guy for six months. Absolutely no intimate contact whatsoever. *Zero. Nada. Rien.* A big challenge for Alex, who has never been one to hold back from jumping straight into the sack, hoping it will help a man fall for her.

Will any guys be willing to wait? Will Alex find her Mr Right? And if she does, will she be strong enough to resist temptation and hold out for true love?

Join Alex on her roller coaster romantic journey as she tries to cope with the emotional and physical ups and downs of dating whilst following a lengthy list of rigid rules.

Only When It's Love **is a fun, feel-good, romantic comedy about self-acceptance, determination, love and the challenge of finding** ***the one***.

Praise For *Only When It's Love*

'**Totally unique and wonderful.** Olivia's book has a brilliant message about self-worth and brings to life an important modern take on the rom-com. Most definitely a five-star read.' **- Love Books Group**

'I guarantee **you will HOOT with laughter** at Alex's escapades whilst fully cheering her on. If you like romance, humour and a generally fun-filled read then look no further than this **gorgeous, well-written dating adventure**. Five stars.' **- Bookaholic Confessions**

'Such a uniquely told, **laugh-out-loud, dirty and flirty, addictive novel.**' **- The Writing Garnet**

'**An exciting insight into relationships in the 21st century.**' **- Amazon reader**

'With the right mix of romance and comedy, this is **the perfect read**. Five stars.' **- Love Books Actually**

'I've never read a story so quickly to find out who she would choose and if Mr Right would be the one! Five stars.' **- Books Between Friends**

'**Funny, entertaining and clever.** Olivia is an incredibly talented writer, and definitely one to watch. I cannot wait to see what she does next! Five stars.' **- BookMadJo**

'Cool, contemporary, but still wildly romantic! Yet another smasher from Olivia Spring! There's something about the way she writes that really endeared me to the heroine of this story.' **- Amazon reader**

'WOW WOW WOW!!!! *Only When it's Love* is **a dynamite love fest**. I read the entire story with the biggest smile on my face. In case you might have missed the million hints I've dropped, download the book today and jump straight in.' **Stacy is Reading**

Buy *Only When It's Love* on Amazon today!

AN EXTRACT FROM ONLY WHEN
IT'S LOVE

Chapter One

Never again.

Why, why, *why* did I keep on doing this?

I felt great for a few minutes, or if I was lucky, hours, but then, when it was all over, I ended up feeling like shit for days. Sometimes weeks.

I must stop torturing myself.

Repeat after me:

I, Alexandra Adams, will *not* answer Connor Matthew's WhatsApp messages, texts or phone calls for the rest of my life.

I firmly declare that even if Connor says his whole world is falling apart, that he's sorry, he's realised I'm *the one* and he's changed, I will positively, absolutely, unequivocally *not* reply.

Nor will I end up going to his flat because I caved in after he sent me five million messages saying he misses me and inviting me round just 'to talk'.

And I *definitely* do solemnly swear that I will *not* end up on my back with my legs wrapped around his neck within minutes of arriving, because I took one look at his body and couldn't resist.

No.

That's it.

No more.

I will be *strong*. I will be like iron. Titanium. Steel. All three welded into one.

I will block Connor once and for all and I will move on with my life.

Yes!

I exhaled.

Finally I'd found my inner strength.

This was the start of a new life for me. A new beginning. Where I wouldn't get screwed over by yet another fuckboy. Where I wouldn't get ghosted or dumped. Where I took control of my life and stuck my middle finger up at the men who treated me like shit. *Here's to the new me.*

My phone chimed.

It was Connor.

I bolted upright in bed and clicked on his message.

He couldn't stop thinking about me. He wanted to see me again.

Tonight.

To talk. About our future.

Together.

This could be it!

Things *had* felt kind of different last time. Like there was a deeper connection.

Maybe he was right. Maybe he *had* changed…

I excitedly typed out a reply.

My fingers hovered over the blue button, ready to send.

Hello?

What the hell was I doing?

It was like the entire contents of my pep talk two seconds ago had just evaporated from my brain.

Remember *being strong like iron, titanium and steel* and resisting the temptations of Connor?

Shit.

This was going to be much harder than I'd thought.

Want to find out what happens next? Buy *Only When It's Love* by Olivia Spring on Amazon now.

ALSO BY OLIVIA SPRING

Losing My Inhibitions

Have you read my third novel ***Losing My Inhibitions?*** Here's
what it's about:

Finally free and ready to have fun...

**He's hot, single and off limits. She's just got her life together
after a messy divorce. Should she risk it all for a forbidden
fling?**

A year after leaving her controlling ex, Roxy's divorce is finally
official. She's got her confidence and career back on track and is
ready to start enjoying some no-strings-attached fun.

But just when Roxy thinks she has her dating plan all mapped
out, a hot younger single man unexpectedly appears. On paper,
he sounds like exactly what Roxy's been looking for, until she's
warned that he's strictly off limits. Getting involved with him
will put her career, home and everything she's worked for in
extreme jeopardy. There's a million reasons why Roxy shouldn't
give into his charms. The trouble is, he's just too tempting...

Will Roxy take a chance and risk it all to pursue a forbidden
fling? And if she does, can she find a way to let him rock her
world, without turning it upside down?

***Losing My Inhibitions* is a sexy, laugh-out-loud romantic
comedy with a modern twist. This story is about self-love,
new beginnings, forging your own path in life and being true
to yourself**. It can be read as a standalone novel or as a prequel
to *The Middle-Aged Virgin* and *Only When It's Love*.

AN EXTRACT FROM LOSING MY INHIBITIONS

Chapter One

At last.

I thought it was never going to end.

He'd been pounding away for ten minutes, grunting like a pig, and I'd been listening to the radio playing in the background, trying to figure out what advert the song before last was from. Was it the one advertising car insurance or the one for those panty liners that are supposed to keep you *cotton fresh all day long*? *It'll come to me...*

We should have just called it a night when he'd first struggled to get his machinery working. Based on tonight, it seems like what I'd read about some older men finding it difficult to get it up was true.

It was only about half an hour after he'd popped a little blue pill that he'd been able to get his little soldier to stand to attention, if you catch my drift. Which, unfortunately for me, was around the same time I started to sober up and wonder what the hell I was doing.

But by then, he was really excited, and it had been so long since my last time that I'd got myself worked up and was just as keen as him to give it a go. I mean, when I start something, I like to see it through. *Yep, I'm dedicated like that.*

I'd also read that there are lots of benefits of sleeping with an older guy. Apparently, after years of experience in the sack, they know their way around a woman's body better than a gynaecologist, so I thought I may as well give it a try. *Purely in the name of research, of course.*

But now I was really wishing I hadn't bothered. It was about as exciting as watching a hundred-metre snail race. And this guy wouldn't know his way around my anatomy if I gave him a map.

Still, at least it was over now. I was back in the saddle. First time since I'd left my ex-husband. Frankly, I hoped it got better from here. *Please tell me it does?*

I opened my eyes slowly and glanced up at his crepey skin and flaky bald head, which had tufts of grey at the side. His droopy man boobs hung above my chest, whilst the weight of his large pot belly pressed down on my stomach.

Dear God.

I must have had a lot more to drink than I'd realised.

Don't get me wrong. If I was looking for a relationship and this was a man I'd fallen madly in love with, then I wouldn't be so shallow. It was just that right now, I was looking for fun. To make up for the years I'd wasted with my ex. When I was dreaming of the day that I'd be free from Steve and with another man, this wasn't exactly what I'd had in mind.

I'd pictured a young, hot, sexy guy with abs that would

give a Calvin Klein model a run for his money, with a full head of dark hair I could run my fingers through. A stud who would have me screaming for more, rather than wondering when it would all be over.

It was Colette, my boss, slash landlady, slash house-mate, slash friend, who'd set me up with him at my divorce party earlier this evening. Now that I was officially free, Colette said some male company might be good for me, so she'd invited Donald, her loaded sixty-two-year-old boyfriend, and he'd brought his fifty-five-year-old mate Terrence along.

I knew that I was ready to get back on the horse, and it was already under control. My cousin Alex had been helping me. She'd given me a crash course in online dating two weeks ago, and I wanted to set up my profile ASAP so I could get going on the whole swiping thing, but this big work exhibition kept getting in the way. I'd been burning the midnight oil every night and often over the weekends too, trying to get everything prepared, which didn't leave me with any time for extracurricular activities. And after another long, tiring and stressful day, a hook-up was the last thing I was thinking about. But I guess the booze I'd been drinking all night had made me relax a little too much, so when Terrence had started flirting, my libido had woken up, curiosity had got the better of me, and I'd hastily thought, *Why not just get it out the way now?*

Big Mistake.

Oh well. You live and you learn. We all do things in the heat of the moment that we regret. As long as I didn't do it again, then it was fine. Which meant I better start thinking about how I was going to get this big sweaty oaf of a man off me. *Now.* I'd heard the effects of those pills can last for hours, and I definitely couldn't endure another round.

No way.

Remind me never to drink alcohol again.

Want to find out what happens next? Buy *Losing My Inhibitions* by Olivia Spring on Amazon now.

ACKNOWLEDGEMENTS

Soooo many wonderful people I'd like to thank for helping to bring this book to life.

Firstly, my amazing mum. Thanks as always for reading through numerous drafts and giving honest feedback. You're so supportive and kind. You really are the best!

Thanks to all of my 'career consultants' who gave their time so generously: Irwin for your insight into the music business, Sarah of Charlotte Designs for giving me a glimpse into the world of being a mural artist (your job sounds really cool!) and Pete for filling me in on life as an illustrator. Thankfully the projects you work on are more glam than Emily's! Big thanks also to Sofar Sounds for the info and show invites. Such a brilliant concept.

HUGE thanks to my editor, Eliza, and my proofreader, Lily, for helping me to create the best version of this novel. Big hugs to my cover designer, Rachel, and website designer, Dawn, for making my book and marketing look lovely.

Gracias to my darling PD for your love, constant encouragement and your calming pep talks. You always know what to say to make me feel better!

To my amazing advance readers Brad, Jo and Loz. Thanks for taking the time to read through the book and give such useful comments.

Merci beaucoup Dad, siblings, Cams, Jas and Nene for your continued support.

Cheers to Mike, Kay and my fellow authors for your advice and wisdom.

Big thanks to each and every one of the *wonderful* bloggers who take the time to read and review my books. You rock.

And the biggest of thank-yous goes to *you*, dear reader. I appreciate you SO very much. I'm incredibly grateful that you continue to buy, read and review my books. It genuinely makes my day when you send messages saying how much you enjoyed reading them. You're even better than cake (and you *know* how much I love cake!). Thank you, thank you, *thank you*!

Until the next acknowledgements page...

ABOUT THE AUTHOR

Olivia Spring lives in London, England. When she's not making regular trips to Italy to indulge in pasta, pizza and gelato, she can be found at her desk, writing new sexy romantic comedies.

If you'd like to say hi, email olivia@oliviaspring.com or connect on social media.

facebook.com/ospringauthor

twitter.com/ospringauthor

instagram.com/ospringauthor

Made in the USA
Middletown, DE
08 May 2021